THE KING'S FALL

THE
KING'S FALL

PATRICK RAIN

TEMPEST
LORE

The King's Fall

Published by Tempest Lore Press

Edited by John Gavin IV

Cover Art by Andrzej Pyrchla

Map © Tempest Lore Press

ISBN 978-0-9979789-1-9

First Edition: July 2017

CHAPTER 1

The SILENCE WAS unbroken. The dense, yellow grasses towered over and surrounded Kyle. With every step, he felt the weight of his armor and sword. Then, a shriek came from behind him, but he had no intention of looking back. The shriek seized abruptly, and a howl reminded Kyle that another warrior had perished. The sunlight hit his face, and he continued to trudge ahead with the last strength he had. Soon, he emerged into a small clearing where the wind played with heaps of dry leaves.

His crew was nowhere to be found.

He stood still, panting.

The tall grasses rustled as the wind whispered. Kyle unsheathed his sword, sweat dripping down his temple. His instinct told him that there was no point in running. His grip became firmer.

A swish came from the grass, and a large shadow leaped out. Despite its size, it moved fast like a famished beast. It rammed Kyle with fierce impetus, knocking him back. His foot slipped, and he lost balance. His back slammed against the ground. His grip loosened, and his sword slid away.

The shadow sprung into the air and landed on Kyle's chest, sending a tremor through his body. He screamed as his ribs let out a crack. The shadow's jaws drew closer, dripping with saliva. Its stench reminded Kyle of a long-lost thought. Trapped, he was too weak to fight. His muscles were giving in. He gazed at the knife affixed to his belt. The jaws came closer to his throat, and there was only one thing he could do to defend. Without hesitation, he put out his arm. The shadow happily took a bite, its teeth sinking in, its jaws tightening. Kyle cried out as fear came over him and blood sprayed his face. He grabbed the knife with his free hand and jammed it into the shadow's neck. He twisted it and ripped it out. The shadow squealed and ran off before he could stab it again.

"Run!" screamed a frantic warrior that Kyle recognized as a member of his crew. The warrior had no intention of stopping to help anyone—not even Kyle, his leader.

Kyle staggered to his feet. A stream of blood dripped down his arm and through his fingers. The grass began to dance, and he knew he didn't have much time. He tightly wrapped a dirty piece of cloth around his wound, re-trieved his sword, and ran.

He thought about his crew. Most of those capable men, if any of them were still alive, were probably thinking only of fear and survival. Yet Kyle had a very different notion on his mind. He was irate that a mere beast pushed him into a corner and turned him into prey. His anger was stifled only by his loss of strength.

He could hear whispers in the grass again. Creatures lurked in the dark, ready to devour him. There was that smell again, a tinge of bitterness coupled with the stench of corpses. The sun pierced the grass and goaded him forward. The tall grasses opened up to reveal a mountain. Its imposing crests glittered in the sun, and a single deep brown peak reached high for the clouds. At the foot of the mountain, his crew gathered—or rather, the remaining warriors.

When the warriors saw Kyle, they fell silent. They were trapped. There was no point scaling the mountain. It was too steep even if they were at full strength. Behind them, the sea of grass stretched as far as the eye could see.

Kyle slumped down and closed his eyes.

"Hurry up or we're going to die," a lad cried out. "Hurry!"

Kyle frowned. The warriors formed a circle around him, putting up their shields. They searched the grass for any movement.

Kyle found it hard to focus. The feeling of peace was fleeting. He faced the mountain, put both of his hands in front of him, and then he spread them wide. The mountain heeded his call, and the rocky slope groaned and cracked. A fissure appeared, puffing dust. One by one, the warriors vanished into the darkness. When the lad tried to go in, Kyle put his hand on his shoulder. "You're staying."

"What?" The lad frowned.

Kyle watched the waves in the grass. He stepped closer and put his face to the lad's ear. "Don't ever order me around."

"I won't, I'm sorry."

"Of that I'm sure." Kyle booted him into the sunlight and waited at the fissure.

What came out of the woods was a creature, not unlike a wolf, but much bigger. Its dark blue fur was sprayed with human blood. It had colorful feathers sticking out above its head just like a crown and had two black dots for eyes. Its gaze was lifeless and malicious.

The lad sat in the grass, weeping like a child. His hand kept shaking on the hilt of his sheathed sword. Kyle noticed the intricate design of the hilt—two birds fighting over something. He couldn't see what it was.

"You can't do this to me," the lad begged. "My father will find out. He will cut off your head. You will die if you let me die."

Kyle ignored the threats. He watched the creatures gather around the lad. His hand was still bleeding, but he seemed to have forgotten all about it. His bitter grin made him look like he lost his mind. "Have a great meal." He bowed as he made eye contact with one of the creatures.

"I'm begging you, please forgive me," the lad uttered through tears. "I'm sorry." The creatures gathered around him in an inhuman ritual, circling around and celebrating their meal. Saliva dribbled out from their jaws as their huge tongues rolled out.

The creatures leaped at the lad, covering his body. The lad's hearty scream turned into a pathetic groan that was quickly silenced. As the creatures devoured him, blood sprayed the grass.

The slope murmured and trembled. The fissure closed up; the sunlight vanished.

Kyle conjured a torch and led the warriors through the widening corridor. Everyone was silent for fear of being next.

On the other side was a small chamber. Kyle decided that it was time to take a break. His crew welcomed the idea as if it was a gift of mercy. Maybe their take on the matter wasn't wrong. They might not get another chance to rest for some time. They made fire and gathered around it. It was the only thing they could do to make this obscure place feel like home. They barely had enough food, and most of their supplies were abandoned in the grass.

"That was a little harsh if I say so myself," Burl said, staring at the flames. There was a tinge of disappointment in his voice, which Kyle instantly recognized. Burl buried his bald head in his hands. He looked grateful for being alive. His sword was nowhere to be found, so he must have lost it during the hike. Yet he still had his bow.

"You think so?" Kyle asked. "If you wanted to be a good guy, you could've volunteered to take his place." He gave Burl a malicious smile.

"Years of adventuring, and you're still the same." Burl smiled almost as if he knew what Kyle was thinking. "How many years has it been?"

"Lost track." Kyle ran his hand through his dark shag. He unwrapped the cloth from his wound and cleaned it. There were multiple deep holes in his arm, each one gushing with blood. He thought about the creature and its stench. It reminded him of his past. It was a time when he was livid, wounded, and lost, his path strewn with corpses and blood.

"What now?" Reave asked. He tied his long black hair with a plain white cloth, and after removing his sword, he slipped into a comfortable sitting position next to the bonfire. He was wearing dark green robes.

Kyle gave Reave a suspicious glare. Reave joined the crew only about a month ago. Unlike most warriors, he never questioned a single decision made by Kyle. His adventurous nature as well as his calm personality made him a perfect addition to the crew. But Kyle had his reservations about Reave's obedience.

"We're in the right spot," Burl asserted, "they said that whatever is commanding the creatures lives in the mountain." He warmed his hands at the fire.

"Wasn't that blue creature with the feathers the leader of the pack?" one of the warriors asked. "We could've just killed it and be done."

"The reports clearly said that whenever the creatures attacked a village, there was a man among them," Reave replied, taking a sip of water afterwards. His lips were dry and slightly bleeding.

The chamber fell silent.

"We came here with three dozen men, and now we are down to seventeen. Tell me that you know what you're doing?" shouted a thickheaded warrior, looking brazenly at Kyle.

"Look, you shouldn't concern yourselves with that." Kyle answered and then paused, lying on his back while peeling an apple. "Just think of yourselves as cannon fodder," he said, smirking.

The warrior's hand twitched. He gave in to temptation and grabbed his sword. As he ripped the sword out of the sheath, the blade turned to sand.

"Enough of this," Burl protested, "we should get some sleep." He then volunteered to be the first to stand watch.

Kyle wondered if it was a good idea to take the job, but after months of searching for work, this was his only option. No one wanted to deal with the creatures, and for a good reason. The rumors that a man was controlling them were enough to scare away most warriors. Kyle didn't want to believe the rumors until now. The reason the crew was almost defeated was because the creatures didn't act mindlessly.

Kyle heard the warriors whisper to each other. They always did.

He closed his eyes. No matter what, he couldn't sleep. It was always this way. Every night he would stare into the darkness, and it would stare back at him. He only felt peace when he was focused on his actions, living his life. Perhaps that's why the nights were the worst, filled with uneasiness.

That's when he would remember his only goal—to become the Celestial King.

He could feel the power that flowed within his mind, the power to make everyone bow to his feet. It was the same energy that pulsed through everything in the world—the animals, the people, the land. The energy called mana.

He had the power to manipulate it. He could use the mana inside his body together with his imagination to impose his will upon the world. He could mold the world with the power of his mind alone—the power of Mind Mana.

◆

The crew continued after a brief rest.

The cave, like a labyrinth, consisted of narrow, interwoven passageways. Every intersection looked the same.

Dark. Cold. But Burl soon picked up a faint breeze. He led them down a corridor that only seemed to get narrower. They pushed on, swords clinking against rock. Around the corner, water dripped down the rocks, which gave them a chance to refresh. After a few more turns, the crew finally caught a glimpse of the sun when the tapered corridor opened up to reveal an enormous chamber. The light entered through the narrow cracks above, illuminating the cave as if it was a sacred ritual ground. Stalactites covered the ceiling.

"We're never going to escape," a long-bearded warrior said, leaning against the wall.

"It's your fault," a thickheaded warrior said to Kyle. "We could live in luxury, yet your greed always destroys everything. There are hundreds of easy jobs out there."

Hissing, a tiny shadow passed through a corridor on the other side, and a faint howl was just barely audible to Kyle.

Infuriated by the useless complaints, Kyle made a fist, thinking of what he could do to soothe his anger. Only one thing came to mind: killing them all. Yet, he knew he couldn't do that. He needed them, for now. So he decided that a single death would be enough. He walked away from the crew, focusing his mind. He heard a whisper, and something pierced his shoulder. He grunted, bending down to the ground. Blood trickled down his back. Looking over his shoulder, he saw Burl holding a bow with an arrow ready.

"What do you think you're doing!?" Kyle screamed.

"You have no regard for human life," Burl declared, "so you've forfeited your own as well. You die here and now, for the crew's sake." The warriors were up in arms, enticed by Burl's words.

The only warrior not going for his sword was Reave, who quietly retreated and leaned against the side of the chamber.

"We can't fight more of those creatures," Burl said.

"So you're going to leave me here to be eaten?" Kyle grimaced.

Burl nodded in reply. "If the rumors are true, the man behind it all should be happy with killing you, the leader."

The shadow from the corridor grew bigger.

"Guess I pushed you too far." Kyle grinned, hiding his anger and pride. "But you're all witless fools. I've never asked you for anything. You all came to me, begged me to take you along." Kyle tried to pull the arrow out, but the pain was too much. "Burl..." he said with a pause, "If it wasn't for me, you would've been a delivery boy for that greedy warlord. You owe me!"

"I once thought so too," Burl confessed. "But we will all die if we follow you. I can't ignore that anymore." He pulled the arrow back, keeping the arrowhead steady. "So tell me your deepest desire."

"I want to..." Kyle trailed off, then corrected himself. "I will... I will become the Celestial King."

Burl released the arrow.

CHAPTER 2

THE GREAT TOWER overlooked the entire Kingdom of Narilan. The clouds embraced it like a crown. The sky was perfectly blue. Residing in the City of Zardan, the Great Tower lay by a lake of unblemished water and was surrounded by a ring of mountains. It was the home of the Celestial King, the ruler of Narilan.

Dorrell Sahne's chamber was on one of the lower levels of the Great Tower. He was still sleeping in his bed when the door rumbled. "Young lad, it's time," a hoarse voice called out. Shielded from daylight, he was hoping to get some sleep and ignored the noise.

Dorrell was a preceptor, a representative of the Celestial King. Whenever the Celestial King couldn't attend important meetings, Dorrell would speak on his behalf. But more often than not, Dorrell was just a liaison, relaying information about Narilan to the Celestial King.

The knocking redoubled.

Dorrell opened his eyes to see the darkness of the chamber. He didn't like it. With a single thought, he could clearly see the sky before him, the clouds stretching across the ceiling. He tried to find things in the clouds—faces, shapes, and symbols. The sky was calming, even if it was just an illusion, an old memory he kept around.

He sat up, thinking of the day ahead of him. Although he knew his job well, it never ceased to surprise him. He felt the breeze from an open window, which he forgot to close the night before.

The chamber looked more like a messy study; books littered the floor, wind played with the scrolls, and dust gathered everywhere. There was also a telescope by the window. Stargazing was Dorrell's favorite pastime after all.

"Young lad, it's time," the hoarse voice repeated.

Dorrell sighed. "Didn't I tell you that you can take the mornings off?" he called out. He rubbed his eyes, then went for the door. His long white robes dragged behind him, and his long black hair was unbound.

Behind the door stood an elderly man with thinning hair. His vest was buttoned up to his chin. It was clean, but worn.

"Without me, you would never wake up and the kingdom would fall," the elderly replied with a smile.

"Certainly, Albert," Dorrell said and returned a humble smile to Albert, his servant. "But I'm no morning person."

Dorrell thought about the Celestial King that lived at the top of the Great Tower. He felt a sense of pride for serving the almighty ruler.

Dorrell walked to one of the windows and stuck his head out. The busy market below was a place where he could find people smiling, but those suffering from despair were there as well.

Narilan has been in peace for 4000 years, with only brief periods of instability. All this time, the Celestial King cared for everything within Narilan. He was the source of the kingdom's well-being and its heart. He manipulated mana to provide fertile land, ward off invaders, control the weather, and so much more. Whenever the Celestial King was about to die, his power weakened, and he couldn't provide for everyone anymore. As a result, there was a shortage of food, disease ravaged the land, and despair corrupted the hearts of men. The death of its king was Narilan's only reason for chaos.

Dorrell knew that the current Celestial King would die soon, and just like countless preceptors before him, Dorrell would be tasked with finding a worthy successor. The only person who could ascend the throne and provide for the people was one with immense power, and Dorrell knew very well that power was corruptive. Hence, finding an honorable person to take the throne was the greatest of challenges. This worried him for years.

Albert helped Dorrell dress in elegant robes. "I'm sorry for your loss, young lad."

"My brother isn't lost yet. He's more capable than most people think," Dorrell said, pulling his hair back.

Young lad, Dorrell thought. He didn't like the name. Back in the years, it angered him because he thought it belittled him and questioned his authority. But as he came to know Albert, he realized that there was nothing malicious about it. Albert just treated Dorrell like family, and it was his way of showing affection. It was one of Albert's little quirks. As time went on, Dorrell grew to accept it. It even made him smile sometimes, especially after an entire day of being called Preceptor Sahne.

Albert combed Dorrell's hair, then braided it.

"Have you decided?" Albert asked.

Dorrell frowned. "I already told you. I don't like the idea."

The chamber fell silent as Albert helped Dorrell with his morning routine.

When he was ready, Dorrell walked to the floor below, where an elegant lift made of glass awaited him. The slow ride down made him sleepy. The vestibule was quiet with no one around. The gorgeous mural on the ceiling depicted the Celestial King and his followers. *It was a while since I last saw the Celestial King in person,* Dorrell thought.

He departed the Great Tower, smiled at a passerby on the street, and jumped into a carriage.

He eventually arrived at the courthouse, a large building with a bell tower, where the Grand Court resided. He walked through the antechamber and made his way up the stairs. He entered and eyed the octagonal table covered with an azure cloth. The members of the Grand Court were already seated, each dressed in a black robe. Their faces were hidden behind various masks—most portraying human faces. It was a method of hiding their emotions. However, it made Dorrell feel uncomfortable.

"Welcome," Dorrell announced, taking a seat at the table. "Do we really need to use that gimmick?" He pointed to the masks. "Cold blood is needed in face of danger and decisions must be made while putting emotions on the side, yet those same emotions are what prevent us from making the wrong decisions. Those same emotions make us human."

"Enough already," a stubborn voice said. "Cease the preaching, preceptor."

"They kindle sympathy, honesty, and honor," Dorrell continued with a grin. He didn't have to hide his dislike for the Grand Court. Composed of mainly scholars, it was there to oversee his decisions and to make sure he didn't abuse his power. Some of their other duties included supervising education, monitoring the economy, and judging outlaws. Yet, all those years of peace and stability made them lazy. They had a hard time making even the simplest decision, and when they did, it was already too late.

"Preceptor," a characterless voice came from Dorrell's left. "You know how it is, right? Not everybody can remain indifferent in the face of a morbid issue."

"The Celestial King will die soon, and our resources have been depleting," a tedious voice said, and Dorrell frowned. He disliked being reminded of the Celestial King's fate.

"As you know, for the past few years we have been distributing food and other supplies equally among all of the twelve warlords that govern the areas surrounding Zardan," said a man with a troubled voice.

"How could I not? My brother went missing when a transport was lost." Dorrell remembered that he was the one to initiate the operation. As the Celestial King became weaker, some lands turned sterile. But Zardan's soil remained fertile and yielded exceptional crops, so Dorrell thought it was only natural that they should support the ones in need. If they didn't, Zardan would flourish and its residents would gorge themselves like pigs, while those outside would starve to death.

"Well, two warlords have expressed their disappointment," the tedious voice said. "Two consecutive times they haven't received support."

"Could it be that the transport was lost just like before?" the man with the troubled voice asked.

"I think someone within the city who coordinates the transports must have sticky hands," a headstrong voice said with a big, garish chuckle.

"I'll look into it," Dorrell declared, knowing that it was for the best. If he left it to someone else, the issue would be brushed aside and never resolved.

Without another word, the members of the Grand Court left. Alone, Dorrell wondered if someone would be foolish enough to steal supplies. There was no reason to; Zardan had enough riches. Anyone could have anything, if they really wanted it. Or so Dorrell believed.

The sunlight was intense when he walked outside. He felt awake but wished to be asleep again. He walked through the crowd of people in the bustling market. People were bartering; some paid with gold, others used their mana to create items for trade. He bought an orange, and then felt something tug on his robes. A drifter grabbed Dorrell's leg, but his grip was light. Dorrell kneeled to check the drifter's pulse. It was weak, fragile. Dorrell summoned a carriage.

"Take this man to a doctor," he demanded.

"Sir, that'll cost you, you know?" the driver barked without looking at who summoned him.

"You know who I am, right?" Dorrell asked, and the driver turned around.

"I apologize, my lord." The driver bowed his head in shame.

Dorrell handed him a few gold coins and remained silent. He had no intention of making the driver more uncomfortable than he already was. The carriage soon drove off, and Dorrell started walking to his next destination. He wanted to resolve the problem with the transports as soon as possible.

There were always those that suffered, and Dorrell believed it was his responsibility to supervise and manage Zardan to the best of his ability. He believed that without him, Zardan would derail. It would succumb to greed, corruption, and indifference in the face of immorality.

At the city gates, he saw a couple waiting to come into Zardan. The Royal Veil, a powerful, invisible barrier protecting the city, was the only thing stopping them. People with very little mana could come and go, but those with exceptional mana had to inform the Grand Court of their arrival in advance. Dorrell thought it was a tedious process. The only reason it still worked was because not many people traveled in Narilan.

Yet, it wasn't always like that. The barrier was implemented when a power-hungry warlord attacked Zardan years ago, demanding to take the place of the Celestial King. He nearly destroyed the entire city. If it wasn't for Brayden, the selfless warrior who stepped in to protect the city, things would be very different.

The meditation ground, a plain, grassy field, was tucked away between the city walls and a massive building to the west. Every day, thirty people were chosen to meditate there, channeling their mana to the Celestial King.

When Dorrell arrived, he was stopped by a knight. It wasn't until he introduced himself that the knight stepped aside and allowed him passage.

Dorrell searched for Edrick, a man he knew for many years, the man overseeing the transports. Back when Dorrell couldn't find his way around the city, Edrick was the one person he could always turn to for help. They weren't the best of friends, but Dorrell trusted Edrick.

Dorrell strode through the field, gazing around, but he couldn't find Edrick. He felt the warm breeze and looked up. The Royal Veil that stretched across Zardan was almost invisible, but the wind made it ripple. The thought made him smile. He cherished the idea that the Celestial King was protecting the city, the kingdom, and all its people.

"Welcome, preceptor," a knight spoke, wearing expensive robes instead of armor, as he bowed before Dorrell.

"Today, I found out that there were problems with delivering supplies to some of the warlords," Dorrell said.

"Yes, unfortunately…" the knight trailed off, downcast.

Someone screamed. It was a woman's voice. Feeble and desperate. She ran across the field with terror in her eyes, only to be caught by one of the guards. The knight left to manage the situation, but Dorrell followed.

"Let me go," the woman cried out. "I can't take this anymore. I can hear them."

The guard forced her to the ground as the knight poured some liquid onto a filthy cloth. He aimed to press it against her mouth, but Dorrell interrupted. "Cease this at once." The guards immediately released the woman. She curled up, hiding her face in her palms. Her hands were cold, and her fingers gnarled.

Dorrell realized that something was very wrong. People were overworked, and the management seemed oblivious.

"Where is Edrick?" he demanded, without another thought.

CHAPTER 3

THE SUN PEEKED through the ever-moving leaves, eyeing their every move. Two women rode steadily through the woods, the wind in their hair. The smell of grass was in the air, and the whispers of chestnuts falling through leaves surrounded them.

"I hope we'll find some leads, Hilda," Ellia said, her long deep brown hair tossed by the wind. Her olive dress blended in with the trees, except for the colorful fringe. She was a slim, young lady, who came from a small village in the west.

"Locklair's the last one. We've spoken to all warlords except him," Hilda said. She hid her face under the hood of her dark brown mantle.

"Well," Ellia said playfully, "Lord Elring didn't want to speak to us, remember?"

"That makes two then." Hilda frowned. "You know, there are stories that Lord Locklair killed a thousand lizardmen," she added, then smiled. Her sword had an ornamented hilt—two birds fighting over a gem.

"Oh, don't tell me you believe that?" Ellia looked at the sky. "There are only humans in this world. But maybe we could find a demon or two." Her pace slowed down to a canter.

"Isn't that exactly what we are bound to find if we continue to search for that Dreamer?" Hilda matched Ellia's pace.

Ellia thought about the rumors. They spoke of a man without mercy and without a heart, an ambitious man with power like no other, a Dreamer. That was the name given to those with immense mana.

Ellia turned to Hilda. "Don't be like that. There is goodness in… most people." She bowed her head. It was hard believing her own words when all the rumors emphasized the man's greed, vanity, and disregard for human life.

"And here I was thinking that you've accustomed yourself to the world and grew a hard shell." Hilda moved closer, and poked Ellia in the shoulder with the tip of her finger.

"Don't mock me like that." Ellia hurled her gloves at Hilda, who barely managed to catch them.

They rode in silence for a little while. Ellia was lost in thought until she said, "I'm more concerned about losing my optimism." She made a forced smile and goaded her horse into a gallop, racing out of the woods.

When Ellia escaped into the meadows, she saw an enormous stone structure that put her in a state of awe. Hearing Hilda fast on her tail, Ellia didn't wait for her to catch up.

Locklair's Keep was surrounded by a thin layer of trees, and vines scaled its fortifications. The stone walls had multiple archers stationed around, watching the neighboring areas. The open gate welcomed Ellia inside. The street was lined with carts. Bulky, but almost empty. Yet the goods that were left seemed to be enough to make the residents content. The fervent chatter and bargaining encircled Ellia, making her smile. Breaking through the crowd, she left her horse at the stables and continued to the front of the warlord's manor.

The manor was an imposing wooden structure, much bigger than anything Ellia ever saw. She was captivated by the giant stained-glass window that stretched across the entire second floor. The window depicted various colorful scenes. Ellia liked the middle scene the most, a portrait of the king and queen. It was colorful and majestic.

She was startled as a few warriors emerged from the front door. They seemed to have lost their enmity over the years as they ignored her meandering—something some might've considered an intrusion.

"War is history, you know?" Hilda whispered from behind Ellia. "They wear the armor only to preserve their culture. Just look at their swords."

Ellia watched one of the warriors. The blade in his hand was dull. She grinned, then entered the manor.

There was a couple gossiping inside by the door. It was a man with a mustache and a boyish girl. They kept to themselves, but Ellia heard their conversation as she passed them. She couldn't keep herself from eavesdropping.

"So many people disappeared recently in Elra," the man with the mustache said. "I don't even know who was first."

"I heard Walter was first," the girl whispered. "But it was so long ago that I'm not sure."

"Walter? What are you talking about? He vanished years ago ..."

Ellia was taught not to eavesdrop. It was something her mother told her all the time, but Ellia liked to do it anyway. There was something fascinating about strangers talking of foreign lands and bizarre events. She strode ahead. But she wanted to listen longer or even join the conversation.

"May I help you?" asked a girl in a cherry dress, a mere doll for welcoming visitors, as she smiled behind the counter.

Ellia waited for Hilda to say something, but Hilda remained silent.

"We're here to see Lord Locklair," Ellia said.

"As far as I know, he's not expecting anyone today," the girl rasped. "And you can't just waltz in and expect an audience. Leave." She tried to wave them away.

Ellia looked down, unable to come up with a reply. She wasn't used to how things were done in the world. Arguments were not her forte. Sometimes, she thought that she would never learn how to put up a fight, but Hilda insisted that she just needed some practice and a bit more confidence. Ellia, however, thought it was strength that she needed.

"Look, we've traveled for days, and we're tired," Hilda interjected. "From what I understand, your job consists of just looking pretty. So would you do something for a change, and go tell your lord that we're here to talk about Kyle?"

Hearing Kyle's name irked the girl in some weird way. She dropped the unmindful act, then led Ellia and Hilda behind the wooden counter, through a claustrophobic passage, and up a green-carpeted staircase to the right.

Ellia felt reassured, knowing that Hilda was following behind her. They turned the corner and followed the girl. The light from the stained-glass window colored the floor like a canvas. The colors mixed, flared, and paled based on the strength of the sunlight.

They stopped at an enormous, wooden double door with a sturdy frame. It was decorated with many engravings. Sounds of mirth came from the other side.

The girl tapped on the door and whispered, "My lord, there are visitors here. Kyle's associates."

"Let them in," a masculine voice ordered, and the girl pushed the double door open before walking away.

Ellia took a deep breath and entered.

Lord Locklair was sitting in a chair at the tip of the table, surrounded by two playful women. One sat on his lap, and the other on the armrest. The women had no clothes, but they weren't bothered by it. Locklair wore only a pair of trousers, so the scars that ran through his chest were in plain sight. In one hand he held a bottle of red wine, which was half full. Disheveled, his black shag complemented his demeanor of a warrior.

Before Locklair, there was a man in a tattered tunic with a very soft face. With tight fists, the man stood straight like a true warrior.

"As far as I'm concerned, Udall," Locklair declared in a cold manner, "you have been living here in peace. You owe me. Now get to work. My army needs weapons, lots of them. And don't even think about leaving. I assure you that if you do, I won't hunt you down. I'll just kill your wife and child."

Udall gritted his teeth in silence.

"Now get out," Locklair waved him away.

Udall strode out. The double doors slammed shut.

Locklair turned to Ellia. "How can I help you, ladies?" he asked in a pompous voice akin to that of a confident leader.

Ellia fell silent, tense. His presence was making her uneasy. She felt vulnerable and weak.

"Lord Locklair, my name is Hilda, and this is Ellia." Hilda bowed. "We're here searching for Kyle."

"A lot of people are," Locklair said as he caressed one of the women. He pulled her closer and smiled. "I think I can help you, but why should I?"

"My lord, we believe..." Ellia trailed off after only just mustering enough courage to speak. After a moment, she found her voice again. "He's the only righteous king of this land. He's the only one able to bear the weight of Narilan." She felt short of breath after speaking too fast in a nervous streak of emotions. Her eyes averted Locklair's gaze.

"That sure is about right, but I've heard many people tell me a story like that." Locklair waved his hand. The two women by his side froze for a moment, bowed, and left. "You do know the type of man I am, right?" he asked, and Ellia nodded, tense. "I can see tremendous terror within your eyes, and it makes me believe you. Nothing is as uplifting as seeing someone shiver in fear." Locklair chuckled.

Ellia faced away, her eyes wandering the floor.

"We've spoken to almost every single one of the warlords," Hilda continued. "None could tell us where he is."

"No surprise there. He's been traveling aimlessly for the past ten months, searching for a warlord who would grant him a Blessing. He needs the support of warlords if he is to have a chance at becoming the next Celestial King. My guess is he took it upon himself to investigate the Fields of Nakroh. The creatures there are a new breed, maybe an aberration caused by the dying Celestial King." Locklair swilled the rest of the wine. "They've been attacking the village of Elra."

"How can you be so sure Kyle will be there, my lord?" Ellia asked.

"You see, I'm one of the few who openly support Kyle's quest. He already has the Blessing of eight warlords, but none of them support him like I do. I've been eyeing his every move, and I'm just waiting for the day when he becomes the Celestial King."

"Why?" Ellia asked, her heart beating faster. It wasn't until she spoke that she realized how foolish her question really was.

"You're asking a lot of questions, young lady. Well, you see, in this kingdom time stands still. Nothing ever changes. Every so often, a Celestial King is chosen to make sure everything stays in order." Locklair stood up, stretched, and strolled across the room. "People live in harmony, then once the Celestial King is dying, there are a couple of years when things become problematic. Some starve, some die, but in the end, another Celestial King comes and nothing changes. It's been like that for far too long." Locklair looked out the window. He frowned at the sight of everyday life.

Ellia turned to Hilda with a worried look. Hilda returned a quick glance at her and shook her head.

Locklair turned to them. "Yet I want something more. I want to know what lies outside of Narilan. I want conquest, and I want all the insecurities of life. That's exactly what Kyle will bring to this land." He smiled.

Ellia felt her chest tighten. But it wasn't fear that she felt; it was boiling anger and frustration. What she heard vexed her until she couldn't hold it anymore. "Are you delirious?" she yelled. "How could you risk Narilan's safety and stability, the peace that we've had for such idiotic—?" Ellia was interrupted by a smack across the face. Her cheek burned bright red as she stood in silence, realizing what she had done. Hilda stood before her with a grim stare.

"I sincerely apologize for her rudeness, Lord Locklair." Hilda bowed. "She has the tendency to speak before she thinks. She's still learning the ways of the world."

Locklair remained calm. "We all once had the world teach us a lesson. What's important is that the lesson comes as soon as possible."

Ellia felt his stare.

"As a token of apology, I desire your hand." Locklair had a disgusting, self-satisfied grin. He stood next to the table with a dirty cleaver, its handle worn and its blade chipped.

Ellia stood frozen, unable to move. Her pupils widened at the sight of the sword. She retreated slowly, her heart pounding. She quickly looked at Hilda.

"Don't worry, it doesn't have to be your dominant hand. I'm happy with getting the other one." Locklair sharpened the blade, waiting for a response.

Ellia took another step back. She knew that if they didn't comply with the request, they would never leave the manor alive. She wanted to speak, but she lost her voice. Her words vanished, and she felt a repulsive feeling in the pit of her stomach.

"I'll go in her place," Hilda declared, her voice calm and collected.

It only made Ellia feel worse. Her guilt intensified. Then she thought about using mana. She had the power, even though it wasn't her own. She wanted to jump in and protect Hilda at all costs. Yet, she knew that wasn't what Hilda would've wanted. Ellia already acted on her emotions in the most foolish of ways, and she wasn't going to do it again. She stifled the impulse. Nauseated, she tried to hold off from crying, but she was powerless, and tears started dripping down her cheek.

"Why make the sacrifice for such a foolish girl?" Locklair asked.

"She's a fool all right, yet she's my sister's daughter. My sister wouldn't be pleased if something happened to her." Hilda stood proud without any fear.

"You know, I really like you, Hilda. We're very similar you and I, so let me tell you a secret. Everyone who was sent to investigate the Fields of Nakroh either died somewhere in the sea of grass or made it to the mountain to die at its foot. If Kyle succeeded, he used mana to enter the mountain. That's most likely where you will find him."

"Why help us now?" Ellia inquired hesitantly.

"The thugs that accompany Kyle don't see the big picture. His ambition will soon be too much for them to handle. They'll rebel. I'm not sure that he'll expect the attack." Locklair's insisting stare made Ellia uncomfortable. As the room fell quiet, Locklair turned to Hilda and gestured with the dirty cleaver—a malicious invitation only made worse by his vicious smirk.

Hilda frowned in disgust. "Wine," she demanded.

Amused, Locklair walked to the corner, and soon, he returned with a bottle. "Some of the best on offer here in my Keep," he proudly declared, passing it to her.

Hilda removed the cork and drank hastily. Then, she rested her hand flat on the table, her other hand hidden behind her back. Locklair raised the dirty cleaver. Hilda didn't even flinch, but her hidden hand tightened into a quivering fist where her ever-present fear was perilously contained.

Ellia shut her eyes, her heart throbbing in her tight chest. Her breath was strained, shallow. Her body felt cold, defeated. She wanted to be strong, but the insidious silence only made her shiver.

With one deft motion, the cleaver descended. Hilda hissed as the cleaver struck, wedging itself into the table. Stunned, she could barely hold herself from collapsing, her composure almost lost. Locklair wrestled the cleaver free, revealing the severed hand, which still seemed so alive, its blood staining the tablecloth crimson.

In this moment, Ellia felt like an empty vessel. She didn't have strength of her own, and she yearned for it so that she wouldn't have to bow before anyone. The only thing keeping her from collapsing was mana, and she cherished it with her heart. She felt hate for Locklair, but she didn't act on it.

Then she closed herself to the world.

CHAPTER 4

OUTSIDE, THERE WAS only silence. Ellia was with Hilda, yet Ellia's mind was somewhere else—in the murky maelstrom of her memories. She was powerless to resist it. She succumbed to its overpowering bitterness that made her mind run wild. She was ensnared into rehearsing her words, her actions, her behaviors, time and again. She yearned to claw her way out of the torment of her very own worthlessness. Yet all she could do was languish amidst the hatred which only seethed. She couldn't look at Hilda, for every time she did, she saw the bloody cloth wrapped around Hilda's forearm. And every time she did, she could only feel smothered by disgust.

Hilda was leaning against a tree, watching her closely.

Ellia remembered how lenient Hilda was with her. Hilda never set any rules when they left on this journey, but she had two requests. She wanted Ellia to experience the world and to learn to think before she acts. *I shouldn't have let myself get carried away*, Ellia thought.

She sat in the grass, trying to regain her peace. She meditated for what felt like an eternity. Nothing happened at first, but she finally felt her grasp on her mind return as she connected with her mana. Her breathing steadied, and she visualized her destination. Roots began dancing around her, forming a perfect circle. One by one, every grain of sand started moving, vibrating, until a pool of quicksand swirled beneath her. It consumed her slowly, dragging her downward. With a sad look on her face, Ellia stretched her hand out to Hilda. When their eyes met, she saw that there wasn't malice or regret in Hilda's eyes, only a mixed look of affection and sadness, strength and something else—something Ellia couldn't quite identify. Hilda nodded and joined her.

"I'm so sorry," Ellia whispered in tears.

The quicksand swallowed them whole, and the roots vanished into the ground, never to appear again.

The air inside the mountain was heavy and cold. Kyle leaned against a stalagmite, as arrows rained around him. Most of them landed at his feet, but some hit the spike and bounced off, echoing softly. Kyle closed his eyes and tried meditating. His breathing was unstable and chaotic. His hands were cold, and the only thing warming them up was the blood trickling from his shoulder. He knew he didn't have much time. An arrow grazed his temple, and he fell to the floor. They were trying to flank him, and he was trapped. With his bloody hands, he grabbed the hilt of his sword and stumbled out of hiding.

"I expected more from you." Kyle had a bitter smirk.

"You're dying, but you still turn to mockery?" Burl said with a stern face. The other warriors laughed at Kyle. Burl tightened the grip on his bow, aiming at Kyle's heart. He pulled the bow string back with all his might. The arrow quivered slightly.

Kyle listened as the arrow swished through the air. Suddenly, the earth shook and dust covered the floor. Shadows emerged from somewhere unseen. The arrow spun in the air and hit the rocks on the other side with a melodious clink.

The dust settled, and two figures were visible next to Kyle.

"Who might you be?" Burl asked, preparing another arrow.

"That's none of your concern," one of the figures said with a feminine voice, hiding her face under the hood of a dark brown mantle. She had one arm hidden under her cloak, and the other was brandishing a sword with an ornamented hilt. "We're here for the man you were just trying to kill."

Kyle stifled his feeling of surprise and began meditating. He didn't want to waste this opportunity.

"Do you have any idea who he is? He should've been dead a long time ago." Burl fired another arrow.

Before it could reach Kyle, his thoughts became reality. The arrow stopped in the air in front of his chest. The arrowhead melted into his palm, and it was remade into a dagger. He released it, and it dropped to the ground, then sank beneath the surface. Kyle had a filthy smirk as he watched Burl, who was slowly retreating. The dagger zigzagged through the ground, leaving a faint trail of dust.

At Burl's feet, it shot up, piercing his trunk and gutting him from bottom to top. His brief groan ended when his head fell back, and his arms dropped to his side. He collapsed with a mute thud, soaking the ground in blood.

Kyle watched the other warriors tremble. Their fear took over, and they all ran for the exit. Kyle called forth a tremor. It shook the chamber, rocks cracked and murmured. The stalactites above quivered, and pebbles danced on the ground. Cracks in the floor puffed dust. The stalactites came loose and plummeted down before shattering on impact. The warriors froze as the exit collapsed and everything stood still. Three bodies joined Burl, all impaled.

Kyle smirked with disregard for his injuries, which already took a big toll on his well-being. He was dizzy and barely standing. His wound left a trail of blood on his armor. Everything around was covered in a thin veil of mist as if it was a dream.

The two hooded figures behind him were talking. One of them seemed shaken and began meditating.

"Don't waste mana on those scum," the one with the sword said. "You know she only has so much of it."

"Everyone's life is worth the same," the other replied.

"The sooner you realize that's not true, the easier this journey will be."

Kyle heard a howl. Two creatures emerged from the corridor behind him. With his single thought, the ground quivered and thin pillars emerged around them, meeting above to form a cage. The cage contracted, and the creatures squealed. There was a screech, a prolonged rasp, and a thud as the cage turned into a tiny cube drenched in blood.

Kyle turned his attention to the remaining warriors as they were regrouping. One of the warriors advanced swiftly with his sword overhead, screaming. He swung his sword, but the blade shrank into its hilt and then extended from the pommel, piercing his chest.

"Anyone else brave enough?" Kyle called out.

He stepped closer to the warrior he just killed. The sword stuck in the warrior's chest broke in half, liquefied in Kyle's hand, and formed into a dagger.

At once, the warriors charged. Kyle staggered back to avoid the first attack and pulled out his sword. He swung at the warrior nearby but was too slow and hit the oval shield. Then he slashed heavily. The warrior's shield and armor split under the influence of Kyle's will, opening up for an attack. Kyle's blade cut through the shoulder, shattered bones, and dug deeper still. The warrior groaned, spitting blood. Kyle shoved him back. His sword slipped out, sliding and grating against bone.

Right behind Kyle, there was another warrior, heaving a greatsword. Kyle sprang away, leaving bloody spots. His step was light and clumsy. The greatsword rang as it slammed against the ground. Then the warrior swung again, but his attack was more powerful this time. Kyle parried unsuccessfully. The blade grazed his arm, then he forced his mana into the blade and shattered it. The broken pieces danced around. With a single fast slash, Kyle slit the warrior's throat, finishing him off.

"Too easy," Kyle whispered. *Just a little more.*

Surrounded by three more warriors, Kyle kneeled with his hands pressed against the cold rock. Thin spikes emerged from below, impaling them instantly. Kyle walked closer and touched the blood dripping down one of the spikes. It was warm and dense, but the warrior was dead. He flicked some of it at the two warriors still breathing before him. They hesitated, dumbfounded. The tiny spots of blood warmed, boiled, and grew. They corroded metal. The warriors screamed in agony as they struggled to free themselves from their armor, which was quickly melting, but it was too late. The warriors fell to the floor and yelped in pain until they vanished in a pile of muck. Seeing this, the last few surrendered their weapons and tried to escape, only to die from falling rocks which came crumbling from the ceiling of the cave. Kyle touched his shoulder. The metal from the arrowhead began dripping down from the wound and into his hand. The arrow shaft dropped to the floor. He reshaped the metal into a tiny sphere. He limped toward the last warrior alive, who feigned death and was now crawling for the exit.

"Do you want to live?" Kyle asked, his voice weak.

"Yes, sir," the warrior wept.

"Eat this then." Kyle dropped the tiny sphere into his hands. "It should be small enough to eat, right?"

The man didn't hesitate for a moment and swallowed it. His eyes became misty. He groaned, then squealed. Spikes pierced his head and neck as his last shriek ended. He died with his eyes wide open, blood pouring out of his mouth.

Kyle looked at the hooded figures. One of them had trembling hands.

Reave, who was enjoying the spectacle from the sidelines, stared at the tiny needles protruding from the warrior's head and neck.

"I almost forgot about you." Kyle turned to Reave.

"You should get those injuries taken care of before we fight. Besides, I had no part in this pathetic rebellion." Reave strolled around, taking in the sights.

"You sure are a weird one," Kyle said, wobbling. "I don't want people without clear motives on my side."

"All you need to know is that I want to kill the Celestial King. Nothing else matters." Reave gave a subtle bow.

With the battle over, Kyle turned his attention to his saviors. He was about to ask what they wanted with him, but before he could utter another word, his legs gave in and he collapsed. His body was drenched in his own blood. The sunlight blinded him. His heart was steady, and his mind dazed. He felt cold, very cold.

Will I die here? he thought.

Before he passed out, he saw someone kneeling beside him.

CHAPTER 5

DORRELL FELT NOTHING but anger. Yet, he didn't let it get to him. He saw the estate that Edrick inherited from his parents years ago. It stood surrounded by a hedge that towered over any visitors. The huge gate was locked, but a torchlight swayed in the wind right beside a tiny door to the side. It was a sign of invitation and goodwill. Dorrell sneaked inside and walked across a tiny bridge, listening to the gurgling stream. The way to the estate was lined with torches. They danced in the light gusts of wind, and the emerald grass replied with whispers.

Where are the guards? Dorrell thought, seeing as there was no one around.

In spite of many attempts to speak to Edrick, Dorrell never did. Edrick went missing the moment Dorrell started searching for him, which made him think that Edrick was hiding. Perhaps Edrick was frightened at what might happen if the two of them were to meet.

Dorrell still couldn't get the image of the woman out of his head. He remembered her deranged behavior, her despair-filled eyes. *Was it because of overusing mana?* he thought. If so, it was his first time seeing such a reaction, and he knew he would have to investigate it.

Before Dorrell made it to the door, it started to drizzle. He scuttled ahead, and when he was shielded from the rain, he turned to look at the night sky. Clouds blocked his view of the stars; he considered it a bad omen, which made him anxious. Without knocking, Dorrell entered. He wondered why the door was left open. *Maybe he's expecting me*, he thought.

The inside was dark. Dorrell took off his boots and left them by the door. It was very warm. There was a light emanating from deep inside, and Dorrell's eyes caught a glimpse of something—a shadow against the wall. His step was furtive, but it wasn't his intention. He wasn't a thief or a bandit, yet he certainly acted like one. The fireplace was ablaze, and a strong smell of burning was in the air. There were some charred papers at the hearth. He walked closer and kneeled beside them to try to make sense of the writing.

"Excuse me, sir," a voice came from behind him.

It made Dorrell tense. He moved slowly until he saw the knight behind him.

"I'm sorry if I startled you," the knight said.

"It's fine." Dorrell relaxed and stood up. "Where is everyone?"

"You don't know, sir? Master dismissed more than half of his subordinates." The knight frowned. "But that was weeks ago."

Why is he calling me sir? Dorrell thought. *Perhaps he didn't recognize me in the darkness.* It's not that Dorrell wanted the respect. He liked it, of course, but he was just surprised. Not being addressed as a preceptor felt comforting. It reminded him that he was human—just a regular person. For a moment, he didn't think of the responsibility that was on his shoulders.

The knight paused. "If you're looking for my master, he is upstairs in his study."

"Is Edrick expecting me? I assume that's why you're not concerned about my sneaky entrance." Dorrell forced a smile.

"Sir, just please talk with my master." The knight bowed and disappeared in the darkness.

The stairs were located in the adjacent corridor. Dorrell walked up the creaking steps. The light from the fireside was gone soon, and darkness consumed everything. There was only a faint flicker that stretched across from underneath the door ahead. Dorrell walked closer, knocked, and entered.

"You can leave the door open," Edrick said. Surrounded by scrolls and ledgers, he sat behind a bulky desk with his nose in a book. There was a flask of water with a single cup by his side. The window behind him was ajar.

"We need to talk," Dorrell said, his anger gone.

Edrick swept the books off the table in frustration. He was a tall man with a face full of freckles. His brown hair was the length of his shoulders, and his colorful royal robe was decorated with a few emeralds around the collar. "Well, talk," he rasped.

"I was at the meditation ground today." Dorrell walked to the table.

"So ..."

"Don't give me that innocent look. You know what I'm talking about." Dorrell's voice was tranquil, but his eyes were furious.

"If you haven't noticed, these are desperate times. I'm only doing what I think is best."

"Explain yourself!" Dorrell demanded, slamming his fist on the desk. "What do you think you're doing?"

"I don't know what this is all about." Edrick frowned.

"Not only are shipments missing," Dorrell said. "But people are overworked. They're suffering."

"We need more mana. The shipments didn't arrive because we don't have enough supplies." Edrick snorted. "The Celestial King is dying, but you don't see what is happening to Narilan from the comfort of your home. I had to make a choice. But you'll never understand."

"Make me understand."

"This is the perfect kingdom," Edrick said proudly. "There are no wars, no disease, no food shortages. The Celestial King is the ultimate ruler in the heavens, and he takes good care of his people. But you do realize... the people live in ignorance, right?"

Dorrell hesitated. "That is true," he admitted.

"Well, I'm making sure that the kingdom is still running. What do you think would happen if the Celestial King would run out of mana?" Edrick reclined in his chair.

"The warlords would probably have a hard time getting along. War would break out."

"Chaos ..."

Dorrell shook his head. "Have you tried getting more people to donate?"

"Don't be naive. Most people only give mana when they are forced to," Edrick said.

"Forced?" Dorrell asked, feeling vexed. If the situation was so grim, he believed that Edrick should've informed him instead of making decisions on his own.

Edrick looked away. He then pretended to be nonchalant, but Dorrell recognized the behavior—a fake veneer to hide undesirable emotions.

"You forced people to give their mana?"

"It's not like that." Edrick sat up from his chair and took a step back.

Dorrell jumped forward and grabbed Edrick by the garments. The chair tipped over. Edrick punched him in the stomach, then shoved him back. Dorrell slammed against the desk. Water spilled from the flask.

Dorrell's first urge was to fight back. Out of anger and out of spite. Yet, one glance at Edrick, and Dorrell managed to rein in this impulse for the moment. He didn't see an evil man standing before him. Edrick was a victim of the choices he had made.

Edrick stumbled backwards, tripping over a chair. "There was no other way. We could never have enough mana. That's when we started taking people—people that no one will look for ..." He bowed in shame.

Dorrell sighed. He picked the chair off the floor and took a seat. "You could've just come to me for help."

"I thought that I could work this out." Edrick curled up in the corner.

"Is it true what you said about the shipments?" Dorrell rested his head back. "We need more mana?"

Edrick hesitated. "Over the last few years, many poor regions formed. I redirected shipments from the prosperous to those in need. We do need more mana... a lot more."

Dorrell calmed down. He believed that he had to understand the situation to solve it. He strived to understand everyone, and sympathy wasn't a foreign idea to him. His father saw it as a weakness. He saw it as a strength.

They sat in silence. Neither had anything to say.

"Do what you must," Edrick said at last. "I knew there would be punishment if I was caught."

"It's not so simple," Dorrell said. The only thing running through his head was the thought of the cruel punishment. Within Narilan, outlaws were branded with the Gift of Misfortune, which attracted all the terrible things in the world to them. Yet, those serving directly under the Celestial King were killed in the most painful ways. It was a method of keeping them under control and from abusing their power.

Dorrell looked at the ground.

They knew what had to be done. Dorrell didn't have to say anything. The conversation made him more suspicious of the world around him. The talk began with anger, but it ended with a sad tone as Dorrell realized that he was blind to what was happening.

"Make it quick," Edrick said, his voice weak.

Dorrell stood up. He didn't want to do it, but it was the least he could do for Edrick. A quick death was the only gift he could bestow on the man cowering on the floor, on the man who would otherwise face unimaginable consequences.

"Thank you," Edrick said.

Dorrell replied with only a nod.

"You know," Edrick added, "maybe *he* should become the Celestial King."

Dorrell took a seat on the floor across from Edrick. He didn't say a word and briefly meditated. Edrick cringed as a ring of wan light surrounded him. His fists tightened. The ring grew brighter as if it was starting to burn. It filled with yellow light, shining and warm. Then a pillar of fire surged up, swallowing Edrick in a violent whirl of flames. It burned with an intensive orange hue, then turned blood red. The air around filled with sparks. Dorrell couldn't hear Edrick's cries, but only the crackle of the flames. When the fires ceased, there was nothing left of Edrick.

There was only a ring burned into the wooden floor.

CHAPTER 6

THE TREES WERE very small. Standing on her toes, Ellia could see above them, but there was really nothing to see, except for the tiny chapel in the distance. She felt someone's presence and looked around. The garden was empty. She continued to pick a few more apples. Her pouch was becoming heavy, stuffed with herbs, apples, and anything else she could get her hands on.

Back home, things were simple, Ellia thought. *But here ... all the danger, the blood, the chaos.* It wasn't what she was expecting. She wasn't accustomed to the world. She always believed that there was goodness in the hearts of everyone, but she was starting to doubt herself. The man she saw yesterday—the man who massacred all those warriors—frightened her. Her hands were shaking.

She pressed her palm against a tree, imagining. Moving her hand away, she saw a primitive image of a bear engraved in wood. She liked playing with mana. It gave her comfort and soothed her worries, but it also made her feel guilty. The mana she was using was not her own. Wasting it was forbidden.

Many times Ellia found herself wondering what it would feel like to have the power of Mind Mana. Her heart ached when she thought about it. The thought reassured her that she could become stronger, but it also reminded her of her weakness. *If only I had power, I could've protected us from Locklair and anything else that might happen in the future.*

When she finished picking apples, she turned around, and there he was. His arrival was silent. Sprayed with blood, he eyed her for a second without saying a word.

"I haven't startled you, have I?" Reave asked, tagging a boar behind him.

Ellia quickly shook her head. "We thought you wouldn't return."

"I was just sick of waiting on him," he said, brushing his hair away. "And a hunt was a good distraction."

"He's doing better with each day."

"Thanks to you." Reave dropped the boar to the ground, stretched, then picked an apple. "I'd like some of those herbs as well. You never know when they might come in handy."

"You can have all the herbs in the world," Ellia said, looking away. "Without the recipe, they will do you no good." She swallowed, feeling the beating of her heart.

Reave fell silent. He took a bite out of the apple, then smiled. "Recipe, huh? I wonder what forbidden recipe heals someone so quickly."

Ellia frowned and strode away.

"Well, we all have secrets," Reave mused. "And yours are safe with me. I don't care what you do as long as it doesn't come in conflict with my plans." He lifted the boar over his shoulder and caught up with Ellia. "Don't be scared of him ..."

"You mean Kyle?"

"Who else?" Reave took another bite. "He only looks scary at first glance. Once you do some traveling, you realize that there are men far scarier."

Ellia took a deep breath. "How ... how could he kill all those people?"

"That's how the world works I suppose." Reave fixed his grip on the boar. "You should ask him."

Ellia shook her head, frowning. The thought of Kyle's murderous spree frightened her, firmly engraved in her mind. She was ordered to help Kyle become the Celestial King, but she already had her doubts. Yet, she didn't tell Hilda. She thought it was better this way. She felt ashamed for even having her doubts because the order came from the most important person in her life, and she had no intention of disobeying it. But for a second—for a brief moment—Ellia didn't want to save Kyle.

Reave wiped the sweat off his forehead. "Perhaps it'll take some time to comprehend the world around you. You must've been enjoying the life of a hermit until now."

"What if I don't want to comprehend it?" she asked. "If I do, I'm worried it'll corrupt me."

He fell silent, lost in thought. "Do what you will."

Ellia nodded hesitantly. "I just can't get over the fact that we must help such a man. You seem kind, but he ..."

Reave chuckled. "Time for your first lesson. Don't ever judge people. Wait until you get to know them. The kindest souls are usually the ones most likely to be rotten." He patted her on the back.

Ellia frowned. "How did you get to know Kyle?"

"Oh, it's a very short story. One of his men died, so I took his place."

"Are you not scared of him?"

Reave kept silent, smiled. "My turn to ask questions. Why are you helping Kyle?"

"You ask..." Ellia began, but her voice faltered. Yet soon after, her desire to be strong took over. "You ask difficult questions."

"Maybe so. It's all out of boredom. I hate standing around. It's been five days, and all we are doing is caring for him." Reave looked at Ellia's pouch. "Let me carry it for you." He stretched out his hand.

Ellia held her pouch tightly to her chest.

"Come on. It's not like I'm going to steal it."

"Worry about the boar," she said with a smile. "I can handle this."

"My name is Reave."

"Ellia."

They exchanged brief smiles. Silence followed until they found some open ground. Ellia visualized their destination. The earth quivered, murmuring softly. The trees swayed, bumping against each other. A flock of birds sung in the sky. Then quicksand swallowed them whole.

◆

Kyle awoke to a blinding light of fire nearby. He heard the wind whisper, the breeze cold. There was a lone bird in the sky, the moon illuminated its wings. Dense and gray, the clouds moved stubbornly across.

Kyle shivered and wrapped the blanket tighter around himself. His body was weak, as if someone took all the energy from him. He felt the wound on his back with his hand. It was covered with leaves, dry, but sticky. The pain was dull, but when he tried to move, it came back. He didn't have his armor, just his dirty tunic and trousers.

He looked at the scorching fire nearby and saw a woman reading next to it. She was eyeing him from time to time. Her gaze was emotionless and powerful. She was wearing leather armor that was old and worn out, with a myriad of marks and scuffs.

Two birds fighting, Kyle thought, looking at the sword by her side. *The sword must be from Relien. Same as that lad.*

The cold soon hit him, so he scooched closer to the fire, groaning. There was a boar there, or rather what was left of it. The bones had barely any meat on them, and pieces of the skin lie in the grass. He wasn't hungry. He looked at the woman and saw the herbs around her arm. *Did she lose a hand?* he thought.

Kyle wondered why anyone would take the time to save him. The very first thought that came to his mind was that they wanted to collect a bounty on his head. The only other alternative was that someone wanted to kill him personally, and they're just delivering him. He preferred the latter for some reason.

"How many days has it been?" Kyle asked, searching for his sword. He felt dizzy, and soon his head started aching.

"A few," the woman said.

"Where is Reave and the other… girl?" Kyle cleared his throat, still searching.

"They're getting some sleep." Hilda pointed to a make-shift bunk to her left and further to a nearby tree. "Your weapon is safe with me," she added.

"Why did you save me?" he asked, but the woman ignored him. "What do you want from me?"

There was no answer.

Kyle sighed. He was too weak to do anything. *If they wanted to kill me, they could've done it already*, he thought. *What could they possibly want?* The thought was somehow unsettling. He was in no position to fight, and that's what made him uneasy. He hated being defenseless.

"The young girl sure is good with herbology," Kyle added.

"What makes you think that I wasn't the one who helped you?" the woman asked.

"You don't look the part."

Kyle remembered the mountain and looked around the horizon. The mountains were far in the distance, their peaks lost somewhere in the darkness.

He watched the starry sky and searched for the moon, which seemed to hide behind the clouds. He chose to lie down, gritting his teeth at the pain. He listened to glowing insects buzzing around in the grass. He liked that. With his eyes closed, he didn't care where he was. It didn't matter. He was alive. The shadows didn't stare at him that night.

◆

The sky was cloudy the following morning, but the sun was shining gently. It was a warm day, but there was also a faint breeze. In the distance there was a flash of lightning as the clouds gathered around a humble chapel far away.

Kyle awoke but remained lying flat in the grass. He was watching the sky when a flock of birds flew overhead. It wasn't meditation, but it made him feel peaceful. He rolled to his side and sat up. He still felt dizzy, and the headache lingered on.

"Finally awake," Reave said, sitting in the grass.

"Where are we?" Kyle asked.

"Tranquil Meadows," replied Ellia softly.

Kyle looked in the direction of the mountains, their highest peaks swallowed behind a powerful barrier that enveloped Narilan, The Dominant Veil. It resembled the Royal Veil that surrounded the City of Zardan. Yet unlike its smaller counterpart, the Dominant Veil was more visible and appeared as a soft fabric that mirrored the horizon. The Great Tower stood proudly reflected in it, caressed by the rays of the sun. Kyle frowned at the thought of being unable to see the other side. The Dominant Veil protected Narilan from invaders, but Kyle only saw it as a desperate attempt by the Celestial King to control the kingdom.

"It's a good time to tell me what you want," Kyle declared.

"You'll know when the time comes," the young girl responded.

Kyle shrugged.

The young girl came closer. "My name is Ellia. This is my aunt, Hilda. We're here to …" Ellia stopped herself and looked at Hilda, who was reading a book close by.

"Whatever it is you want from me, you should hurry up. When I regain my full strength, I won't be so forgiving." Kyle forced a bitter smile.

"No need to get all upset." Hilda stopped reading and walked up to Ellia. "Our goals are one and the same. We will help you become the Celestial King for the sake of Narilan."

Kyle chuckled, bowed his head, and ran his fingers through his dark shag. He was suspicious of every one of them. He just didn't know who was worse: Reave or the two women standing before him.

"Give him the medicine," Hilda said to Ellia.

Ellia handed Kyle a sack of water, without looking him straight in the eyes.

Its bitter taste made Kyle almost vomit. But with only a couple of sips, he felt invigorated. His mind was cleared, and the dizziness was gone. He felt slightly stronger too. "There is one problem," he said. "I hate to owe anyone anything."

Hilda frowned. "You already do. You owe us your life."

Kyle chuckled. He didn't like being pushed around, but he knew he had to restrain his anger. There was a time for rage, and a time for watchfulness. He kept his pride in check. "Ellia, right? What do you hope to achieve when I become the Celestial King?"

"Narilan needs a strong ruler who is capable of providing for the people," Ellia said, full of hope. "You have enough mana to achieve that. You are powerful enough to be the Celestial King. Without a king, Narilan will fall."

"What makes you think that I will be a righteous king?" Kyle observed Ellia's reaction to see her eyes wandering around. "You don't have an answer." He smirked.

"Enough," Hilda snapped, and Kyle smiled. In some ways, she reminded him of the women from the town of Aylmar. Stubborn and rough, they didn't hesitate to smack their husbands over the head with a wooden stick to goad them to work.

"So what are you planning?" Kyle asked.

"When you're well enough, we will head into the mountain to finish the job," Hilda said.

Kyle pondered a moment. "Fine," he casually agreed. "But I have a word of warning. I will do what I decide. I won't share any of my plans with you. You might accompany me, but make no mistake, we're not allies. You say we share a common goal, but I have my way of doing things, so don't ever stand in my way."

Hilda shrugged. Reave ignored him. Silence followed.

"I have a question," Ellia whispered.

"I'm listening." Kyle said, assuming it was directed at him.

"How can you be so lighthearted? We saved your life, you nearly died, and you killed ..." she trailed off, her voice strained.

"You'll get used to it." Kyle said with a smirk.

"Why did you kill all those men?"

"Why not?" Kyle asked. To him, it was just the way the world worked. There was nothing wrong with fighting, with conflict. Anyone with a weapon should be prepared to die. He certainly was. *Scum kill scum*, he thought, recalling Burl's favorite saying to justify bloodshed.

Ellia looked away. "Don't you feel any appreciation for what we have done?"

"Is that what it's all about?" Kyle asked, his voice calm. "I didn't ask you for anything. You didn't save me out of a kind heart. You're here for a reason. For all I care, you could've left me there. At least I wouldn't have to listen to you now." He leaned back, arms crossed.

"Such bitter words." Ellia went to her bunk, found the medicine she had made earlier, and tossed it at Kyle.

Everyone fell silent. The sun was shining. Numerous bees were buzzing in the air. A bird was warbling a tune that Kyle liked. Reave started making some noise as he sharpened his sword. Hilda returned to reading.

"Hey, Ellia," Kyle called out.

Ellia didn't pay attention to him.

"Thank you for saving my life."

Ellia was sitting in the grass, troubled. With a hundred thoughts, she struggled to pick the right words to say to Hilda. Everything she came up with sounded foolish or meaningless. Perhaps she didn't know what to say, overwhelmed by emotions.

"Spill it," Hilda tapped her on the head with a book before placing it down. "What's on your mind?"

Ellia looked around. Kyle was sleeping, and Reave was stargazing. "What do you think about those two?" she started with the easier question.

"I don't like Kyle, but she told us that he will make a fine Celestial King. That's all that matters to me. As for Reave, I don't have an opinion. I told him to leave, but he didn't."

Ellia fell silent. She didn't want to admit that she questioned helping Kyle. But she felt that Hilda figured it out already. Hilda's gaze had that spark to it as if she could see through everything.

"Are you worried about what Reave said in the cave?" Hilda cocked her head.

"No," Ellia said. The Celestial King's death was inevitable, even without Reave's aim of regicide. "We haven't talked since..." she confessed.

"I know." Hilda nodded, clutching her arm. "Things have been rather hectic, but we're making progress and that's what counts."

"I'm sorry—" Ellia whispered.

"Enough." Hilda waved her hand. "You don't have to apologize. I did what I thought was right. Of course, I could have stood back and let Locklair have his way, but I didn't. It was my choice."

"I know, but it's so unfair," Ellia said softly.

Hilda leaned closer, putting her hand on Ellia's shoulder. "That's just how things work. But listen, I'm proud of you. I'm proud that you didn't use mana. I know you wanted to. I'm proud that you are slowly becoming stronger. But you must learn from the past," she insisted. "You will remember that day, and I will try to forget it. We will not speak of this again."

Hilda's words were meant to be reassuring. Ellia knew that, but she could only see them as a hidden refusal to speak of what happened. She sighed heavily, incapable of shaking off her concern for Hilda. "If only I was more powerful. If only I had mana of my own, I wouldn't have to bow to the likes of Locklair." She looked up at the moon. It was larger today, as if it was coming closer to Narilan to stare at its inhabitants. Cracks showed up on its surface. Its craters were large and deep.

"You will." Hilda smiled gently. "One day, you will have your own mana, and when you do, you'll be free to do what you desire. It's just a matter of time. I think that once the ritual is concluded and you're not using her mana anymore, yours will awaken. You'll just need a little push."

Ellia perked up slightly, but remained silent. Hilda pulled her closer and embraced her tightly. She held Ellia for a brief moment before walking away. Ellia grabbed her pouch and started preparing herbs for Kyle. It was the last batch.

◆

The storm came the next morning. Rain pelted down the meadows. Gales shook trees, apples falling down. Day resembled night in a dark and gloomy way. Animals hid in holes, ditches, and gnarled tree trunks. It was on that day that Kyle was ready.

He still felt pain from his wounds, but his strength was back. He didn't want to waste any more time. *I can rest when I become the Celestial King,* he thought.

When everyone was ready, they set out in a flurry of dust, roots, and quicksand.

CHAPTER 7

THE DARKNESS WELCOMED them inside the mountain as they arrived in the same chamber where Kyle eliminated his old crew. It had a different feel to it now. The sunlight was absent, which made it darker. A vile smell reeked in the air, and blood painted the ground. The bodies of the dead warriors weren't the same. Some had their faces massacred, disfigured. Others had limbs severed, or big chunks of flesh torn off. There were those that still had their eyes open as if they were staring, hoping that someone will save them. One thing was certain; it wasn't the work of a human.

Kyle searched for Burl's body, but it was gone. Reave looted a few corpses, collecting silver and gold coins. His step was light and carefree. Hilda led Ellia, who had her hood up. Ellia's eyes were downcast, her head down. She was tense and frightened. Yet from time to time, she would look up as if challenging herself to stare into the face of violence.

They crossed the chamber and continued through the dim corridor on the other side. When it was too dark to see, Kyle and Ellia conjured torches.

"What if there's a man truly behind controlling the creatures, how does he do it?" Reave mused, rubbing his chin. His voice came off as sleepy. "Do you think he turns into a wolf?"

Kyle chuckled. He found the idea absurd. He was told long ago that monsters didn't exist in Narilan. Yet, he did face men far scarier than any monster he could imagine—among them were noblemen and warlords.

"I doubt it," Ellia said in a timid voice. "I think I might have an idea about what happened here."

"Care to share your thoughts?" Reave insisted.

"This man might just be using mana in ways that are forbidden. Mana can be unpredictable after all."

Reave rolled his eyes. "How so?"

"Influencing someone directly with your mana is not recommended," Kyle said. "You can form a dagger, then use it to pierce someone's heart. But imagining someone's heart exploding... would probably lead to your own death as well. When mana is used on a living being, it'll lead to nasty consequences."

Reave tried to hide his grin.

"I once heard a story," Hilda said, "where an evil traveler used mana to corrupt a villager with a pure heart. He succeeded, but things didn't turn out how he expected them to. Good became evil, and evil became good." Hilda looked at Ellia, then at Reave.

"I think we all heard that bedtime story," Reave said, brushing away his long hair. "So maybe the man we're searching for will be a beast... or perhaps a monster."

"We'll find out when we find him," Ellia said.

Kyle thought about the unspoken law. Using mana directly on yourself or on another living being was forbidden in Narilan, even for the purpose of healing. It was said that whenever mana was used this way, you ran the risk of bringing upon yourself something unwanted, some part of the one you were trying to influence, or something else entirely. Frequently, it was something that ignited a negative emotion within you, or the very thing you were trying to change with mana. Mana was capricious that way. It could even bring death to you when all you wanted to do was live. Yet, rituals were different. They attempted to mitigate these negative effects by distributing them between the person and the physical world through the use of various props, writing, and even sacrifices. *Maybe that is how he's controlling the creatures*, Kyle thought.

He considered leaving his companions behind. He felt strong enough to escape.

Then a deep howl rang through the corridor. It was followed by a chant that was too soft to be understood.

Kyle sprung ahead, his step clumsy. He heard Hilda call out, but he ignored her. Cries that pierced the walls and echoed in the distance led him forward. The wind began to blow intensely, extinguishing his torch—the only guiding light. Darkness befell him, but Kyle didn't stop. He couldn't. His mana relit the torch, but it was pointless. The wind strengthened and gusted through the corridor again and again. He continued through the darkness until he hit a wall, where a thin ray of light came through a narrow crack.

Kyle peeked through it, his heart pounding with excitement. On the other side was a softly lit corridor, which led to a chamber. The cries grew louder, turning into moans and shrieks. They were coming from the chamber ahead. Kyle focused his mana. The wall quivered, and dust fell from the ceiling. The crack widened, letting him in. When he was on the other side, he heard Ellia's shriek. He let go of the wall, and it trembled, then the crack ceased to exist.

Focused and determined, Kyle strode ahead. The ground turned into mud, and his feet sank in. Or so he thought. Chunks of deteriorating flesh mixed with blood coated the ground like a thick layer of mud, forcing Kyle to put up a piece of cloth to his face out of extreme disgust. When he made it out of the corridor, he saw a circular chamber below. He dropped down and landed lightly.

Most of the torches along the wall were extinguished. There was a squalid table in the middle. Kyle then noticed the glowing, azure moss. A highly toxic substance, clustered in every corner and along the ceiling.

"Help," a mumble came from the side. "Please help me!"

More cries echoed, but it was too dark to see where they were coming from. It wasn't until Kyle used mana to light the torches that he noticed the chamber was filled with cages, filth dripping from them. Inside were people— peasants, knights, and even nobles. Their clothes were mucky, and their voices almost muffled as if they were dying. They all stretched out their arms with hope that he would free them. Their cadaverous faces gazed at him, the light reflecting in their blank eyes.

Kyle frowned, and then turned his attention to what looked like a throne deep within the chamber. It was hewn out of rock, and was very primitive with sharp edges, cracks, and bloody stains.

Creatures, like those he encountered earlier, encircled the throne, their overgrown wolf-shaped bodies casting ghastly shadows in dim light. Some were feasting on their prey, blood dripping from their large jaws; others were patiently waiting, their vivid blue fur painted red. Yet, there were also those that had the look of malicious satisfaction as they eyed the cages, their pitch-black eyes reflecting nothing. In front of the filthy throne was something much bigger. It was kneeling on the floor, digging its head into a plate and spilling blood.

Kyle whistled to get its attention. His goal was within reach. For all the days of struggle he endured, he was about to be rewarded with a hefty dose of adrenaline and the possibility of his ninth Blessing. *Finally*, he thought.

The beast stood up and howled at all of the creatures around. A call to arms. Their blue hides bristled, and all of them began to growl. The beast had the stature of a man, the skin of an animal, and the head of one of the creatures.

Kyle unsheathed his sword and waited.

The beast charged at him on all fours, its movements slow but steadily increasing in momentum. Kyle ducked away, skidding across the bloody floor. Noticing how powerful the charge was, he created a stone barrier to prevent the other creatures from joining the fray. Waiting for an opportunity, he watched the beast as it circled around him.

The beast rushed him again. Kyle evaded, spun, and dug his blade into its head. The blade barely cut the skin of the beast. As Kyle added more force, blood trickled from underneath the head as the beast rolled away. Yet Kyle knew his attack was too shallow. It lacked power, which made him wish he was back at full strength.

Kyle readied himself as the beast rose from the ground to the sound of dripping blood. Its bulky hide rustled as it came undone, dropping at its feet and revealing a figure of a human. Kyle chuckled, realizing that the beast was just a man, hiding underneath the hide of one of the creatures.

The man was tall yet very thin, starved. His figure was clothed in tattered, filthy villager's rags. A bluish shade adorned his neck and shoulder, the color of the creatures. His tiny pupils protruded from his bloodied, wrinkled face, which was obscured by a thick beard and outgrown hair. His savage appearance brought to mind a recluse who scorned humanity long ago.

The recluse grunted as if he was trying to speak. He had the mind of an animal, and the only thing that separated him from a beast was his human origin.

Looking at the recluse, Kyle didn't see him as a monster or a fiend. All he noticed staring at the mindless beast before him was a lost soul. It was a man who lost his way playing with mana. It made Kyle feel at peace. He knew he could defeat a man, no matter how powerful. Yet, he also saw it as a warning. Kyle had the tendency to overuse mana too. The thought unsettled him.

Kyle relaxed and watched. The recluse's hands quivered, and his eyes rolled up. He mumbled something, falling to the ground, and then howled. The shaking in his hands redoubled. Cracking, they slowly reshaped into blue paws.

"Some claws you got there," Kyle mocked, but he didn't think the recluse could understand him.

The recluse growled. He shook his head and at once jumped in Kyle's direction. Kyle dodged the attack to the side and countered with a fast slash. The claws grazed his shoulder. As the recluse landed, he rolled uncontrollably with a powerful wail. Kyle chuckled, staring at his blade, which was dripping with blood. This time, Kyle had managed to cut flash—to slice the stomach. As the howling recluse tried to stand up, Kyle pointed at the ceiling and moved his hand in a downward motion. A huge stalactite came loose and fell right on the recluse. It shattered into a thousand pieces, and a dense cloud of dust covered the chamber.

The people in cages began to cough. The chamber fell silent.

"Is that it?" Kyle said, disappointed.

When the dust settled, he dismissed the stone barrier he put up earlier. The creatures weren't there anymore. Right behind him, Ellia and Hilda emerged from an alcove above, dropping into the chamber. Reave followed soon after.

Seeing the suffering of the captives, Ellia froze, aghast. She then ran to a cage where a couple of children were crying for their mother.

"I'll get you out." Ellia forced a smile as she searched for a stone. The stone she found was not enough to break the rusty metal lock on the cage. "I'll get you to your mom," she said. "Would you tell me where she is?"

"There." One of the children pointed at the throne. Ellia looked over her shoulder. She saw a big plate filled with blood. In the middle of it, something was sticking out—a bone with a bit of flesh. The sight made Ellia lose all her will to go on. It made her sick, but she was unable to look away. She felt short of breath.

Kyle watched her all this time. He then took his sword and started opening the cages. He noticed a stack of books in the corner. They had wet pages and broken spines. He recognized countless symbols on the covers which meant the books contained old rituals. There were also a few loose scrolls there.

"Here, use my sword." Reave passed his sword to Ellia, but she kept staring, her eyes blank and hazy.

"What was that all about?" Hilda snapped at Kyle.

"You should pay more attention to Ellia," Kyle said.

Hilda frowned. "Is it over?"

"Not until I get its head." Kyle heard something. He came to a halt, scouting out the area. He was firmly gripping his sword.

"Don't kill the other creatures," Hilda insisted.

"There is no need," Kyle said.

"My head?" the voice of an elderly man filled the chamber. His shadow stretched across, spreading from his body which stood before the throne. "Don't make me laugh."

"Oh, so you're still alive," Kyle said, his shoulder throbbing. "I have to say I'm glad. I was a bit disappointed after our battle. But I must praise your use of mana. It's… fascinating."

The recluse let out a cough and hunched forward. "I remember now." He cupped his face in his hands, whispering to himself, "I remember."

Kyle watched his transformation unfold.

"How are you able to regain your humanity?" Reave interrupted suddenly. "You've been controlling the creatures which means you inherited some of their traits, behaviors, and more."

"That's true." The recluse wheezed, feeling his abdomen. It was bleeding. "It took me nine years to regain my humanity after I've lost it completely while trying to control animals. I became a beast who didn't think. Yet, there were traces of mana within me, and I had brief moments of consciousness. With luck, I realized something. By making a human inherit some of my beastly traits, I could take some of his humanity. From a beast to an infant, from an infant to a child, and from a child to a grown man." The recluse put his hands behind his back, stepped forward, and then howled. All of the creatures gave a thunderous reply. "That's why I have slaves of all ages within this chamber," he said and paused. "Just watch," he added as he took a seat on the throne.

Ellia let out a subtle shriek, then retreated, falling into Hilda's arms. She had a shallow stab wound through her thigh. A child in the cage next to her held a bloody piece of metal. His eyes were different, feral.

"It gets easier each time," the recluse continued. "It used to be all about luck. Trial and error. But then I realized that many times the trait that I inherited was the exact thing I was trying to change."

Kyle frowned. The thought that this man could reclaim his humanity by influencing a human—a child—just as he did with an animal was utterly disturbing. It disgusted Kyle. "Once a beast, always a beast." Kyle grinned. He watched the displeasure creep up the recluse's face. *I didn't think words could hurt him this much*, he thought.

The recluse brooded for a moment with a blank look. "I'm sure you're talking based on your own experience," he retorted, putting out his hands and grabbing a pair of swords that emerged from the floor. With a vexed look, he dashed forward, the swords in his hands, his movement erratic and fast. Their blades clashed. Despite his age and neglected appearance, the recluse was strong. More so than before. He stared at Kyle with a feral, lunatic gaze as he slowly overpowered him in a struggle of pure physical strength. With a kick, he shoved Kyle back. The recluse jabbed with his sword. Kyle parried. The recluse feinted an attack, and then with a fast swipe slashed Kyle's face.

Kyle wiped the blood from the shallow cut right beneath his right eye. "Is that all?"

A few more creatures prepared for an attack, and Kyle saw Reave and Hilda joined the battle. Reave unsheathed his blade just in time to jam it into the jaws of a creature that leaped for his throat. He dodged another and killed it. Then, something shoved him off his feet. Reave plunged to the ground, and his blade slid away. As he saw the black pupils of the creature, he grabbed his knife.

Hilda killed two but struggled to do so with only one hand. Pain rushed up her leg when a creature bit her foot. She fell to the ground and saw another creature just above her. Then a blade was rammed through its skull, and she saw Reave.

Kyle was holding his own against his adversary. Their blades clashed again. The recluse tried to prick Kyle's foot. Retreating a step, Kyle countered with a horizontal strike. The recluse ducked down, and the blade passed over his head. With a fierce gaze, the recluse drove both of his swords into the ground. The steel dissolved, sipping through the cracks, and then formed a cage around Kyle. Kyle reacted with an earthquake that passed through the chamber, leaving countless fissures. The bars on the cage bent until they snapped. Kyle took this opportunity to attack, swiping his sword. The recluse attempted to jump away with an evasive maneuver, but his foot was caught in a fissure. Kyle smiled as the fissure contracted under his will, trapping the recluse's foot. Then there was a harsh crack, and he screamed. He fell to his knees, groaning, and used all his strength to stagger to his feet.

"You should be happy. You'll die like a beast." Kyle moved behind the recluse and kicked him to the floor. With a single precise strike, Kyle beheaded him. As the head rolled, a creature jumped on Kyle's back. He shook, tossing the creature off. He touched some of the blood on the ground, turning it into fire. The flames grew bigger, sweeping across the chamber.

The creatures scattered, squealing. The flames let off sparks. They were bright red, the color of the sun. Kyle played with the flames, leading the creatures into a corner. Squished between stone and fire, the creatures huddled together. Their howling and squealing redoubled.

"You and Ellia had saved my life." Kyle turned to Hilda. "If I let them live, is that a fair enough repayment?"

"No, it's not," Hilda rasped, tired from the battle.

Kyle shrugged.

"That's enough," Ellia screamed an instant before another slaughter took place. "Stop!"

The fire ceased. Reave opened the only door, and all of the creatures escaped.

Kyle sighed. He felt a profound throbbing in the back of his head. His step was light and dazed. He walked to the captives and continued opening cages. Soon, they were all free. "Let's bury the dead," he ordered.

"Do you intend to escort them all?" Ellia turned to Kyle.

"Only until we make it out of the mountain. They're on their own after."

"You can't." She hesitated. "I'd like you to take them to safety."

"And why would I do that?" Kyle retrieved the recluse's head and stuffed it into a filthy bag he found lying around. "You should be more concerned about your own life."

Ellia rested her hand on Hilda's shoulder. Her leg was bleeding, but she was thankful the wound was shallow.

To Kyle, Ellia looked frail and weak. Her sight irked him. Her foolishness was something he could never accept. Her uselessness could only hinder their progress, nothing more. When he met her gaze, he grew even more irritated. "You should have been more vigilant. Your incompetence is a danger to the mission."

Ellia froze, unable to resist the urge to lower her gaze.

"This is not the time, Kyle," Hilda instantly objected.

"This is exactly the time," Kyle insisted as he approached the trembling Ellia. "Heed my words. Make yourself useful or prepare to die."

Ellia swallowed hard, clenching her fists. After a moment, she met his unyielding stare. "You know that you might not get the Blessing even now after completing the mission," she spoke in a subdued voice.

"Your point?"

"You can't force a warlord to do anything, but the citizens can. Get the people's appreciation, and you might just get the warlord's support."

Kyle gave her a cold look, then frowned.

CHAPTER 8

DORRELL GAZED AT the flames. He felt them staring back at him. The warmth only made the cold within his heart feel ever colder. There it was—his own reflection within the bursting pillar of fire. He tried to leave, but he couldn't, he was attracted to the warmth. He watched as his hand melted without any pain. Then, he found himself inside the pillar of fire and was set ablaze.

Dorrell screamed, springing up from his bed. He was gasping for air, sweating. His breath was heavy, and his chest tight. Dorrell imagined the sun, and it illuminated his chamber. *It was just a dream,* he thought. *Relax.* His loose, messy hair covered his entire face, and sweat covered his body. He sighed.

No matter what, he couldn't forget about Edrick. The memory of that night followed him wherever he went. He couldn't escape it. He was worried that it would torment him forever. He regretted what he did, even though he thought it would be best for Edrick.

Why is it that pleasant moments don't make such an impression? Dorrell thought.

Yet deep down, he felt he did the right thing. A quick death saved Edrick a lot of suffering. Dorrell had no doubt about that. He already approached the Grand Court about it. He didn't want to act like a crook, hiding his deeds. He told them everything, and they reacted with anger before voicing approval. And all of Edrick's responsibilities fell temporarily on Dorrell.

He walked to the window and watched the city. Seeing people shuffle on the streets had this hypnotizing effect on him. He felt tranquil, for a moment. He knew exactly why he couldn't get over Edrick's death. There was something very important that Dorrell didn't think of that night; he never killed anyone before. He never gave much thought to how much of a price he would have to pay for taking someone's life, how heavy a burden it would be. He didn't feel guilty. He felt bitter, disgusted with himself.

Dorrell dressed in his robes, fixed his hair, and went outside. He didn't want to stay home more than he needed to.

His destination was the market. He chose not to take a carriage and walked. It wasn't far, only a short walk. There were people at the market, but it wasn't busy. He dismissed intrusive thoughts again and found a stand with his favorite fruits, pineapples.

"You've missed another lecture," someone behind him said.

When he turned around, he saw one of his students. "Hello, Cwen," Dorrell said.

"What's with you recently?" Cwen dropped the respectful manner of speech. She was a tall, young girl, and was a lake of never-ending advice for Dorrell, especially when he was in trouble. Her long green skirt was decorated with colorful jewels of various shapes and sizes. The thick gold bracelets around her ankles and wrists were something that she loved to wear and could never do without.

"It's Professor Sahne to you," Dorrell said, handing a few gold coins to the merchant.

"Well, "all-knowing" Professor, why are you so depressed?" Cwen poked him in the elbow.

"I'm sorry," Dorrell said. "My life has been hectic recently."

Cwen came closer and studied Dorrell with her small brown eyes. He didn't like that. He felt under suspicion as if he had done something wrong, which he didn't. "We were waiting for you the other day. You could at least tell us there would be no lecture."

"I'm sorry about that." Dorrell forced a smile.

"Finding a successor giving you trouble?" She played with her bracelet.

"You have no idea."

"Ever since I met you, I knew you were passionate, but I never considered that it would be to this extent." Cwen cocked her head, studying him again. "What about Kyle? He should be strong enough."

Dorrell shrugged. He was reminded of Edrick's last words. "Supposedly, every one of the previous Celestial Kings was noble, but I have yet to find a Dreamer who isn't corrupted by mana—the absolute power." He let out a faint sigh. "Kyle is the prime example of that problem."

Dorrell looked at Cwen. She was one of his most diligent students. She cared for Narilan just as much as he did. He thought that she would do anything to help the kingdom. That devotion was something he valued her for above all else.

Dorrell strode ahead.

"Maybe you're looking at it in the wrong way," Cwen said, stopping Dorrell from leaving. "You should realize that finding a noble person with extreme power is absurd. We both know power corrupts, so maybe the other Celestial Kings weren't so noble after all."

As always, Cwen stirred up Dorrell's emotions and thoughts.

He couldn't argue with her.

There was nothing he could say. He left. He had work to do today. He had to figure out how to resolve the problem with the shipments as well as investigate what was happening to the people who overused mana at the meditation ground.

CHAPTER 9

THE BONFIRE SWAYED morbidly. The tall grasses whispered, dancing in the wind, but they weren't as intimidating without the creatures lurking around. The sky was clear, with the stars shining brightly—a sign of good luck. Ellia was sitting on one of the large logs surrounding the bonfire, arms crossed on her lap. Her injured leg was straight, her wound covered with the same herbs she used on Kyle.

The people who languished in the mountain formed a crowd around the bonfire. They looked tired, sick, and withering as if any moment they might collapse. Yet they continued in silence, without complaints. Sometimes, they would look in the direction of the village—Elra. Within reach now, it seemed to give them hope. Perhaps without the dream of returning to their families, most of them would've perished in the mountain.

Ellia admired their strong will.

She tried to find familiar faces in the crowd. Kyle sat across from her in silence, listening to the people gossiping. The fire reflected in his eyes. Reave was eating an apple reclined on a log closer to the fire, one foot dangling from the edge.

Hilda took a seat next to Ellia after standing watch. She then wrapped her cloak around the two of them.

"I still remember when I went hunting with your mother." Hilda cleared her throat. "It was our first time outside the village. We caught a couple rabbits, and we decided to sell them in another village."

"And what happened?" Ellia curled up.

"We never made it. Good thing we knew how to hunt. We got sidetracked… lost. When we made it back, everyone was worried. We're all foolish… at one point or another I mean."

"How can I make it up to you?" Ellia asked, looking at Hilda.

"You can do so by becoming the person you were meant to be." Hilda gave her a soft smile.

Ellia held the cloak tightly.

"I'm not sure if I can ask," Reave said to Ellia. "But care to shine some light on that teleportation technique of yours? It must take a big toll to use it, especially with so many people and that's not even taking into consideration the distance." Reave cut a large piece of a red apple; the juice dripped down his knife.

"I probably shouldn't even be standing after something like that, huh?" Ellia asked, her voice troubled. Every day she practiced stifling her emotions and dealing with stress. She knew she was improving slowly, but she still had a long way to go if she was to be strong and learn to control her feelings.

"Let me guess," Reave said. "You underwent a ritual to acquire this power, and now, someone is suffering instead of you." Reave smiled, then finished his apple. "But that would require tremendous amounts of mana. It would require a Dreamer."

"I don't really like talking about it," Ellia said. "It's only temporary. Soon this gift will be no more." Ellia held her tears back. She didn't like talking about personal matters. She felt vulnerable doing so.

"Gift?" Reave frowned. "I don't think so. There is probably something you have to do in return, right?"

Ellia fell silent.

"You're quite perceptive," Hilda interrupted. "Is that why you want to kill the Celestial King? Because he had you do something you didn't want to?"

"The Celestial King is dying," Reave declared. "He's pathetic. He should've been dethroned long ago."

"Have you ever thought of challenging the Celestial King yourself?" Kyle asked, turning to Reave.

"Me?" Reave asked. "Ruling a kingdom is not my thing. I prefer adventuring. To be honest, I could go on like this forever. I love nature, and the vast landscape that surrounds us fascinates me."

The fire was weak, and it would soon begin to smolder, so Reave went to gather some wood. Kyle stood watch, restless. Everyone else reluctantly tried to sleep, but most of them couldn't. The murmurs of those that did only made it worse. Nightmares of their lives in the mountain tormented them in their sleep. There were feeble cries and pleas that resounded through the camp. Some begged to be free or prayed for a divine intervention. Others cursed someone in the worst ways possible, their voices harsh. The same name, a very common one in Narilan, came up often. Walter.

Before dozing off, Ellia remembered what she heard in Locklair's Keep. Walter was the name of the man who turned into a beast.

◆

The next morning, Kyle was closing in on Elra with everyone lagging behind. The village was surrounded by a dense field of corn, and there was only one dirt path that led there. The path was muddy, and soon, his armor was soiled. He regretted taking the path. He had no other choice though.

Kyle didn't see any soldiers guarding the area or archers preparing to strike. The village stood wide open, without any fortifications. The wooden houses there looked fragile and dilapidated. *War in Narilan is nothing more than a folktale,* Kyle thought. *No wonder they're not afraid of an attack.*

Kyle watched as the people hurried ahead in search of their families, and a huge crowd formed in the town square. Kyle sneaked away with a filthy bag in one hand, looking for the tavern. He knew it was a place where he could find the warlord—Lord Elring. When Kyle found a squealing sign of a maiden that swayed above a squalid wooden door, he entered the tavern. Inside, it was empty, except for a fine lass who was cleaning the tables, her head wrapped in a plain white scarf.

Thundering cheers and cries echoed from the outside. The lass quickly finished her job, then left in the direction of the noise. Kyle shrugged.

Perhaps he knew what would come next and chose to hide, Kyle thought, then smiled.

He wasn't on the best of terms with Lord Elring. Their beliefs frequently clashed, which resulted in many verbal confrontations, but never a fight. However, they met frequently enough that Kyle knew Elring's habits. The next place Kyle intended to check was a tiny schoolhouse in the distance away from the busy street. It was Elring's favorite place, a bright orange building with a bell tower and an almost flat, brown roof.

Kyle made his way through the short maze of wooden huts, up the incline, and stopped at the base of the steep stairs that led to the schoolhouse. The bell began pealing. Kyle hurled the blood-soaked bag—the man's head—into the bushes. He wanted to spare the kids the sight of something so horrid. Their minds were yet to be corrupted by the world, and he didn't want to have any part in that. The doors sprung open, and the kids spilled outside. They zigzagged past Kyle, chatting, screaming, and cheering. Kyle walked upstairs and through the door.

Elring was seated and pretended to peruse a book. He didn't wear armor, and instead wore frayed rags, which made him look more like a peasant than a warlord. There was no sword by his side, but that's not to say that he wasn't proficient at using one. There were those that believed him to be a master swordsman. Kyle thought it was only a bedtime story—something you tell your kids when they're scared. Despite his young age, Elring had a furrowed face.

"So how was the hunt?" Elring asked without turning away from the book.

"Cruel," Kyle said. "Just like the world we live in, but the mission is done." He took a seat at one of the small desks. The wind slammed the door behind him shut.

"Proof?" Elring asked, rubbing his eyes. They were red from allergies.

"Corrupting the youth is not my style, so you'll have to do some digging around the bushes." Kyle smirked.

"I considered everything, and I have decided," Elring said.

"You're not going to give me your Blessing, I know." Kyle frowned, overcome by a profound disgust toward Elring. Kyle disliked him the moment he heard the rumors going around. They spoke of Elring's love for his village, as well as his lack of greed and price. They painted a picture of a humble man who believed in the good of the world. Kyle never believed any of those stories. He doubted Elring had any of those traits from the moment they met.

Kyle was inclined to kill Elring where he stood. He knew the deed would give him a sense of satisfaction. He had that same urge every single time, but he never acted on it. He rested his hand on the pommel of the sword that was at his belt. *There will be a time for that,* he thought. *But not yet.*

When Kyle opened the door, he saw the whole town gathered in front of the schoolhouse. The people were cheering in an outburst of hope and joy.

Ellia stood before them, ready to speak. "Kyle is a vicious warrior with disregard for human life." She paused, and glanced at Hilda, who was by her side. "Many have heard of the rumors. That he is a callous fiend, a brute without remorse, but I want to ask you something here and now. Can a man change? Can a man be greater than his past? Today, Kyle returned your loved ones to you. That is an act of good." She preached in a firm voice.

Kyle saw her hands trembling. She then made a fist.

"I know you are afraid of making wrong choices. I am, too." Ellia hesitated. "But can we allow ourselves to follow a single man's judgement? To forfeit our right to choose? To let another make decisions in our stead?"

The people listened patiently to Ellia's speech. It made them quiet down and consider something that doesn't happen often in Narilan—questioning a warlord.

"I met Elring only once," Ellia continued. "But there was one thing I was certain about—he cares for all of you. He would do anything to save you, yet he is still human. He has strong prejudice toward Kyle. So I ask you all to form a verdict of your own. Should Kyle get Elring's Blessing? Consider everything you know and answer. Is Kyle worthy of becoming the Celestial King if he strives to be a better man?"

A hundred voices murmured, and the atmosphere became heavy. The villagers spoke among themselves. Reave was watching from afar.

Elring strode out of the schoolhouse. Kyle noticed worry on his face. He knew that Elring was losing his footing. Kyle grinned. Elring's strength—his love for the people— was used against him. Some warlords were known to be harsh, but Elring wasn't. If he didn't do what the people asked him to do, he would lose credibility.

"Give him the Blessing, our lord," the villagers declared in unison.

Kyle stretched out his hand to Elring as a gesture of cooperation. He was hiding a bitter grin. He didn't take Ellia for a person so cunning. Her words were manipulative, bending the people to her will. She wasn't the pure, naive girl he thought she was.

Elring hesitated. He slowly stretched out his hand.

Their eyes met. They didn't say a word, but they understood each other perfectly. With a brief handshake and with a single thought, Kyle received Elring's Blessing.

The ritual began.

CHAPTER 10

THE TAVERN WAS full. The crowd was roaring with strident chatter. In the center, a bard was trying to string together a new tune. So far, his attempts were fruitless—the words nonsensical. Yet, he did succeed in one thing—making the crowd chortle every single time he opened his mouth. He didn't have to fight for attention. A lass nearly tripped, spilling some ale. Her white dress was dirty at the fringe. The sound of wooden mugs resounded. Kyle made his way through the crowd to the table, where he found his companions.

"Nine Blessings, only one to go," Reave said and began eating his stew. "So a man was behind all the attacks. I'm kind of disappointed." He sighed.

The round table had a bowl of stew for everyone and a mug of ale. Kyle could smell the pig being roasted in the back. The smell of fresh vegetables was in the air as well.

"Isn't that for the best?" Hilda asked, looking at Reave. "The world wouldn't be so peaceful if monsters were lurking around."

Reave frowned, then smiled.

"If you look hard enough, you can still find malicious humans, scary ones," Ellia said. "There is no need for monsters." She made a childish smirk. Kyle noticed that she was slowly getting used to everyone. "That elderly man… the recluse… do you think what he said was true? About controlling the creatures and his consciousness?"

"The man was insane," Kyle said, grabbing a mug, leaning back in his chair, and propping his feet on the edge of the table. "I don't know if he did it all with mana. I saw some ritual books there as well. Unless somebody tries it, there is no way to be sure. Maybe you, Reave?"

Reave sneered. "Elring must be quite upset. He was tricked, but he was not forced to do anything. I guess if he really wants to blame someone, he can blame Ellia."

"I'll just tell him Kyle forced me to say everything," Ellia said without looking from underneath her bowl.

Hilda smiled at Ellia. It was the first time Kyle saw Hilda in an upbeat mood. He thought that Ellia was the center of her world, the only good thing. The thought wasn't foreign to him.

"I must admit I never took you for the conniving type," Kyle said with a grin. He finished his ale, then took a spoonful of the stew.

"You're mistaken," Ellia lashed out. "Everything I said was true. You helped the people, and I believe that there is goodness in everyone. I think you can become a better person."

Kyle shook his head, smiling in disbelief. He was impressed with her when she spoke to the people, but all that flare was gone now. She was the same naive girl he saw before. "But I must thank you, Ellia," Kyle said honestly. A young lady poured some ale into his mug. "Without you, I would never get that Blessing. For that, you have my gratitude."

"I would much prefer that you acknowledge the value of good deeds," Ellia said, munching on a piece of meat. "He was forced to give you his Blessing because you truly helped. Not because you killed some beast, but because you saved those people."

"Oh, enough with the preaching." Kyle pulled the serving lass aside and whispered into her ear. She chuckled. "Let's celebrate. I ordered more." He was in a very good mood. *Just a little longer,* he thought. *Just a few more steps, and my goal is within reach.*

"If it's mead, I'll pass." Ellia waved her hands.

"You don't drink?" Reave said, surprised.

Ellia nodded. "Only water."

"Tough luck." Reave rolled his eyes. "Not even a sip?"

"Unless you want to see me cry, I'll pass," Ellia whispered to Reave, and he smiled.

When the roasted pig was ready, it was brought to their table—a gift from Elring. Its skin was dry and slightly burned, but it was much better than anything Kyle had in the past few months. The vegetables, however, were delicious. The lass brought some mead.

"What do you think of Elring?" Ellia turned to Kyle. She finished her meal and pushed the bowl aside. She was sitting in her chair, tense and slightly timid.

"You really don't want to know," Kyle said, looking around. He felt calm and collected, yet still suspicious of his companions, especially of Reave. Kyle couldn't explain it, but he knew Reave was hiding something, lying every step of the way.

"He seems like a good guy," Ellia said.

"Not when he is angry," Reave interrupted.

Hilda put her mug down. "Is he the type of man that cares only about holding appearances?"

"Something like that," Reave said. "He can get pretty violent, or so I've heard. No wonder. When you're hiding so much frustration, there has to be a way to vent off."

"There was something up with him." Hilda pushed back her hair. "I felt it when I first spoke with him."

"Anyway..." Reave stood up. "Where is a good place to sleep around here? Upstairs?" He pointed up.

"No, the beds are full of bugs," Kyle said. "Elring invited us to his manor."

"Really?" Hilda prepared to leave. "Does he intend to poison us or something?"

Kyle ignored the question and searched the crowd for a familiar face until he established a connection with someone in the shadows.

Ellia watched as Kyle's expression softened, the hostility melting away. She kept her eyes on him as he stood up and strode away without a word. A few jolly patrons blocked her view. Once they were gone, she saw Kyle at a table in the corner, his companion veiled in darkness. Kyle leaned in, whispered. His companion drew closer to him too. For an instant, Kyle appeared to have the faintest of smiles. Gone was the brute and left was only a man.

The next moment, he was already on his way back. Ellia hastily pretended to be absorbed in the conversation at the table.

"Our mission is done," Kyle declared suddenly. "You are all free to do as you please. We'll be leaving tomorrow morning."

"Where to?" Hilda asked, but Kyle ignored her again.

"I'll stay a bit longer," Reave said. His plate was empty of anything eatable, only littered with tiny bones. "I'll be staying upstairs for the night." Without another word, he left the table and mingled in the crowd, oblivious to his companions.

Kyle decided to leave the tavern. Outside, he watched the moonlight. The pale light hid behind the clouds. Stars formed constellations, many of which he recognized. He took a breath of the fresh, mild air of the night. The night was warm—pleasantly warm. He saw the manor in the distance, overlooking the tiny huts of the villagers. Its chimney was puffing out smoke.

Ellia stopped behind Kyle. Downcast, she kept silent.

"I must say that I don't trust you, but I do owe you. You've helped me twice now." Kyle stretched, his back sore. "If the future allows it, perhaps one day I will be able to return the favor." Kyle entered the night. The shadows led him to the manor. He left Ellia standing there in the darkness.

◆

The party disbanded, and the feast ended without a boom. Reave chatted with some lass in the corner, but he soon felt too tired. He went up to his room, but not before grabbing some ale. It was a long way up to the third floor of the tavern, the steps creaking. The wooden door screeched as he went in. The modest room had no luxuries: a single bed in the middle with a tiny box for storage nearby. The smell of ashes from a nearby hearth wafted through the open balcony. Reave removed his outer, deep green robes and went out. He leaned over the railing, stargazing.

Reave felt nostalgic. He could still remember looking at the people below from his home. He remembered Zardan, the Celestial King, and the Great Tower.

He watched the villagers scatter to their homes like frightened prey. The faint fire from the tavern brightened the outside, a couple shadows stretching across the ground. The most loyal of patrons were still drinking. A confident knock came at the door.

"It's Hilda," a voice declared, and Reave invited her in. He led her to the balcony, where they overlooked the tiny figure of a drunkard who couldn't find his way home.

"So, what brings you here?" Reave asked, suspicious of Hilda's intentions. Suddenly, he realized that ever since he arrived outside of Zardan, he's been surrounded by people whom he shares no bond with. Perhaps, he could never form a bond to begin with. *Such a depressing idea,* he thought.

Hilda disclosed a concealed bottle of wine and two petite cups. "Just a friendly visit. I have nothing else to do."

"What about Ellia?" Reave asked.

"She's doing her own thing. She wanted me to give her some freedom."

"She might be with Kyle," Reave suggested suddenly. "Is that a good idea?"

"She's an adult. I can't keep her on a leash. The only way she will learn anything is by being out there." Hilda pointed to the horizon, which was very hard to see. Within the shadows, everything looked the same, and the boundary between the horizon and the sky was lost.

"I'll drink to that." Reave smiled.

Hilda placed the two cups on the railing and carefully poured the wine.

Reave sipped from the cup. "White wine, huh?" It wasn't his favorite, but he didn't mind it.

"Any problem with that?" Hilda finished her cup and started pouring some more.

"No, it's not like that." Reave placed the empty cup on the railing. "Women always liked white wine where I come from. It's their drink of choice."

"Conclusion?" Hilda leaned against the railing, staring at the moon.

"Fear the white wine. You can easily drink too much." Reave chuckled. "Do you like stargazing?"

Hilda nodded. "Do you see that there?" She walked closer and pointed at the sky. "That's the Brayden constellation. You know who that was?"

"Some warrior from ages ago. I much prefer the Shahana constellation for she is a symbol of fortune. See those three stars making an arch?" He pointed to the right. "They make up her bow... and those, the fringe of her dress."

"But she stands for good and bad luck, why her?" Hilda turned her back to the sky. Light peeked in through her long hair.

Reave grew silent. He didn't like talking about himself. He didn't like confessions, but even more so, he didn't want to lie to Hilda. "It gives me a sense of peace inside. When you're out there, things don't always work out. I can tell myself that I can't control everything, and something... up there... already decided my fate." Reave bowed his head.

"I like that. Maybe I should revere Shahana then." Hilda poked him in the arm. "So how long have you been away from home?" She poured them some more wine.

"To be honest, I've lost track. Life is very different here than it is at home. At home, everything is organized. Neat and clean. But here, things are spontaneous… different."

A loud thud came from below. The sound of glass breaking, wood creaking, and a scream.

"Looks like somebody doesn't want to leave." Hilda looked down from the balcony. Two villagers were kicked out by the owner. On their way out, they tripped, plunging headfirst into the mud. After some time of struggling to stand up, they sobered up and went home. "Anyway, I know what you mean. Life in my village was so peaceful. I didn't need to have my sword by my side all the time or constantly look over my shoulder." She frowned.

"But you like fighting. I can see that." Reave looked deep within her eyes. Her expression was calm and relaxed.

She chuckled, turning away. "Nothing like breaking a skull."

"That's the spirit." Reave chuckled, but then he realized that she wasn't like him.

"Enough with the wine." She set her cup aside. "So tell me, are you from the city?"

Reave looked at the ground. *Should I tell her?* he thought. *I really don't want to lie to her. She's already figured it out. I'm sure of it.* The thoughts all showed up in his mind. He hesitated, then looked at Hilda. "What gave it away?"

"Well, you said that your home is organized and clean. Only Zardan is liked that." Hilda patted him on the shoulder. "So why keep it a secret?"

Reave remained silent.

"Want to hear my story then?" Hilda leaned closer. "You see, where I come from, the head of our village is a woman of great power. She is the most noble of rulers, yet also the most unforgiving when dealing punishment. She once sentenced a man to be buried up to his neck and left for dead because of something he said."

"I think I might like her." Reave smirked. "Such a merciless and vicious lady."

"She isn't that bad. She has a favorite type of punishment though. She marks a person's wrist in a ritual. The mark burns if the person disobeys her order. She only had to do it three times so far. One person is in exile. Another is dead." Hilda smiled, enjoying the tale, which made Reave question if it was true.

"And the last one?" Reave asked.

"Could you help?" She placed her arm on Reave's lap. He rolled up her sleeve to the elbow. There he saw herbs wrapped tightly around her forearm. She gestured for him to continue. Reave peeled back the leaves to uncover an ugly wound. The skin was heavily burned, bleeding, and liquid seeped from it. Hilda sighed, thinking of her past. She dug her face down as her unbound hair fell down. Reave helped her cover the wound again.

Reave paused. "And the other hand?"

"I sacrificed it for Ellia."

"You have sacrificed so much for that girl." Reave felt sad. Looking at Hilda, he realized that she didn't regret anything. At first, he thought Hilda was forced to take care of Ellia, but now, he realized that she really cared for the young girl and all her decisions were her very own. Hilda was never forced to do anything. She crafted her own fate.

Reave pondered the value of sacrifice. *I have never sacrificed anything for another person,* he thought. *Does that make me evil?* he wondered. No answers came to him. He just sat there, looking at the brave woman sitting beside him.

Hilda soon noticed Reave's robes which he left on the bed. He never wore armor, and it made her curious. The robes were a simple green article of clothing which provided no defense, yet they endowed Reave with the freedom of movement. "What kind of a warrior wears something like that into battle?"

"One that has many tricks up his sleeve."

"You seem to have knowledge of mana." Hilda said.

"Do I?" Reave grew silent again. He didn't want to lie, but she insisted on knowing. He rolled his eyes. "I was a historian in Zardan. I was thrown out because they didn't want me to dig and uncover some fact that would make the city crumble," Reave said with a reminiscing look.

Narilan was made into a kingdom of no history. It had no past, nor a future. The only thing that mattered was the present. All records of what happened for the past 4000 years were kept in the Great Tower, locked away from prying eyes. Of course, the individual towns had their history and some remnants of tradition, but all of that was slowly fading away. The people didn't mind it. Living in the moment was firmly engraved in Narilan's way of life, but dwelling on the past and thinking of the future wasn't.

Hilda poured some more wine, and they shared a toast in hopes of a sympathetic future.

Reave's cheerfulness was gone. He felt bitter. He tried to fight it, but he lost. He was forced to lie yet again in order to hide his true intentions, but he was used to it.

CHAPTER 11

AT THE EDGE of town, Ellia was climbing the hill toward the schoolhouse. Darkness had befallen the landscape, and her one and only guide was the faint glow coming from the top of the tower, where the bell was located. The doors to the schoolhouse were wide open as if someone carelessly left them so. She heard the soft sound of a flute coming from above. The inside was dim, yet a faint glow of light crept up from the back of the classroom to guide her. Everything inside was organized—the perfectly-spaced, miniature desks, the pencils on top—except for the black board, which was covered with scribbles. Ellia found her way to the back and climbed a ladder up the tower to the belfry, where she saw Lord Elring. He was seated in the corner, playing the flute. Countless insects were magnetized to the music. The insects danced around him, emanating with a vibrant purple light. Their wings were translucent, occasionally puffing up some powder.

Elring stopped playing. "Good job today."

Ellia didn't know how to respond. The comment sounded ironic to her.

"Isn't that what he told you?" Elring added, then continued playing.

"Yes, it is, my lord." Ellia took a seat in the opposite corner, their eyes met for only a second. "I was informed you wanted to see me?"

"Yes," Elring acknowledged. "Have we met before?"

"We have," Ellia said. "At the time, you didn't want to see me."

Elring nodded with a morose look on his face. Ellia remembered her first visit to Elra. Elring didn't want to see them, going as far as ordering his servants to escort them out. She lied today when she spoke of her first encounter with him. Her first impression wasn't good in any way. Yet, she heard all the rumors that spoke of a noble and kind Lord Elring, and she wanted to believe them. *There must be some truth to them,* she thought.

"Please tell me why you didn't want to see us?" Ellia asked.

"Perhaps I wanted Kyle to die, to be devoured by the monsters, to perish in despair." Elring bowed his head in shame and defeat. "Ever since I first heard about you, I pondered… why would someone like you choose to help him?"

Ellia wavered as her confidence weakened. "Because I must face someone," she said, her voice soft. She imagined her village, a secluded place populated by only a tiny group of people, a tranquil land on the western side of the kingdom, where people strived and succeeded to live without mana. She remembered Nalza, her home.

"You should've found a better way. Kyle will just get you killed... or kill you himself." Elring played a slightly faster tune, and the bugs began whirling in a tornado.

Ellia felt disturbed and uneasy. Her chest became tight, and she was losing conviction. *I can do this.* "I once thought so too. Yet, over the last few years, about ten others tried and they never succeeded in defeating the Celestial King despite his weakened state. They say Kyle is the strongest. For my plan to work, I need him to win." Ellia shared her inner thoughts with Elring, believing that he might be an asset in the near future.

"Have you ever wondered why no one can defeat the Celestial King? I mean, he must be over a hundred years old now. Shouldn't be too hard to kill an old man, right?" Elring said with an upset look.

Ellia didn't put much thought into it. She believed that a ritual was involved or mana. Another idea that she had was that the Celestial King had someone to fight in his place. "I'll be sure to find out when I make it to Zardan."

"Please tell me when you do," Elring whispered, and began playing his flute again.

Ellia hesitated and looked at the ground. Her breathing became tense again. "I would like you to tell me everything you know about Kyle." Her voice was strained.

"I know about him as much as anyone else. He's narcissistic, egoistical, and he has no respect for anyone." Elring leaned forward as he took a break in playing. "Let me share something with you. I have no proof, but I have a feeling he has another goal. Sure, he wants to become the Celestial King, but I think there is another reason behind it all. It's not to be a tyrant. That's what scares me the most... individuals that I can't fathom." Elring sighed. "He has one weakness though. Be obedient and make him think you're on his side. Maybe that way, you'll gain his respect. Maybe with his trust, you'll be able to influence him."

"Do you know who he might have met with in the tavern?" Ellia asked.

"Avril, most likely. The only person he loves."

Ellia fell silent. The thought that Kyle had someone he loved made her feel more confident. It strengthened her belief that people are a blend of good and evil. "Please aid me in making Kyle the Celestial King," she whispered.

Elring chuckled and took out a small flask hidden behind his back. He gulped its contents down in one go. "Naive girl, truly naive." Then, Elring sprung up and leaned from the tower to look down.

"What is it?" Ellia asked.

"I thought I heard something." Elring sighed. "I once cherished being a representative of the people, but I've come to understand that they're just a brainless mass. They often lack the capacity to think. Bugs and school children, they are the only ones that listen to my preaching."

"They're certainly easier to sway," Ellia said, and the comment bore fruit to an ill will.

"Perhaps you're not as naïve as I thought. Is that because of his influence?" Elring finished his solo, and the bugs spread out. Light diminished, and darkness consumed the place. The moon glowed in the sky. Its craters looked like shadowy blobs or little specs. "I would like you to tell me something. What happened to Kyle's crew? A certain warlord asked me. Apparently his son was a part of it."

Ellia hesitated.

"That's all I wanted to know. You're free to leave." Elring stayed motionless in the darkness.

Ellia found the ladder.

"In the north, there is a warlord whose people struggle with disease," Elring interrupted before Ellia could leave. "Go there, go to Relien. They might have work for Kyle there."

"What's with the change of heart?" Ellia whispered.

"You might still have something that I've lost a long time ago."

"Hope?" Ellia asked, but she heard no answer.

Kyle walked into the circle. He could feel the cold water with his bare feet. It was covering the ground. He listened to the chanting of the priestesses that surrounded him. Their soft but kind voices merged into one—a devoted summon. Kyle looked up at the oculus above him. He could see the cloudy night sky that heeded the chanting and cleared. He identified the Brayden constellation. *Some warrior*, he thought. *What did he even achieve?* Kyle didn't know, nor did he care.

He felt the cold air of the night around his bare back. The many battle scars he had forgotten about long ago stopped hurting. He closed his eyes. The shallow water around him began rippling. He felt something overcome his body—a peculiar sensation. It was as if the Celestial King himself was staring right at him.

Kyle looked up. He knew he shouldn't, but the oculus was there for a reason. Chambers like these were built all over the kingdom. They were called heavenly grounds and believed to be places you could visit to speak directly to the almighty Celestial King. Kyle looked and looked at the sky, but he didn't see anything. No matter how much he wished to see the Celestial King, he just wasn't there.

A burst of air passed through the room, nearly knocking Kyle over. The chanting ceased, and he knew he had to look down again—submit himself to the ritual.

There was also another reason these chambers were special. It was said that the Celestial King bestowed his power upon the priestesses, allowing them to break the rules of mana. It was the only place, a special ritual ground, to bestow a Blessing on someone.

Kyle always wondered what was so special about the ritual—the Blessing. He always heard the usual. A Blessing was a pact between two or more people. It could be formed by a simple handshake, which initiates the ritual. It's almost like leaving a scar on someone's psyche. It was used by warlords to mark their favorite successor, by the Celestial King to punish transgressors, by ordinary people for very important agreements, and much more.

Kyle felt warm. Then the chanting started again and redoubled. The wind swished around. He felt his body overwhelmed by something, which brought him to his knees. He felt a profound aching gather around his chest and then up into his head. Then, he collapsed into the water. His head was aching, pounding. He felt pain in his hand. He held it up to see a tattoo around his finger—a ring.

The ritual was done. His body marked yet again.

He didn't have any strength to get up. He just remained there, the cold water rippling.

CHAPTER 12

KYLE AWOKE MIDWAY through the night, the sky was weeping. His head was still aching, but the thought that he went through the same ritual many times before gave him comfort. He grabbed his tunic and sword, then left. The path from the manor led him back into the village. At the square, he continued left and down a muddy path, leaving a trail of footsteps. In the distance, Kyle saw something, a shapeless object which sank into the ground. When he was closer, he noticed that it was a caravan, but the horses were gone. All of the wooden wheels were drowning in a pool of mud, but none appeared to be damaged. Still, there was no chance that the caravan would be moving any time soon. *This must be it,* he thought.

Kyle pulled open the door and precariously leaped inside, the caravan swaying in the mud. He saw a figure sitting on a bench, legs crossed. As soon as he closed the door, a tiny lamp lit up.

"I haven't seen you in what feels like forever," a female voice said.

"I know, Avril," Kyle said. "But look at you. You've done well." He was unable to find a place to sit, so he chose the floor, his back against the wall. Avril sat close by.

"I'm holding up." Her hair, the color of a night's sky, was weaved into a single braid that drooped almost to the floor. She was wearing a leather jacket and a brooch fastened to her chest. Her girdle had many pouches and knives fastened to it. She also had a pair of boots that went up to her knees. Some expensive robes lie tangled at her feet.

"What about the little mark on your shoulder?" Kyle looked at Avril with concern.

"Just a minor scuffle," she quickly brushed him off. "I took care of it."

"I know you did." He looked up at her. "But I'd like to hear what happened."

"Some peasant was being terrorized by marauders. I took the job, but I didn't expect to encounter so many of them."

"Where was this?" Kyle asked. "Here?"

"In Aylmar." Avril rubbed her eyes.

She must've been waiting for me all night, Kyle thought. "That's not far," he said.

Avril frowned. As Kyle started snickering, she punched him in the shoulder.

Kyle could sense her irritation. He made her wait all this time for his return. "How many?" he asked.

"Nine against one, but they didn't see it coming," Avril said, and Kyle sensed a bit of pride in her voice.

Kyle was satisfied that Avril could handle herself. She accompanied him wherever he went, so he knew she had the necessary skills, but recently something had changed. He had a lingering thought that something might happen to her, and he didn't want to take that chance. He couldn't bear the thought of losing her. And so, instead of taking her on the last mission, he sent her off on an errand. Yet, he had the feeling she knew exactly what he thought. And he knew exactly what he would do if she were to die. Nothing would matter, except the death of the one responsible.

"Did you encounter that beast?"

"No, just a man who lost his mind," Kyle said, stretching. "A really strong man though, a little primal too." He went on to tell her about the mission, Burl's betrayal, and Ellia saving his life. He also admitted he probably pushed Burl too far.

"So the girl who saved you, Ellia, wants to help you become the Celestial King?" Avril looked at Kyle with suspicion. "You shouldn't trust her. What are you going to do about her?"

Kyle sighed. At first he wanted to get rid of Ellia and Hilda as soon as possible, but he changed his mind. "I owe her my life and she helped me get the Blessing. She can stay as long as she wants to."

Avril nodded skeptically. Kyle expected that she wouldn't argue against allowing Ellia to come along. Avril owed Kyle her life, and it was one of the reasons she traveled with him. He knew Avril would understand his obligation.

"You know, I eavesdropped on Elring while you went through that ritual. He met with Ellia. I have a bad feeling about it. She might be up to something."

"Did they notice you?" Kyle looked Avril in the eyes.

"No." Avril grinned. "I don't think so, but I nearly twisted my ankle when escaping. Even with mana, climbing that tower wasn't easy."

Kyle untied her boots and slipped them off. He pulled her closer. She slid into his arms, giggling, knives ringing at her belt.

"Elring is scheming again, isn't he?" Kyle asked.

"He wanted to know what happened to one of your men. He said there was a son of a warlord among them." Avril tossed her hair back. "Then he told Ellia of another place where you could get a Blessing."

"We can discuss it later." Kyle paused.

Avril leaned closer. "Can I see the tattoo?" She had a curious look about her.

Kyle stretched out his hand. There was a tattoo around his index finger, as well as two rings on others. One of them was an elegant silver ring that Kyle received from Kendryck, a warlord from Razan, when he set out on his journey. It was said to protect him. The other ring was much more precious to him; it was a plane copper ring bought in a town called Orrzol as a gift from Avril. Every time Kyle looked at it, it reminded him of her.

Avril eyed the tattoo around his finger. It was completely black, with some inscription that neither of them recognized. Her eyes glittered with excitement.

Kyle watched Avril, and he took pleasure in it. But her empty eyes hindered any attempt to unravel what exactly was going through her head. She had a tiny physique, yet she still had the look of a mature woman. Her curves made it easy for her to manipulate others. Kyle liked that about her. Avril was a challenge, even for him.

"We're almost there." Avril finally said, letting go of his hand. She leaned in, kissing him. She cuddled closer, her breath on his neck.

Kyle kissed her lips.

He noticed that Avril had this peculiar, hidden sadness within. She was trying to conceal it, but Kyle always felt it. She was worried about him. "Just one more," he said, reassuring her.

"And then we can escape," Avril said with a profound sense of disgust that appeared on her face. Kyle easily recognized it. It was that same look she had whenever she looked in the direction of Zardan. The Celestial King's dwelling that stretched up into the clouds only reminded her of her wretched past—Kyle knew that feeling very well.

"We can keep our promise. We can leave Narilan too." Avril put her finger to her lips.

"We might not be able to do both," Kyle said.

Avril shoved her elbow into his ribs. "I can dream, right? But I'll be fine as long as we keep our promise."

"Either way, we'll live the life that we chose to live." Falling silent, Kyle succumbed to musing. This was his ninth Blessing. Each one was a sign of support from a warlord, but many also saw a Blessing as a symbol of goodwill, of helping the people.

I must hurry, he thought, remembering the rules that governed Narilan. To enter Zardan and challenge the Celestial King, a contender for the throne needed ten Blessings. Yet Kyle knew very well that he wasn't the only one. Others were also striving towards the same end. A warlord could have many favorites after all, bestowing upon them the most honorable of gifts—a Blessing.

My aim is almost within reach, he reminded himself. The thought gave him confidence and strength. It was a light of hope that guided him.

They sat cuddled together for a while, gossiping and laughing. Avril was the one person that Kyle trusted above anyone else. He didn't have to pretend or be strong around her. Neither of them had to hide anything because they knew each other inside out.

"This wasn't your caravan, was it?" Kyle ran his hand through Avril's hair.

"No, it was probably Elring's," Avril said. "Why? Is that a problem?" Kyle shrugged. Avril fingered her pendant. A small blue stone hung around her neck. "It was almost empty when I found it. There were only some expensive robes and a few boxes. I know Elring has expensive taste so I couldn't resist looking around."

Kyle nodded with a grin. Despite Elring's humble nature around his people, he had expensive taste and stashed hundreds of luxurious goods in his manor. Perhaps they left the caravan thinking that no one would take the goods. There really weren't that many thieves in Narilan. "I'd like to see his face when he realizes someone emptied his stash," Kyle said, smiling.

"You know," Avril began with an amused look, "I actually gave it all away."

Kyle chuckled, then kissed her.

"It was very nice of you to save those people," Avril said, giggling softly.

CHAPTER 13

DORRELL WAS SITTING in his study. His hair was unbound, and his robes were disheveled. He was dizzy and had a peculiar headache. He took a sip of wine, leaning back into his chair. The stacks of ledgers were more intimidating than usual. Read and finished, books were scattered across the floor.

Albert strode in. "Did you think about it? It might be a good idea."

After Dorrell told Albert about what happened at the meditation ground, Albert kept asking the same question, a question that Dorrell didn't want to hear. It was one of those questions that tempted you and seemed like a great idea. But Dorrell knew otherwise, and he didn't even want to consider it.

Dorrell shook his head. He spent the entire day at the meditation ground, donating mana. Yet it was not enough.

He even gathered as many people as he could, which wasn't much. People in Narilan just weren't keen on sharing their precious mana with others. What little mana they did have, they kept to themselves in case of an emergency. He didn't blame them as these were uncertain times.

"Just think about it," Albert said, his voice friendly. "You could save Narilan. You could protect the people."

"I'd like to be alone, Albert," Dorrell said, then picked up a book. It started to drizzle outside, thunder murmuring afar.

Ever since Dorrell saw that woman at the meditation ground, he wanted to know more about what could happen to someone if mana was overused, but most of all, he wanted to know how he could help. He searched his library all day, but information on the topic of mana was very limited.

There was the obvious talk of mana flowing through everything in the world. It was in people, animals, nature, and everything else. All things were soaked in this invisible energy.

Dorrell did find many topics on overusing mana. Many of them give simple advice on how to avoid suffering—all of them came down to refraining from using mana after noticing any discomfort. Yet none of them gave a solution on how to help someone who was already past that point and suffering.

Dorrell felt his head throbbing. He leaned back in his chair, agitated. *Guess I overused my mana,* he thought, smirking. The dazed state and headache were signs of it.

He tossed another book across the chamber. Even with the largest library in Narilan, he felt blind to the truth and uninformed.

Albert came back with a single book in hand. "Have you read this one? It might have the info you're looking for?"

Dorrell nodded, staring at the book cover. It depicted mana in its purest form—a pale moonlight. "I have. Say, these works go back over 3000 years. What about books before that time?"

"They were lost," Albert said. "I believe it was during a time when a Celestial King died. There was a huge earthquake. Things were truly bleak back then. Only oral tradition remains which was passed down through the generations. My grandmother used to tell me about it."

The storm was closer, rain pelting down. The wind intensified, gusting the windows.

"Is there any chance I could talk to her?"

Albert bowed his head. "She passed away."

The lift groaned, echoing through the chamber. Dorrell fell silent. When the lift stopped, a man came out, the knight from the meditation ground. He had neither his sword nor his armor. He was wearing silk robes and rings on all of his fingers.

"What's the news, sir?" Albert asked.

The knight kneeled and bowed his head. "Preceptor Sahne, I'm extremely sorry to bring bad news. The shipment problem is beyond our control. There just isn't enough mana. I'm sorry."

Dorrell sighed, slouching in his chair. "Stand up," he said, waving to the knight. "You have far more experience working at the meditation ground. Your ancestors have supervised mana donation for centuries. What would you have me do?"

The knight grew silent. "Wait," he said feebly.

"Wait? That's all you have to say?" Dorrell stood up. Then thunder struck and lightning shined through the window. "People are dying out there, and you're telling me to wait?"

The knight hesitated, his eyes wandering around the room. "May I speak from the heart, my lord?"

"Speak," Dorrell declared, then Albert handed him a glass of wine.

"Find a successor, or pray that Kyle will get his tenth Blessing, and he will arrive on time. Help him get here. He should be strong enough to ascend the throne."

Dorrell gritted his teeth. "Get out." He waved his hand.

The knight left in silence.

The thought of a bloodthirsty brute ascending to the throne made Dorrell sick. He was too proud to allow someone to defile the throne. He wouldn't stoop so low. He thought the only viable option was finding someone noble and kind, someone who will care for the people of Narilan.

Dorrell hurled the glass to the floor, shattering it into pieces. His heart pounded as he turned to Albert. The sky roared as lightning struck. Dust fell from the ceiling, the tower quivered slightly. The sky murmured. The storm was intensifying.

"Fine," Dorrell agreed. "Let's do it."

◆

Albert took Dorrell upstairs. They were almost at the summit when the lift stopped. The door opened into a dark chamber. Dorrell stepped forward. It took some time for his eyes to adjust. When they did, he saw circular pools of water, shallow and big enough to house an adult human. They were scattered around the floor, forming concentric rings.

"As you can see, I have made progress," Albert said, and Dorrell sensed pride within his voice. "I was working on it ever since our initial talk months ago. I thought that we would need it eventually. And if not, no one would find out anyway."

"So that's where you intend to keep them?" Dorrell asked.

"Yes, all those who strived to take the Celestial King's place but failed will be here. They will donate their mana to a great cause."

"How long until it's working, Albert?"

"Some time… but I'm close. Just one word and we will proceed."

Dorrell hesitated. He killed Edrick, and for what? He condemned Edrick for abusing his power? For failing to follow laws? Or for treating people like slaves and draining their mana? Yet, here he was making those same mistakes. He felt like an utter hypocrite. "Do it," he declared, his voice strong and determined.

"We always knew you would make the choice when the time came. Your brother was the one who pushed me to start working on this." Albert stood with his hands wrapped behind his back. "It was your idea, you know?"

Dorrell stood silent. He came up with the design for this chamber. Years ago, he shared this idea with Albert and his brother. It was only a suggestion back then, but ever since that day, Albert would ask him about it.

"How does it feel, young lad?"

"What?"

"Making the decision to take the fate of the kingdom into your own hands?"

Dorrell sighed. "It feels rotten, pathetic. Especially since I just killed a man for doing in essence the same thing." Dorrell strode out of the chamber. He felt anxious, but he had already made his choice. He chose to endure the guilt and the ferocious doubt that corrupted his resolve. He chose to fight it all. No matter what, his path was set. There was no backing down now.

CHAPTER 14

ELLIA FINISHED SADDLING her horse, then played in the sand, drawing with her mana. It made her feel calm and relaxed. She knew she had to refrain from using mana; it wasn't hers after all. Yet, she thought it wouldn't cause much harm to use a little of it.

Hilda pulled her aside. Hilda had a serious look, but Ellia didn't mind it. In some peculiar way, it reminded her of home. Hilda was just always like that—even around family she would have a serious expression. It was only from time to time that she would smile and open up.

"Are you sure it's a good idea?" Hilda asked, holding Ellia by the arm.

"I am." Ellia nodded. "Lord Elring told me about the place, and I trust him."

"That's not what I meant." Hilda frowned, then tightened her grip on Ellia's arm. "It's dangerous. You might get hurt."

"When will you stop worrying about me?" Ellia asked, but immediately found the question immature. She regretted asking, and looked away. "I believe that everything will work out for the best. Nothing will happen to me."

"I already told you that people are different here. They might be kind sometimes, but they can also be cruel and mindless." Hilda paused as if to weigh her words. "I know the king of Relien, but he won't be able to do anything if things go wrong. The people will decide."

Ellia nodded. "I have made my decision. I must be strong."

"I respect that." Hilda let go, then frowned. "I just want to know that this is your decision. I don't want you to make foolish mistakes because you didn't know what you were getting yourself into."

"I know." Ellia smiled. She felt pleased that she was making her own decisions—that she was, hopefully, getting acclimated to the world around her. Yet, she still felt tense and powerless.

"I'm proud of you." Hilda patted Ellia on the back, then started walking away with her horse. "To answer your question: I will stop worrying about you when I see that spark within your eyes."

Ellia recalled her mother saying the same thing. When Ellia was at a young age, she couldn't fathom what that spark was, but by now, she believed that she had a good idea. It was a certain state of mind that could be seen in one's eyes. It was a sense of confidence and power that was far more than brute force or mana prowess. Sometimes Ellia saw that spark in others—in Hilda and her mother, Vivianne.

◆

Kyle sauntered through the town square, leading his light brown horse by the reins. It was the same horse he left weeks ago as he headed for the mountains, the small scar was still there on its muzzle. Kyle was trying to reacquaint himself with the horse after such a long absence. He didn't know what was more surprising—that the horse remembered him, or that it was still in Elra.

Kyle strode ahead. Sleeping in the caravan wasn't the best idea, and his back was sore. Yet, catching up with Avril was more important to him. He felt rested as he woke up late. Passing the tavern, he went inside. The stew was served cold, and the bread was stale. He ate them anyway as he needed the energy to travel.

Walking back through the town, Kyle watched the villagers going about their menial tasks as mandated by the Celestial King. A bell resonated in the distance, and the children rushed out of their homes, forming a swarm. Running, they surrounded Kyle, and soon, they were gone somewhere up the grassy incline that was speckled with various flowers and trees. The schoolhouse was visible on the horizon like a beacon of knowledge.

Kyle soon made it back to the sunken caravan. He heard Ellia and Hilda talking, sitting on a dirty rug nearby. Avril was there too. She exchanged a word with them and then tended to her mount. Reave was missing.

Kyle slumped on an old tree stump and drank some water. "I see you've met Avril. She will be with us from now on." He exchanged a glance with Avril.

"Yes," Ellia agreed. Hilda nodded with distrust.

"I know where we're heading to next—"

"I have a suggestion," Ellia interrupted. "To the northwest of Zardan, there is a disease-ridden castle, Relien. I think we should go there."

"Not a chance." Kyle shook his head, pretending to know nothing. "It's too far."

"Why?" Ellia stood up. "There is a chance that helping Relien might get you the last Blessing. I think I could cure their sickness."

"You think your herbs will do the trick?" Kyle towered over Ellia.

Downcast, Ellia froze. Kyle watched her succumb to her timid nature. The flare that he sometimes saw within her was completely burned out—gone. She was just standing there, helplessly trying to come up with something to say.

Reave appeared out of nowhere with his boots covered in mud. His neat green robes were soiled in filth, water dripping from his sleeves. He was completely soaked.

"Where were you?" Hilda said to Reave.

"I was hunting… but it was a very unlucky day."

"Should have thought about the rain," Kyle said.

"Well, I had to wash my face." Reave found a piece of cloth from his sack, and dried his face.

"Nothing like a bucket of cold water." Kyle saddled up his horse.

Reave ignored his comment. As he noticed Avril, he nodded, acknowledging her return.

"So what's it going to be?" Ellia asked Kyle in a trembling voice.

"I wouldn't recommend it," Reave said, brushing off

the mud. "I heard you want to go to Relien. You'll probably be labeled as a witch there. Most of the kingdom treats death as a natural occurrence. They don't fight against it. Helping the dying is forbidden in Narilan." Reave then vanished, looking for his horse.

Kyle remained silent. He heard the vague adage before. It was based around the belief that this life was just a transitional stage; people lived as long as the Celestial King allowed them to live. If they were sick or dying, they just accepted it as a calling. Dying was treated as invitation—as if they were wanted in the next life. But the application of this belief varied. To some, it was only an unenforced notion—a call to accept whatever life throws at you. Some, like the people of Relien, frowned upon and punished any kind of healing—be it herbs or something else. Yet others embraced extreme callousness where the only time anyone was allowed to intervene was in cases of extreme suffering, and the only resolution to that was a warrior's death. Kyle experienced it all; he saw it with his own eyes. He was familiar with the beliefs of Narilan, but to him, they were unconvincing.

"I heard." Ellia turned away.

"And you still want to go?" Reave rolled his eyes.

"Why not?" Ellia insisted, chasing after Kyle. "Tell me."

"Are you really prepared to risk your life for the people?" Kyle turned around to face Ellia. "For the same people that might later kill you?"

Ellia fell silent. A tear dropped down her cheek. "I can't say... I don't know." She looked up. "But I will try. I won't let fear stop me. What about you?"

Kyle chuckled. "You see, King Breneon's son was in

the mountain with me. He died by my hand. As soon as I make it to Relien Castle, I'll be detained. Going there is suicide." Kyle recalled the lad he sacrificed to the creatures in the Fields of Nakroh. He didn't fear Breneon; he didn't fear anyone. But Breneon was impulsive and angry. Even without a son to avenge, Breneon had more than enough reasons to hate Kyle. Kyle then realized he had made quite a lot of enemies over the years.

Everyone grew quiet.

A horse was prepared for travel on the opposite end of the street. Heavy luggage was tied to its saddle, a blade by the side. Elring was arranging for a journey. He mounted the horse and made his way past Avril, bowing his head just a little. Kyle noticed that Elring's eyes were dashing anxiously to meet Ellia's feeble glare. Elring was clearly distracted. A couple steps forward, and the bags suddenly slipped down from his mount. They plunged into mud with a massive splash, then disappeared, submerged.

Kyle hurried to help Elring. He meditated, and soon the bags were spat out by the earth. The two men had to lift them together to place them on the horse. Elring began tying up the ropes by the side.

"So where are you heading?" Kyle asked.

"None of your concern, wretched fiend." Elring snorted.

"Such bitter words." Kyle put on a triumphant smile, but he felt profound contempt for Elring. "I hope to never see you again."

"Likewise. Yet, we both know we will see each other." Elring mounted his horse and trotted away.

Kyle spat, watching Elring. Then there was nothing but anger. Contempt. Kyle really wanted to kill Elring as he did many times before, but he always thought it wasn't worth the hassle. Now, nothing would bring him more joy. Yet, Kyle had enough problems, enough enemies. The only thing stopping him now was the Blessing. He was worried of losing it if he killed the man who just bestowed it on him.

Then Kyle decided. "Let's follow Ellia," he said in a comfortable voice.

"You can't be serious." Avril protested.

"Maybe she will be right again." Kyle gazed at Ellia, but she didn't say a word. "Besides, it's not like Maedr or Leor will ever give me a Blessing." Out of all of the twelve warlords, three hated Kyle, and nothing would make them happier than killing him. Breneon was seething with anger on the first day he met Kyle. Their conflict has only escalated since. And like Breneon, the other two warlords had genuine reasons for hating Kyle. After all, Kyle nearly killed Maedr in their last scuffle a few months back, eliminating most of Maedr's trusted guards in the process before stealing some goods. As for Leor, Kyle seduced his beloved wife. Leor's touchy pride was irreversibly hurt. In the end, it seemed like Kyle was out of options. Getting his final Blessing required approaching one of these three men. No matter what, he knew it wouldn't be easy.

"And if she's not?" Avril asked with a worried look on her face.

"She will burn like a witch should." Kyle snickered softly at Avril. Her complaints stopped, and she returned a self-satisfied grin. Kyle put his arms around her, then pulled her closer. "I know you don't want to go to Relien, but trust me. I'll tell you everything soon."

"There will be bloodshed?" Avril asked.

Kyle nodded.

Reave came back with his horse. "Any chance you

could use mana to... you know, get us to Relien?" He turned to Ellia.

Ellia shook her head. "It's too far. I've already spent too much mana."

When everyone was ready, they left. The sun was shining, and the day was bright. The mild breeze made travel comfortable. The journey started in a very relaxed manner.

Kyle led them north from the village. The lands that surrounded Elra were friendly toward travelers. They had good dirt roads, and travel was safe, but recently, they were cursed with heavy rain. After only a day of travel, the rain started, and it intensified from then on. It was the worst out in the open, but even in the woods the treetops couldn't protect them. When it started to pelt down even harder, the horses refused to continue. They would occasionally let out a grumpy nicker, shaking their heads, water splashing from their manes.

Yet, it wasn't until their hooves started sinking in the mud that Kyle decided to stop. He found a small alcove near a moss-covered boulder. It was a primitive and dirty place, but it protected them from the rain.

Reave leaned against the wall. "Finally a break."

"Whose turn is it to make fire?" Avril tossed her cloak to the side, water dripping from her braid.

"Didn't realized it was this bad." Hilda took off her hood.

"Too bad you haven't seen the Woods of Blood." Kyle tossed his drenched cape in the corner and ran his hand through his wet hair. He then placed his sword against the wall and dropped to the floor.

"Never heard of it," Hilda said, turning to Kyle. "I'll

make the fire."

"I heard of the woods where blood rains from the sky." Ellia took a seat.

"Where did you learn about them?" Reave asked.

"I used to read a lot of books." Ellia wrapped herself in her cape. She was cold.

Avril searched one of her bags, finding a flute. She started playing. The melody that came out was a harsh, discordant string of notes.

"Isn't that Elring's?" Ellia asked.

Avril shrugged. "And what if it is?"

Ellia paused. "It would mean you're a thief."

Kyle watched the scene unfold. He couldn't put his finger on it, but Ellia was changing. There was something going on within her mind that made her different. He thought that she was finally getting used to the world.

"Can I see?" Kyle turned to Avril and pointed at the flute. He closed his eyes and played. A soft melody filled the air—a harmonious yearning for peace that made everyone recall their best memories. When the gentle tune was over, Kyle smiled.

Avril looked at him. "That was lovely. You keep it. I doubt I'll get any use out of it."

"Where did you learn that?" Ellia asked.

"I once had an encounter with the law. I was stuck in a prison cell for a few months." Kyle reclined against the back wall of the alcove. "I needed something to do. And a thug in the cell had a flute."

Ellia frowned.

"Something on your mind?" Kyle gave her a carefree look. "Speak up. It's not like anything dangerous can happen to you."

"What is it with you two and stealing?" Ellia looked up.

"Wait until you see more of the world. You'll realize that this is a battlefield and anything goes." Kyle sat up. "Would you like me to teach you to play?" Ellia slowly scooched closer. Kyle explained how to play a simple tune, but his mind was concerned with something else. He was watching the people around him. He wanted to know his companions a little bit more. They were very different from his usual crowd. They lacked the resentment, the vulgarity, and the bloodlust of most of the other people he was around. Instead, they showed signs of peace, courtesy, and kindness. At least, that's what he would have thought if he trusted his feelings. He didn't, and so he just watched.

Hilda finished making the fire, which enveloped the alcove in a warm light. She rested flat on the ground, and Ellia returned to her side. "So your name is Avril, right?" Hilda asked.

Avril nodded.

"How does it feel being new to the group?" Hilda fixed a bag acting as a pillow under her head.

Avril brushed aside her hair. "Oh, I'm not new. I was the first one to help Kyle. But I only know Reave out of this new group. Does that make me new, then?" She put her cold hands out to the fire. "Tell me, why are you helping Kyle?"

"I want what's best for Narilan." Hilda looked away. "The kingdom needs a strong ruler."

"We both know you're lying," Avril said in a childish and meek way.

Reave came closer to the fire, dragging his bag behind him. "And what's so bad about lying, huh?"

"Exactly." Hilda nodded. "I once traveled to the Tranquil Meadows. They say that all the people there are liars. They will never say anything to upset another human."

"Because all they care about is peace." Avril crossed her arms. "I know that story. Loved ones would live together without knowing anything about one another."

"My point exactly," Reave said. "Why say something if it'll upset someone."

"Maybe to nurture a relationship?" Avril asked sarcastically.

Hilda smiled. "Avril, I think we can come to some sort of understanding."

"But you're still not going to tell me anything."

"Maybe some other time, Avril." Hilda grinned. "Some other time."

Avril frowned, then stood up and came to Ellia. She put her lips to Ellia's ear, "Thank you for saving Kyle."

Ellia nodded with a soft smile.

The fire crackled, and the chatter continued. It redoubled when everyone was sleepy. As if sleep loosened their tongues, the harsh yelps and laughs conveyed nothing important. Kyle watched smiling from time to time. He frequently joined the conversation. He felt peaceful and relaxed. He really didn't want the night to end. The tranquility was something Kyle wasn't accustomed to. The relaxed nature of the chatter made him forget about his ambitions and plans. Yet, he wasn't deceived by any of it. He knew it was only temporary, a fake occurrence that would soon vanish. In its place would return the grim world Kyle lived in.

Distrustful and reserved.

Kyle just kept watching.

CHAPTER 15

KYLE KNEELED ATOP a small hill that overlooked the woods, surveying the area. The rain ceased, but a storm could still be heard in the distance. He waited still, looking for prey. There was none. The woods were empty. All the animals hid or escaped.

"Nothing," Avril said behind him with a tinge of frustration in her voice.

Kyle raised his hand. Everything fell silent. He eyed the bushes that swayed, hoping that it was an animal, but it was only the wind. He sighed.

"Would you finally tell me what you're planning?" Avril poked him in the rib.

Kyle looked around for Hilda. She went her separate way when they began their search for food. She wasn't around, but Kyle wanted to make sure they were alone. "How long has it been since we started this journey?" Kyle asked. "How many challenged the Celestial King before me? Sooner or later, someone will become the next Celestial King, and it might not be me."

"I know." Avril leaned against a tree. "You're not on the best of terms with the last three warlords so that's not helping."

"Exactly," Kyle admitted. "I'd like to say that Ellia's plan will work, but it won't. Breneon will arrest me on the spot. I think Elring will inform him of his son's death."

Avril hesitated. "I didn't know one of his sons was with us."

"Breneon has way too many children." Kyle smirked. He didn't see worry in Avril's eyes. Perhaps she grew accustomed to his way of going about things. He was always engaging in fights and getting involved in all sorts of dangerous situations.

"Why do you want to go?" Avril asked.

"I'm only sharing this with you; Breneon is impulsive and mad. If I can confront him outside of the castle, I will force him to give me his Blessing."

"What?" Avril asked, her voice bearing a tinge of anger. "How do you plan to do that? Besides, even if you get his Blessing, he can take it away before you find a place to perform the ritual."

Kyle agreed. He knew it was a big risk, but he didn't have any other ideas. He couldn't wait much longer. Brute force was all that he had left. Kyle didn't know any other way. Either he would die in Relien, or he would get his last Blessing—those were his only two options.

"Breneon already hates me," Kyle said. "He will do everything he can to kill me once he realizes I'm close to becoming the Celestial King. His emotions are eating him up. I think I can use that."

Avril hesitated, biting her lip. "But is there any way I can help?" she asked, her voice was sad and powerless.

Kyle dug into his bag. He took out a sword. The blade was broken, and the hilt was damaged, but it had an intricate design—two birds fighting over a gem. "I know one of Breneon's sons has a sweet spot for you," Kyle said, teasing Avril. She frowned. "You probably won't get arrested then. If you stumble upon Elring, plant this on him. The broken sword is only a replica I made with mana, but it looks just like the real thing from Relien." Kyle handed her the broken sword.

Avril hesitated, then nodded. "Anything else?"

"When I'll need your help, I will say a specific word. When you hear it, I'd like you to do everything in your power to save me. But don't take unnecessary risks."

"Fine, but I have a request." Avril said.

"Does it have something to do with Breneon's son, the one that, you know?" Kyle smiled.

"His name is Ronn." Avril faced away. "I'd like you to promise me that nothing will happen to him. I don't care about Breneon and anyone else, but Ronn is important to me."

"I can't promise you that." Kyle rested his hand on her shoulder. Avril shivered and he wrapped his cape around her.

Kyle knew Avril had a history with Ronn. Ronn was someone dear, someone Avril could always turn to for help. The one time that they stayed in Relien, Ronn begged Avril to stay. Breneon was furious at his son for such a disgraceful act.

"He will get hurt," Kyle said. "But I can promise you that I won't kill him." He pulled Avril closer, and wrapped his hands around her. He could feel her heart beating. "You don't have to come along if you don't want to. I know Relien brings back memories."

Avril shook her head. "What's the word?"

◆

The morning was cold. Ellia was shaken away by the sound of thunder. She opened her eyes to see the fire smoldering and smoke making weird shapes in the sky. Ellia felt rested and ready. She was still in the woods. Reave was packing. The thunder was far away, whispering something.

"Good morning," Reave said.

"Good morning." Ellia stood up, brushing off the dust from her clothes. "Where is everyone?"

"They're hunting, but they should be back soon." Reave stretched. "I miss a comfortable bunk. How about you?"

"Sometimes." Ellia examined the woods. "Oh, there they are!" She waved to Hilda.

Soon everyone gathered around the smoldering fire.

"We found nothing," Kyle said, walking to his horse.

"Nothing?" Reave asked, raising his brows. "I had no luck the last few days, but I was hoping it was just… bad luck."

"Well, we found a dead boar, but that's about it." Avril said, and Hilda agreed.

"It might have something to do with the Celestial King dying," Reave said, lost in though. "Something is happening to the land. It's the first time in my life I have heard such a violent storm."

"Same here." Hilda nodded, looking at the dark sky in the distance.

The dark clouds clustered together on the horizon. They sometimes lit up with an ominous radiance as lightning stuck.

"Thankfully, we still have water," Kyle said, preparing to leave. "But travel will be very difficult if you're right."

Ellia was silent. She tried to conceal her worry, but she wasn't doing a very good job as Hilda noticed right away. "How will we travel?" Ellia could only utter a whisper.

"Kyle," Avril said. "Remember Razan. Maybe we should head there?"

"We could, but it's a long way from here." Kyle mounted his horse.

Ellia knew the quickest way to Relien was to travel west, then cut through the forest. She even wanted to offer the chance to rest at Nalza. Her people would surely welcome them. Yet, Ellia didn't say anything. She wasn't ready to return until she finished her mission. She had to make it to Zardan. She had to save Narilan and confront someone.

◆

Ellia trotted on her horse behind Hilda, but her eyes were staring at the peculiar flowers that lined the dirt path. Their buds glowed red, yet an open flower had orange pedals with blood-red edges. At the first sight of the flowers, Ellia started sneezing, and her eyes became itchy. Soon, Avril, Kyle, and Reave started having the same symptoms as well

The flowers caused an allergic reaction in people with significant amounts of mana. It started with fiercely red, watery eyes and ended with trouble breathing. While Kyle endured it all in silence, Reave complained. He became lazy, low-spirited, and moody. It was the first time Ellia noticed him complain about anything. Reave almost reminded her of a child in this moment.

Ellia was happy. She thought that the allergic reaction might be a sign that there was mana dwelling deep within her. *Maybe I'm a Dreamer,* Ellia thought. The idea that she had mana enticed her and made her happy.

Suddenly, a ghastly stench hit Ellia, and she covered her face.

"It's coming from over there," Hilda said.

They turned from the path into the woods and carefully descended the grassy slope. When they emerged from a patch of thick bushes, they saw the grass was layered with carcasses. A whole herd of deer was lying in the grass— dead. Blood everywhere, entrails ripped out, their lifeless eyes open. The flies were buzzing around.

Ellia saw some movement. She watched as Hilda walked to a lone survivor and ended its misery.

"Disease." Reave looked around. "I feel sorry for the predators," he said, after noticing that something was feeding on the carcasses.

"It's settled." Kyle watched the sky roar. The thunder was coming from the direction of Zardan. It was moving west. "We'll go to Razan. I'll lead us through the mountains."

Ellia felt sad, but only a little. Soon, she felt nothing. She didn't mind looking around. The ghastly sights didn't bother her. Ellia felt neither disgust nor fear. *It is the world after all,* she thought. She wasn't scared. Her worries vanished, and she relaxed.

◆

Out of the woods, Kyle led them northeast, and soon he saw a village. Its humble houses had straw roofs, and smoke was billowing in the sky. A small lake was nearby too. There was a piece of land in the middle of it that vanished behind the Dominant Veil, along with the lake. The village was Hunt's Hamlet. Kyle remembered being there once; he even had their warlord's Blessing.

Hunt's Hamlet was famous for its minstrels and bards. Many of whom even traveled to Zardan to play during various celebrations and ceremonies. Music was just a key component—and the only remnant—of the village's culture. Children were forced to select an instrument at a very young age and practiced until mastery.

The village was poor. Beggars scrambled for food in the square, and the warlord was nowhere to be found. The people were unwelcoming too. The tavern was empty of patrons. Everyone bought a humble meal, except Ellia who ate nothing in silence, then they left soon after.

The further away they were from the flowers, the less intense were the symptoms. Yet, they didn't go away completely. Kyle felt as if they would never diminish. He looked at Reave. "I'm wondering why you had a reaction to those flowers," he said, thinking of a time long ago when Reave claimed he had no mana.

"Not sure." Reave rubbed his red eyes. "Maybe I have a tinge of mana within me." Kyle sensed that Reave wasn't pleased about the sudden inquiry.

Kyle gave Reave a final look, then frowned at the reply. It was just another mystery—another lie—to associate with Reave. It made Kyle consider ditching him. Despite Ellia's obvious but unknown ulterior motives, Kyle wasn't worried about her nor Hilda. Perhaps he knew he could handle them both. He could anticipate what they would do, but Reave was different. He was a complete mystery. Kyle didn't trust him. He suspected Reave of the worst. He believed that it's only a matter of time before Reave will stab him in the back.

Trotting, Kyle eyed the rivers that flowed down the enormous mountains like veins. The summit was concealed by clouds. To his right stretched the Dominant Veil protecting Narilan from something. It resembled a water bubble—soft and malleable. Kyle wondered what was on the other side, but he couldn't see in. The closer he came to the Veil, the more vivid was his reflection. He saw his own tired eyes and the enormous Great Tower behind him.

Kyle recalled a few times when he tried to tear the Dominant Veil open with his mana. Every time, he failed. He just wasn't strong enough at the time.

When they reached the mountains, Kyle found one of the hidden passages without a problem. He led them down a corridor, decisively making each turn. He didn't even need to think; he just followed the warmth. The further he ventured, the warmer the walls became until the air was heavy with heat as well. When he exited the corridor, he saw steam rise up and cluster above. The sweltering chamber was an empty pit filled with melted rocks, burning crimson red. The rocks murmured something from time to time, scorching below. Poles of rock stuck out above, unfazed by the hellish fires below. The poles were all differed in thicknesses, some having a tip as tiny as a needle's head.

"We're almost there," Kyle said. He spent a fair amount of time in the mountain on one of his adventures. While it was overpowering at first, he grew accustomed to the heat, the oppressive corridors, and the feeling of being boxed in.

As Kyle crossed the pit, he had a smile on his face.

Avril was nimble, and easily made her way across, dancing. Her step was light and swift. Reave was clumsy. He nearly tripped, but Hilda managed to grab him by his robes. He didn't thank her until later, but his eyes were full of fear. Ellia had no trouble crossing, which surprised Kyle. He expected her to panic and slow the group down. Yet, Ellia kept up, and Kyle was impressed.

They continued through a very long corridor until they emerged on the other side of the mountain. The fresh, cold air was refreshing. A humble village was seen in the pale green meadows, its chimneys were spitting out gray clouds of smoke. The wooden huts were inviting after such a long journey. The sun settled behind the village, sinking down. It was blinding, yet like a glimmer of hope, it attracted Kyle.

CHAPTER 16

RAZAN WAS DARK, muggy, and dirty. Scraps littered the ground, and the streets were empty. There was a heavy reek in the air, the stench of corpses. The huts were all occupied, but no one wanted to open their doors. The residents were hidden in their safe havens—warm and cozy.

"This is not how I remember this place," Kyle said, looking around.

Reave snorted. "I'm sure they'll relinquish their food with a smile."

Avril rolled her eyes. Hilda and Ellia said nothing.

"You think this is funny?" Kyle looked at Reave.

When they made it to the stables, they left their horses and continued in silence. The fountain in the center of the square had long gone dry. Next to it was a lone barking dog, forever abandoned. When they made it to the warlord's manor, they were stopped by two sentries. One with a thick beard and a droopy look. The other with a dull sword and a stern expression. The sentries were ready to attack, sword and shield in hand.

"My name is Kyle. I have come to speak to Lord Kendryck."

"Lord Kendryck isn't awaiting any guests," said the sentry with a stern look. "Leave."

"Do you know what this is?" Kyle rolled up his sleeve and put his hand out, palm down. The sentry with a thick beard seemed to want to retreat, but his back was already pressed firmly against the wall. The other one stood his ground. "I'll say it again, I'd like to speak to Lord Kendryck."

The sentry with a stern expression left.

"Do you think he'll agree to talk to us?" Ellia asked behind Kyle.

"I do," Kyle reassured her. "He was the first one to give me his Blessing. He'll see us."

"But will he be able to help...?" Avril looked at Kyle.

The sentry with a stern expression returned. "Lord Kendryck will see you," he said. "But only Kyle and Avril can enter."

Kyle looked at Avril, then at Ellia, Hilda and Reave. Hilda shot him an angry gaze, but he didn't give much thought to it. He entered through the large door, Avril right behind him. They were led down a corridor which was decorated with paintings. The paintings were all depictions of royalty—deceased but remembered. Kyle recognized one man, a cousin of Kendryck, a jovial old fellow with a bald head and a powerful voice.

Inside the Great Hall, the fire was burning. Lord Kendryck was alone, hunched in his throne, and scratching his beard with his gnarled hands. His crown was on the floor, right at his feet. His long ashen hair drooped down his royal robes.

"Greetings, Lord Kendryck." Kyle bowed his head.

Kendryck let out a hearty laugh. "Kyle! Oh, drop the formalities." He coughed, waving his head. "Glad to see you decided to visit Razan. Have you decided to finally return and marry one of my daughters?"

Kyle looked away, grinning. Avril gave him an unpleasant glare. Kyle expected the question. He heard it many times before, each time he visited Razan, but he wasn't offended in any way. It was just a question. Kendryck never tried to force Kyle to do anything. He never bargained with Kyle. Perhaps that's what Kyle liked about Kendryck. If the old man really wanted something, he would just take it. No questions asked. But he wasn't a thief, just an ambitious man following the rules of Narilan.

Kendryck smiled. "So what brings you here, Kyle? Have you given up on becoming the Celestial King?"

"Far from it. I'm traveling to Relien." Kyle walked to a table and left his sword there. "It's my last stop before Zardan."

"Nothing brings me more joy than to hear you say that." Kendryck wiped his face, saliva dripping down his chin. "I would embrace you like a son, but you probably noticed I'm not well."

"I have also seen your withered village," Kyle said with a frown.

"Did Elring treat you well, or was he trouble?" Kendryck asked.

"Troublesome as always. He had no intention of giving

me his Blessing, even after I completed the mission. But things turned out all right." *Thanks to her,* Kyle thought.

"Glad to hear at least one of us is doing well." Kendryck rubbed his forehead. "So tell me, you're traveling from Elra, right? Wouldn't it be faster to go directly to Relien? Don't tell me you've come all this way just to see old Kendryck."

Kyle remained silent. He didn't want to admit it, but the truth was that he avoided the western regions since they were crawling with guards and knights patrolling the areas. He didn't want to fight more than he had to. He wanted to save his mana for when it's really needed, for a real fight.

"The western regions are swarming with knights, Lord Kendryck," Avril said. "We have very little food left. Razan is one of few places that openly supports Kyle."

Kendryck sighed.

Kyle was disturbed thinking about the village and its surrounding areas. Disease was destroying everything. Kyle quickly reshaped the thought into an idea that gave him determination. He couldn't allow himself to be downcast. He needed all the strength he could muster. "Tell me, what is happening here?"

"Disease… famine…" Kendryck trailed off. "It all started suddenly. Plants withered, a storm hit us. I didn't take it as anything special. I mean, we have been living in harmony all this time. I knew that the Celestial King would die eventually, and things might be tough, but this is different. I'm helpless."

"Shouldn't Zardan provide aid?" Avril asked. "I mean, it does so whenever a warlord needs help."

"Well, I received no shipments for the past few

months, and my pleas for help seem to be ignored."
Kendryck shook his head.

"Bastards." Kyle frowned.

"Don't be like that." Kendryck paused. "You can't afford to be led by anger. You must be thoughtful. Whatever
you do, let it be your decision, and not a thoughtless act of
anger."

"I know, I know." Kyle looked away, then nodded.
"How do you plan to work this out?"

"I don't. I'm hoping things will pass when a new Celestial King will be crowned." Kendryck leaned back, his
breathing strained.

"Well, old man, this is not how things work. You're the
one that taught me that if we want something done, we
need to act." Kyle's words, while uncourteous, were honest.
Kendryck valued honesty. It motivated and flustered him.
Kyle was expecting Kendryck to lose his temper or give in
to his histrionic tendencies, but instead he saw no reaction
from the old man. "How bad is it? Tell me."

"People die every day, Kyle. You should see the mass
graves. I tried to hide it for as long as I could, but people
found out. It's impossible to hide it when numerous
people vanish each day."

"Have other places received goods from Zardan?" Avril asked.

"I know for a fact that Relien and Orrzol did."
Kendryck nodded, then leaned back.

Kyle took a seat. Razan was a place important to him. It
was the only place that accepted him. Unlike most warlords,
Kendryck didn't react to Kyle's extreme mana prowess with
aggression or fear. He smiled, welcoming Kyle into his
home. Kendryck saw it as a chance, an opportunity to leave

a mark on the history of Narilan. Slowly, Kyle learned things about mana. It was in Razan that Kyle learned how to wield a sword. The knights taught him how to fight. Of course, it was all under Kendryck's supervision. Without Razan, Kyle wouldn't have the skills necessary to survive in the world. He knew that.

"I think I have an idea," Kyle said.

Kyle walked outside. It started raining again. He summoned Ellia, Hilda, and Reave to the Great Hall. They all took a seat, and a young lass in a fringed dress began serving some mead. It was cold and refreshing. When Ellia's turn came, she refused and asked for water.

"I told Lord Kendryck that we will help him with the food shortage," Kyle declared, sitting at the table.

"And how do you intend to do that?" Hilda asked, arms crossed.

"In two days, there will be a shipment to Orrzol. We will capture it." Kyle watched Reave's eyes flare up. They were glowing with excitement.

"What?" Ellia asked, pushing her mug aside. "You can't do that? If we attack it, people will die."

Again with the preaching, Kyle thought. "You can try doing something about the disease if you'd like... to take your mind off of the slaughter that will be taking place."

Ellia snorted. Kyle saw that she wanted to protest again, but when their eyes met, she fell silent.

"And you intend to do it for..." Avril trailed off.

"As always." Kendryck laughed, then coughed. For a moment, his face was lively and full of mirth. "The young lass won't do anything for free, but I assure you there is a reward. I promised Kyle a portion of the supplies. You take whatever you need. The rest belongs to me."

"I'll pass," Hilda said to Kyle. "I don't want to have any part in the attack."

"Hilda, your sword is from Relien, right?" Avril asked. Hilda nodded, but didn't say anything more.

"Reave, you seem to know a lot about Zardan." Kyle asked with a calm, yet fierce, stare that scrutinized Reave. "Do you know how many knights we can expect to encounter?"

Reave frowned. "Maybe a dozen, maybe more."

Kyle turned to Kendryck. "I assume you will provide some backup."

"You can have all the men that I have... which isn't much, but it'll have to suffice." As his coughing redoubled, Kendryck leaned over the table, pushing his mug off the edge. The mead spilled on the floor. A knight rushed to his side. Kendryck whispered something to him, then nodded to Kyle and left.

"You're free to do as you please," the knight declared. "I'll make the necessary arrangements."

Kyle nodded.

There were fruits on the table, but none dared to touch them. Even drinking the mead was uncomfortable. Kyle was probably the only one without the fear of falling ill.

Reave placed his sword on the table. "When we were inside the mountain, how did you know where to go?" He turned to Kyle. "Most people would lose their way and never return."

"A certain person and I..." Kyle smiled to Avril, "...we got lost there. It took me some time to find my way. We ventured too close to Zardan. At the time, I didn't know that you can't use mana in the region. Looking around, I encountered some guards, and I was injured... quite seriously—"

"But I was the one who found that room full of lava," Avril interrupted.

The sanction on mana. That's another reason why I wanted to avoid going west and getting close to Zardan, Kyle thought.

"I wish I met you earlier," Reave confessed. "You had adventures while I engaged in everyday nonsense." He tipped back in his chair.

Kyle and Avril grinned. It was a rare time when Reave seemed honest, Kyle thought.

"I liked my life," Ellia said. "The peace... and every-thing about it, but adventuring is something else. You don't really have time to think, you just act."

"Do you ever want to go back?" Kyle asked.

"I'm growing fond of life as it is." Ellia bowed her head. "But I do miss Nalza... but I can't go back yet."

"I understand." Kyle reassured her. "Avril and I, we have no home of our own. At least not yet."

Avril perked up. "What about you, Reave?"

"I do have a home, but I'm in no hurry to go back." Reave fell silent.

Kyle looked at Reave. As a warrior, Reave was just too well-mannered with his soft demeanor. Kyle never en-countered a person like that... at least not a real warrior. Reave seemed educated and thoughtful. *Maybe he's from Zardan,* Kyle thought.

"All right. I'm tired after the journey. Let's meet up in two days." Kyle stood up and stretched. He felt his body aching from the constant travel. He was yearning for a warm bath and some tranquility.

CHAPTER 17

HILDA SAT BY the window in Kendryck's manor. It was already dark outside. Placing her hand on the hilt of her sword, she thought about Avril's sudden question. Hilda wondered if she should have revealed her relation to Relien. *My sword says it all,* she thought.

Hilda looked at the hilt of her sword. The battle between the two birds felt like an accurate representation of her internal struggle—and the gem was a symbol of her heart. A part of her was honest and didn't want to hide anything unnecessary. Yet a different part rebelled. Rattled, it didn't want to reveal anything. It didn't want to bow to the likes of Kyle. It wanted to do things its own peculiar way. But what way? Hilda didn't know. It was just the rebel inside her speaking, a rebel she frequently subdued. It lay dormant as she adventured, the thought of the mission fully consuming her heart.

Hilda didn't know what Kyle was planning in Relien. *Maybe he thinks Ellia will heal everyone,* she thought. Yet, her intuition was telling her Kyle had something else in mind. Again she was worried about what might happen to Ellia.

She thought of King Breneon, the ruler of Relien. Many years ago, she saved his life. It was a fluke, a chance encounter. She was hunting when he was attacked, and she managed to ward off the marauders. She wondered if King Breneon would even remember her.

Hilda hoped so. Deep down, the thought that King Breneon owed her his life made her feel stronger and secure. But she was worried about what the people of Relien might do.

Then it hit her, the reason she was so anxious. She was worried about Ellia. They've traveled together for so long that they grew close. Hilda couldn't imagine a life without Ellia. Yet, she knew she couldn't get too attached. She was already too close, too caring, and she couldn't help it. Ellia was the center of her world. She was her niece, but also a reminder of the deep, inseparable bond she shared with her sister.

Then Hilda made a choice. Ellia wished to be treated like an adult. She chose to go to Relien. Hilda decided to respect that choice. Putting everything aside, she decided to support Ellia as she always did, and let Ellia make her own decisions.

Hilda sighed. She knew the time had come. *I won't be able to protect Ellia forever,* she thought.

In the window, she saw someone walking out into the field. She thought it was Kyle, but she wasn't sure. The figure sat down to meditate.

I'll keep a close eye on Kyle while we're in Relien, Hilda thought, lost in her tempest of thoughts.

◆

Ellia knocked on the door. She tried to make a strong impression, but instead the knock came out feeble and indecisive. She walked in, swallowing.

Lord Kendryck's chamber was lavish. The huge bed he was sitting in had white, silk sheets and crimson red blankets. There were many pillows, a couple on the bed and the others cluttering the floor. The thick, brown carpet had various intricate designs in red. The wooden chair tacked in the corner had a plain blanket on it.

Ellia took a seat, then wrapped the blanket around herself. "You called for me, Lord Kendryck?"

"Yes." Kendryck nodded. "Have we met before? Are you from Nalza?"

His eyes seemed piercing to Ellia, as if he knew something she didn't. "Yes, have you been to my village?" she asked anxiously.

"Well, I've been to the Cluster, and I've met with the Lady of Benevolence," Kendryck confessed with a proud smile.

Ellia was content hearing his words. Formally, Nalza was known as the Nalza Village Cluster, a group of neighboring, tiny encampments that were united under the rule of the Lady of Benevolence.

"Which village do you come from?"

"The most western one," Ellia said.

Kendryck brooded for a moment. "I'm sorry for your loss. I'm sorry about what happened."

Ellia hesitated. She had never met anyone before who

would've heard about the tragedy that struck her village. Most people didn't care for Nalza. Yet Kendryck visited her village and knew what happened. "I can't believe that the Celestial King would allow such a thing," she said, her hands tightening around the blanket. "I think the Celestial King abandoned us."

Kendryck smiled, scratching his beard. "Perhaps not. Look at what is happening here in Razan or Hunt's Hamlet. As far as I know, the rest of Nalza is safe. It's not suffering from disease."

Ellia perked up after hearing his reassuring words. "Thank you for telling me that."

"I'd like you to be careful. People are not fond of Nalza in the north. They're tired of Nalza's preaching."

Ellia nodded with a sad expression. People throughout Narilan looked down on Nalza. They viewed it as an insincere place, frequently calling the Lady of Benevolence a hypocrite. Perhaps people just couldn't fathom how Nalza had an absolute ban on mana, yet its ruler was a Dreamer.

"Can I ask you about something, my lord?" Ellia inquired. "Please tell me about Kyle. What kind of a man is he?"

"There are many tales of atrocious acts done by Kyle. Ask any bard, and he shall tell you. I, for one, will tell you only a single thing. Kyle is an animal..." Kendryck trailed off with a pause. "Stand in his way, and he won't hesitate to kill you. Trick him, and he will come after you. Stand aside, and he will pass."

Ellia nodded.

"One more thing," Kendryck said, then coughed. "There is a rumor going around of a Dreamer who is using mana to teleport, searching for Kyle. Rumors spread quickly, you know? They say the Dreamer's name is Ellia."

Ellia exchanged a sincere smile with Kendryck. She knew he was trying to warn her. She enjoyed his company. Unlike Kyle, Kendryck wasn't intimidating; he was normal. There was nothing about his behavior that set him apart from all of the other people Ellia met, and she liked that. Despite being a king, Kendryck was honest, and his behavior was simple.

◆

Kyle's heartbeat was steady, slow, and harmonious. His breath was shallow and light. He sat in the field; legs crossed and palms up. His body felt heavy, weighed down as if it was about to sink into the ground. He had that peculiar sensation that irked him to move, an eagerness to act. The longer he kept still, the more powerful it became. He liked that feeling.

With each breath, his body became heavier. With his mind empty, he lost sense of his surroundings. He saw a pale white light. It was inching closer to him, but not blinding him. He could look at it, the eyes of his mind wide open. It was powerful and bright. Soft, yet overwhelming. Its warm touch swallowed him.

Kyle took another breath, then opened his eyes. He felt rejuvenated.

Avril was sitting beside him, her eyes closed and breathing relaxed. He wanted to whisper something in her ear, but he didn't want to ruin her meditation.

Kyle saw a knight coming their way. He stood up and sneaked away.

"I apologize for disturbing you, sir," the knight declared. "We are ready and awaiting your orders. Lord Kendryck wishes you the best of luck."

Kyle nodded. "Tell the rest of my group to prepare." He looked in the direction of the nearby village of Darga. It was where he was born. He even considered visiting, but quickly dismissed the thought. He had no relatives there anymore. There was nothing to come back to. While he could visit the graves of his parents, he wanted to do so when his battle was over, when his mind wasn't clouded with all the nuisances.

"Ready?" Avril whispered into his ear. He shoved her gently in the shoulder, frowning.

The two days were over. They passed quickly, but they were enough to rest. Kyle strode in the direction of Razan, Avril right behind him.

◆

The woods were whispering with excitement. The clouds were dark and crying. Kyle was hidden in the bushes. Avril and Reave were by his side. He saw Razan's knights across the path in the bushes. The subtle murmur of the caravan could be heard in the distance. The sentries' rhythmic footsteps intensified. The cadence of steel could be heard moving through the forest. Kyle watched the caravan crawl closer as he emerged, blocking its path.

"You are in the way of an official transport. Identify yourself at once," the sentry in charge declared. Yet his words were only met with silence. "Step aside or you shall die," the sentry rasped.

"It's pointless to waste my breath on you," Kyle brushed him off. "This will be over in a heartbeat." Then

Kyle resolved to give the order. With one quick step, and a fast slash, the sentry was beheaded before he could draw his sword. As his head rolled off his shoulders and his limb body collapsed to the ground, Razan knights screamed, spilling out of the bushes.

Kyle slaughtered those that crossed his path, his eyes intently watching as most of the sentries died in the initial frantic charge. Some failed to react, ignorant of their impending death. Others struggled hysterically. This only hastened their demise. When the transport was surrounded in blood, some fled. Those were quickly dispatched by Reave or Avril.

When all was said and done, Kyle rummaged through the supplies and loaded his horse with bags. Avril did the same. He watched as Reave looted a dead sentry, quickly and discreetly.

"You can have everything else," Kyle told the knight of Razan in charge.

"Thank you." The knight bowed. "This means a lot to us. Razan is in your debt."

"You're mistaken," Kyle said. "I'm just paying a debt of my own."

When they finished, Kyle trotted away with Avril, and Reave trailed behind. They rejoined Ellia and Hilda, then followed the path that ran parallel to the mountains that surrounded Zardan. They crossed a makeshift bridge, the river gurgling, and continued down the path.

They traveled in silence. In the end, Ellia was unsuccessful in curing the disease. Perhaps with more time, she could have understood its workings. Perhaps with much more time, she could have succeeded. Kyle saw tremendous disappointment in her eyes.

He turned to look at the goods they had just stolen. He felt a sense of satisfaction. As much as he didn't want to admit it, Razan felt more like a home to him than Darga. Deep down, he felt indebted to Razan and Lord Kendryck. He was content with helping them in these harsh times. It was the least he could do.

Kyle took a dirty cloth and wiped his hands. The blood didn't want to come off.

He was used to it. The battles, the bloodshed, he knew it all.

He was grateful for that.

CHAPTER 18

DORRELL DUG HIS head into his hands, sitting half-awake at his desk. Trying to forget his usual delight in sleeping, he was constantly reminded of the sleepless night behind him. He lifted his head and skimmed the ledger—one of hundreds. The masses of paperwork turned into thin corridors around his entire chamber, making any trek feel claustrophobic. Albert maneuvered an antique cart with some breakfast on it through the chamber, the wheels yelped for some oil.

"Had a long night again, young lad?" Albert asked.

"You can't even imagine." Dorrell dug himself out of the paperwork, staring at the breakfast. It was a simple one, a couple of slices of bread matched with a few boiled eggs. Dorrell could never digest any kind of meat right after waking up. If he tried, he would feel sick, and it almost felt like his body just rejected that type of meal.

Forcing a smile, he blindly searched for something buried in the pile of papers on his bed. He pulled out a red folder. It contained the names of all the Dreamers who failed to defeat the Celestial King.

"That seems to be the only thing on your mind nowadays," Albert complained. "I also wanted to report that we've acquired fourteen samples so far."

Dorrell perused the list. "Good. We're just preparing, so let's not make any rash decisions."

"They're just awaiting your judgement." Albert tried to reassure Dorrell. His face had a concerned look.

Dorrell took a seat, ready to begin breakfast. He wasn't very hungry, but he didn't want the food to go to waste. "This will probably sound weird, but make sure to have an eye on Cwen and her assistant. I can't put my finger on it, but I have a feeling she might do something."

Albert nodded, then watched as Dorrell gobbled up the breakfast until the plate was empty.

"I know you want to say something." Dorrell wiped his lips with a handkerchief. "If so, say it."

"Are you sure about what you're doing? You've been acting differently recently."

"I have. I'm more determined. Ever since Edrick..." Dorrell's words gradually faded. He realized Albert was the only person he could open up to, even though he didn't most of the time. It still felt comforting to have someone to talk to without being judged. Dorrell sighed, and smiled lightly. "We're just looking at alternatives."

"I'm not criticizing your work," Albert immediately replied. "I just don't want you to lose track of what's important. I have been working on this idea for a while now. I'm just worried that you're making rash decisions.

This has to be your decision. Not mine."

Dorrell shrugged. He signed a few more ledgers, then read a few more manuscripts. "I'm not about to lose myself. I will do what is necessary to ensure that this kingdom survives," he declared formally and forced a smile. He feared disclosing his honest feelings. He was worried that it was already obvious he wasn't up to the task. He was kneeling, forced to the floor by the weight of his decisions and the future.

The thought that he was bending the laws of Narilan felt disheartening. He really didn't want to proceed with the plan. Yet, he thought that Narilan might fall if he didn't. He chose to act tough, ignore his personal feelings, and continue.

"Oh, your work is splendid indeed," Albert said, pouring some tea. "One might even see it on par with the throne." He took the cart away, hiding it around the corner.

Dorrell trusted Albert. Their lives intertwined multiple times, and Dorrell had known him since childhood. Yet at times, Dorrell felt like the servant, and not the other way around.

"Narilan is just too dear to me. I'll do anything to save it, even if I'm labeled as evil," Dorrell said, walking to his telescope.

Suddenly, a trumpet blared above. Its sound strong and vibrant, resounding through the entire kingdom. It indicated that the workday was over, and all citizens could go home. Through the telescope, Dorrell watched as all flying creatures—birds and insects—danced to the harsh rhythms coming from the Great Tower. They flapped their wings joyfully as they gathered, surrounding the Celestial King's dwelling—his place of refuge. Without a warning, the tune ceased, and the animals stopped dancing. They did a final loop around the Great Tower, making it disappear as if surrounded by a hurricane. Then they disbanded, flying in all directions of the world.

Albert hesitated. "Evil, you say? Maybe to the ignorant eyes, maybe to the unwatchful, but your intentions are pure. You have nothing but the best in mind for Narilan."

Dorrell frowned.

Albert rubbed his forehead. "If it helps, imagine that maybe the Father of this kingdom had to face the same dilemma."

"Do you know where I could read more about Him?" Dorrell asked, but his question was never answered as Albert escaped through the door. Sealed inside his chamber, Dorrell realized that it was late afternoon. The sun was slowly hiding behind the horizon.

He fell onto the bed for just a second.

He was asleep before he could fight it.

CHAPTER 19

THE FIRST THING Ellia heard was the powerful blare of the trumpets from the Great Tower. She was riding on her horse right behind Hilda, with Kyle, Reave, and Avril only slightly ahead. Castle Relien stood before them, and an imposing, wooden gate greeted them. The cold stone walls that surrounded Relien towered over them, and the archers gave them crestfallen stares, peeking from the arrow slits. The four towers that surrounded the castle reached high up into the sky and were crowned with battlements. Unlike most of the other regions of Narilan, Castle Relien had some of the grandeur of Zardan, but it was also firmly grasping to its own traditions.

Fully armored, knights patrolled the streets, making sure order was rigidly upheld. Their spherical helmets had two tiny holes for the eyes, and a pair of horns on top—

each decorated with thorns. The rest of the armor imitated the round shape of the helmet in an attempt to make everything uniform—all at the cost of hiding any signs of a muscular physique. Each knight also had a double-edged sword hooked to their belt. Although Relien was not in a state of war, every post was occupied.

After leaving their horses at the stables, they made their way to the town square, and Ellia was startled by discordant noises—cheers and cries.

Kyle walked slowly. "I wonder what they're celebrating." He looked around. The streets were full of mirth. People were drinking outside, their laughs booming. Women were gossiping, their aprons neat and clean.

A girl merrily strode past them, a garland on her head.

"Well, it's not coming from the castle," Avril said.

"Could be the cathedral," Ellia said, and Hilda agreed.

"But it doesn't look like they're suffering like Razan," Avril added.

"They might be doing a better job hiding it." Reave looked around.

They continued in silence.

Deep within the walls, there was a cathedral, which was only overshadowed by King Breneon's imposing castle looming overhead. Lively cheers and stringent clamor echoed through the courtyard. Music was playing in the background. It reminded Ellia of a wedding. The cathedral was too small to fit everyone, so the crowd spilled into the courtyard. Some people tried to fight their way to the front, while others stood on their toes, hoping to get a glimpse of the majestic ceremony inside.

Ellia watched Kyle stand impatiently before the crowd. She saw a glimmer within his eyes—a sign of ambition and greed. *What is he doing?* she thought. *Is he going to rush in there?*

Before Ellia could say a word, Kyle vanished.

She then saw a boy weeping in the grass. The boy looked scared. His knee was bleeding, and Ellia noticed the bloody cobblestones. The boy's eyes widened as he was about to cry.

Ellia felt a familiar sensation that she couldn't resist. She had to follow her heart. She couldn't just look away. She overheard Hilda whispered behind her, "I'll keep an eye on Kyle."

"I'll watch Ellia then." Reave bowed his head, giving Hilda a soft smile. She didn't reciprocate, her face stern.

"Why leave me now?" Ellia called out to Hilda.

"You already have that spark. I can see it in you." Hilda smiled lightly. "And because I know that I can't help you anymore." Ellia watched Hilda walk away slowly—in that bereaved, yet hopeful pace.

Ellia bowed next to the boy. She wrapped some leaves around his knee, their juices dripped down. Ellia's treatment proved to relieve pain, and it pacified the boy. His eyes showed a sign of relief. Ellia smiled. She felt warmth within her chest. She was scared coming to Relien, but she never admitted her fears to anyone—not even to herself. Yet, they were all gone now. She felt at peace, for she knew she was doing the right thing. The boy's relaxed look turned into a frightful grimace. Ellia turned around to see a disheveled peasant behind her.

♦

Kyle pushed his way through the crowd. The candles from the chandeliers were smoldering, extinguished by the fierce gusts of wind coming from the south. The smoke gathered below the ceiling before it escaped through the stained-glass windows, which depicted various figures— all from Relien and none from Zardan.

The people of Relien were giving their full attention to the head of the cathedral, a cleric in humble white robes with an image of two birds fighting embroidered on his chest. He recited a few litanies in a pompous tone, his face hidden underneath a hood. His unmoving eyes contradicted his fervent voice. He then whispered something to the couple facing each other in front of the altar.

King Breneon, the ruler of Relien, stood right beside the man who was getting married. Kyle instantly recognized the man as Ronn, Breneon's youngest son. He bore a striking resemblance to his brother, whom Kyle had killed. Ronn had an honest smile. His black, uneven haircut was brushed back, patted down close to his head. His hands were trembling with fear. Kyle wasn't sure if Ronn was scared of the ceremony, or of getting married. Ronn's bright eyes were glued to the woman standing before him. Her face was hidden under a veil. The pallid dress made her look like a true angel.

When the cleric uttered the final words, Ronn pulled up the veil and kissed his new wife. The citizens of Relien cheered, then bowed and murmured a prayer to the Celestial King, the divine being sitting at the summit of the Great Tower, asking for good fortune on behalf of King Breneon and his son.

Kyle stood his ground. Hilda kneeled, showing respect. Avril hesitated for a moment when Ronn looked their way. Kyle watched as she hid in the crowd. He waited until Breneon finished what Kyle considered a farce.

Suddenly, every person from the crowd applauded and shared the happiness of the moment. Breneon finally faced Kyle and stared him down from under his thick black eyebrows, hiding any hint of surprise. His pupils wandered around the hall until he made eye contact with the guards. Without any kind of signal, the guards sprang into action. Kyle was well aware of their practices.

The celebration came to an end, and the peasants moved slowly to the back of the cathedral, where they formed a bottleneck and struggled to exit.

"You have guts showing up here," Breneon said with his back to Kyle. "Do you have anything to tell me before I make any rash decisions?" He ran his hand through his long grey hair. His movements were slow, weak. The spherical crown over his head was decorated with only a couple of jewels—tiny emeralds and large sapphires. His thick, violet cotton cape drooped down to the floor. Kyle sensed that Breneon wanted to grab the ceremonial sword at his belt.

"I've come to lament over the death of your beloved son," Kyle lied, then watched as irritation crept up Breneon's face and his calm behavior changed into a struggle to restrain frustration. Hilda listened closely, and Kyle had a disgusting smirk all this time.

"If I didn't know you better, maybe I would've believed you." Breneon walked closer to Kyle, leaving Ronn and his wife behind. "Tell me what happened."

"We were ambushed by some vicious creatures in the Fields of Nakroh," Kyle said. "My whole crew was separated. I lost over half of my men. I didn't even realize your son was part of my team until we made it to Mount Nakroh."

"Give me a reason why you shouldn't be executed tomorrow?" Breneon said in an ugly, hoarse voice. His hand rested on the pommel of his sword.

"Would I come here only to lie?" Kyle asked, looking at Breneon. He had a history with Breneon. Each of their brief meetings in the past ended with a scuffle and a few dead Relien knights.

"Then why come to Relien?"

"Looking for some work."

"Impertinent fool." Breneon chuckled. Yet, his face showed no mirth. It was full of disgust, subdued anger, and restrained hatred.

Kyle fell silent.

"I see it written all over your face. You have killed my son. Unfortunately for you, it's your testimony against mine. I should be merciful, but I'm the king here and I know you all too well."

Something crashed into the back of Kyle's head. He felt a sharp pain that resonated through his skull. He fell to his knees, grunting. The guard behind him was stoic, and the hilt of the sword in his hand had blood on it. Kyle gritted his teeth, then forced a smile. He didn't put up a fight as the guards disarmed him. The anger flared inside his chest, but he restrained it. He knew this would happen. He was prepared for it.

He saw the mistrust in Breneon's eyes—the fear and suspicion. Breneon was struggling with the emotions inside.

"You'll be executed tomorrow, first thing in the morning," Breneon rasped. "Where is the girl that travels with you?" he added without looking at Kyle.

Hilda stood surprised.

Before Breneon ordered the knights to search for Avril, Ronn intervened." Father, let me take care of it."

Breneon hesitated, then nodded. "Fine, but if you find her, she's your responsibility." Breneon frowned at Hilda, ignoring her. He strode out of the cathedral. His pace was fast and determined. He didn't look back at Kyle.

◆

Reave watched as the crowd gathered. He took a step forward, but just as he did, someone shouted for the guards. Reave shoved aside a person who blocked his way, catching sight of Ellia by the boy. Yet his eyes dashed quickly to the arrow slits and the battlements. The archers were already watching.

He wanted to intervene—to keep his word. Yet his mind was too fixated on the heavy metallic footsteps. The guards were already here. And with their arrival a deeper, more entrenched part of him—a part that rebelled against his good will—took over. His urge for self-preservation so seductively made him feel that this was not his problem, that this situation didn't involve him.

Why should I risk my freedom for the sake of another's foolishness? He shrugged with a bitter frown.

As he caught a glimpse of Ellia, Reave stilled. For a moment, he thought she was looking his way with a plea for help. That's when he averted his gaze and steadily retreated.

◆

Hilda was about to leave the cathedral when she heard a feeble scream. She fought against the crowd, trying to push through. Outside in the courtyard, she saw that the crowd formed a ring around a new commotion. At once, she forced her way until she could see what was going on.

"Leave my son alone, you filthy witch," a peasant screamed. His tattered clothes made him look overworked and mindless.

"I was just trying to help," Ellia pleaded.

"Guards!" a woman screamed; her soiled long hair fell down her face as she bowed before the boy.

Many guards were already present, forming a loose ring around the commotion. Yet they didn't intervene. Most of the guards gazed ahead with a distant look. Only occasionally did a glance wander to the one in charge—a closely-shaved knight who sat at a table, eating stew. He was in no hurry to act. With every hateful comment, he seemed to titter, relishing the escalating conflict.

Hilda placed her quivering hand on the cold pommel of her sword. Her unsteady grip tightened. The more she struggled to still it, the more it trembled.

"I'm fine, mom," the boy said before the woman could ask. The peasant stood his ground.

A single, weightless pebble struck Ellia's back, and then another—and another. Ellia shrank to the floor, covering her face with her hands as the pebbles turned to stones. Hilda froze and watched Ellia. She saw Ellia's face—the anger.

Ellia staggered to her feet slowly. "What is wrong with all of you?" she called out, her voice enraged. "Don't you feel compassion?" A rock with a sharp edge hit her in the forehead, and she collapsed to the ground. Her face was dirty from the soil, and blood dripped down her right eye. She wept.

Hilda was watching the whole scene unfold, unable to move. She yearned to rush in and protect Ellia no matter the cost. Yet something held her in place. Motionless and cold. She desperately thought about what she should do. Fighting her way out of Relien was out of the question. She could beg King Breneon to intervene, but he would never listen. He didn't even remember her after all. A thought crossed her mind suddenly—the idea of leaving Ellia. The thought made her cringe within. It made her feel ashamed.

Abruptly, Hilda hated herself for not stopping Ellia. They visited so many places together, yet none made Hilda feel this way. She tried to grasp this very thing which insidiously crept in and thwarted her resolve. Aimlessly searching for an answer, a tear dropped down her cheek as she saw Ellia bleeding—crawling. Their eyes made brief contact, but Hilda quickly turned away in disgrace. And then she understood.

This thing which ensnared her in this very instant was always there, but she smothered it within, amidst her cold bravery. She refused to acknowledge it time and again. But it lingered, festered. Now, it surfaced at last. And it broke her. Hilda seethed at her own helplessness. Her cold, trembling hand was about to senselessly grab the hilt of her sword.

"Dying here won't help her," Reave said in his usual, indifferent voice. He seized Hilda's hand and held her with full strength.

"Let me go!" Hilda demanded. Reave didn't respond.

Not ready to listen, Hilda propelled her head back, striking Reave in the face. His grip loosened as he retreated, blood gushing from his nose. Hilda pulled out her sword. The metal shrieked, then turned into a metal snake which writhed itself around Hilda's arms and forced her to the ground with its weight.

"You said you would look after her!" she barked.

Yet Reave kept silent, unable to meet her gaze.

Ellia's shrieks and cries were muffled by the cheers and shouts of the crowd.

The closely-shaved knight finally stood up and walked forth with his second-in-command, the crowd opening up for them. He first listened to the testimony of the peasant woman, then walked to Ellia, who was surrounded by a circle of rocks. Ellia elbowed the second-in-command as he tried to restrain her. Before she could move, the closely-shaved knight punched her in the stomach.

Ellia let out a feeble cry, then fell. "You should all be in my place," she rasped. "I chose to be here, and you have chosen too. You have chosen to suffer." The knight grabbed her by the arm, yet she wriggled free. Seething within, Ellia lashed out, planting her fist in his face. He grunted, eyes wide open, blood trickling out of his mouth.

At once, all the guards stepped forward, ready to intervene, yet the knight simply lifted his hand and they stilled.

Ellia whimpered, hugging her bloody hand, as she collapsed to her knees.

The knight groaned, coming back behind her with his blade unsheathed. "You suffer because—" Ellia screamed as he dug the pommel of his sword into the back of her head. Ellia fell to the ground like a broken doll, her limbs lifeless.

The closely-shaved knight had a broken jaw. He tried spitting, but most of the blood dripped out of his mouth, down the chin, and either to the ground or down the neck. He spat out a tooth, and then another. The other guards watched him in awe. He gave them a single glance, and they knew not to stare.

Hilda looked at the guard with the broken jaw. She knew she would never forget his face.

CHAPTER 20

ELLIA STRIPPED OFF her dress and relinquished her belongings. She was forced to wear some old, filthy rags instead, and then a pair of guards led her down a spiral of stairs into the dungeon. Her bare feet shackled in chains, she had to watch her step. It was very easy to slip and fall. The cold stone floor made her shiver. When she made it to the bottom of the stairs, she saw far more guards than she expected.

"Twenty years and so far we have only had three prisoners. Today must be our lucky day," a guard spoke in a lighthearted voice, ready to laugh.

"Two in a single night, huh?" a second guard said eagerly. "When was the last time something like that happened?"

Ellia listened, but she wasn't scared. Her anger dwindled as well. She was already thinking of a way to escape, a way to use her mana to leave Relien.

"In the last 4000 years?" The guard chuckled. "Never."

"That's probably why King Breneon ordered all of us to watch the prisoners today."

Unlike all the other guards who were carefree, the two guards that escorted Ellia wanted to leave the dungeon as quickly as possible. Their faces were concealed by their helmets, but their voices revealed the tension that they felt. As soon as Ellia was shoved into a tiny cell, they left. She wondered if they were scared of her.

The cell was small and dark. The tiny window above opened up to the street, and its bars were repulsively greasy with the sewage of the inhabitants of Relien. The dense, foul muck dripped down the walls and onto the one and only bench right underneath. Ellia frowned, then took a seat in the opposite corner. It was the least dirty place.

She tried flexing her bruised hand. At once, she hissed. The hand wasn't broken, but every move was painful.

We've visited so many places. We've been here before. I never could've imagined that people could act so horribly, Ellia thought. She felt disappointed in the choices she made. Then she felt something else emerge in her mind, a much more overwhelming feeling—sadness. She felt calm, but defeated and foolish.

"Relien looks well," a muffled voice penetrated the wall to her right. She leaned against it, oblivious to the filth dripping down.

"The disease is gone, Kyle" Ellia said. "I don't even know if it was here in the first place."

Elring might have lied, she thought, cringing inside. *He tricked me. I was a fool.*

"It's my fault I'm here," Ellia said. "But I didn't think you would just come to Relien to get arrested."

Kyle was silent.

Ellia realized why the two guards wanted to leave. They feared not her, but Kyle. *That would mean that the rest of the guards outside were unaware of the identity of the man they were supposed to be watching*, she thought. "Do you think we could escape?"

"I wouldn't try using mana here if I were you," Kyle said.

Ellia knew he was right.

While Narilan didn't have many problems with Dreamers breaking the law, they came up with a tactic to detain those who did break it. Somewhere nearby, there was a Dreamer who meditated, focused on the dungeon. It was a Dreamer who spent his entire life monitoring the world, a Spectator. A Spectator's consciousness was much more sensitive and in tune with mana. He felt the world on a deeper level. He could also spread his mana over a very large area and keep it that way for a prolonged period of time to monitor it.

The whole dungeon was most likely drenched in a Spectator's mana. He could thus detect anything and everything that went on inside. If a prisoner tried to use mana, the Spectator would know about it and could alarm all the guards. If the prisoner was too dangerous to approach or tried doing something suspicious, he could also be killed on the spot by the Spectator. There also no way for the prisoner to locate the Spectator without using his mana. It was the perfect trap. Furthermore, if a prisoner did escape, which was nearly impossible, he would have to face all the knights outside. There were very few Dreamers who could defeat them all without losing their life.

Yet all those fears were not what was keeping Kyle here. Ellia knew he wasn't forced to be here; he chose to be locked up. At least, she chose to believe that.

"Care to hear my story?" Ellia asked the very moment the memories of Hilda, Reave, and her violent arrest slithered into her mind. She couldn't endure them, and she knew very well that with more disheartened pondering came only bitterness and dark musings.

"Now?" Kyle asked. "Fine, let's kill some time."

"I already told you I'm from Nalza. It's in the western region of Narilan."

"Nalza Village Cluster." Kyle nodded. "I know that place."

"It's a place that's very much different from the rest of Narilan," Ellia spoke in a soft voice. "We strive to abstain from using mana. We believe it clouds the mind, and it's ultimately like playing God."

"Nalza isn't so different," Kyle whispered. "Just like the rest of Narilan, the ruler of Nalza is a God among man."

Ellia blew warm air into her bruised hand as it grew cold. "You're right, but only partially. The Lady of Benevolence is an exceptional Dreamer, but she uses her mana only in emergencies. She's not like the Celestial King who is considered a God."

"I couldn't disagree more," Kyle said. "I visited Nalza a few years ago. The Lady of Benevolence was a stingy hag who thought she was the center of the world."

Ellia snorted. "Don't speak about my mother like that."

"So that's why..." Kyle chuckled lightly. "You're using her mana."

"Yes."

"But why don't you have mana of your own?"

"It's that obvious, isn't it?" Ellia mused sadly. She knew most people were born with little mana. The more their ancestors used it and expanded on it, the more potent will be the mana of their children. Of course, there was also chance involved. People with a lineage empty of its power were sometimes born special. They were gifted with extreme mana prowess. Ellia frequently wondered why she didn't have a lot of mana of her own. She was the daughter of a Dreamer after all.

"Anyone with enough experience with mana would know," Kyle said after a brief pause. "With overuse, you start feeling lightheaded, dizzy, tired, but you didn't have any of that."

Ellia didn't say a word. She thought about Kyle. She was curious if his parents had a lot of mana or if he was just gifted. She guessed it was the latter.

"You were saying something," Kyle added.

Ellia's voice grew sad. "One night, I woke up to the screams of my brethren. Hilda was helping my sickly mother stand as she told me to dress quickly. Walking outside, I saw white flashes in the sky. The Dominant Veil—the mighty barrier that protects Narilan—trembled, weakened, and began to travel east. It glowed in a pale light. The villagers ran in panic, screaming. Most of our straw huts were destroyed. Some were burning from the roof, others were covered in countless spears. The three of us sprinted out of the village as the ground quivered underneath our feet. Before our eyes loomed the colossal and arresting Great Tower. I looked back, but could see no other villagers behind us." Ellia felt her throat turn dry, hoarse. She swallowed.

"I didn't hear of the incident, but I did hear of the kingdom... shrinking," Kyle said. "But go ahead."

Ellia felt a sense of compassion coming from Kyle, which

made her feel a little better inside. She touched her heart to realize that it was beating restlessly. A single thought rattled her to the core, shaking her grip on emotions.

"The darkness, the never-ending shrieks, the sound of flames mesmerized me," Ellia continued. "I lost my footing and fell. My head sank in the sand. Lifting it up, I realized that a red soaked spear landed next to me, scraping my thigh. Hilda was screaming something, but I couldn't understand what. She pulled me away as arrows covered the ground, then threw me on her black horse. Resting on my stomach behind Hilda, I had a final look at our village dipped in blood and flames—painted crimson. The screams had ceased as I closed my eyes and realized that Hilda saved my life." Ellia fell silent, and tears dripped down her red cheeks. There was nothing she could do about it. Her body tensed as she pressed her knees tightly to her chest and rolled into a tiny ball.

Ellia recalled the last meeting she had with her mother. She still remembered her mother's hopeful eyes. Even though only two dozen people made it out of the village, her mother insisted that she shouldn't foster a grudge or feel hatred. Her mother taught her that the only way to defeat malice was with kindness. Ellia remembered her mother's Blessing—the ritual. She eyed the spiral tattoo on her thigh. Until her mother dies, Ellia could use all of her mother's mana to fulfill their last wish—making sure no one has to face the same fate they did. Ellia was instructed to find Kyle. She sighed, thinking of how little guidance she received. Her mother insisted that fate will lead her.

In my dreams, you could make the right decision, in reality, you will too, Ellia thought, remembering her mother's last words.

"Tell me," Ellia said. "Did my mother also gave you her Blessing?"

"She did," Kyle admitted. "It was a small job. I just had to deal with some bandits." He cleared his throat. "But before that, she asked me to show her my power. When I did, she asked me if I could promise her that I won't let this kingdom fall."

"And did you?"

"No," Kyle said.

The dungeon fell silent.

"Looks like we're not so different after all," Kyle said. "We were both ignored by the Celestial King in our time of need."

"Why do you think so?"

"The Celestial King is believed to be the catalyst for making Narilan flourish. But is one person really capable of such a feat?" Kyle asked. "All over the kingdom, deep underground, there are caves. They're designated for a group of ten people who will give their mana to the Celestial King. I was forced to live in one of those caves."

Ellia listened as Kyle spoke with a complete lack of emotions, or rather with all of them hidden deep within.

"I didn't know..." Ellia trailed off. Rain began drizzling, then pouring. The mass of nastiness inside her cell dripped from the bench and onto the ground.

"Most of the people there are volunteers. They work out of free will. Their families are told that they traveled to work for the greater good of the kingdom. Then there are those that are forced to give their mana when there are not enough volunteers. Mostly orphans. But of course, exceptions are made due to negligence and to meet the needs of the system. And once you're in, you can't leave. They drain you of mana until you go crazy or die."

"Couldn't anyone save you?" Ellia felt pity for Kyle. "What about your parents?"

Kyle chuckled at Ellia. "They were killed in order to persuade me that I had to give my mana." He fell silent. Ellia recognized it as an attempt to hide his feelings. "To this day, I can still remember how I crawled, crying that I have parents and how I don't want to go. That was all a mistake. A big man with countless scars laughed as he gestured. His assistant summoned two people—my mother and father. My parents didn't show any signs of fear. They concealed that emotion with a smile." He took a deep breath. "They were killed there... on the spot... right in front of me. I still see their smiles. At first, I thought that it was a way of cheering me up, but over the years, I realized the true meaning behind it. Never bow to anyone, laugh at those who tower over you."

Ellia held her legs tight to her chest. "I really pity you."

Kyle chuckled. "Don't do that. I'm the bad guy here. No need to be sympathetic."

Ellia frowned, a tear dripping down her cheek.

"And here I was thinking that you're growing thick skin." Kyle sighed.

"I'm not crying," Ellia protested falsely.

"I meditated in that cave for fifteen years. That's where I met Avril—the girl born from the darkness. We believed that one day we would escape from the cave and from Narilan. Years passed without any hope. Volunteers were replaced, faces changed, yet everything remained the same. I held on to that seed of hope. It wasn't until Avril fell ill that I lost all motivation. She had a bad fever and was really weak. Life was evaporating from her, and I couldn't help her. Hope changed to disappointment, anger to frustration, and love into despair. At one point, she was so weak she couldn't stand up, and the guards instantly knew what to do. I tried to hold them off, but I was too exhausted. They restrained me. As I watched them take Avril, all her life stolen from her, an earthquake shook the place." Kyle stifled a chuckle. "Avril and I were the only ones to emerge from the ashes of that cave, my hands drenched in the blood of those I had to kill…" Kyle trailed off. The air fell silent. After a moment, he banged on the wall. "Hey! No sleeping."

Ellia giggled lightly. "Is that why you're so determined to become the Celestial King?" She whispered abruptly. "Is your incessant need to escape the very thing driving you to kill others?" She spoke faster than her mind could process her thoughts. "Why not concentrate on killing the one responsible for your grief instead?"

"First of all, I've only killed wretched scum—bandits, thieves, and killers… well, mostly. A few other men who made the wrong choices too." Kyle snickered.

"And you think that makes it all right?"

"I do. Anyone who stands in my way armed with a sword will die."

"Would you kill me?" Ellia asked, but Kyle didn't answer. "Would you?" she repeated.

Kyle remained silent. "Second, getting to the throne is a means to an end, an end where I keep my promise… where I am free—"

"Is there a third point?" Ellia interrupted. She really didn't want to talk to Kyle anymore. She wanted to end the conversation.

"The one responsible for my anguish died deep within

that cave. I made sure to give him the most miserable death. But I'd like to kill the Grand Court too. They're the ones who oversee the caves."

"What about the preceptor?"

"He's probably involved too, but I doubt I'll be able to kill him if I become the Celestial King. I'll need his help until I can find a replacement."

Shaken, Ellia couldn't utter a word. Their pasts were filled with sorrow. However, Ellia had something which Kyle did not—a feeling that there was still an essence of good within everyone. In this tranquil cell, Ellia was left to herself. Her mind was her greatest adversary. It rehashed everything that she didn't want to see, and tormented her with images that she yearned to forget. She regretted talking with Kyle. With her optimistic view of the world challenged, she felt defeated.

"Remember that plant that caused an allergic reaction in Dreamers?" Kyle asked suddenly.

"What about it?"

"Do you know if the intensity of the symptoms a person experiences is directly proportional to his power?"

"I don't," Ellia replied quickly. She tried to lie, realizing that Kyle was thinking of Reave who claimed to have little mana. "But you already know otherwise."

Kyle paused. "Say, what do you think is out there... on the other side of the Dominant Veil?"

"I don't know, but whatever it is, it's hostile," Ellia admitted, gently hugging her hand. "I think the Veil is there for a reason. It might very well be that Narilan is the only world for us."

Kyle didn't say another word. Ellia sat there alone, listening to the rain.

CHAPTER 21

DORRELL STOOD ON the podium consumed by his work, teaching. "You are the future," he declared to all his apprentices. "Please remember that. When a new Celestial King ascends the throne, he will choose a preceptor to take over in my stead—one of you." His pompous voice spread through the miniature classroom, ending the lesson. His apprentices had their eyes fixated on him. They aspired to be just like him one day. Every one of his words seemed to sink into their minds, never to be forgotten. It was something Dorrell was pleased about since he didn't see himself as a teacher. More so, he hated to preach. Most of his memories of passing on knowledge weren't satisfying. Before he became a preceptor, no one listened. They yawned, questioned, and mocked—pushing Dorrell into frustration. There was a thick line between an insolent remark and a philosophical inquiry. More often than not, Dorrell faced the former.

Dorrell walked off the podium with his head held high, a sign of confidence. It was his first lecture in a while, and at first, teaching felt foreign. For the past few months, he was devoted to selecting a successor to the throne, so he had to call off many lectures. He was known to be a workaholic, and his social life meant nothing to him, yet preparing his apprentices so that one day one of them might become the next preceptor was a huge part of his duty as well. *It feels right be to teaching again*, he thought.

The classroom was echoing with idle murmur. A subtle breeze sneaked into the classroom through the open door.

"How's life, professor?" Cwen blocked Dorrell's escape. With her hair tied back, the dozens of piercings on her ears were easily visible.

"Duty calls." Dorrell attempted to be casual, angling the corners of his lips to form an unconvincing smile.

"So it does." Cwen followed him outside. The clouds have mostly cleared out. The sky had a deep blue color, which was getting invaded by the early morning sun—a smear of orange that steadily took over the heavens. Stillness encircled the institute, where the lectures took place. Around every corner, students and faculty settled into groups of around twelve and meditated for various reasons—personal or not. Some even chanted, embracing the stillness. Others prayed for Narilan's well-being.

"Anson insisted on talking with you," Cwen said. "He said he found some evidence which should be brought to your attention."

Dorrell shrugged. He never admitted it, but he considered Cwen his one true apprentice. She had the same love for Narilan that he embraced, and her devotion surpassed even his own. In any case, Cwen's apprentice was Anson.

"You should tell your servant to back off." Dorrell dropped the respect for a more practical response.

"He's just doing what he thinks is right."

"Not what you think is right?"

"Maybe a little." Cwen smirked, twirling a lock of hair. "After all, it's stated in the Charter of Narilan that if the preceptor goes astray, his apprentices are obligated to put him back in his place." Cwen proved to Dorrell that she had every bit of the Charter memorized. However, he didn't even wink as if expecting the argument.

Then Dorrell left Cwen. He sneaked past a meditating couple in the garden and made his way to the street, then waved his hand at a carriage and jumped inside. The voiceless driver stuck his palm open. Dorrell slipped a piece of paper with his address written down on it.

Cwen caught up to him. "You know, I love you too much to let you get swallowed up by your sense of duty."

"Try to stop me." Dorrell reclined in the back seat, and closed his eyes.

"I will, if it comes to that."

The carriage crawled forward. Although the ride home was smooth, the busy streets and mild bartering kept Dorrell awake, despite his honest intentions of getting some rest. If sleep was a method of turning off the mind, Dorrell just wasn't able to do that. His mind ran rampant—thinking, calculating, predicting, and planning. Spacing out was the best he could do to empty his head. Suddenly, the carriage came to a halt. A dense crowd of people gathered on the street. Dorrell was anxious that something happened, but his worries were put to rest when he saw a few happy faces cheering from a balcony above.

"I'll walk," Dorrell said. He moved through the crowd and made his way to the fountain. Its limpid water rippled lightly, revealing a vivid reflection—a proclamation of the arrival of a new contestant for the throne. A young man with a triumphant smile and blond hair, his eyes set on the Great Tower. He was already on the way. *Guess he received his tenth Blessing,* Dorrell thought. *Let's see how this turns out.*

"Good luck, my prince," a girl called out, aiming her confession at the blond lad. Her words couldn't reach him, of course. He couldn't hear a single cheer from his massive audience from all over Zardan.

Dorrell honestly hoped that the lad would succeed—that a new Celestial King would be born. He sighed. *If he doesn't, I'll just add him to my collection,* he thought. He pushed through the crowd and walked home. When he arrived, he rode the lift up halfway to his library. Although he had most of his work materials already in his chamber, the library was where his mail arrived, so it was only natural that he visited it from time to time.

The lift stopped, and the door opened to reveal Anson leaning over the railing on the upper level of the library. Anson was a bald-headed, thick-skinned man whose timid nature contradicted his muscular appearance. Dorrell always thought Anson was a man scared of being wrong or making a mistake.

"Pleasure to see you here, Anson." Dorrell put on his indifferent expression. He slipped off his shoes and walked across the room. The lavish red carpet with a yellow fringe was warm.

Anson slammed the lift closed with his mana, and the groan of the door filled the room. He had a letter in his hand and an anxious look about him. "How could you do something against the Celestial King?" he complained, refusing to make eye contact.

"I don't know what you're talking about." Dorrell guessed that the letter contained something that disclosed his plans.

"The letter arrived some time ago. I couldn't muster up enough courage to open it until today." Anson dropped the letter to the floor. "One of our shipments was attacked. The letter was on a dead knight, so that's why it's blood-stained."

Dorrell walked to the letter, picked it up, and read it.

> *Dear brother,*
>
> *I apologize for my absence. As you know, I was attacked during my travels. However, there's a good side to the story. Your plan will come to fruition. Don't ever give up. I found a Dreamer who would make the perfect donor of mana for a noble king of your choice. He already has nine Blessings. When we make it to the capital, I'll defeat him. I know you're hesitant, but don't be. Your plan is perfect.*
>
> *Reave*

Dorrell snickered. He was pleased that his brother was alive. He let out a chuckle, then saw Anson's perplexed gaze.

"Sorry, you don't even know how much I've been waiting for this," Dorrell said to Anson. "You should've come earlier. We could've talked this over. That way you wouldn't have to be so disturbed about the meaning of the letter."

"Please explain, professor." Anson backed down a little as sweat dripped down his chin and neck in thick droplet.

"You made too many assumptions when reading this. You know about the Celestial King and how much responsibility he must bear, right?" Dorrell waited until Anson nodded. "Remember how I've taught you about the caves all over Narilan."

"I do." Anson hesitated. "They are places where citizens can donate their mana."

"Exactly," Dorrell agreed. "All this letter means is that my brother has found another volunteer who will support the future Celestial King."

"But it says that you will select a future Celestial King of your choice," Anson spoke, struggling with his faltering voice.

"I'm obligated to search for a righteous successor, am I not?" Dorrell forced an honest grin. He knew that Anson most likely confessed all his suspicions to Cwen. He needed to persuade Anson that everything was fine.

Anson walked downstairs. "I'm so sorry."

"Happens to everyone," Dorrell said. "Don't worry. I'm impressed you confronted me. This is what a true preceptor should be like." He patted Anson on the shoulder. "Say, have you made copies of the letter?"

Downcast, Anson lowered his gaze. "I have made two copies, but I haven't given a single one to anybody, not even Cwen," he explained. "So... I'll bring them tomorrow." The lift grated as someone called it down. Dorrell's eyes met Anson's pathetic stare one final time.

"I would appreciate it." Dorrell smiled.

Below, someone walked into the lift with a heavy pace and began riding upstairs.

Anson swallowed, waiting. His hands gripping his keys so tightly that the sharp edges pierced his palms. His feet were firmly planted on the carpet, somewhere in the center. Dorrell kneeled to touch the ground; his hands were cold. The carpet's four edges sprung up to meet just above Anson's head, trapping him. Dorrell ignored Anson's screams and spread his hands wide as the stone floor murmured, opening up one stone brick at a time. Gravity did the rest as Anson plummeted down and was ingested by the darkness. Dorrell waved his hand, and the keys were spat upward. The stone floor closed up almost instantly as Dorrell let go of the floor and sprung forward to catch the keys.

"I'll pick up my letters personally," Dorrell said, with the keys in his hand.

The lift opened, and Albert walked into the room, his face pale. "I think he's dead. I think the Celestial King is dead!"

CHAPTER 22

KING BRENEON SAT in his chair, looking at the crackling fireplace. He was eating supper, but the wine tasted stale and the chicken insipid. He couldn't forget Kyle's disgusting smirk. It mocked him every time he closed his eyes.

He hurled the plate across the room, and the glass smashed into the fire. "What is this?" he rasped to his servant. "Tell the cook that he has a single day to improve. If he doesn't, I'll cut him down myself."

"I understand." The servant bowed.

Ronn walked through the door. "You called for me, Father?"

Breneon reclined in his chair. "Have you found the girl?"

"Avril? Yes. She will be staying with me."

Breneon frowned. He couldn't understand why Ronn fell for Avril. With so many beautiful women around,

Ronn could have anyone. Yet, he chose a thief and a crook. Breneon felt disgusted, but he restrained himself around his sons.

"Thank you, Father, for being understanding," Ronn said. "I know you have never approved of my relationship with Avril."

"Since you like her so much, convince her to stay," Breneon suggested. The thought of taking something away from Kyle, something that he loved, was simple yet overwhelming in its enticement. Breneon chuckled, then coughed briefly.

Ronn paused. "Would you stoop so low as to use your own son to get back at an enemy?"

Breneon fell silent.

"How did it happen that one of my brothers, Eric, was with Kyle anyway?" Ronn asked.

"He was the son of a king, he did whatever he wanted." Breneon didn't look sad. The thought of his son dying was terrible, but he could live with it. He couldn't live, however, with Kyle as the Celestial King. *I will die before I allow that wretched scum to ascend to the throne of Narilan,* Breneon thought.

"May I speak from the heart, Father?" Ronn asked, and Breneon agreed. "Why are you so obsessed with Kyle? Why does his death matter so much to you?"

"He killed my knights," Breneon rasped. "He spat on the insignia of Relien. He came to my castle as if it was a filthy barn, smiling in my face. And I could never do anything about it. By the time I set out to kill him, he already had his first Blessing, and no one can intervene in the journey of a Dreamer on his way to challenge the Celestial King because of some quarrel."

Ronn walked to an empty chair and took a seat. "If he is so evil, why doesn't the Celestial King curse him with the Gift of Misfortune? Or why doesn't the Grand Court curse him?" Ronn called for the servant and demanded some mead.

"It's too late now," Breneon said. "He's on the path of becoming the Celestial King. That's why he's not cursed. As for earlier, perhaps the Celestial King ignored Kyle. Perhaps he had more important matters at hand or knows something we don't. But in truth, I don't know." Breneon chuckled. "Maybe Kyle is wondering that as well. He should have been languishing in misfortune and suffering long ago."

The servant brought the mead. He had a bruised face, which reminded Breneon of one of the guards, Raun. His violent tendencies sometimes got the best of him.

Ronn took a sip of the mead. It was cold just as he liked it. "One thing that's making me worried is the reason Kyle came here. He's powerful, self-centered, and bloodthirsty. Why would he allow himself to be caught?"

Breneon gritted his teeth. "That's why I want to have him executed quickly. I was once afraid of the consequences, but not anymore. I always thought Kyle would perish someday, but he has come too far. I can't allow him to become the Celestial King. I should've killed him long ago." He cleared his throat.

"Father," Ronn's voice was sad and quiet. "I'm always by your side. If you think Kyle should not be allowed to live, I'll support you."

"That's what I wanted to hear." Breneon raised his glass with a smile. He had many sons, but he always gave Ronn preferential treatment. Most of his other children were scattered, only Ronn remained in Relien. Breneon kept Ronn close, despite being his youngest son and sometimes a naive boy. Breneon thought that having someone like that by his side made him a better man, a better king. "Let's avenge Eric's death," Breneon added after a long pause.

◆

Avril watched the dancing flames as she made her way down the corridor. The cramped space triggered various feelings and memories. She didn't like that. She always told herself that thinking of the past was a waste of time. There was only one moment that demanded her attention—here and now. *I am certain the chamber was this way,* she thought, searching for the one place where she hoped to find Ronn. Even at a time like this. Scared of being overwhelmed by her memories, she continued.

She turned left around another corner to find yet another stone corridor. Then it happened.

She looked outside and saw a lone tree in the field. The dark, gnarled tree made her memories flood her mind.

Avril recalled the hazy images of sitting behind Kyle. He was taking her to Relien at the time since it was the closest place from the cave they escaped. She desperately needed help; she was sick and dying. By the time they made it to the castle, Breneon already knew about the cave. At the square, they were approached by a few knights. They were separated. The knights dragged her away as she watched Kyle struggle to defend himself. Yet, she was sure that he would live, escape. At least she hoped so. She barely remembered anything after that, only the fever. However, she believed she could hear Ronn begging King Breneon to save her.

Avril was shaken awake by the realization that she made it to a massive, wooden door. The key was already there. She walked inside to see the same chamber where she spent over a month in bed. She tossed her bag on the chair, then walked further in. The bed was neatly prepared with clean, white sheets, and a vivid red quilt with pillows on top. The curtains had the same red color. A faint but familiar scent of flowers stimulated her memories.

Every night Ronn would sit by her bed, reading to her. She remembered many of the stories by heart. Ronn told her of a young warrior that spent the nights under a gnarled tree in the grass. One night, when Avril was strong enough to stand up, she walked to the window and saw that same image. The only difference was that the warrior she hoped to see—Kyle—wasn't there.

She noticed a small wooden casket on the nightstand. Beside it was a note. *For the one who knows me best.* She lifted the lid to find a small silver pendant in the shape of a heart.

Avril held it dearly in her hand. She was almost certain Ronn would be here. He always wanted her to be with him. In the past, he strived to persuade her to stay, and his gift was a sign that tonight he still felt something. His affection was the only reason she recovered back then.

Avril awaited Ronn, but he never came.

I could have been a princess, she thought. The idea brought a playful smile to her sad face. Yet, she didn't want that. She wanted something more, something different. She always looked inside for answers, and every time she was told that there must be a meaning to her life. She had to accomplish something great. That's why she traveled with Kyle.

A knock came at the door. Avril rushed to the door, hoping it was Ronn, but it was only an old servant.

"Lord Ronn wants to apologize," the servant said. "He has important matters to discuss with King Breneon. He will be late." The servant vanished soon after.

Slightly disappointed, Avril walked back to the bed.

She took a deep breath and thought about what she would say to Ronn if he was here. *Could we really have a regular conversation?* she wondered.

She was curious what Breneon might be planning. Breneon never admitted it, but it was common knowledge that one of his greatest dreams was for his son to become the Celestial King. Yet rumors claimed that none of his sons were powerful enough. And so he had to settle for another dream that he had—seeing Kyle executed. Avril couldn't understand it, but Breneon nurtured a deep hatred toward Kyle and would do everything in his power to have a chance of cutting Kyle down. The only thing that stopped him so far was fear of the consequence of such a vendetta.

Avril thought that Breneon most likely called for Ronn to arrange Kyle's execution. That's why Ronn wasn't with her.

"What are you thinking?" she said aloud, hoping that Kyle would hear her words.

A subtle creak came from the corridor. With the door ajar, she spotted an unlikely guest—Elring—exiting a room. At once, she rummaged through her belongings and found the broken sword that Kyle gave her.

◆

The anger from the day before settled deep within Hilda's heart, and it fed on her ever-lasting feeling of regret. The memory of how powerless she was when the guards took Ellia away enhanced this awful feeling, making her, for the first time, feel truly helpless.

The night was about to come to an end. The sun was hiding right behind the horizon line, spreading its timid yellow and orange rays throughout the deep blue sky. Hilda was eyeing the street with a blank stare from the second floor of the tavern. She kept to herself all night, sitting in silence.

Reave sat right behind her at a round wooden table. He held a cold bottle of mead to his face. His nose wasn't broken, but there was a large purple bruise on his cheek. A piece of cloth that he had in the other hand was stained in the blood that gushed from his nose until midnight.

"Breneon is afraid of Kyle," Reave finally said. "That's why he'll execute Kyle today. Ellia will probably be in that prison for another month."

"What is that bastard planning?" Hilda murmured, thinking of Kyle. She still couldn't shake off the surprise she felt when Kyle was taken away.

"Kyle and Breneon had some serious quarrels." Reave placed the bottle of mead on the table, revealing his face. "I saw Elring today. He might be the reason Kyle was arrested so swiftly."

Hilda frowned. "Kyle was arrested for killing Breneon's son."

"You want to know my honest opinion?" Reave asked, but Hilda didn't respond. "I don't know how, but Kyle is here to kill Elring and Breneon. He will try to force Breneon into giving him a Blessing." Reave smiled, showing his teeth white. "For now, think about Ellia. She's just imprisoned."

"And I should be happy about that?" Hilda asked, then hid her face in her palms.

"Exactly." Reave stood up and stretched.

"You had the mana. Why didn't you save her?"

Reave shook his head and sighed. "I don't know who you take me for, but I'm not a hero."

"I wonder what Kyle will say once he learns that you can proficiently use mana," Hilda said. "Hiding something so important. There must be a reason for it."

"Who would be stupid enough to reveal something so vital to their survival?" Reave frowned.

There were sounds of a commotion outside. The chatter coming from below was slowly intensifying. The people of Relien started swarming the street. Drums boomed to summon anyone and everyone.

"What do you mean?" Hilda watched Reave carefully. Something seemed to irk him.

"I have a goal, and so do you. Our adventure isn't over until we reach it. However, Kyle is unpredictable, and I might be the one and only person who can stop him. How long do you think it'll take him to kill you both?" Reave chuckled.

Hilda shrugged. "You're too sure of yourself. Kyle underestimates Ellia, but she has a lot of power too." *Thanks to my sister*. Whenever Hilda thought about her sister, the Lady of Benevolence, she would catch herself thinking of her sister's well-being. The thought wouldn't be so troubling if it wasn't for her sister's impending death. They were never close, but the thought of just how out of touch they were made Hilda feel even worse.

"I would like to see timid Ellia punch Kyle in the face." Reave smirked. "I'd give everything to see that." He then walked out only to return with a new bottle of mead in a few minutes. The murmurs of the patrons gathering for a morning glass of booze echoed from the floor below. "You know, I never told Kyle my reason for heading to Zardan because he wouldn't let me join his group," Reave continued. "I was born in Zardan. I was... guarding a shipment when it was attacked. I was the only one to survive. I didn't make it back in time, and the Royal Veil was closed when I got to Zardan."

Hilda never realized just how isolated Zardan really was. It strived to separate itself from the rest of Narilan like a fearful coward. It hid behind mountains, behind the Royal Veil, behind its walls. It didn't allow people to migrate from other parts of Narilan. It tried everything to stifle travel.

Hilda rubbed her eyes. "Don't you have any family? They must be on the lookout for you. They could allow you into Zardan."

He nodded.

"Well, leave Kyle, get back to Zardan, and wait. They'll notice you, and you can get back to your peaceful life."

"I don't know if I want to go back," Reave confessed.

"Adventurer, huh?" Hilda looked up at Reave.

"I enjoy it here. I feel much more alive here than I ever felt in Zardan," Reave said. "That's why I volunteered to protect those shipments. I was hoping something interesting would happen. I don't question Kyle because I saw him do some crazy things. I saw him risk it all... and it was very entertaining to participate in those events."

Silence filled the room.

"I somehow pity you," Hilda whispered. "You can never live unless you are risking your life." Hilda was a fighter herself, but fighting was just a part of her life, a fraction of it. For Reave, it seemed as if it was the center of his life, the totality of it.

"Your turn to confess."

Hilda hesitated as she collected her thoughts and recalled memories. "Our village was destroyed, forgotten. I want to confront the one who's responsible for it and kill him."

"So the person responsible lives in Zardan?" Reave sipped some mead.

"Yes," Hilda admitted, letting the room grow silent. "He lives in prosperity and makes decisions on behalf of the Celestial King."

"You're talking about Dorrell Sahne, the preceptor?" Reave leaned forward.

"Yes, I want to kill the preceptor for abandoning my village," Hilda confessed, then noticed the sadness in Reave's eyes. Like a bitter revelation, her words troubled him.

"So what exactly did he do?"

"The Dominant Veil stopped protecting our land." Hilda sighed. "But I don't really want to talk about it."

Reave stood up, then started walking away. "Be careful. Sooner or later Kyle will try to kill you both, and he will start with Ellia," he said with a depressed look in his eyes.

Hilda nodded morosely. She decided to grab something to eat downstairs before the execution was underway.

◆

Kyle was escorted outside by the guards, their faces blithe and their gossip garish. Both were a sign of their inexperience. The sun hit Kyle in the face, blinding him. His eyes slowly adjusted to the light. He felt the rough surface of the ground with his bare feet—wet soil and cold cobblestones. He was in a pathetic mood. He was angry and frustrated. A guard goaded him onward. When Kyle didn't react, one of the guards prodded him between the ribs with his sword. The pain was dull, but cold and uncomfortable. With a single step, Kyle felt something prick his foot. He grimaced, leaving bloody marks as he strode ahead. *Just a little longer*, he thought.

Kyle wasn't scared. He knew he could escape. He had enough mana. The challenge was grasping his anger as it seemed to grow with every single strike that he had to endure.

At the square, a crowd of people gathered, encircling a wooden podium. The guards shoved Kyle through the dense crowd. When he emerged on the other side, he saw Breneon's triumphant smile. The executioner was waiting there as well, dressed in a dark robe, hood up and axe in hand. A few knights were stationed around. Kyle turned in the direction of the castle. *Are you watching, Avril?* he thought. He was led up the steps and forced to kneel.

In Narilan, barbaric deaths were forbidden. An execution that caused unnecessary pain or was extremely violent was believed to affect the mind. It was said that it corrupted all the enlightened minds of Narilan's citizens. Breneon believed otherwise. He didn't shy away from brutality.

Kyle studied the crowd for some familiar faces, but all he could observe was the anger of the crowd. The madness he saw exceeded his wildest dreams. The people shoved, screamed, swore, and some even hurled things at the podium. He didn't mind it. Quite the opposite, he found it entertaining.

◆

From his position deep within the back of the crowd, Reave could see Kyle. Reave wasn't sure what he should do. He was content with Kyle being killed, but then he remembered his obligation to his brother. *Such wasted potential,* he thought. *What are you planning?*

Reave counted the guards at the podium, and then surveyed the arrow slits and battlements. He was feeling restless, ready to fight. Then he realized that he was concerned about something else. He was worried what would happen to his brother if Hilda made it to Zardan. He sighed. *What about Ellia?* he thought. *She probably hates my brother too. And Kyle.* He had to do something about it; he knew that. *If we make it to Zardan, I might not be able to stand a chance against them all.*

With a grim expression, Hilda approached Reave. He remembered her words, and they reminded him of his bloodthirsty tendencies, which maliciously mesmerized him. He just loved to fight, and for the past month, there was very little of what he adored. He realized the real reason why, for a brief moment, he wanted to aid Kyle; he was just making excuses to massacre a few knights. That was his only reason; there was nothing else.

"I tried speaking with Breneon about Ellia," Hilda said. "But he didn't even want to see me."

"Remember what I told you in the morning?"

"I don't want to hear it." Hilda frowned. "Not now."

"Kyle is planning something," Reave said. "Something

is telling me that when he gets the tenth Blessing, he will intend to kill you and Ellia."

"And he won't try to kill you?" Hilda gave Reave a suspicious gaze. "Look, I don't know what has gotten into you, but you're not yourself."

"Fine, but if you see me arguing with Kyle, it might very well be for Ellia's sake," Reave said, almost honestly. "Don't forget that. Don't waste the opportunity to pierce his heart."

◆

Kyle was on his knees, eyes on the floor and hands tied behind him. He listened to Breneon's speech about the atrocities that he committed, but his mind turned off sometime after Breneon mentioned a long list of deaths. The crowd listened to every single word of the revered king. Upon finishing, Breneon glanced at the executioner, who started preparing his axe. Elring, accompanied by an escort, made his way up the podium with a vulpine smirk, looking at Kyle then at Breneon.

Kyle wanted to kill Elring very, very much. Yet, he chose to return a disgusting grin.

"Breneon, my friend, I see you've captured the fiend," Elring said with a smile.

"Yes." Breneon smiled as well, running his fingers through his beard. "I'm sorry I couldn't see you last night, but I'll be right with you once I finish this."

Just you wait, Kyle thought. *You won't be laughing much longer.*

Elring came closer, then put his hand on Breneon's shoulder. Kyle could hear everything. "You know, executions have to be permitted by seven warlords to be valid." Elring rubbed his brow. "Quite an outdated custom."

"We don't have time for such sentiments." Breneon shook his head.

"That's why I'm here," Elring declared, his hand holding a scroll. "Six signatures. All we need is your own."

Breneon grinned, his thick eyebrows obscuring his wicked eyes. He bit his lip in excitement. The crowd awaited Kyle's judgement patiently.

"Father, wait," Ronn charged up the steps. "Stop this at once. This man had this in his room." Ronn, holding a broken sword, pointed at Elring.

Breneon looked at Kyle, who returned a bitter smirk. "You bastard! Is this some sort of scheme of yours?" Breneon sprung forward, fist clenched. With a powerful swing, he punched Kyle, and his ring tore through Kyle's face, leaving a bloody mark. Kyle was surprised that the old man still had that much strength.

"What is going on?" Elring asked.

Kyle spat blood. He had to fight against the urge to free himself. He looked around for Avril.

"Don't say another word, son." Breneon embraced Ronn. "I'll tell you everything later."

"You know about him?" Ronn murmured, pointing at Elring. "You know he killed your son?"

"Is that Eric's sword?" someone from the crowd yelled. Everybody's eyes were drawn to the design of the hilt. The mutters escalated.

"What is it, King Breneon?" someone screamed with a lack of respect.

"Tell us!" the people demanded together. Their screams redoubled and merged into a discordant string of noises.

"This means nothing! The one responsible is this man here." Breneon pointed at Kyle.

The crowd called out with more questions and suspicions.

Breneon was at a loss for words. Elring tried to sneak out, but he was stopped by a guard with a broken jaw. His words were barely understandable. "You shouldn't have come here," the guard said with a sadistic grin.

"It's all his doing, Raun." Elring frowned at the guard. "Who would kill someone, and then carry incriminating evidence? You take me for a fool?"

"That's no argument," Raun said heavily. "Remember that woman from ten years ago. She collected fingers of those she killed." He then restrained Elring.

Breneon suddenly coughed blood and bowed forward. Ronn hurried to his side. He helped Breneon stand, then ordered Kyle and Elring imprisoned until he can investigate further. Breneon tried to protest, but his coughing intensified.

Elring ran to Kyle with a clenched fist. "You, fiend!"

Kyle sprung away as Elring swung and missed. He waited until Elring was at his eye level, then butted him with his head. Elring fell back, his nose bleeding. The guards restrained Elring, but he wrestled out of their grip. He ran to Kyle, and landed a punch. It was strong and painful. Kyle fell on his side, angry. Elring booted him in the stomach—and again. The boot had a metal shell which dug deep into Kyle's skin. Kyle spat blood, his guts throbbing as if ripped apart. He then rolled on his back and shoved Elring back with a fast kick. Elring fell to the ground, his knuckles scuffed. He spat at Kyle as the guards shackled him.

The guards laughed.

Breneon, still on the podium, called Raun. "Take a few knights and make sure you kill that bastard, Kyle, you understand?" He grimaced, noticing Kyle's prying eyes.

"Any means necessary?" Raun spoke in a stoic voice.

"Exactly. Just execute him and be done with it." Breneon smiled, putting his hand on Raun's shoulder.

Raun bowed, then turned to his trusted knights. He murmured, giving them the order. Then he led the way, cautiously rubbing his swollen jaw.

"No more, no more," Kyle shouted as the knights lifted him from the floor. His head was heavy. The throbbing in his stomach made standing up a real challenge. The pain emanated all over his body. He ignored it and spat on the ground as he stood up. His breathing was deep and strained. He walked down the steps and off the podium. Then he was shoved in the back and kneeled down onto the cobblestones.

"Move it," one of the guards said, pushing Kyle.

Kyle fell to the ground. He used all his strength to subdue his anger. He could feel it boiling within, clouding his mind. He stood up and continued, eyes closed. The cold cobblestones soon gave way to a muddy road into a courtyard. As they turned the corner, a hooded figure leaped down from a tall hedge. It jammed its knife into a guard's throat, dodged a sword swing, and killed another guard.

Raun, who was ahead by a few steps, tensed up as he looked back to witness the slaughter of his men. Motionless, he ordered his remaining knights to attack.

At once, Kyle glanced at Raun and the ground growled. It yielded under his feet, swallowing Raun with another guard like a famished beast. The two yelled, struggling to crawl their way out, but in vain. All that remained where they once stood was a small burial mound. When the last guard began escaping, Kyle stretched out his hand. The guard froze. Kyle clenched his fist, and the guard's armor quivered. The metal contracted quickly. His yelp was short-lived as the metal shrunk with a crack—into a ball, drenched in blood.

"Thanks." Kyle nodded, tossing the corpses over the hedge.

"I've got your belongings too," Avril said after taking off her hood.

"The Spectator's dead, right?" Kyle asked, melting the shackles around his hands and feet.

Avril nodded. "What's next?"

"One more thing." Kyle closed his eyes, thinking. All he saw in his mind was a battlefield, blood, swords, and combat. As his heartbeat steadied, he thought about Elring. He didn't care about losing the Blessing as much as he did earlier. *It was time*, he thought.

Screams erupted behind Kyle. Some strong, others weak and frightened. There was a peculiar shout that resounded through the air like an angry roar. There was a weep, and then silence.

"Lord Elring!" someone cried out.

CHAPTER 23

RAUN CHARGED INTO the Great Hall, covered in mud. He was struggling to hold on to his emotions. He had failed and he feared the consequence. He didn't know what King Breneon would do faced with the news that his prisoner, Kyle, had escaped. Raun had just crawled out of one grave, and he knew very well that he could easily end up in another.

"Your Majesty," Raun said, bowing before the king. "I'm sorry to disturb you, but there is an urgent matter."

Breneon was seated, making another one of his grand speeches. A servant by his side was meticulously writing down all his words.

At the first sight of Raun, the Great Hall fell silent.

Raun looked up at Breneon but only for a brief moment. He sought consent, but there was none. Unable to withstand the silence, Raun gasped, "The prisoner... Kyle has escaped."

"What?" Breneon asked aloofly. Raun observed the anger consume the king, his face growing more and more contorted. "What do you think you're looking at?" he roared at the servant. "Get out before I have you beheaded."

The servant strode out.

"Kyle had help. All my men died," Raun continued. His jaw was still hurting, even more so now. "I nearly died as well."

His face warped with displeasure, King Breneon stared at Raun without a word.

"An archer saw Kyle escape into the woods," Raun carried on helplessly.

"Very well," King Breneon said suddenly. "This might be our last chance to kill that bastard." Breneon grabbed a flask, then poured some wine into a glass. "You want some?" He looked at Raun.

"Your Majesty is very generous, but I could never..." Raun trailed off. He wasn't a fool. He knew he wasn't worthy of drinking with a king, and Breneon knew that as well. Breneon just had a habit of offering wine to Raun every time they were discussing something. Was it courtesy or mockery? Raun didn't know.

Breneon frowned. "One of my people told me that the girl we imprisoned is in Kyle's group. We can use her. Gather your knights and tell Ronn to get ready as well." Breneon waved his hand as a sign that Raun must leave. "And grab Satia as well."

Raun didn't move. The words he wanted to say were stuck somewhere in his throat.

"What are you waiting for? Move!" Breneon came closer to Raun, then backhanded him. "All right, speak if you must."

Raun hesitated. "I don't think that it's smart going after Kyle. I heard stories that he is the most powerful Dreamer of them all."

"Stories? That's what you heard?" Breneon gave Raun a malicious glare. "Kyle killed my son, disrespected my family, and laughed in my face," he screamed. "And you are telling me that you heard stories. There are stories about me too. What are they? Speak."

Raun hesitated, tense. "They speak of a noble and kind king who loves and cares for his people."

Breneon chuckled, then finished his glass of wine. "Do you really believe them?"

◆

Ellia slept on the floor, unconscious and oblivious to the bugs that crept around the cell. By now, she was accustomed to the filth and subdued her disgust. *Everything will work out,* she thought. Yet, it was very hard to believe that. Deep within, she felt anger. It was her first time being truly angry, and she didn't know how to deal with it. Left alone, she ran in circles. She recalled her memories, boiled with frustration, subdued her anger, and then repeated the process.

She had a hard time falling asleep. The only thing that helped her regain her tranquility was the subtle sound of rain hitting the puddles of water above. It was calming.

A muffled sound echoed through the cell. She was never a light sleeper, but she woke up as if expecting it.

She promised herself that she wouldn't cry or panic. She struggled to get a hold of her emotions and forced a stoic expression. The muffled sound turned into a clinking of keys. She heard footsteps—heavy footsteps.

A guard opened the door. The darkness was obscuring his face. There were three other men with him. "Move it," he said to Ellia. One of his men grabbed her by the arm and pulled her out of the cell. She turned around and recognized the guard with the broken jaw. The others called him Raun.

Raun put a bag over her head and shackled her hands. He pushed her. She hesitantly took a step and another. Something cut on her leg, and she fell headlong onto the floor. He snickered, and she gritted her teeth. The other two guards were silent.

"Move it," Raun said, still smiling.

Ellia stood up without a word. She bit her lip and took another step. This time, she walked slower and with more care. Raun put his hand on her shoulder and led her right, then left. She was led through a door and a faint breeze caressed her. Someone shoved her in the shoulder. Walking slowly ahead, she bumped into another person and nearly fell. She lost her sense of direction. A door and another corridor. More doors. The air inside was heavy, noxious. She was suddenly pulled back.

"Watch your step," one of the men said.

She felt the floor with her bare feet. There was a staircase in front of her—steep and narrow. She put her hands out to the wall to support herself. Like a clumsy old woman, she struggled to get down with each step being a challenge. With each stride, she would wobble, hoping that she wouldn't fall. The smells were getting stronger.

Ellia could smell all the different herbs. She could even identify many of them among the heavy odors of the room. *Are they practicing medicine here? Alchemy?* she thought. *If so, why did they toss me in a cell?*

She took another step and wobbled, then someone pulled her forcefully to the side.

"Oh, it's you, Raun," a girl's gloomy voice asked. It was slightly hoarse.

"I need your help," Raun replied.

The girl cleared her throat. "Sorry about that. I was experimenting yesterday, and things didn't turn out how I wanted them to." The girl shuffled through scrolls. "What is it this time?"

"You'll accompany me on a mission. I need to hunt someone down."

"Who are you hunting for?"

"I don't have time to explain it to you." Raun frowned. "I just had a bitter conversation with the king. He's upset one of our prisoners escaped, and he wants us to hunt him down. The prisoner escaped into the woods, so he's still close."

So Kyle escaped? Did they just leave me? Ellia felt disappointed and flustered.

"Who's our guest?" the girl asked.

"Doesn't matter. The king is preparing. He's coming along and so is his son."

"What will I get in return?" the girl asked, mixing something in a jar. "Aren't you scared that I might try to escape?"

"You'll be able to continue your work," Raun said. "Besides, this is the best place for you."

The girl snorted.

"Hypocrites," Ellia said calmly. "You condemn me for practicing medicine, but you do the same thing here."

"Shut up." Raun backhanded her.

Ellia wanted to free herself—to fight. Yet, the thought of a Spectator watching was holding her back. She was scared of dying. She wanted to live, to travel, and to discover mana of her own. The shackles dug into her skin, scuffing it and drawing some blood.

"Would you mind taking that thing off?" The girl asked, but Raun didn't react. She came closer and took off the bag from Ellia's head. "Look at you." She put her hands to Ellia's cheeks. Her hands were cold and decorated with a few rings.

Where am I? Ellia thought. She looked at the girl standing before her. Judging by the girl's voice, Ellia expected her to be the same age she was, but the girl was older— Hilda's age. Her long, curly, black locks had pale tips. Her eyes were dark with a few lighter freckles, like a night sky full of stars. She had a candid smile too.

"Unfortunately, I can't practice medicine out in the open as well, but King Breneon allows me to work here." The girl spread her arms wide. "Not the most extravagant workshop in the world, but I've got my herbs, flasks, and a cauldron." She smiled.

Ellia turned and looked at Raun. She didn't know why he was so lenient with the girl, but she guessed that he didn't want to tempt fate. The girl didn't look dangerous by any means, but she could still cause him many problems.

"The people got you good." The girl shook her head, looking at Ellia's bruises. She vanished in the back of the workshop, then came back with some herbs. "Here, drink this. It'll help with the pain." She shoved a mug into Ellia's arms.

Ellia drank the mixture. She wasn't scared. She knew exactly what was in it. Tasting it, she was reminded of home. Her mother taught her to make the exact same mixture.

"My name is Alsatia, but call me Satia." The girl smiled. "What is your name?"

"Enough of this. We don't have time." Raun took a hold of Ellia's arm. His fingers tightened around until Ellia grimaced in pain. "King Breneon is waiting."

"It won't do you any good if the girl collapses during the journey, right?" Satia asked, and Raun backed off. "So?" She turned to Ellia.

"My name is Ellia. Where are you taking me?" She looked at Raun.

Raun kept to himself. He didn't say a word until Satia gazed at him with her onyx eyes. "I think Kyle will want you back. Having you around, we can force your group to surrender."

"What makes you think Kyle will do that? He left me here." Ellia frowned. She noticed a change within Satia's eyes.

Raun didn't answer. Satia placed her palm on the shackles around Ellia's hands. The metal lost shape and dripped down her wrists. It wasn't hot, nor cold. Once it was off it hardened into a thick crust. "Could you give us a moment?" Satia asked, without looking at Raun.

"Just don't make me come back here." Raun strode out.

Ellia looked around the room. There was a cauldron in the back, the flames bright red. The room was lined with shelves filled with many different ingredients—herbs, animal parts, insects, and much more. There was a table in the middle that was loaded with journals, books, and scrolls. Some of them on the floor as well. A heap of clothes was spilling out from underneath a messy bunk in an alcove to the right. Ellia walked to a purple screen beside it and pulled it open. On the other side, she saw a cadaver, its chest ripped open and held by fishhooks. The heart and liver were gone.

"What is this?" Ellia put her hand to her lips.

"Don't worry. He was dead before I had a chance to work on him." Satia walked to the table.

"This is deranged," Ellia said, yet she didn't feel disgusted. Ignoring violence was easy for her now. It didn't bother her, but it didn't mean that she had to support it.

"Don't judge. Thanks to my experiments, many people are alive. What's wrong with studying the human flesh anyway?"

The chamber fell silent.

"You probably heard that Relien was struggling with disease. But it's all behind us now. Thanks to me." Satia had a triumphant smile just like a child after venturing into the dark woods and returning.

"That's why I came to Relien," Ellia said. "Lord Elring told me that I could help out."

"He was wrong." Satia sipped something from a mug. "Want some more?" She pointed to a jar in the back.

"No, thank you."

"I apologize for how they treated you," Satia said. "Raun is careful not to disclose the location of my workshop to outsiders. People can be quite cruel, as you probably know."

"So how did you end up here?"

"I helped a few people. When King Breneon found out, he most likely thought that it would be smart to keep me around." Satia put on her cloak. She took a few pouches and tied them to her belt. "But to tell you the truth, I would do anything to escape. I want to see the world. I don't want to be confined to this squalid work-shop.

Ellia saw a scar around Satia's wrist, but she kept it to herself.

"I really wanted to meet you." Satia looked at Ellia. "If the chance comes around, would you be interested in joining my workshop? I mean, it gets kind of lonely here."

"I... can't. I have other things to attend to."

"That's fine. I have your clothes. They're over there." Satia pointed to her bunk.

"Where are you from, Satia?"

"I'm not from Nalza if that's what you're wondering," Satia declared. "I just studied in Nalza among many other places."

Ellia found her clothes neatly placed on the bed. She didn't even notice them earlier. She tossed the dirty rags and changed. Her olive dress had dirt all over, and the fringe was soiled, but it still felt good being in her own clothes. She felt herself again.

"Shall we?" Satia asked.

They walked outside. King Breneon was already on his fine horse, a black stallion with a white mane. More than a dozen knights surrounded him. All of them were fully armored. Ronn was talking with a few men close by.

Raun came to them with a horse. It was dark brown with a pair of droopy eyes. "This one's for you." He handed the reins to Satia.

"I know what I want in return," Satia said to Raun. "I'd like you to let Ellia go."

Raun grinned, looking at Ellia. It was the most sickening sight she ever saw. He emanated with a repulsive pride as if he came up with a number of wicked ideas that made him feel delighted. She cringed at the thought of what might come out of this man's mind.

"I have an idea how we could use you," Raun said to Ellia with another repulsive smile.

CHAPTER 24

DORRELL'S WORLD FELT as if it was falling apart. He just couldn't imagine a world without the person he admired most—the Celestial King. However, he faced the notion that someday it would come to be, but he couldn't prepare for it. The only thing that made it easier was the thought that there really was something after this life—that death wasn't permanent. Yet, just when he believed himself ready for the inevitable, his heart ached again. No matter how he prepared, he would never be unmoved—he would never be indifferent in the face of the Celestial King's death.

The Celestial King was still alive—barely. His pulse was weaker than ever. Dorrell was kneeling by his side, weeping. The other people in the chamber had the same blank faces Dorrell saw every day. *They don't care,* he thought. He felt lonely. No one seemed to care for the Celestial King as much as he did.

"The King's Fall," someone whispered.

Dorrell looked around the chamber. It was secretly called the King's Fall among members of the Grand Court. He was almost at the top of the Great Tower. It was dark, but some light sneaked in through the open door. He could hear the whistles of the wind. The air was lighter, clearer. Water burbled in the background.

"I'd like to have a word with the Celestial King," Dorrell said in an unforgiving voice.

One by one, the people left. Some gave him peculiar looks, others struggled to hide their scorn. In some ways, they were right. Why should they care for a Celestial King who was almost absent from their life? They never heard him speak or make any decisions. The Celestial King was alive all these years, yet he was also absent from the world. Even if he was the heart of Narilan and his mana fueled the world, all the citizens of the kingdom seemed distant from him. They always were. *They never appreciated him,* Dorrell thought.

It was all because of the comfort of their lives. The people of Narilan lived in peace, happiness, but also stagnation. Nothing changed in Narilan until the Celestial King was dying. Everything was perfect and stable until then. Everyone grew too comfortable. They never felt fear or insecurity. If they had, they would revere the Celestial King.

A thick red blind separated the Celestial King from the rest of the chamber. The curtain was so thick that Dorrell couldn't even see the outline of the throne, let alone the Celestial King.

The soft murmuring of the water gave the chamber a peaceful atmosphere. Water flowed from the roof through countless miniature openings and spilled into the ponds directly below. The floor was covered with tiny, intricate ridges and pools for the water to run through.

Dorrell remained on his knees as he always did when he came to the Celestial King's chamber. It was a sign of respect and humility. Ever since he became the preceptor, he had countless meetings here. Much of that time was devoted to shaping Dorrell into a righteous person, yet some of it was dedicated to simple conversations with the Celestial King—banter and chatter.

"I would like you to know that I am hard pressed for time," Dorrell said, but he didn't know if the Celestial King was listening. "You'll leave me soon, and I have yet to find someone worthy of the throne." Dorrell felt awkward. He felt like he was talking to a corpse. The Celestial King, as expected, didn't respond, but Dorrell, for some reason, was reminded of the Celestial King's laughter.

Dorrell paused. "I have decided that I will not let a savage occupy the Great Tower," Dorrell declared. "I will do whatever it takes to honor this sacred place, even if my choices go against tradition. Even if my right to ascend to the next life is taken away, I don't care. I will continue even if it kills me. I'll follow your teachings and my heart." Dorrell fell silent, then listened. He hoped that the Celestial King would utter a single word or nod. Then he stood up, bowed, and pushed the massive door open.

Outside, Albert was waiting with his hands behind his back. He looked at Dorrell with his old, wrinkled face. "What now, young lad?"

"Have you been taking good care of our donors?" Dorrell whispered.

"Certainly, all of them are safe."

"In a day or two, we'll catch another one, so please continue as planned."

"We'll be finished soon, but I don't think I'll be able to finish modifying the Celestial King's chamber until he passes away," Albert said in an uncomfortable tone.

"Fine," Dorrell said. "Just make sure we're prepared." He walked to a nearby window, which overlooked the whole kingdom. *I will do exactly what I was assigned to do,* Dorrell thought. *I will select a worthy successor, but power will not be the deciding factor—the heart will. All the Dreamers we've gathered so far wanted to sacrifice their life for the kingdom. They will be able to do so as donors of mana to the weaker but noblest of kings.*

CHAPTER 25

KYLE TROTTED ON his horse through the woods with a hood over his head. Avril was right by his side, but Hilda and Reave were lagging further behind in silence, as if unwilling to catch up. Hilda was pulling Ellia's horse with her as well. The horse was stubborn as if it knew that Ellia was left in Relien, and it yearned to go back.

The woods had a deep emerald color, a healthy green hue. The vine-bound trees towered over them, motionless in the wind. Their massive trunks ware encircled by fragile, barren bushes. A few birds sang in the background, but no other animals were around. The place was peaceful—too peaceful.

Kyle slowed down, then looked around. "How was it with Ronn?" He looked at Avril to see her frown.

"We didn't get to talk much," she said.

Kyle wasn't jealous. Avril wasn't his property, of

course. She could do anything she wanted. Yet, having her come back meant that she was still on his side, that he had won her over.

"How could you?" Hilda abruptly caught up, blocking the path. She then jumped off her horse.

Kyle looked over his shoulder for a moment, then turned to gaze around the woods.

"How could you leave her there?" Hilda clenched her quivering fist.

"I'm not her guardian," Kyle said in a cold voice. "Did you really expect me to take care of Ellia in your stead?"

Hilda sprang closer, grabbing Kyle by his leather armor. She pulled him down. Kyle slipped from his horse, and barely managed to land on his feet in a puff of dust. Hilda tried to land a punch, but he grabbed her fist, and shoved her back. Avril wanted to intervene, but Reave stopped her.

"I thought it was obvious that we're not allies. We're not companions. Everyone is responsible for their own actions." Kyle spat on the ground. "Besides, I am not the one who left her."

Inflamed by his words, Hilda unsheathed her sword. She sprung forward with a powerful overhead swing. But she was too slow. Before her sword could come close to hitting Kyle, it turned into a cloud of dust. Kyle grinned, his hands wide open. Hilda snorted, hurling the hilt at him.

It hit Kyle hard in the chest with a subtle thud.

"Where is your will to fight?" Hilda asked. "Where is that bloodlust that I once saw?"

Kyle chuckled. "I am desperately trying to save it for someone else." He ran his fingers through his dark hair.

Staring into Hilda's frantic gaze, he could no longer see

the same warrior he once saw. Gone was the steel resolve and cold focus. Ever since Reave dragged her out of Relien, Hilda was different. She had lost something there. Something burst within, and it could not be easily mended. He doubted she would be of any use in battle.

"Enough of this," Avril interrupted. "This isn't leading us anywhere." She turned to Kyle. "Tell us, what do you intend to do? I think we all deserve to know."

Kyle sighed. "Breneon will not let me leave. The anger is eating him from the inside. The thought that I could become the Celestial King makes him sick. He probably thinks today might be his last chance to kill me. He'll come after us with Raun and his knights. He will most likely take Ellia with him for... protection." Kyle spat blood. "Hilda, tell them why I think he'll do that."

Hilda hesitated. "Breneon is known for using other people. One time when a peasant disrespected him and hid in the woods, Breneon took the peasant's lover in order to make the peasant come to him. After that, he killed both of them."

"Breneon probably thinks he can use Ellia as leverage," Kyle said. "He's hoping he can make me surrender."

"But how do you intend to fight all of his knights?" Reave asked.

"I came to Relien because I want to confront Breneon. I'm hoping that I can force him to give me his Blessing. That's why I endured the imprisonment." Kyle paused. "If I defeat Breneon, the knights will all retreat."

Avril looked at Kyle with a worried expression.

"I will need your help, Reave." Kyle looked at Reave, who returned a suspicious glare. "We both know you can use mana. I think you are strong. Am I mistaken?" Kyle waited, but Reave didn't object. "I'd like to use that to our advantage. I want you to draw their attention. They will be on a lookout for any signs of large mana use. I can't fight them all, but if you draw some of them away, I think I can manage."

"What would you have me do?" Reave asked.

Kyle grinned. "You'll figure something out."

Reave let out a lifeless snicker, then nodded. Long ago, Kyle noticed Reave's desire to fight. It was only natural that Reave would agree. He would have a chance to fight, to cause chaos.

A weak, but gradually more violent, tremor came from the direction of Relien. The woods were sent into motion as they started to sway in the gale, leaves falling down. A harsh groan resounded through the ground as a tree toppled down.

"What was that?" Avril asked.

Reave climbed a branch and swung to another. He continued to leap from branch to branch, delicately and naturally. The large trees obscured his vision. "It must be another cataclysm. The Celestial King should be dead soon. Was this your first time hearing an earthquake, Avril?" Reave dropped down. "You looked scared."

"No, it just reminded me of an unpleasant memory." Avril frowned.

Kyle patted his horse. "Hilda, this might be your chance to save Ellia. You know Relien. Think of what Breneon might do."

Hilda remained silent. She looked at Kyle with disgust.

Kyle saw profound worry on Hilda's face at the sound of the tremor that shook the woods. He thought he heard such a sound somewhere before. It was weaker at the time, but still resembled the crushing force of this one. Then he remembered, it was on the day he almost died. On the day he met Ellia.

"What if we get separated?" Avril asked.

"We're all going our separate ways," Kyle said. "It'll be harder to catch us that way. You should hide the horses, Avril. It would be a pity if they died in the fray."

"If you think I'll sit this one out, you don't know me," Avril replied, shaking her head.

"Your choice." Kyle shrugged. "Join me when you're done." He looked at Avril. In her eyes, he saw a mixture of feelings. He could sense displeasure, anger, and guilt. They were overwhelming her, and she had every right to feel them all. Kyle slightly regretted bringing her to Relien. Yet, coming along was her choice, and her choice alone. Kyle thought he had no right to tell her otherwise. He respected all of her choices.

Kyle paused. "Once Breneon is dealt with, we should regroup. There is a waterfall close by. Travel west, and you'll find it."

Reave nodded and left without his horse. Without a word, Hilda tied Ellia's horse to hers and rode away, taking both horses with her. Avril imagined a bow, it came into existence and slipped into her hand.

Kyle looked up at the sky. He could barely see it beyond the treetops. *The King of Relien will come for me,* Kyle thought. *And he will suffer defeat.*

◆

The ground trembled. The bushes retreated, and the grass opened up to reveal a patch of dry soil. Roots came out of the ground, dancing around and about. Puffs of dust covered the woods, billowing. The soil was stirred until it turned into quicksand. More and more roots protruded out of the ground, hiding in the dust. The large pit opened up. It became larger and larger, then everything stood still.

When the dust settled, Breneon took a step forward. Raun was behind him, holding Ellia cruelly by the hair. She was at his knees, dizzy. Ronn was there too with more than three dozen knights and archers. Satia was hidden in the crowd of swords.

"I told you she could do it, Ronn." Raun smiled, eyeing Ellia. "She has a lot of mana, I tell you."

Ronn nodded stoically. He had a large horn hanging from his belt, a gift from his father.

Breneon turned to Raun, "Send the scouts. Let them scour the area. Remember that the other three are secondary objectives. We're hunting specifically for Kyle and no one else."

"Yes, Your Majesty." Raun bowed, then walked away. After giving out orders, he took a seat. He took a vial, which contained a dark blue liquid, out of his bag. He dipped his arrows in it, then poured it on his sword.

Satia kneeled beside Ellia. "Have some." She passed Ellia some water. "We're going to be here for a while."

Raun turned his attention to Ronn. "Lord Ronn, I know King Breneon is tolerant of your behavior, but if I see you helping the enemy, I promise I'll kill you." Raun heard no response.

Ronn stood still, lost in thought. Then after a long pause, he looked up at Raun. "Thank you for not telling my father of Lord Elring's passing. I thought it would only further enrage him. If we are to succeed, he can't lose his grip on himself."

Raun bowed his head.

Then a harsh tremor came through the ground. A tree swayed in the distance, hitting the crowns of the surrounding trees. The ground murmured, then cracked open everywhere. Uprooted, the tree toppled to the ground with a powerful boom, and a dense cloud of dust spread through the woods.

Breneon stood still with a disgusting frown. "Raun, it must be him. Take the girl and all your knights. Kill him."

CHAPTER 26

REAVE SPRINTED THROUGH the woods, the massive tree he knocked down fell behind him. It started to drizzle. The wet soil splashed with every step he took. A few knights saw him and had no intention of letting him escape. They pulled out their bows and fired. An arrow landed right in front of Reave, and he froze. Another one coming, he dodged to the side, then hid behind a tree trunk and noticed that the arrow grazed his leg.

How I hate archers, he thought.

Reave darted to the right through a patch of shriveled bushes. He could hear the knights following behind. He slid down a steep slope, his cloak torn by the parched branches and withered bushes tagging on it.

Sunlight soon pierced the trees, and he saw the edge of an enormous pit. He didn't know if he could stop in time, the momentum propelling him forward. When his feet hit flat ground, he tried to grab a hold of something, a branch or anything. But he was moving too fast. Realizing that he couldn't stop, Reave summoned vines from a nearby tree. They wrapped around his torso and pulled him back just in time, returning his balance.

Reave sighed with relief. He turned around to see a knight charging with his sword overhead. He seized the knight's hands, which were gripping the sword, then put out his foot. The knight's momentum did the rest as he tripped and rolled off the edge. A pair of knights appeared, steadying their bows. Reave deflected each of their arrows with his sword and stood his ground, but the barrage of arrows was unyielding. One broke through his defenses, slitting his cheek.

He bowed forward, and blood dripped from his face. "You don't know who you're fighting against, you maggots!"

More knights joined the fray, surrounding him. He counted twelve. None were brave enough to attack just yet. He closed his eyes to meditate. He could hear their feeble murmurs. Then, a circle of rough, dry soil formed underneath Reave's feet. The circle propelled him up into the air, mud trickling from it. His body levitated upward and into the center of the pit. He steadied his breath, arrows flying in the sky. The soil around the edge of the pit started to tremble softly. Then it was set in motion. It spilled down, flooding the pit with a large mass of dirt, mud, and rocks.

All of the knights were carried down by the landslide—falling, tripping, getting killed by the rocks and root. Their screams echoed in Reave's ears. He enjoyed it. It made him feel a sort of satisfaction that he rarely felt outside of combat. He felt power and joy.

When the soil settled at the bottom of the pit, only a handful of knights were left. Some screamed, alive but gravely injured. There were those that struggled to dig themselves out, only to find out that they're stuck. Those capable of fighting patiently waited for Reave to make a move.

Reave landed in the pit, unsheathed his sword, and walked slowly. A panicking knight screamed when sand, controlled by Reave, ferociously crushed his leg. His scream was silenced by Reave's blade, and the knight's head rolled off his shoulders. Another knight, who was ready to cry, sprung forward to attack. Reave ducked down, grabbed his knife, and jammed it into the knight's throat. Then pivoting around, he deflected multiple sand daggers.

Another Dreamer, he thought. *No, too weak.*

"So you can use mana, huh?" Reave said to a knight standing before him.

The knight remained silent, sweat dripping down his neck. Only his fear-struck eyes were visible behind his round helmet.

Sand began to gather around Reave's ankle. He tried to move, but it was too late. He grimaced as the pain kicked in, then focused his mana. The knight rushed in for an attack. Yet roots surfaced from the ground, wrapping around the knight's chest. He cried feebly as the roots dragged him back and then slowly underground. His screams redoubled as the sand dissolved around Reave's foot. The knight was buried up to his head. Reave chuckled, ran closer, and kicked the helmet, hurling it away. Underneath, he saw a face with a torn lip—a face of a woman.

"Please let me go," she begged, tears running down her face. "I have a family."

"Should've thought about that earlier." Reave walked away, unmoved. She groaned, then shrieked. Soon, there was nothing left of the woman, her body swallowed by the land.

Reave prepared to leave, but took his time finishing off every one of the knights, listening to their feeble and helpless screams.

When he was done, he sighed. He looked around, almost hoping that someone would still be alive. He felt bitter and unsatisfied. He wanted something more. He wanted to fight a true adversary, a monster that would push him to his limits. He yearned for something he couldn't have, and that thought made him feel disappointed.

◆

Hilda advanced through the woods slowly, her eyes searching for Raun and her ears picking up the smallest whisper. She avoided any paths and clearings where she could be easily seen. Attacking head-on wasn't an option. She looked at her arm—the lost hand—and wished to have it back. She felt much weaker without it. She pacified her two horses, pulling them closer by the reins.

Hilda remembered her first encounter with Ellia. At first, Ellia wasn't easy to get along with. Her impracticality when dealing with life outside of Nalza was something that Hilda could never understand. Yet, Ellia became her only family. Perhaps Hilda got used to Ellia's personality with time. Or perhaps Ellia changed and became corrupted by the world.

Hilda was shaken awake by the sound of something coming. She peeked from the bushes to see a knight wobbling, barely holding himself from collapsing. Gasping for air, the knight was holding his arm and leaving a faint trail of blood.

He must've faced Reave, she thought, looking in the direction the knight came from.

Hilda followed him.

Soon, she heard footsteps, then marching.

An adamant voice echoed through the woods, giving orders to knights. *Raun,* she thought. There was nothing Hilda wanted more than to rush ahead and confront him, but she decided otherwise. She followed the knight while keeping her presence hidden. Soon, she caught a glimpse of Raun on his horse and knights marching behind him. She hid behind a barren trunk of a tree and observed.

The knight fell to his knees in a puff of dust, right before Raun's horse. "I'm sorry. We failed." The knight gasped for air.

Hilda peeked from behind the tree trunk to see Ellia tied to Raun's horse. Her clothes were tattered and muddy. Her face was grazed, cheeks red. Anger boiled within Hilda. A hooded figure who was riding behind Ellia retreated and vanished as everyone's attention was drawn to the wounded knight.

Raun dismounted. "Don't worry. You did a good job." He came closer, knife in hand. He patted the knight on the shoulder with a smile, then crammed the knife into the knight's neck. The knight squealed. Raun pulled the blade out, wiped it, and sheathed it. The knight at his feet stopped moving—dead.

Raun paused, looking around.

Hilda instinctively hid behind the tree trunk. Something pulled on her armor, then jerked her to the side. With not enough time to react, she collapsed to the ground, slipping from her hiding spot. Her horses dashed away, startled by the commotion. Her armor drawn to Raun, Hilda was dragged across the ground and couldn't fight it. One of her arms was useless and relinquishing her blade wasn't an option. When she stopped, she rolled on her back, throwing dirt at Raun. He flinched.

She staggered to her feet.

"So you must be the caretaker of this worm, right?" Raun asked in a disgusting tone, then pulled Ellia closer, forcing her to the ground. Ellia had countless dark bruises. No matter how much Hilda wrestled against Raun's hold, she lacked the strength to stand up.

"You bastard," Hilda said, her sword ready.

Raun glanced at a pair of knights by his side. They dismounted and advanced, sword in hand. One of them was reserved and hesitant, but the other was headstrong and determined. Hilda waited for them, her fingers numb from the cold hilt. As the headstrong knight attacked, Hilda rolled away and mustered enough strength to leap back on her feet. The knight's sword dug into the soil. Unable to pull it out in time, the knight was an open target. Hilda drove the tip of her blade into his foot. With a scream, the knight leaned back. Hilda swung her sword upward, grazed the knight's armor, and hit his helmet right at the chin. It sent the knight into a dazed state, but he didn't release the hold on his sword. Before the knight could regain his bearing, Hilda spun and finished him off with a strike to the back of the knee. The knight groaned, then slumped to the ground, grimacing from the pain. The other knight stepped aside, forfeiting the fight. The cavalry was silent.

Hilda panted. "So much for your knights."

At the sound of the comment, Raun gnashed his teeth. He took his bow and fired off two arrows, killing both knights. They didn't expect the attack. He sighed.

"I must say I'm quite disappointed. My knights defeated by someone like you. You can't even comprehend how humiliating it is." Raun's voice was fueled with frustration. "But I must admit, your allies are something else." He held on to Ellia by the hair—tighter. Ellia wept.

"They're not my allies," Hilda confessed. *They were never my allies,* she thought, thinking of Kyle.

"Right." Raun looked down at Ellia. "Freaks from your village regard everyone else in Narilan as animals, animals that pretend to be gods."

Hilda couldn't disagree with that. She felt bitter just thinking that her people really did believe that. She was against that mentality, the mentality that she suspected might have been the cause for the annihilation of their village. But that was just her guess.

"Freaks?" Hilda asked. "At least I don't kill my comrades."

"But you sided with Kyle. He killed many." Raun smiled.

Hilda remained silent.

"Oh, don't give me the silent treatment." Raun sauntered forward. "I have heard of your village. Pitiful. I truly feel sorry for you. You could have lived in peace forever. At least, you believed you could."

Hilda forced herself not to look away.

"Yet, you were all killed... forgotten... abandoned by the Celestial King." Raun smiled again. "Like the worthless filth you are."

Hilda lashed out with a sword strike. Raun sprung away in time to avoid the blow.

"You think you know what happened?" Hilda accused. "You have no idea."

"People talk, you know. I heard stories. One of them said that Zardan was sick of dealing with you. That it was sick of listening to your preaching." Raun drank some water from the flask at his belt.

Bastard! I heard those stories too. I heard many stories, most were false. Hilda didn't feel like continuing to talk. She knew what he was doing. "We're done here," she said. "Let her go."

Raun shook his head. "Just how do you intend to fight all my knights?"

Hilda leaped forward. Her attack was cut short when a large axe appeared and rammed into her abdomen. She was shoved back and lost the grip on her sword. The blade clanged as it hit the ground. Roots enveloped Hilda's remaining hand and pulled her to the ground, then contracted until blood gushed from her. The large axe returned to Raun.

"A traitor surrenders his right to live," Raun said, then he made the large axe that levitated around him vanish. "You've betrayed Zardan, so the end is near."

A Dreamer, Hilda thought. All her hope was gone.

More roots wrapped around Hilda's feet, forcing her to the ground. With only a single arm free—the arm without a hand—she eyed the sword. She couldn't even reach it. She was stuck, imprisoned. Raun kneeled next to her and grabbed his knife. He licked the edge. The saliva dripped from the blade, trickling down to the ground.

"How does it feel to be killed by an animal?" Raun asked. Then he drove the blade into Hilda's stomach. She wailed, and her eyes met Ellia. With a final bit of strength, Hilda kicked the sword in Ellia's direction.

"I'm sure Zardan will thank me," Raun whispered. "All citizens of the Nalza Village Cluster should be killed."

Hilda watched Ellia free herself. Their eyes met one final time. Hilda nodded, and Ellia returned a defeated look.

Raun looked over his shoulder. He saw Ellia running away. The cavalry was still. "Get her!" he screamed, then stood up.

Hilda wrestled against the roots. She felt them digging deeper, making her bleed. The pain wasn't getting to her anymore. She didn't care. A tiny knife slipped out of her pocket. She managed to grasp it with her hand, but struggled to cut the roots. The more she moved, the more blood she lost. Yet, it didn't matter. Nothing mattered.

Raun was already standing over her. Before she could react, he grabbed a hold of her hair, and shoved his knee into her face. She fell to the ground, spitting blood, but her hand was finally free.

Then with a quick swipe, she drove the knife into Raun's leg, just above the ankle. The blade dug deep, and Raun screamed. He fell on one of his knees and backhanded Hilda. Yet she managed to stab him again twice in the shoulder. Ruan bashed his elbow against the ground as he fell on his side. The knife was still left in his wound.

The effects of his mana vanished, and Hilda was freed from the roots. She stood up, covered in blood and feeling dizzy.

"Let's stop this. Go tend to your wounds." Raun said through gritted teeth.

"We both know how this ends." Hilda looked at the cavalry, but none of the knights moved. They just kept watching.

Raun grimaced. "You're already dead. You'll die today."

"But you'll die first."

"I'm just doing what I was told," Raun declared in a stoic voice. "Dying is an honor. I'll die for my beloved kingdom."

"Your beloved kingdom?" Hilda kicked him in the face, forcing him to fall on his back. She retrieved her sword, then returned to Raun. He looked at his knights as if calling them to intervene. His eyes were blank and filled with awe. Hilda lifted her sword. Raun smirked— dazed and defeated. His final chuckle ended with a quick groan as Hilda sunk the tip of her blade deep into his chest. She took a step back, and the blade slipped out of her hand.

The cavalry didn't move.

Hilda took another step. Light and soundless. The dizziness stopped, but she felt cold.

"Finally someone dealt with him," one of the knights said.

"Sadistic bastard." Another shook his head.

Hilda listened. Their words turned to whispers that vanished somewhere in the distance. The sun's rays were dull. The air was dry and insipid. She couldn't hear her heart beating anymore. Then, Hilda saw Ellia. Ellia was safe, but most of all, she looked happy. Her innocent smile and kind eyes were enough to soothe all of Hilda's worries and fears. Hilda felt no yearning to go back to Nalza and no motivation to keep going. She just stood there with her best friend. Then, her knees hit the ground.

The world stood still.

Hilda didn't move. She just stayed there, looking at the sky—silent and still.

With Ellia by her side.

Chapter 27

KYLE WALKED WITH a heavy step through the graveyard of corpses. His leather armor was stained in blood, and his blade was in hand. Most of the knights were dead, but some still grunted and grimaced in pain. There were also those that wept, fearful for their life.

Kyle frowned, hauling a knight behind him. The knight was wounded in the leg and unconscious. Yet before he passed out, he told Kyle Breneon's location. Kyle wanted to just leave the knight, but then he came up with an idea.

Kyle climbed a small, barren hill and followed a lone path. Then he heard sounds and finally saw Breneon's camp. Dragging the knight behind, he whistled.

The camp echoed with noise as the knights armed themselves, archers steadied their bows, and Breneon emerged at the helm with Ronn. Breneon had a proud grimace as if he was ready, as if his victory was inevitable. Ronn, on the other hand, looked worried.

The knights were unnerved. It wasn't a surprise to Kyle. No matter how much practice they had in swordsmanship or archery, they couldn't prepare themselves for the chaos of a real battle. They were weak and inexperienced. Gruesome sights and the screams of their fallen comrades overwhelmed them. Years of harmony in Narilan gave them no opportunity for real combat. They were already defeated.

Kyle took a few more steps, then stopped. "You really thought I'd fall for such a trick?" Kyle asked as he sensed the mana pulsing through the land, the trees, and everything else. A circular area around Breneon's camp was drenched in mana, and a Spectator was watching. Kyle was standing right at the edge, where the Spectator's influence ended.

Breneon frowned. He looked in the other direction, where the sounds of battle escalated. He didn't look caught off guard or surprised. "He must have another Dreamer with him," he said to one of his knights.

"You should've listened to the stories, Breneon." Kyle pulled the unconscious knight closer. With the corner of his eyes, he caught a glimpse of a hidden archer outside of the Spectator's area of influence and forced the ground to swallow him whole. The archer's death was inaudible and quick.

Breneon gestured to his son, then strode in Kyle's direction. His knights hesitantly tagged along. "I'd much rather see you for the ruthless brute you are with my own eyes." He coughed. "Stories mean nothing."

"I agree with you there," Kyle said. "Tales of Breneon

from Relien painted a beautiful picture of a just and noble ruler. What I see before me is a man of many evil deeds... such as myself."

Breneon shook his head. "Don't judge me, boy. I'm not like you. My actions were all meant to help Relien. Your adventures are a meaningless chain of violence fueled by your greed."

"Greed, anger, hatred. We're both familiar with it all. The difference is that I can admit it, and you can't." Kyle felt the influence of the Spectator grow, and took a step back. "Why would you come here if it wasn't out of anger and hatred?"

Breneon fell silent, gnashing his teeth.

"I know you all too well, Breneon." Kyle grinned. "Was it worth it? You sacrificed so many lives for the sake of... for the sake of what?" Kyle ruffled his hair.

Breneon chuckled. He looked at Ronn and reassured him that they had the upper hand. "I confess. I came here out of anger and hatred, but those were not the main driving forces behind my actions. I can't fathom how such a worm collected nine Blessings. I feel disgusted just thinking that you might become the Celestial King. Today might be my last chance to kill you, and I can't let that pass me by." He cleared his throat. "Now tell me, why did you come to face me, just to die?"

"I need your Blessing." Kyle smirked.

Breneon snorted. "I should just let my son kill you on the spot."

"Is he the Spectator?" Kyle looked at Ronn then at Breneon. He wondered who might be the one proficient at using mana. He looked at each of the knights. It was true that everyone had some mana inside of them, but these men were terrified and overcome by panic. There was no way they would be able to enter a state of meditation, let alone influence the world with their mana. These men were ready to run and abandon their king.

"So what do you intend to do?" Breneon asked. "We can stand here all day. When Raun returns or my reinforcements arrive, we will kill you. I already sent a messenger to Orrzol. How long do you think it'll take them to arrive?"

Kyle fell silent. He knew that the Spectator was either Breneon himself or Ronn. Maybe both. Yet, he wondered why Ronn was here in the first place. Breneon would force Ronn to stay in Relien if he didn't need him. Ronn was just too precious, too dear to Breneon. *He must be here for a reason. If Ronn is the Spectator, he is Breneon's only advantage, but he can also be Breneon's downfall,* Kyle thought.

Breneon commanded his archers with a wave of his hand. Arrows rained from above and whistled in the air. When they reached Kyle, they burst into glittering dust around him, leaving almost nothing behind and surrounding him in a thin cloud.

Then, three consecutive arrows swished passed Kyle. Precise and swift. Three archers collapsed with arrows sticking out of their heads.

"Hold your ground," Breneon declared at the first sight of his knights backing away.

The thought of Avril watching him comforted Kyle. Her archery skills were as sharp as ever. It was quite some time since she fought by his side. He didn't even realize how much he missed it. Having her there gave him a person to depend on. It was something that stood in sharp contrast to his frequent, lone struggles. Yet, Kyle knew that for Avril this was a very different battle, an internal fight. Having her still on his side meant that she was his true ally.

"Did you kill my brother?" Ronn demanded. "Tell me."

"And what if I did?" Kyle asked. The knight at his feet started to mumble. Kyle kicked him, and the knight opened his eyes, grimacing. Kyle pulled him up and hid behind him, holding a sword to his neck. "The next person to attack will be killed by my archer."

"What do you think you're doing?" Breneon asked.

"How many men has your son killed?" Kyle asked. "How many?"

Breneon looked away, frowning. He waved his hand, but his knights hesitated to advance. The remaining archers surveyed the treetops in search of Avril.

"Attack!" Breneon screamed at all of his knights.

Kyle marched ahead.

"I order you to attack!" Breneon roared, yet no one reacted.

Kyle tossed Ronn an evil grin. Ronn's hands quivered, heart throbbing in his chest. Ronn tried to steady his breath.

Kyle took another step. The ground beneath his feet throbbed with mana. It was mediocre by his standard, but still dangerous.

"Kill him." Breneon unsheathed his sword yet took a step back.

The mana stood still and gathered underneath Kyle. He could feel it. As the earth began to tremble softly, he sprang back, pulling the knight with him. The knight slipped and fell on his back as a stone spike emerged from the ground. It ripped through his armor, and surfaced out of the chest in a stream of gushing blood. His limbs lifelessly drooped down. His open mouth was stuck in a perennial scream, eyes wide open.

The sight forced Ronn to his knees.

Kyle felt the mana wither away. He kneeled and forced all of his mana into the ground. The earth groaned, spitting puffs of dust as it cracked. Breneon panicked and tripped. The knights scattered, armors clinking. A powerful quake passed through, earth shattering and trees shaking. The ground fissured, forming a deep, dark chasm that looked like an entrance into an abyss. It puffed warm, nasty clouds of dense air.

Kyle heard something coming. A knight charged him. Kyle sidestepped and spun, dodging and cutting through the knight's leg. The cut was shallow, but it was enough to send the knight to the ground. With a swift sword swing, Kyle beheaded the knight.

Another one appeared from behind a tree, coupled with two others. They didn't have helmets. One had a scar running down his cheek, a remnant of the past. The other two didn't have armor and resembled peasants, rough and tattered.

Kyle picked up another sword from the dead knight.

The scarred knight attacked first. His attacks were calculated, but weak as if he was testing Kyle. Kyle blocked each of the attacks with ease. Then suddenly, the knight put all of his strength into an attack, nearly sending Kyle's sword down to the ground.

Kyle stood his ground as they went into a standstill. He saw the peasants circling around. They were trying to flank him. One of them attacked. Kyle saw it as a chance to finish them off. He shoved the scarred knight back, evaded the peasant, and then parried the peasant's follow-up attack. He countered with a swift blow to the shoulder. The peasant grunted, then collapsed. The other one tried to attack, but Kyle spun and jammed his blade between his ribs, leaving it there.

Before the scarred knight could attack again, he was dead—impaled.

Kyle heard the sound of arrows, then everything fell silent.

Kyle saw the roots gather around him. *Old trick, Ronn,* he thought. He sidestepped around the roots and charged at Breneon. The ground quivered, and dark pits appeared everywhere. They were small, but large enough to consume a man. One appeared underneath Kyle, and he fell down. He grabbed the edge of the pit, and his hands bled as he struggled to hold on. He forced a root to wrap itself around his arm and pull him out. There was no time to rest as a spike emerged from the ground. He rolled out of the way, but his ribs were grazed. Breneon tried to attack, but he was too slow. Kyle cut upright through his chest and face, splitting his eye. Breneon screamed, dropping his sword. He knelt, his face in his hands.

Kyle grinned at Ronn, taunting him. Ronn sprang forward fueled by his emotions. Kyle parried the clumsy attack, and countered with a pommel to the head. Ronn collapsed to the floor, blood trickling from his face. Kyle stomped on his stomach, and Ronn let out a faint, feeble squeal as roots restrained him.

"Stop this!" Avril screamed, emerging from the woods. "Stop this at once."

Kyle looked up to see her gloomy expression. It was solemn and resolute.

Kyle ignored Avril and gave Ronn a kick in the back, then turned his attention to Breneon. "The Blessing." He stretched out his hand.

"I will die before it happens," Breneon rasped. "You will never get my Blessing."

"I won't ask again. I don't want to do this because Avril is here, but I will if you force me to."

"Don't do it, Father," Ronn screamed.

Breneon gnashed his teeth, looking at his son. "Was this your plan all along? You think you can force me to submit? You think you can murder all my knights, and then I'll try to save my son by giving you my Blessing?"

"Time is running out. What's your answer?"

"Kill me now, boy, or I will find you anywhere you go," Breneon declared. "I won't stop looking for you no matter what."

Kyle took a hold of his sword, the tip down over Ronn.

"I beg you, Kyle," Avril pleaded. "Stop this."

Kyle ignored her and steadied his sword. With a precise, downward thrust, the blade pricked Ronn's leg. Ronn let out a pathetic scream that echoed thought the woods. His screaming redoubled as Kyle twisted the blade and pulled it out, then turned into a long, feeble squeal.

Breneon didn't look away. He tried to be strong. A bloody teardrop fell down his cheek.

"You can stop this, Breneon," Kyle said. "It's your choice." He lifted his sword once more.

Then something rammed Kyle. He fell to the ground, puffs of dust around him. He saw Avril with her knife sitting on him, but he didn't fight. Kyle waited to see what she would do. He guessed that she wouldn't have the courage to use the knife. Avril sighed and tossed the knife away. Kyle was right and smiled. It was a mistake, as it provoked Avril into throwing a punch. It was painful, despite her small size. She didn't stop there and continued. It was only after numerous attacks that she noticed Kyle wasn't defending himself. She hesitated after seeing his bloody face, and that's when he seized the opportunity. He easily shoved her off and stood back up.

"You can't do this," she declared, standing up. "We're not like that!"

"Scum kill scum, remember?" Kyle said.

"Let's just leave," Avril begged.

Kyle shook his head. "Then everything we have done so far will be for nothing. There is no way the other two warlords will ever give me their Blessing out of kindness."

"We're not savage beasts. There is a difference between killing someone in a fight and torturing them to death." Avril looked at him, with hope in her eyes.

"This is the only way," Kyle insisted and recovered his sword from the ground. He stood over Ronn, holding him at sword-point. His hands trembled at Avril's pleas. He hesitated, then closed his eyes.

When he was ready with a final attack, he heard Breneon call his name. "I'll do it, I'll do it," Breneon said, weeping on the ground. "Just don't hurt my son." Poignant tears dripped down his face.

Kyle came closer, then stretched out his hand. Breneon looked up and swung his sword at Kyle, who effortlessly evaded, and, with a powerful swing, sunk his blade deep into Breneon's shoulder. The old man spat blood. Kyle could hear Ronn thrashing around, trying to free himself.

Kyle frowned.

Then, in a gesture of submission, Breneon put out his

hand. "Listen to me, boy," Breneon whispered. "Your plan won't work. Don't you remember that the Blessing isn't enough? You still need to perform the ritual. Did you know that each warlord has a different chant?" Breneon smiled, blood dripping from the corners of his mouth.

They shook hands, and the old man collapsed to the ground.

Kyle sighed and kept silent. He didn't know of the different chants. He thought that he could just go back to Razan or another place with a heavenly ground to complete the ritual.

He thought about Breneon. With him dead, Kyle didn't know what would happen. He still felt the fragile mana that symbolized Breneon's Blessing. It was still there—thriving. He thought about Elring and all the other things he had done. He wondered if the Celestial King was watching.

Kyle waited there, thinking of the Gift of Misfortune. The moment felt like an eternity, but nothing happened. There was no grand judgement or revelation. Nothing.

Kyle looked around, but Avril was gone. A part of him wanted to run after her and bring her back. Yet, it was all a weak impulse, a childish thought. He knew Avril wouldn't be coming back any time soon, if ever. He disappointed her, and she needed time.

"I might be able to help, Kyle," a soft feminine voice came from the woods. A hooded figure appeared from behind a thick tree trunk. Upon putting down the hood, Kyle saw a woman. Her curly, black locks had white tips.

"How dare you!" Ronn screamed. "We should have never trusted you!"

"Who are you?" Kyle asked. "How do you know my name?"

"My name is Satia, and I'm an alchemist. I know you, Kyle. I saw you when you first arrived in Relien. I saw you for the powerful Dreamer you truly are." She smiled lightly. "I know all the chants needed to perform the ritual. Not all of the heavenly grounds are within villages and castles. I can lead you to one that isn't."

"And in exchange?" Kyle asked.

She came close enough to whisper. "Narilan doesn't like my approach to the world. I question, investigate, and analyze. I'd like to be able to study the world when you become the Celestial King. I think it's my only chance to get what I want."

Kyle didn't want her help. Yet, he realized that if she was telling the truth, he couldn't do without it. Without Breneon's chant, the Blessing he struggled to receive was useless. "Done. But make no mistake, if I see you doing anything suspicious, I will cut you down."

"I know," Satia said without fear in her eyes.

Kyle claimed the horn from Ronn's belt and whispered to him, "You are only alive because of Avril. Remember that." He handed the horn to Ronn and walked away. Satia followed right behind him.

"Lead the way," Kyle said. The horn resounded through the woods with a powerful blare. It was a sign that the battle was over—lost. A call to retreat.

It started to drizzle. Satia put up her hood.

Kyle looked up. He felt exhausted and dizzy. He frowned at the idea that there was a punishment for his actions. The Celestial King really was watching, and today, Kyle was cursed with losing Avril, the only person that mattered in his life.

Red raindrops fell on his face. The clouds cried in blood.

CHAPTER 28

ELLIA KEPT RUNNING, but the knights were gaining on her. They were unyielding and determined. Strength was slowly escaping her. She felt a profound headache, which gathered around her forehead.

Suddenly, Ellia tripped, falling headlong onto the grass. She staggered back up, coughing with a throbbing sensation in her ribs, but she quickly bowed down again. She could hear the knights behind her. She imagined a wall between herself and her oppressors. Yet nothing happened. She imagined it again in much more detail, but her mind felt empty. Taking a step back, she fell on her back. Her heart began to race. She felt weak and insecure. *My mana is gone,* she thought.

The knights caught up to her. One of them drew his sword, but before he could attack, he heard something. He recognized the powerful blare, and sheathed his sword.

Then, he gestured to the other knights to follow him. The blast of the horn was their sign to retreat.

"We're just going to leave her?" one of them asked.

"You heard. We're retreating."

Then the knights left. Yet, Ellia didn't have any strength to stand up. A bitter realization took over her mind, and she was faced with an overwhelming idea. Her mother was gone. Dead. Ellia lay there, but she didn't feel like crying. She didn't feel anything, except for the profound emptiness. She thought about her mother's impending death for so long now that it had no impact. There wasn't a cathartic flood of emotion that would set her free. There was only a lifeless void. Nothing more, nothing less. It was a cold emptiness that lingered deep within her heart. All she wanted to do was stare at the sky.

I wonder what happened to Hilda, she thought. *I should go back soon. The knights will most likely be gone by now.*

The rain of blood came down.

◆

The woods were still. Ellia didn't encounter anything of interest. Occasionally, she stumbled upon a corpse, or a cloven shield, or armor, but they were no longer a surprise to her. She didn't care. The red raindrops that fell from the sky looked like blood, but diluted.

Looking within herself, Ellia wanted to use mana.

She thought about the void that she felt within. She didn't want to admit it, but she knew why it was there. She lost something today, something dear that made her life worth living, a spark that gave her life meaning. Without it she felt empty and weak. She lacked the confidence and strength to keep going.

To her, mana wasn't the energy that flowed through the entire world. It wasn't a divine power, but a flame that kept her going. Mana gave her life. Without it, she had nothing.

Ellia continued her stroll through the woods as the rain stopped. She knew the general direction she came from, but she was too focused on her thoughts and still lost her way. She walked through a patch of thick bushes, then past a few withering trees. Hidden in the distance, she spotted something.

I think that's it, she thought.

The path was strewn with only a few corpses. Everything was quiet. Ellia assumed the knights left. *But why wouldn't they bury the dead?* she thought after seeing two more corpses in the middle of the path.

Then Ellia saw her. The black hair, the cape, the sword, Ellia recognized it all. She ran ahead, then froze. She looked at Hilda's face, her eyes closed as if she was sleeping. The void within Ellia grew. She felt overwhelmed, angered, and disappointed. She stifled it, hiding it deep within, but it didn't help. It hurt much more than anything she felt before. It was something she wasn't prepared for. Bereaved of everything that mattered, Ellia didn't know how to withstand her pain. She wanted nothing more than to hide, to escape.

"There you are," a voice came from the other side.

Ellia looked up, then nodded to Reave. He came closer, but didn't say anything when he saw Hilda. He tried to remain calm, but Ellia noticed that he was shaken.

"Are you not going to say anything?" Reave asked.

"What do you want me to say?" Ellia noticed that he relaxed as if some great weight was taken off his shoulders.

"You know, people should express emotions." Reave tried to smile, but what came out was a bizarre grimace.

Ellia shrugged. "You never do," she said in a cold voice.

"That's because I express my emotions through actions. I don't need to cry to feel better but—"

"But what?" Ellia interrupted. "A weak village girl has to cry on someone's shoulder?"

"You don't have to be bitter." Reave frowned. "May I?" He gestured with his hand at Hilda, and Ellia nodded. He bowed before Hilda, placed her sword in her hands, and began a soft, slow, phonetic chant. He almost whispered, so Ellia came closer. She repeated after him.

The mellow tune had a soft sense of melancholy, which Ellia identified with. At first, it evoked lost dreams, proud victories, and noble aspirations. Then, it stressed a loss of a loved one. Ellia tried to hide it, but the tune spoke to her. She understood it. More and more, she had trouble rehearsing each word after Reave for fear of losing control of her emotions. She held on to them—that's all she could do, and even that seemed like it was too much for her.

Reave stood up and walked to Raun's dead body. He focused his mana, and the soil, imitating the waves of an unsteady ocean, slowly carried Raun's body away. Then Reave meditated for a brief moment, and the ground opened up. As it swallowed Hilda, Ellia prayed to any god that would listen. When Hilda's burial was finished, Reave drew an image of the Shahana constellation in the dirt.

"Where did you learn that chant?" Ellia asked, trying to think of something else.

"My brother sang it at our father's funeral," Reave said, but there was no sadness on his face, his voice relaxed. Ellia wished she had the ability to distance herself from the world. She disliked being influenced by events outside of her control.

"Can I ask you something, Reave?"

"You don't have to ask for permission."

"When was the first time you used mana?"

Reave chuckled. "It was nothing special. I..." He hesitated. "I wanted something that I couldn't have at the time."

"Was it a sword?" Ellia looked up at Reave.

"I'd like to say it was." Reave grinned. "I wanted a pendant, so I sat there in front of a wall. I meditated until it opened up, and I could steal the pendant. Unfortunately, I couldn't control mana at the time. I was only a child, so I left the wall open like that... and I was quickly caught."

"They say that anyone can use mana. Do you have any ideas why I can't use it?"

"You probably can." Reave patted her on the back. "Like any other skill, you need practice. You come from a place that forbids using mana, that's probably the reason. I know people that learned it at the age of eight, but I also know some that first used mana when they were seven."

Ellia nodded.

"Would you like me to bury the other knights as well?" Reave asked.

"Why would you think that?"

"Well, I thought you might consider it appropriate."

"No." Ellia shook her head. "Leave them here, let them rot."

She strode away. Her pace was heavy and slow. Reave shrugged, then followed her. They went in the direction of the waterfall that Kyle told them about. Ellia didn't say another word, struggling to handle the weight of her own feelings.

CHAPTER 29

THE MAN WITH the blond hair collapsed. His sword was broken. Many pieces of the blade were scattered across the cold floor of the Great Tower. The blood from his wounded hand spilled into the tiny ridges and grooves on the intricate design of the floor.

"Are you ready to give up, Graeme?" a voice called out to him. It came from a tall man standing at the door leading up to the Celestial King's chamber—the summit.

Graeme ignored the question. His eyes were fixed on the grotesque monster towering over him. Only its lower half seemed human. Its upper body, however, was a skeleton glazed in a mix of blood diluted with some clear bodily fluids. The skin and flesh, which should conceal bone, hung loosely from the waist in thick folds. Within them hid the myriad of organs which were still functioning. Its skull had a small, already mended, crack from a previous battle. Its lidless eyes gazed incessantly, red from dryness. Its tongue occasionally crept out from behind its bare, yellow teeth to feel a chipped incisor. One of its skeletal arms held a bizarre and oversized axe in its hand—a tusk secured to a wooden club. It lifted the axe, its pupils set on Graeme.

Graeme's heart skipped a beat. He remembered his promise to his little brother. His brother's hopeful eyes and innocent smile were firmly engraved into his mind. Graeme swore to his brother that he would become the almighty Celestial King. Yet kneeling on the floor now, Graeme was defeated. His dream was lost. He was tormented by the faces of all the people from his hometown. Their disappointed gazes made him sick.

Graeme hesitated. He didn't know what was more honorable—surrendering, or fighting until the end.

"I give up!" Graeme screamed. "I give up!"

The man applauded. As he moved closer, Graeme recognized him as Preceptor Dorrell Sahne.

The monster put down its weapon and relaxed. Its skin crept up until the monster regained a human appearance. It looked like a tired, unassuming man with parched, bruised skin and a long, narrow face hidden under thick, long, dark hair.

"Drink this!" Dorrell tossed a bottle that dropped to the floor with a subtle thud, twirling like a snake in Graeme's direction.

"What is this?" Graeme asked.

"You wanted to serve Narilan, right?" Dorrell asked. "If you still desire to do so, drink."

Graeme hesitated. The first thing he wanted to do was leave and return to his brother. His brother needed him much more than Narilan. Yet the thought of returning defeated worried him. He wanted to make his little brother proud.

Graeme sipped on the liquid. It had almost no color, and it tasted like water. It was light, but there was something suspicious about it. Graeme finished the bottle, then turned around, ready to ask questions. His hands fell to his side, and he slipped to the floor. The fresco above him illustrated the almighty Celestial King—divine and omnipotent—above a crowd of people dressed in pale white robes. *They revere him,* Graeme thought. His consciousness started to drift away as his body rested on the floor. He could still hear voices.

"You have my gratitude, my friend." Dorrell looked at the monster.

"I'm only repaying my debt. Have you, by any chance, acquired those leaves?" The monster spoke in a tired, sleepy voice. Gasping for air, it spat blood as its body quivered. "I could use something for the pain."

"Are you all right?" Dorrell put his hand on the monster's shoulder. "Here are the herbs. Please tell me if there is anything else I can do to ease your pain."

"Thank you," the monster whispered, searching the sack. He pulled out a piece of willow bark and began chewing. "I heard about your brother."

"He'll return when he is ready. At least, I hope so." Dorrell smiled lightly. "Again, thanks for fighting for Zardan. Ever since the Celestial King fell ill years ago, Reave stood in for him, but now..." He fell silent.

That means anyone could kill the Celestial King in his current state, Graeme thought.

"I'm a masochist, so it was a pleasure," the monster

said. Its tone was sarcastic, but it also had a serious touch to it.

Dorrell gave the monster a final look. "Cor, I'll take care of the transport, so you can return to your cell."

The monster nodded. "Don't feel bad about this whole set up. If it wasn't for you, I'd be dead already. And I admire Reave for how powerful he is. I'd do anything for him. I feel honored helping you." It started walking away. "And my name is Corbit. I hate to be called Cor."

Graeme fell asleep.

CHAPTER 30

THE WOODS WERE barren. Leaves covered the ground, coloring it brown, yellow, and red. The only thing alive was the playful wind that whistled every time a powerful gust passed through the woods. Sometimes it would form tiny hurricanes, playing with the leaves. Other times, it would weave between trees like a harmless ghost.

"Do you know where you're going?" Kyle asked, pulling the reins of the two horses behind him. He chose to retrieve them before going with Satia.

"Just a little longer." Satia pressed her hand on a tree trunk. A symbol was carved there—a circle surrounded by a few crosses. "I know we're getting near. I carved this when I was a kid. A moon and its stars."

Kyle felt dizzy. Just like every time he used too much mana, the fatigue was overpowering. There was a direct connection between his current state and his use of mana.

Every time he went overboard, he would suffer. That's why Kyle thought he needed to hold himself back. He did abuse mana, but he tried to restrain himself, especially after seeing what happened to the man in Mount Nakroh. He didn't know what would happen if he ignored the symptoms and continued, but he wasn't eager to find out.

Satia ran ahead, and Kyle followed.

A structure emerged, stuffed between the barren treetops. Its dome was collapsed, and a part of the wall was open with stones piled in the grass. Kyle caught a glimpse of the inside and recognized the design; it was a heavenly ground.

"The place looks abandoned," Kyle said.

"Give it a chance." Satia climbed the two steps, and knocked on the door. "Audene, it's me Satia. Open up." She pounded on the door—harder.

Kyle waited briefly, then walked to a nearby well. It looked like it had dried out a long time ago.

A priestess opened the door, dressed in plain white robes.

"Audene, it's been a long time." Satia opened her arms.

"Satia, it's great to see you." Audene walked out, then embraced Satia with her gnarled hands. She wasn't old, but the physical labor she had to endure took a toll on her. She turned to Kyle and gave him a hard look. She had a furrowed face with thick hair tied back.

"This is Kyle," Satia said. "We have a favor to ask you."

"Audene, what do you want us to do now?" Two priestesses called out simultaneously. They ran out of the door—one carrying a dirty broom, the other a bucket full of water.

"Ladies, behave yourself." Audene frowned.

The two priestesses bowed their heads.

"Please meet my pupils. This is Rosa." Audene pointed to the one with the broom. "And this is Fay." She gestured to the other.

Rosa had big, green eyes and a small face. Her gaze was fragile and innocent. Fay was broad-shouldered and taller. With the stature of a man, she looked more like a guard than a priestess. Both of them bowed in unison.

"All right, enough of this," Kyle said, and Satia gave him an unhappy look. "You know who I am, right? I need you to perform the ritual," he said to Audene. He was worn out from the battle. He wasn't about to beg for help if things didn't work out, so there was no point in hiding the truth.

"You see what happened to the dome," Audene said. "Nothing I can do."

"We both know that it's not the dome that matters, but the physical location itself."

"That's true, but my answer remains the same." Audene stood with an emotionless face.

"Please reconsider, Audene," Satia said. "Or at least tell me why you won't do it?"

Kyle leaned against a tree. "She's probably scared that the Celestial King will curse her or this place."

"No, that's not it," Audene replied. "The Celestial King has already cursed us. The earthquake destroyed the dome recently, but we had our fair share of problems before. Many of my pupils left. There is really nothing I can lose anymore, but there is also nothing you can give me that I might want in exchange for helping you."

"I could fix the dome," Kyle said, loosening his cape as the wind weakened.

"You said it yourself, Kyle of Darga. It's not the dome that matters."

She knows where I come from, Kyle thought. *Does she know about the caves too?* The memory of his past unnerved him. But only for a second, then it was gone, forgotten for the time.

Rosa pulled on Audene's sleeve and whispered. Fay joined in as well, whispering and eyeing Kyle from time to time.

"It appears we have a bit of a problem." Audene declared without emotion. "My pupils have... opposing views. Why don't you stay overnight? We don't have much, but we can share whatever is left."

Kyle nodded. He could use some rest.

"Thank you, Audene." Satia smiled.

Just as Kyle expected, the inside of the structure was a circular room with an intricate floor design. There were also two little side rooms. He was in one now, sitting in an old wooden chair at an even older table, with a candle on it and some mead. The room didn't have any windows, except for a tiny opening in the ceiling. The stew was simmering in the cauldron behind him. There were many shelves around. The room served as a dining room and a pantry.

Satia left a while back.

Kyle was satisfied. He had the time to care for his minor wounds and rest. His leather armor was on the floor in the corner, and he was wearing a plain tunic and trousers. He stretched, and his back ached.

I wonder what is on the other side of the Dominant Veil, he thought. *What if Ellia is correct? Maybe there is no life for me and Avril on the other side.* It was the first time he considered it. The thought didn't discourage him, but it was a little disappointing. Yet, he knew he couldn't abandon his goal. He came too far—too close—to give up.

I just have to adapt to the situation. If I can't escape the kingdom, I'll change it to suit my liking.

Satia entered and walked to the cauldron. "What do we have here?" She stirred the stew, then ditched her cape to reveal her bare shoulders and arms. There were marks around her wrists and elbows. They resembled stitches. The corset she wore outlined her beautiful figure.

"I was surprised they didn't want me to fix the dome," Kyle said.

Satia took a seat across from him. "They're a little grumpy here sometimes, but the priestesses have hearts of gold."

"I'll believe it when I see it."

"I really hope Audene will change her mind."

"If not, then you can help me with the ritual."

"It doesn't work that way." Satia leaned in her chair. "We need three people to do it."

"Well, if my companions get here, we'll have enough." Kyle stood up, grabbed a wooden bowl and spoon from the shelf, then walked to the cauldron for some stew. "Do you think they would let us use the heavenly ground then?"

"We can always make them." With a childish grin, Satia teased Kyle.

He stared into the fire. The feeble flames swayed softly, but there was some bravery in their will to fight, to survive. Kyle liked that. He returned to the table.

He looked at the scars around Satia's arms. "What happened?" he asked.

Satia walked to the door and closed it. "It's a story I'd rather not share with Audene and the others. You know what I mean?" Satia waited for Kyle to nod. He did. "You must have had your own escapades?" she whispered.

"I did, but I'm not ashamed of them." Kyle leaned back in his chair, the bowl of stew in hand.

Satia frowned. "Who says I was ashamed? I just care about my friendship with Audene."

Kyle drank some mead. "So?"

"I was once labeled as a witch, and I lost my hand. When I was in jail, there was a person languishing there. All he would ramble about is how much he wanted to die." Satia leaned closer. "He could use mana, so I asked him to try to heal my hand. He tried, and nothing happened. One night I woke up to his screams. The man was bleeding, his hand gone. I can still remember the knights dragging him away. That night I had my hand back, but the scars were there."

Kyle chuckled, surprised and interested. "Little thief."

"I am not." Satia crossed her arms.

"You tricked the man. You stole his hand." Kyle frowned. "I didn't know something like that could be done."

"Narilan banned the use of mana to influence people and animals, but it can be done. It's just that it's… dangerous and unpredictable."

Kyle finished his bowl of stew. It was tasteless. "I've seen a madman control beasts. He even had some of their features."

"Too bad I missed that." Satia sighed. "I think that when you influence another being, you become connected in some way. When you change a person, you inherit some of the things you wanted to change in him."

"I heard about that." Kyle nodded. "Which leaves one question. How come the Celestial King can do whatever he wants?"

"I'm sure we'll find out when we make it to Zardan. Keep in mind that rituals have no rules. That might be the reason."

Then a ruckus came from the main chamber. There was clamor and echoes. The priestesses were arguing. Rosa screamed in frustration, then ran out. Audene called out to her. Fay did too.

"Guess Rosa is on our side," Satia said.

"Say, do you know what is on the other side of the Dominant Veil?" Kyle asked, finishing eating.

Satia shook her head. "The curiosity is just killing me though."

"I'd like to know that too." Kyle poured some mead into his cup. He felt worn out, his head heavy. "When I use mana, I sometimes feel dizzy. Do you know anything about that?"

"Dizziness and fatigue, right?" Satia smiled proudly. "I think a lot of people get that. It's a symptom of overusing mana. But if you're asking me what would happen if you ignored it, to be honest, I don't know."

Kyle frowned. It wasn't the answer he was looking for.

The fatigue kicked in. All he wanted was some sleep. He didn't care about anything else. The thought of the battle and the location of his crew passed through his mind. He stood up, and without a word, strode out of the room. He found his bunk in the adjacent one and comfortably fell on his back. He closed his eyes, and darkness consumed everything.

CHAPTER 31

REAVE WALKED BESIDE Ellia. She hadn't said a word since they left, which made him uneasy. He was hungry, so he looked around. The trees were bare, and the sky empty. Ellia was clenching on to something.

"You know, nothing will happen with that pebble no matter how hard you hold on to it," Reave said.

Ellia didn't even glance at him and continued to look ahead. Then she opened her hand and looked at the tiny, round pebble.

Reave rolled his eyes. He grabbed a flask of water tied to his belt. It was almost empty.

Reave watched Ellia. To him, it was obvious she was struggling with the events that transpired. Yet, her way of coping was something he couldn't understand. It seemed as if she was trying to subdue her feelings inside, as if she was trying to pretend she was fine.

It wouldn't be so unsettling if Ellia was a different person. Yet, Reave saw goodness within her... fragility as well. Having a delicate person like Ellia tortured by these events made even Reave upset.

"What's with you?" Reave asked. "I know Hilda died, but I've seen weaker people take a hit and shake it off with some dignity. Contemplating sadness won't do you any good." He wanted to say something meaningful, but the words came out foolish and cold.

"I'm not sad." Ellia shook her head. "I'm... I don't know what I am. How would you feel if someone close to you died?"

"Probably vengeful." Reave grinned.

"See, I don't feel anything like that for Hilda. I'm tired of the world. When I look deeper inside, I'm empty. I don't have that flare that I once had."

Reave looked away. "Maybe what you are lamenting isn't the loss of your family, but the loss of mana."

Ellia snorted. "And what would you do in my place?"

"I wouldn't be in your place... ever."

Ellia threw a punch. Reave easily grabbed her fist with his hand and stopped it. "You must try harder if you want to hit me." He smiled. *That's the spirit,* he thought, looking at Ellia. Reave wasn't offended by her behavior. He considered it a natural thing. He preferred a person who freely expressed emotions, even anger or hate. The ones hiding them were the worst. Or so he thought.

"You might be right," Ellia admitted.

"About?"

"Having no mana makes me uneasy," Ellia confessed, her voice cold. "I'm tired of the world because I lost so many people, but it's the lack of mana that makes me lose all hope." She brushed back a strand of hair. "I think that I miss it. I need it to keep living… to become strong."

The barren woods opened up to reveal a lake. The water was unsteady, rippling. A few leaves, like little boats, were on the surface of it. There was a soft but lively burble of moving water in the background, but the waterfall was nowhere in sight, obscured by the Veil. A girl that looked like a priestess was gathering water into a pair of wooden buckets at the edge of the lake.

Reave came closer to the water. "Greetings," he said to the priestess. "I was supposed to meet here with my companions. Have you seen them?"

The priestess shook her head.

"One of them is Kyle."

The priestess looked up and gave him a distrustful glare.

"My name is Reave, and this is Ellia."

"He is staying with us," the priestess said after a long pause.

So he succeeded? Reave wondered, then smiled. On his way through the woods, he encountered countless dead knights, yet he didn't find Breneon's corpse. He wondered how things played out.

"I can help." Reave kneeled and gently grabbed the other bucket from Rosa. Then he filled it up. The water was cold, but clean. "He told me of a waterfall. Is it …"

The priestess hesitated. "It's behind the Dominant Veil. It vanished a few months ago."

"But," Ellia said. "That would mean that Narilan is shrinking."

"Yes." The priestess sighed. "That's what happens when a Celestial King is dying."

"So are you performing the ritual for Kyle?" Ellia asked.

"He asked my master to perform it, but she declined. I tried to convince her otherwise, but things turned into a fight. She's quite the purist."

"Always following the rules," Reave added. "She's probably afraid of getting cursed by the Celestial King." Then Reave realized that the same was true for him. He loved to fight, and he could go on a rampage anytime, but he didn't want to spend the rest of his life with the Gift of Misfortune. Even if the chances were slim, the thought of the suffering unsettled him. That's why he helped Kyle. Fighting alongside a successor to the throne gave him an excuse, a reason to kill. Maybe it was a good way to protect himself, or maybe it was just a way to trick his mind into standing down. He didn't know, and he didn't care as long as it worked.

The priestess filled another bucket. "Kyle offered us his help with fixing our ruined dome," she said. "But my master believes that we should wait until a new Celestial King is crowned. But before that happens, the heavenly ground might be on the other side of the Veil. I tried to reason with her, but she never listens."

"I know that feeling," Reave said, thinking of someone close.

The priestess smiled. "My name is Rosa. Please come with me. I'll lead you to Kyle."

"I'm Reave." He smiled. "This is Ellia."

Ellia looked at Reave. "I'll stay here. I like the place. It's... peaceful. Besides, all I need is a little push, or so I heard from Hilda."

"Suit yourself." Reave patted her on the back, then pulled her closer. "Don't use force. Let your mana surface on its own. It's there, flowing through your whole body. You're the daughter of the Lade of Benevolence, after all." It was the best advice he could give her. He wanted to see her bloom into a Dreamer.

Ellia nodded and thanked him.

He grabbed the two buckets full of water and placed them on his shoulders, one each. "Shall we?" He turned to Rosa, then started walking away. He looked over his shoulder to see Ellia one last time. She took off her boots and sat at the edge of the lake, her feet in the water. Reave wanted to wish her luck, but he didn't. Somewhere deep inside, his intuition was telling him that there was more to Ellia. *She's a fighter,* he thought. *I know it.*

Then, Reave followed Rosa.

CHAPTER 32

KYLE WAS LYING on his back. The humble bunk was clean, but hard. Through the tiny opening above, he could see the dark sky. Fay was silently cleaning the main chamber. Satia left some time ago to try to persuade Audene to help. The two have been spending a lot of time talking together, gossiping. Kyle could hear the door open behind him, and then someone walked into his room.

"Finally found you," Reave said, then grabbed a stool from underneath the table. "Where is Avril?"

"She left," Kyle said.

Rosa knocked on the door, carrying a bowl of stew and some mead for Reave. Her step was light and timid.

"Thank you," Reave said with a smile.

"There is more in the pantry," Rosa said, blushing, as she left.

Kyle chuckled. "Looks like you've made an impression."

Reave grinned. "Rosa told me you want to perform the ritual. Fill me in on what happened."

Kyle sat up. He never considered Reave an ally, but Reave did help in the last battle. Kyle thought there would be no harm in telling him what happened. He was brief and to the point, telling Reave about how he killed Breneon, tortured Ronn, received the Blessing, and encountered Satia. Yet, he deliberately avoided mentioning Avril.

Reave swallowed a spoonful of the stew. "It's good," he said. "I didn't think you'd succeed. You should have killed Ronn too. We wouldn't have to worry about them coming after us."

Kyle frowned. He was worried about that too. That's why he thought it would be best to leave the heavenly ground soon. Yet, he decided that they had time. *It'll be some time before Ronn will be able to walk again, considering his injuries,* Kyle thought. *Even if he uses herbs or some other method of healing, it'll take days for him to recover.* Kyle wasn't worried about the reinforcements from Orrzol either. He doubted that they'll have any interest of coming after him after hearing that he already has ten Blessings.

"Do you think Avril returned to Castle Relien?" Reave asked.

"It would be foolish. Who knows how Ronn would react." Kyle didn't feel like talking about Avril, especially with Reave. "Now it's your turn."

Reave finished the remainder of his stew quickly. Then he told Kyle of his encounters with the knights and Ellia's behavior. When it came time to talk about Hilda's burial, he spoke briefly, and his voice was emotionless and grim.

Kyle didn't ask any more questions. Ellia's reaction seemed strange to him as well. He expected her to cry and become emotional, and not bottle up all those feelings. He didn't know what to think until Reave told him about her apparent love for mana.

"There is something more," Reave said.

"What is it?"

"If you expect me to take part in the ritual, I must decline." Reave finished his mead.

"Don't tell me you're afraid of the Celestial King's curse." Kyle frowned, looking at Reave. The fearless liar had a pathetic grimace for a face. Not many people still feared the Gift of Misfortune. The Celestial King's imminent death was an opportunity to cause chaos for some. It was as if the Celestial King couldn't see everything anymore. Some people did whatever they wanted, hoping that their transgressions would go unpunished, overlooked. Yet no matter how sickly the Celestial King was, Reave seemed to fear his judgement.

Reave hesitated. "I am, actually."

Days passed slowly. The winds redoubled, and the dome became colder. Kyle awaited Audene's decision, but it never came. At first, he hated the pointless waiting, but he came to appreciate it. It gave him time to recover, and the dizziness was slowly withering away as time passed. The headaches were now gone, and soon, he even came to enjoy the tranquility of the woods.

When Kyle was better, he killed time by playing the flute and even decided to help around the dome. He fixed the wall, although not without using his mana. Reave helped a little too, but he devoted most of his time to practicing with his sword. On most days, he was out in the woods, doing whatever he wanted. Satia spent her time on long, superfluous discussions with Audene that failed to convince her to help each and every time. No matter how long they continued on for, the result was the same. Rosa promised to help in the ritual, no matter what. Fay remained stoic and completely devoted to Audene like a blinded follower.

The days were long and unexciting. Nothing ever changed, except the weather became colder. Although one day snow fell from the sky in tiny, fragile flakes. Yet it melted as soon as it reached the ground like an unkempt promise. Each night, Kyle gazed at the sky, thinking of the future.

He accepted how long he has been running and appreciated the time of stillness as a true blessing. Each night when he closed his eyes, he didn't have any dreams. He didn't have to face the darkness. All that he felt was a profound sense of tranquility.

◆

Something resounded through the room, clattering and bumping around. Kyle was a light sleeper so he sprang up, reaching for his sword. It was dark, but his eyes were used to it. An echoing thud sounded again. He saw a rock dancing on the floor. He smiled, grabbing his boots, armor, and cape.

As Kyle left, he noticed that Reave was gone. *He's probably practicing outside,* Kyle thought. The door squealed as he walked out. He saw a dark figure outside and strode in its direction.

"There you are," he said to Avril.

"I figured I'd find you here," she said in a stern voice.

"You always find me."

"Ten Blessings, huh?" Avril said.

"Almost. But I'm afraid that our dreams won't come true. I heard there is no life for us on the other side." He paused. "Ellia told me about how her village was destroyed. The Dominant Veil is protecting us from something."

"You believe her?" Avril touched her lips.

"Why wouldn't I?" Kyle asked, then went on to repeat what Ellia told him.

Avril frowned. "That's a pity. So much struggle… so much pain for nothing."

"Not exactly. We can still change this world. We can keep our promise, make sure no one ends up like us." Kyle and Avril rarely talked about the promise they made when they escaped the cave. There wasn't a need for it. It was hard to forget since it was surrounded by some of their worst memories. It was a simple promise; they swore to make sure no one would have to suffer in the caves. It was one of the two reasons Kyle wanted to become the Celestial King, second only to his desire to leave Narilan.

Avril nodded with a faint smile. "Please don't forget our promise when you become the Celestial King." She hesitated. "I'll be brief. I'm only here to say farewell. This is the end."

"That's fine." Kyle said, honestly. He had no intention of forcing her to do anything. He knew he pushed her too far. Trying to justify his actions would be childish and pathetic. "I won't ask you to stay. It's your life, and you decide what to do with it."

Kyle heard Reave practicing in the woods nearby. His sword whistled with each swing.

"I don't think I can ever continue to travel by your side," Avril admitted with a gloomy smile. "I can understand fighting, but torture… why would you stoop so low? How could you do that to Ronn, the person who saved me?"

"I thought it was the only way." Kyle bowed his head, then looked away.

They fell silent.

Avril gave him a concerned look. "You've used a lot of mana. How are you holding up?"

"A bit weak. The headache is there too, but it'll pass."

Silence filled the air again.

"I was with you on all those adventures," Avril said. "I helped you so many times. I never asked for anything until now. Before I leave, I have a wish."

"I'm listening," Kyle said without hesitation.

"Remember that saying you told me?"

"Scum kill scum?" Kyle paused. "You don't have to say anything more, I already know your wish." He understood the implications of the statement. Avril didn't want him to turn into the rumored brute without remorse who kills anyone for any reason. She wanted him to control himself. She wished for him to be a better man and not a monster.

Avril came closer and embraced Kyle. He felt her heart beating, calmly. He held her tight for a moment before letting her go. He really wanted to keep her, to have her back.

"You should visit me when all is said and done," Kyle said.

Avril smiled, kissing him on the cheek. Then she slipped one of her small knives into his hand—her way of telling him to be careful—and retreated into the woods until the shadows nearly consumed her.

"Goodbye, my queen," Kyle said with a faint smile. "Take care of yourself."

Avril nodded, then smiled lightly. Before vanishing, she gave him a final passionate look. It was the same look Kyle saw in her eyes back in Relien when they escaped the cave. It was a look of hope and sadness. He stood still, knowing that he lost her. Yet a part of him wanted to believe that history was just retold. He lost her again, and he was bound to get her back. He noticed that the sun was starting to come out. The day was just beginning.

CHAPTER 33

THE BASEMENT REEKED of spoiled food and vomit. Water ran through the cracks in the brick walls, gathering into puddles on the ground. The place was stuffed with cages, most large enough to house a grown man. Most of them were empty, but mumbling came from some of them. Light crept in through the door that was slightly ajar.

Anson shook his head. He was still dizzy, but he could make out the man that stood before him. "Dorrell? What is going on here?" he cried out.

There came no answer. Dorrell was standing at a desk full of various flasks and colorful mixtures. He had a troubled look about him.

Anson realized that he was in a cage. His heart sped up. His hands became cold and sweat dripped down his face. He kicked and thrashed around, yelling. Nothing. He looked around and recognized the imprisoned blonde man, Graeme, who yearned to become the Celestial King. Graeme was sleeping and continued to mumble.

"Dorrell, what are you doing?" Anson shouted. "Let me out!"

"You know I can't do that," Dorrell said.

"I won't tell anyone!"

"Yes, you will." Dorrell wrote something down.

Anson grabbed the metal bars and meditated. The bars glowed red, then turned almost malleable. His fingers sunk in slightly as the heat intensified. His skin started to burn, so he released his grip, screaming and writhing in pain.

"I had some practice as a Spectator," Dorrell said, "so don't do that ever again."

Why did I bother getting involved? Anson thought. *I should have stayed quiet. What do I do? What do I do?* He kicked the cage once more before giving up. He sighed as all strength left him. "I'll join you," he said. "I'll do anything I can to help you, just let me out."

"That's an interesting proposal, but… I don't trust you." Dorrell stirred something in a tiny jar.

"Why? I promise!" Anson came closer and reached out with his hand, pressing his chest against the bars. "I swear I'll be loyal."

"Tell me, Anson, why are you so interested in me?"

Anson paused. "My loyalty lies with Narilan. I suspected that you were doing something forbidden."

"Really? So you're telling me that you spied on me because of a selfless desire to care for Narilan?" Dorrell looked at Anson with a piercing gaze as if he saw through all lies. "I heard you're envious of those who found something they love in life."

Bastard, Anson thought. "That's not true!" he roared.

"A master sees in their apprentice what the apprentice doesn't see," Dorrell said. "The Celestial King once told me so."

"I'm not envious, I admire you," Anson declared. *He saw through me,* he thought. *He knows, he knows.*

"So you wouldn't feel better if you humiliated me?" Dorrell faced the cages and took a seat on the table, arms crossed. "It wouldn't make you feel better if the Grand Court took away my position as preceptor from me?"

"Of course not. I swear. I swear to you that I'll do anything just let me out."

"That's the problem," Dorrell said. "You'll say anything to persuade me. You'll do anything. I know, but you're just a worthless scum. A gutless bag of bones without a purpose. You watched me for the sake of the kingdom? Don't make me laugh."

Anson gnashed his teeth, his hands quivering. "Cwen will notice my absence. She'll find me."

"You really think so?"

"Let me out," Anson screamed. "Somebody help me!"

"Tell you what, be honest and I'll tell you what your future holds." Dorrell stood up.

"Fine," Anson looked away, his head down. "I followed you because I hate you. I hate how everyone is inspired by you. I hate that I can't be just like you." He fell silent, the anger throbbing in his chest.

"Not too hard, was it?" Dorrell asked, walking up the stairs.

"Will you let me go?" Anson asked.

Dorrell frowned. "I'm sorry to leave you, but we have a critical problem in Zardan that requires my attention."

He said in a troubled voice. He strode out and closed the door. There was no light, only darkness.

Anson screamed, thrashing in his cage. With his anger unshackled, he booted the door, but it didn't yield. His knuckles bled as he hit the rusted metal bars time and time again. It wasn't until the anger left him and despair took over that he fell silent.

CHAPTER 34

AVRIL SCANNED THE woods. She didn't know her
destination, but she didn't mind wandering around.
She had the map in her pocket, but she didn't need it. She
remembered most of the places that might interest her.
Maybe I should visit Zoll's Village, she thought. *I haven't been
there yet.* She wanted to do something new. She needed to
travel to a place that she never visited, but not because a
mission required it. She wanted to journey, to feel free.

Avril tightened the cloak at her neck and wrapped it
around herself. The wind was strong and cold. She trotted
through the woods until she found a dirt path.

She heard a buzzing sound, then a stronger, jarring
din. At first she wanted to ignore it, but she found herself
drawn to it.

Something was telling Avril that she couldn't ignore it.

And so she followed the sounds. When she made it out

of the woods, she saw a kaleidoscope of colors. The Dominant Veil flickered like a dying star. Its colors were reflected in the lake at its feet. Then the Veil started to ripple, and a tiny opening, which emanated with a pale, pure light, appeared in the center. The light crept in slowly—greedily.

The water swelled and spilled over the ground. Stones led to a sunken boulder in the center of the lake. Its tip peeked out just above the surface. On the boulder stood a slight figure, its olive cape and brown hair blown away by the intensity of the wind.

Avril came closer. "Ellia," she called out. "What are you doing? Stop this!"

Ellia didn't react.

Avril watched as a rift was torn in the Veil. *Kyle once tried it,* she thought. *He failed. He wasn't strong enough. Is Ellia capable of tearing the Veil because she's so strong, or is it because the Celestial King is so weak?* The thought made Avril uneasy.

She remembered what Kyle told her, and she knew she had to stop Ellia.

Avril picked up a stone and tossed it at Ellia. It smacked against Ellia's back, then fell into the water with a plump. The winds ceased, and the Veil returned to its natural, motionless state. The light vanished as the rift closed up.

"It's you." Ellia gazed at Avril.

"What are you doing, Ellia? This is dangerous."

Ellia had an emotionless look. "So what?"

Avril hesitated. "Kyle told me everything. Whatever is on the other side, we might not be able to fight it."

Ellia paused. "For the first time I can face whatever is

there without fear," she declared. "I'm not going to back away."

Something is different about her, Avril thought. "What happened to you? You seem different."

"I grew tired of the world after I lost everything," Ellia admitted with a frown.

Avril looked at Ellia and saw a person shaken and overcome by something powerful. Avril didn't know what. Yet, she knew that she wouldn't gain anything by arguing with Ellia. "You shouldn't exert yourself so much. Take it easy with the mana."

Ellia snorted. "I'm not going to turn away from the only thing that brings me joy. Finally, I don't have to conserve my mana. I'm a Dreamer, at last." She spread her arms wide, and the water churned. Then it started moving in a circular motion around her as if she stirred the water with her thoughts. Ellia smiled.

"There is something you don't know," Avril said.

"I do. You're going to tell me about the dizziness, and the headaches, and everything else. But I don't care. I don't want to hear it." Ellia faced the Dominant Veil. The winds redoubled.

"Listen, Ellia!" Avril called out. "Let's talk this over!"

Ellia ignored her.

Avril sprung toward Ellia, leaping across the stones. Ellia gazed over her shoulder, and a wall of water surged before Avril. The Veil jerked, and the light appeared again—stronger.

This is bad, Avril thought. *I must do something.* She closed her eyes and focused on the sunken boulder. The boulder quivered, making Ellia sway. She nearly lost her balance, but managed to reclaim her footing. Then the boulder started to submerge, and as the water crept up around Ellia's feet, she slipped. Avril exchanged a gaze with Ellia and saw her panic-struck eyes before she disappeared in a splash of water. Everything stood still.

Avril waited. She hoped that Ellia would emerge from the water any second. She didn't want to hurt her. Something gathered around her, deep in the ground. Avril sprung away as a spike emerged from the stone she was standing on. She retreated. Before she could make it to land, she felt something pull on her cloak. She grabbed her knife and sliced the knot at the neck. Speeding away, she landed on the ground, then looked back.

Ellia was standing on a thin stone pedestal, levitating above the water. Her clothes were soaked. She opened her hand, and a myriad of water pillars surged up, surrounding her. She divided the water from the pillars into large blobs, then molded them into spears before turning them to ice. Surrounded by a sea of glittering, frozen spears, Ellia smiled. With a single hand swipe, she shoved them all at Avril.

Avril kneeled, and the earth covered her like a blanket as the spears rained down on her. She closed her eyes in the darkness. She heard a swish and felt something prick her arm, her leg, and then her chest. The pain was sudden and piercing. She felt needles all over her body, thin but sharp at the tip. She tried to move, but she felt immobilized as if she was impaled by a thousand spikes.

Avril forced the ground to withdraw a little. Through the small gap she saw the sky, the freedom.

She slowly let out a breath.

CHAPTER 35

THE DOME WAS completed late evening after only a week. The debris was out, and the wall sealed. Kyle stood there, looking at the sky through the oculus. He could identify all the stars and constellations that had anything to do with Zardan. His father taught him that.

"You did a really good job," Satia said behind him.

"But they'll have to do without the fresco," Kyle replied and smiled, pointing up.

Satia shook her head. "Are you sure Reave isn't an artist?"

"He is, but in a very different craft," Kyle was ready for Reave to stab him in the back at any time. Yet now, he wasn't worried about that. He continued to keep his guard up at all times though, as he always did.

"A peculiar fellow. For some reason, he doesn't talk to me much." Satia put her finger to her lips. "I think he doesn't like how perceptive I am. I guess it makes him feel uneasy."

"No idea," Kyle said. He felt rested and vigorous. On his way out, Fay and Rosa thanked him and bowed.

"It's time," Audene said in a hoarse voice, with her hands behind her.

"Ready to perform the ritual?" Kyle put on a disgusting smirk.

"Indeed," Audene said, "I am ready."

Kyle didn't feel impatient anymore. Honestly, he came to relish the mundane life in the woods. It was good while it lasted. He didn't want to stay there forever, but the temporary disruption felt good. "Why wait all this time?"

"I believe that all people have goodness inside," Audene declared, her eyes studying Kyle. "They have wickedness too. I needed to see if you are capable of being human with my own eyes. I needed to make sure you hadn't completely lost your way."

Kyle frowned. "Your verdict flatters me."

"There are many stories about you, Kyle. The citizens of Narilan live normal lives, but you are different. You've seen evil. You did evil. Yet, you proved that you can be civil and human. You have earned my respect."

"Maybe I'm just pretending." Kyle grinned. "Maybe Satia told me about your little scheme."

"That's unlikely," Audene said with her eyes closed. "Satia didn't know about it. I'm a good judge of character. I see what you might not. Inside each of us, goodness and wickedness collide and entwine."

Kyle didn't want to listen to her preaching. He faced away. "When do we begin?"

"Tonight your wish will come true," Audene said, the

two priestesses behind her. Fay was looking at the ground. Rosa had a cheerful smile.

"Call for me when you are ready," Kyle agreed, then went outside. He looked at the Great Tower, something he hadn't done recently. Clouds of dust were gathering around it, and the sky was dark. There was a flash of lightning and a soft murmur of a storm far away.

"Congrats," Satia put her hand on his shoulder.

"Did you know about it?"

"Even I have trouble figuring out what is inside Audene's head. She's a mystery." Satia smiled.

Kyle nodded. "So you knew."

"I don't know what you're talking about." Satia played with her hair.

Kyle chuckled, shaking his head.

"But I'm surprised," Satia said in a serious voice. "I thought that you would use brute force. Yet, you didn't. Could you tell me why?"

"I needed to recuperate," Kyle said, thinking of the headaches and the dizziness. "This was a good place to do it." He looked at Satia with a little more trust. So far, all she did helped him. *If I do get my tenth Blessing, it'll be thanks to her,* he thought.

Kyle hesitated. "When we're done here, I'd like you to do something for me. We're going to split up. I'll go to Zardan, and you will wait by the Dominant Veil. When I ascend the throne, the very first thing I'll do is make an opening. I'd like you to witness what is on the other side."

Satia looked at him with a smile, but remained silent.

At first, Kyle wanted to wait until later to find out what was behind the Veil. But because of all the chaos that's been going on, he thought no one would notice if the

Veil goes down for a brief moment. He decided it would be better than waiting until he settles in as the Celestial King and has to deal with the Grand Court and the preceptor.

Satia's eyes glittered with excitement. "I'll gather a few men and find a suitable location. How will you find me?"

"Take this." Kyle placed an elegant silver ring into her palm. "It's infused with my mana. I heard the Celestial King sees and knows all, but it'll make finding you much easier. I'll know when you are ready. That's when I'll open the Dominant Veil."

◆

Kyle listened to the chants, which echoed through the chamber. The three priestess and Satia formed a circle around him, whispering and chanting. He was familiar with the ritual; he could even pick out words and phrases, but only that.

He felt the cold wind on his skin. The sky was full of clouds, so he couldn't gaze at the stars. He felt the overwhelming feeling in his body. The mana pulsed through him. Then he sensed the Celestial King. He could feel his presence in the Great Tower. The presence was faint and pathetic like a withering flower. In his thoughts, Kyle could hear the Celestial King weeping and begging. The meaningless mumbling of a dying man resounded through his mind.

He fell to his knees. The begging redoubled. It became clearer until he could make out the Celestial King's words.

Help me. Save me.

The mana culminated in Kyle's chest. It burned with vast intensity until his chest bled. He screamed as the mana left a scorching, bleeding mark around his heart.

The ritual was complete. The pain was worse than anything Kyle had experienced before. *It's over,* he thought, looking at the mark—a circle of mana symbols.

He stood up. Satia came closer with a blanket. He rejected her help and just stood there. He didn't know what to think of the Celestial King. He didn't know what to expect in Zardan.

That's what worried him the most.

CHAPTER 36

THE FOLLOWING MORNING, they left early, traveling light. It was the coldest of days. The ashen clouds gathered above them. Snowflakes fell from the sky, covering the ground in a thin layer of snow that melted the moment the sun came out. The winds faded.

Kyle led the way, occasionally surveying the woods for any knights. Right behind him, Satia complained about the weather. She didn't mind the cold, but hated how the wet snow stuck to everything. Reave was trailing behind her silently. He was relaxed and calm.

They trotted down a dirt path through the woods, eyeing the imposing mountains. Soon, they outran the snow, and the path led them to a crossing with a worn-out, wooden post. The post swung on a single nail, ready to fall down. They continued in the direction of the mountains. When they arrived at the base of the towering peaks, they noticed that the path vanished somewhere in the darkness of a cave.

"It's time for me to go," Satia declared.

Reave looked at her. "You're not coming with us?"

"I have something to take care of." She loosened the reins.

"What could be more important than Zardan?" Reave insisted.

Kyle interrupted, "Satia was locked away for quite some time. It's only natural she has things she wants to do."

Satia nodded. Kyle came closer and pulled her gently by the arm, putting his face to her ear. "I hope I made the right decision to trust you. I wish you luck. Let us see the kingdom for what it really is."

Satia smiled. "I won't let you down, my king."

"Before you go, tell me one thing." Kyle paused. "During the ritual, I heard the Celestial King. He was begging for help. What do you make of it?"

"I don't know," Satia confessed. "You should be very careful in Zardan."

"I was hoping for something more."

Satia frowned. "Are you sure you don't want me to come along?"

"I'll feel better knowing what is out there," he reassured her. "I can handle anything that happens in Zardan."

She nodded, then put up her hood. She left silently, traveling down the dirt path.

Reave gave Kyle a bitter glare. Kyle knew it was because he left him out of their discussion.

"Shall we?" Kyle led the way.

The inside of the mountain was much warmer. Yet, it was a very uncomfortable warmth. The air was hot and heavy, but also completely dry. The walls were glowing in a crimson hue, as if they were ready to melt. The lava inside of them was pulsating.

How many days have I spent here? Kyle thought. The memories of his travels with Avril returned. He could still recall the countless days he wasted here, trying to map out the maze of corridors. Yet this time, he knew where he was going.

"Another irregularity," Reave pointed to the lava. "It was never this hot in here."

"So what are you going to do when you get to Zardan?"

"I'll kill the Celestial King," Reave said, trying to hide his amusement.

"That shouldn't be so hard." Kyle returned a bitter smirk.

"Are you implying something?"

Kyle didn't say anything. He just continued. The hooves hitting the ground made a rhythmic sound like that of a clock.

◆

The sun was waiting for them when they made it out. It hid in the distance behind the Great Tower, illuminating it like the heart of Narilan that it was. Its height rivaled the mountains. Its appearance was intimidating and powerful. Its battlements reached up high into the sky as a dense cloud of dust formed a ring around the Great Tower.

There were trees nearby too—pine trees. Healthy and green. They surrounded the back of Zardan, forming a semicircle and hugging the city walls. A huge lake stretched across the land, its color green. All the rivers from across the kingdom gathered there.

Kyle stood in awe at the perfect sight of Zardan. It wasn't like the rest of the kingdom. Its impeccable, powerful appearance made him tense. He knew the brutality of the world and the struggle. He could handle it all because he knew how it worked. Yet he had never seen such a flawless sight of supremacy, and he didn't know what to expect.

Reave dismounted from his horse and pulled the reins, leading it to the lake. He bowed, ready to drink. Then he noticed something swimming in the water and immediately pulled the horse away.

"What is it?" Kyle asked.

"There is something in the water."

Kyle dismounted, then came closer. The water, although light green, looked fine at first until he noticed little white freckles. They were moving, shuffling around. Like little insects, there were many of them, and they gathered into big, white patches at the bottom of the lake.

"First time I've seen anything like it," Kyle said in disgust.

"Let's hurry," Reave insisted. It was the first time Kyle noticed a sense of urgency in his voice.

They climbed their horse, then galloped in the direction of Zardan. When they made it to the city walls, they faced a huge, wooden door. It was sealed—barred from within. Kyle surveyed the area, but he couldn't even see the Royal Veil that was protecting the city. Yet, he knew it was there. Standing in the shadows of the massive city walls, he stretched out his hand. Nothing.

He took a step forward, and felt his hand touch a soft fabric. As his hand sunk in, the fabric became more tangible. It was invisible, but he could feel it. He spread his arms wide as if he was drawing the curtains, and it opened. He walked inside, and Reave followed right behind him.

When they were on the other side, the fabric closed up and vanished. The massive door was already open, welcoming them to Zardan.

Kyle had a triumphant smile.

CHAPTER 37

ARMED IN SPEARS, the guards stationed at the gates nodded as Kyle and Reave entered Zardan. Instead of armor, the guards wore robes. Similar to the ones Reave always had, but made from a stiffer fabric and lighter in color. One of the guards sprung closer with a surprised look. His skin was parched.

"Sir, your brother is looking for you." The guard looked at Reave.

"I'll go see him soon." Reave nodded.

"Brother, huh?" Kyle said. *He must be someone important,* he thought.

Reave didn't respond.

Zardan was exactly what Kyle expected—very different from the rest of Narilan. Pure white cobblestones covered the streets. There were lampposts decorated with vines and flowers. Occasionally, he encountered sculptures—large marble statues honoring powerful warriors and selfless martyrs. The buildings, while most were short and unimpressive, were made of stone with windows of fine glass. Most of the homes on the upper floors also had balconies, while the ones on the ground floor had tiny gardens. Citizens hid from the sun under arcades, sitting at tables and bantering.

Arches and pillars supported bridges above the streets. The bridges connected large buildings in a myriad of ways, forming simple yet intricate maze-like designs and obscuring the sun.

Kyle followed the scent of fruits until he reached the market. It was empty, except for the carts, which were full of fruits and vegetables. Yet, there weren't any people around. He grabbed a red apple, then noticed it was rotten. All of them were.

"It's most likely from the disease in the water," Kyle said to Reave. He looked at a lone stream that passed through the market in the direction of the Great Tower. *It must come from the lake,* he thought.

Reave had a worried look. "I never even considered things would be this bad."

"Looks like Zardan didn't escape the devastation that comes with the Celestial King's death." Kyle smashed the apple against the wall, leaving an ugly stain.

"You say this as if it was nothing, Kyle."

"What's with you?" Kyle asked. "You didn't seem bothered when every other place was suffering."

Reave frowned.

They followed the street in the direction of the Great Tower, which was being consumed by the cloud of dust. Kyle looked at someone peeking at them from a second-floor window. Another person was eyeing them, lying in the street and drinking ale.

Kyle knew the Great Tower was huge, but standing right in front of it was intimidating. The monstrous structure loomed over the city. There was something majestic about it, but there was also something terrifying too. The Great Tower was a beacon of hope for Narilan. It stood as its protector and caretaker. Yet, now it was just a reminder of how powerless the Celestial King really was.

Someone pulled on Kyle's foot. "Please save us," a man with a pale complexion uttered, his hands quivering.

"Come on," Reave insisted.

Kyle strode ahead. His heart started to beat from the unyielding anticipation. The thought of becoming the next Celestial King kept him going all this time, and his time had finally come.

Elegant, marble stairs led them up to the Great Tower. There were guards stationed at the rails — ten on each side of the stairs. They bowed as Kyle made his way up. He wanted to think they were bowing to the future Celestial King, but that wasn't the case. They were bowing to Reave.

The entrance was a pair of stone doors. Kyle recognized the images engraved in stone; they depicted the Celestial King, his arms spread wide and his followers at his feet. There were also countless symbols of mana, each separated into pairs.

One of the guards bowed, looking at Reave. "Welcome to the Great Tower, sir," he said, then turned to Kyle. "I presume you are here to challenge the Celestial King."

"Yes," Kyle said, his voice determined.

"Put your hand to the door." The guard pointed to a circle at the base of the doors.

Kyle stepped into the circle, then pressed his hand on the door. The image of the Celestial King lit up in a pale, white light. The door murmured, and without any external force, started to open.

"Follow the stairs up," the guard said.

The darkness welcomed Kyle when he walked in. His eyes adjusted quickly. The inside was a vast circular chamber with stairs leading up. The stairs looped around the outer edge of the chamber.

"I should thank you," Reave said to Kyle.

"For what exactly?"

"I yearned to return to Zardan because of my ties to this place, but I can't say I enjoy the world I live in. So here I am bowing before you for killing some of my boredom." Reave smiled. "You have made my life quite enjoyable."

"I'd prefer to finally hear you speak the truth."

"What truth?" Reave asked, frowning. "That I wanted to return to Zardan because of family ties? That I hid my connection to Zardan because I thought I wouldn't be able to travel with you? It's all true." Reave cleared his throat. He was stern and honest. "Why did I want to return? I'd like to save Narilan. I can't do the things I love the most if the kingdom perishes. And you are here to help me with that."

Kyle studied Reave. For the first time, his intuition was telling him that Reave wasn't making anything up. "I think you would be better off in a world of anarchy. You could fight all you want."

Reave seemed to entertain the thought. "I once thought about abandoning Narilan, but I think I would be way too weak for whatever is outside the Dominant Veil."

They reached the top of the staircase.

The ceiling was cracked in countless places, blocks precariously loose and ready to fall. Countless blocks were already scattered around, but their original shape was lost on impact as they shattered into pieces. The place was littered with broken blades and cloven armor. The walls were stained with blood, yet no bodies could be found.

Across from Kyle, there were more steps that led to the next floor. A man stood on a balcony above, leaning over the railing. He started sauntering down.

Reave strode ahead. "Preceptor," he called out with a smile.

The two met at the base of the stairs.

"It's good to see you, brother." Dorrell spread his arms wide as a welcoming gesture. "I knew you were alive." He smiled honestly.

Kyle was certain Reave was from Zardan for quite some time now, but the idea of him being the preceptor's brother was a surprise. That's when it became clear why Reave made up that silly story about wanting to kill the Celestial King. Kyle would never allow him to be a part of his group if he knew about his deep connections with Zardan.

Kyle watched the two men; they were like twins. They had the same thin stature and the same height. Their black hair was equal length, but Dorrell's was braided at the tips. The only difference was in their clothing. Dorrell wore long, impractical robes made of silk and dyed in many vibrant colors. Reave, on the other hand, had humble and filthy green robes.

"Have you received my message?" Reave asked.

Dorrell nodded. "I did. I see you have brought company?"

"You have no idea what I have been through," Reave said aloud, then pointed at Kyle. "Anyway, I have found another donor."

"Donor?" Kyle rasped. "Explain yourself." They ignored him. He was instantly reminded of the caves. The memories corrupted his mind. He knew Dorrell and Reave were up to something. The very first thing that came to his mind was that becoming the Celestial King was just a lie, a trick to get Dreamers to come to Zardan, so that they could be enslaved. His mind unnerved, Kyle knew he had to get a hold of himself. He couldn't let anger and fury lead him. He took a seat on the cold floor and listened to the conversation.

Dorrell shook his head. "That won't be necessary. I've got more than enough donors. But we can imprison him and use him later." He took a few steps up, and Reave followed. "We're almost ready. I'm sure you saw the water, but don't worry. Everything will be back to normal soon."

Reave seemed to entertain some thought. "So I can do anything I want with him now?"

"You know how I hate your bloodthirsty tendencies," Dorrell gave Reave a concerned look. "But there is no use fighting against human nature, so help yourself."

"If he survives this, he'll be a donor," Reave said. "If he dies, it's the end of his story."

Dorrell sighed, then shrugged. "You do what you have to do."

Kyle felt a sense of tranquility. Within this feeling, he found an overwhelming surge of mana. He sensed the energy within him and stood up. "Are you two finished?"

"Sorry to keep you waiting," Dorrell declared, his voice pompous. "I'm Preceptor Sahne."

"Where is the Celestial King?" Kyle demanded. "Is it all a lie? A trick to gather Dreamers?"

Dorrell rubbed his eyebrows. "Of course, it's not a lie. You can become the ruler of Narilan, but as you can see, the Celestial King isn't here. You will be fighting my brother instead."

Reave frivolously stepped down the stairs, tightening his hair back into place. Kyle noticed a spark of passion in his eyes. Reave looked uplifted and jovial.

"So the Celestial King needs someone else to fight his battles for him?" Kyle asked. He expected that the Celestial King wouldn't be able to fight, and there had to be some other way to test a successor to the throne. Yet, he never would've imagined that Reave would stand in for the Celestial King.

"Yes," Dorrell agreed. "It's been like that for the past few years. Ever since the Celestial King fell ill. Win, and you will get the throne."

"You called me a donor," Kyle said, but Dorrell left before he could continue. He frowned, detesting the preceptor.

Reave drew his sword. "Perhaps being the Celestial King isn't what you expect. But don't worry. You'll learn soon enough." He meditated, eyes closed. "Let me know when you're ready."

With a nod, Kyle drew his sword.

Dorrell reached the balcony above and prepared to watch the battle.

"I've always wondered why you hadn't killed Ellia yet," Reave spoke softly, making sure his voice didn't reach Dorrell.

"Is there a reason I should kill her? You seemed very

pleased when she was gone." Kyle grinned. Then he forced the rocks that surrounded him into the air. They glided in Reave's direction, then surrounded and enveloped him in a sphere. Before it could harden, Reave pierced it with his sword. The sphere soundlessly burst like a bubble, turning into dust.

Reave tossed his long hair around to get rid of the dust. "You're going to need to try harder if you want to hurt me."

You shouldn't do that, Kyle thought, looking at Reave. *Imposing your will on an object already filled with mana is dangerous.*

"Can't you muster enough courage to tell me the truth?" Kyle asked.

Reave frowned, but answered. "The truth is that Hilda and Ellia wanted to confront my brother, to kill him." He took a sip from a jar of water that was at his belt. Planning his next attack, he hurled the jar high up, making it burst in midair. Enormous amounts of water, hundred times what was in the tiny container, spilled out from the jar, covering the floor. It almost looked like a cloud formed at the ceiling as water continued to rain down. Reave charged, turning the drizzle into hail, which pelted down on Kyle. Each ball of ice was hard and heavy. Kyle used his mana to lift a huge block from the floor, then hid behind it. The hail bounced off of it, then bumped around on the floor.

Closing in, Reave pierced the block with his sword, forcing it to explode in a puff of dust. As the dust covered the ground, Kyle sprung forward with an overhead attack, but Reave parried and spun around, ready to counter. He aimed at the foot. Kyle retreated as Reave's blade sunk into the marble floor right before him. The blade was pulsing with Reave's mana, light reflecting from it. Kyle kneeled as Reave attacked; the horizontal strike passed above his head. Before Reave could swing again, Kyle made a stone wall to shield himself. Reave's blade sunk into it. To his surprise, the wall wasn't hard, but soft and malleable like wet clay. Then Kyle turned the wall solid, trapping Reave's blade. Reave groaned while tugging on his weapon, but before he could pull it out, Kyle snapped it in half.

Reave let out a faint chuckle as the hail ceased. "You know, mana is a capricious thing. We can't use it instantly, but with a bit of meditation, it's almost as if we enter a trance. It then takes a lot to shake someone out of that trance."

"If I ever need a tutor, I'll know who to turn to," Kyle said with a grin. "You know, maybe you shouldn't try so hard to impose your mana on mine."

Reave smirked. "But emotions disrupt our concentration, which makes me wonder about something. You've done so well fighting me; could it be that Avril means nothing to you? Her disappearance didn't impact you that much. If it did, you wouldn't be able to use mana so effectively."

Kyle was irritated by the insolent remark. As much as he wanted to kill Reave quickly, he knew he couldn't. He knew that if he mindlessly charged in, he would die—his dream would die. Reave wasn't a regular opponent. He had skill and experience. He was just like Kyle—born for battle and anointed with blood.

"So the preceptor is responsible for the tragedy that struck Nalza?" Kyle asked.

"I have no idea what you're talking about. My brother

does everything and anything for the people of Narilan." Reave tossed away his broken sword.

"So you're not denying it?"

"Whatever happened, it was for the best," Reave declared with confidence. He pressed his hand against the ground, and it sank in. Then he pulled out an object. It had the shape of a bow, but it was covered in thick chunks of rock. With a bit more patience, Reave cleaned the remaining rocks and debris from it. He also tightened the string, then aimed an arrow he created from stone. "I hate bows, but I'm proficient at using them. Kind of ironic, don't you think?" He put on a cheeky smile.

The arrow left the bow with astonishing speed. Kyle didn't have enough time to react. As he tried to evade, the arrow grazed his side, cutting in between the ribs. He kneeled to the floor, pressing his hand against the wound. He gritted his teeth, anger intensifying.

Reave imagined another arrow and steadied his bow, aiming. Kyle touched the ground, focusing his mana. The water provided a catalyst for a thick mist, which filled the chamber. It was as if the floor had tiny little pores which oozed with vapors. The thick mist interrupted Reave's attack. He fired an arrow where he last saw Kyle. It struck a wall, then rang as it hit the floor.

Reave closed his eyes and listened, meditating. "Did you make a run for it? I didn't take you for a coward."

A cloud of mist shook slightly behind Reave. Kyle soared with his blade over his head, the cloud trailing behind him.

Then, a colossal pole emerged from the ground and plunged into Kyle's stomach. On impact, his sword broke into tiny shards, which showered Reave. With great force,

Kyle was shoved back, his limbs lifelessly dragging along. Reave let out a scream of agony, hiding his face behind his hand. There was an echoing thud as Kyle fell to the floor.

Cringing on his knees, Kyle couldn't think. For a moment, he felt fine. Then the pain throbbed through his entire body. But he knew worse, much worse. It wasn't until he vomited blood that the torment intensified, and he was overwhelmed by the excruciating pain in his stomach. He traced his stomach with his hand. He felt his insides pricked by something. *Broken ribs,* he thought.

Barely holding his weapon, Kyle looked up at Reave.

Reave's head was down, one hand on his face. Blood was dripping down his cheek. He was holding a piece of cloth, his hair free. He tied it around his eye. "Bastard," he muttered.

Kyle put on a disgusting smirk.

Reave gnashed his teeth. He imagined two swords, then charged at Kyle. Kyle's clumsy attack was caught between Reave's two swords. Adding pressure, Reave forced the sword out of Kyle's grip. He spun around and attacked.

Helpless, Kyle blocked with his hand. Reave's blade jammed into his forearm, and he screamed. The blade tore a piece of skin off and cracked bone, pointing at his neck. Kyle groaned, gnashing his teeth as he could barely hold up his arm. He was on his knees, and he had no more strength to fight.

Reave lifted his other blade, his eyes mad. Kyle wanted to attack, to use his mana to tear Reave apart, but it was too late. His mind was filled with chaos, clouded and disordered. The mana he wielded was dispersed and out of focus. He panicked.

Reave's sword was filled with his mana, emanating with a powerful presence. With a swift upward strike, it tore through Kyle's elbow, ripping through flesh, shattering bone, spilling blood. Kyle screamed, falling on his face in a pool of blood. Reave kicked him over, and he fell on his back.

Kyle could see the cracked ceiling—the Celestial King in the fresco. He had no strength to get up—to fight. He could only feel his whole body pulsing in a burst of brutal pain. He wanted to scream, but what came out was a mute murmur. *Is this how my life ends?* he thought.

Reave was standing over Kyle, ready to plunge his blade into his chest. He was drooling at the thought of killing a great adversary like Kyle.

"Reave, stop," Dorrell called out.

"What is it?"

"We're not executioners," Dorrell argued.

"This is mercy killing," Reave said. "Who knows how long he'll have to suffer before he dies. Look at him."

"We both know that the only reason you want to kill him is to sate your own bloodlust," Dorrell said with a sad look. "I don't want that to happen. Summon the clerics. I'll see if I can do anything for this man."

"I don't understand. How can you help him when you explicitly stated your contempt for Kyle?"

"This is not a discussion," Dorrell declared.

Kyle couldn't see anything. There was nothing left but the ensnaring, vicious pain that tormented him as he drifted off.

CHAPTER 38

SATIA ARRIVED IN Locklair's Keep on her horse. The archers gave her wary looks, gossiping above the gates. There were many knights in town, most training at the time. Their brief scuffles usually ended with a pommel to the head, or a kick in the gut.

Teaching your men to fight dirty, Satia thought, looking at the manor clad in stained-glass windows. *That's your style, Locklair.*

She dismounted her horse and led it by the reins. In the center of town, she looked around. All the wooden houses seemed the same. In fact, they were the same. The dilapidated huts were falling apart. Many of the slanted roofs had holes the size of a fist.

"I'm looking for Udall," Satia said to one of the villagers who was passing by. Downcast, he didn't respond.

She repeated the question to a village boy running by. He didn't stop, but pointed her to a hut with no windows. She came closer and knocked. There was no answer, so she went around the back.

Behind the house was an open yard, where a man sat by an anvil in the shade. She recognized the man as Udall. He was wearing thick, black gloves, with a hammer in one hand and a sword in the other. Its blade was dull.

"Alsatia." He bowed his head.

"Didn't think I'd find you working." Satia came closer, tied the reins to a post, and left her horse behind.

Udall smiled. He only wore a tattered tunic, showing his muscular arms. He was a slender but imposing man. His face was a little too soft to be the warrior that Satia so vividly remembered. "What bring you here?" he asked.

"I'm on a mission."

"Last time I agreed to go with you, we ended up in a prison, and I almost lost my life." He scratched his head. It was almost bald, except for a thick patch of hair at the tip that resembled a flame.

"But we survived," Satia said, "and had a lot of fun."

"Speak for yourself." He shook his head. "I've got my own life now."

"The future Celestial King sent me. What could be more important than the affairs of the kingdom?" The thought of seeing what was on the other side of the Dominant Veil excited Satia very much, but she knew she couldn't do it alone.

"Father," a voice came from the hut, and a young girl stopped out of the door, tossing back her long braids. "We need your help."

"Tell your mother I'll be right there." He nodded, stood up, and turned to Satia. "You should find someone else. And don't look so surprised."

Satia hesitated. She remembered Udall as a headstrong warrior, who never backed down from a mission, but the man standing before her was a doubtful villager. "What is going on here? What happened to you?"

Udall gave Satia a serious look. "Since we're longtime friends, you can stay the night. I'll let my wife know to prepare a bunk for you." He stopped at the door. "You can leave the horse there."

Satia sighed.

♦

Satia was surprised at how small the inside of Udall's house was—only two rooms and a single tiny window. The air was just as cold as outside. It was only when his wife, Emma, started to cook that the hut warmed up. Satia took off her cloak and was offered a meal. She politely rejected, thinking of how poor Udall must've been, but Emma insisted.

The meal was delicious. The chicken was slightly dry, but that was to be expected from such a humble place. The soup, on the other hand, was delicious. Satia never heard of cucumber soup, but she fell in love with it after only a single taste.

She found out Udall had three daughters: Annabella, Dia, and Nelga. They were all named after people Satia met during her travels with Udall. Satia didn't bring it up as she didn't want to ruin the mood.

When the dinner was over and the town covered in darkness, she found Udall working outside.

"Making a ruckus again," Satia said, holding a mug in her hand.

"You shouldn't drink so much." Udall hammered on the sword. It was glowing red and yellow.

"Want some?" Satia asked as she pet her horse.

Udall shook his head.

"This isn't some ordinary mead, you know? I bought it in Relien from Ronn, King Breneon's son."

Udall paused. "You bought it?"

"Well, I took it as a reward for my work." Satia smiled.

He chuckled. "You never change."

"What happened here? What made you change?"

Udall sighed. He hammered down on the sword again, sparks flying. When he was done, he put away his hammer and took a seat. "It's been tough here. You either help Lord Locklair, or you perish. That's why most men joined his army. The rest of the people were assigned menial tasks."

"What is he planning?"

"You haven't heard?" Udall asked surprised, but she didn't answer. "Where have you been?"

"Locked up in Relien." She finished her mead.

"Locklair believes that if Kyle succeeds in becoming the Celestial King, he will be able to attack and conquer the lands on the other side of the Dominant Veil." Udall took off his gloves. His hands were parched, the skin dry from all the labor he had to do in his life.

Is that why Kyle sent me to investigate the Veil? she thought.

"You said something about a future Celestial King, right?" Udall asked, and she nodded. "You're talking about Kyle? When he received his tenth Blessing, everybody saw his image… in the water. What exactly does he want you to do?"

Satia saw curiosity in Udall's eyes. It made her hopeful. "He wants to know what is on the other side of the Dominant Veil. When he ascends the throne, he'll open a rift. We'll be able to peek inside."

Udall frowned. "Does that have anything to do with Locklair? You could just ask him for help."

"I don't like Locklair. I don't trust him." Satia tightened her cape. "Do you know if Kyle promised Locklair anything? I'm curious."

Udall went inside and returned with a coat made from a bear's hide. "I heard Locklair complain about Kyle ignoring him for the past few months. Maybe they're not on the best of terms." He put on his coat and gloves, ready to continue his work. "You should go inside. It's getting cold."

"Come with me," Satia said. Her words came out selfish and ignorant, but she couldn't hold herself back. She needed allies, and no one could take Udall's place. She just knew what to expect from him, and that's why she wanted him on her side.

"Even if I wanted to, I can't leave my family. What will they do without me?"

So you do want to come, she thought. She didn't say it aloud, knowing that it would make persuading Udall even harder. He was a stubborn type. She could never win an open argument with Udall. Even if it was obvious she was in the right, he would lock himself up and refuse to acknowledge it. She needed to approach him peacefully.

Satia went to her horse and grabbed a sack of gold. It was everything she had left, save for a few coins to cover travel expenses. "Take it. Your family will have enough until we return."

"It's not about gold. What if something happens to the village? My wife and daughter can't protect themselves." Udall frowned.

"Locklair is here. He might be a brute, but he cares for his people. Locklair's Keep will never fall."

"To be honest, Locklair is already sick of me," Udall said with a chuckle. "He wants me to make swords, and I'm already falling behind."

"Then come with me and be free of Locklair. When we return you can live in Zardan. I'm sure Kyle will reward you." Satia placed her hand on his shoulder.

"You put a lot of faith in him. Why?" He gave her a sad, long look.

She lost herself in thought. "Underneath his harsh nature, he is honest, unlike most."

Udall fell silent. He was lost in thought. "That's not true," he said in an irritated tone. "I don't want to hear the common answer to the question. Tell me the real reason."

Satia took a seat next to Udall. "Because he is just like us. He isn't a purist or a Narilan fanatic." Her words were honest—fragile—right from the bottom of her heart. She regretted not telling Udall the truth earlier.

Udall perked up as a faint, kind smile showed on his face.

"I can help you with the swords," Satia said. "We can pay whatever debt you have, then we'll leave. You don't have to live in this filthy place." She couldn't promise anything, but thought that life in Zardan would be better for Udall than staying in Locklair's Keep. She knew the city didn't allow people to migrate, but she figured Kyle could make an exception.

"Think about it, you could live in Zardan," she continued.

Udall hesitated. Satia saw within him two opposing forces fighting. On one hand, Udall didn't want to pass the opportunity to live a better life, yet deep down inside, he feared losing the precious things he already had. He wasn't the brave warrior she remembered, but that didn't put her off.

The memories that they had together were as vibrant as ever. Satia could still recall that one time when they were imprisoned. Udall had a chance to escape, but he stayed. When she asked him why he didn't leave her behind, he simply said that she would've done the same thing. At the time, Satia didn't want to admit it, but she wasn't so sure about it. That changed, however. She would do anything for Udall now.

"Fine," Udall declared. "I'll help you. But first, the swords." He turned to his wife, who was standing in the door. Emma had a glimpse of sadness in her eyes as she nodded at her husband. "You can leave the gold inside."

"Greedy bastard," Satia said openly, then smiled.

CHAPTER 39

ELLIA WAS WALKING down a dirt path, shivering in the cold. Snow was lightly covering the ground. Her hands were dirty and had traces of blood, especially under her fingernails. She couldn't rid her mind of the image of Avril's empty gaze. It was staring back at her every time she closed her eyes.

She kept telling herself that it was just an accident, but she couldn't convince herself. She felt like a murderer—the lowest type of scum. She couldn't even give Avril a proper burial. She just left her there, buried underneath a thin layer of dirt. Everybody on the path would walk over Avril's corpse. The thought disgusted Ellia. She wanted to go back, but she wasn't sure what she would say if someone saw her. She was afraid of getting caught.

At first, Ellia wanted to rejoin Kyle when she learned to control her mana. Yet now she feared what he would do if he found out about Avril's death. She could never be a part of his cause again, and so, the mission she was entrusted by her mother was over as well.

The world is already rotten, Ellia thought. *Why should I be any different?*

She fell to the ground and pounded on the earth, screaming, until her hands bled.

Then she heard the sound of hooves drumming on the ground. Someone was coming up behind her. Five horsemen stopped when they saw her. She didn't pay attention to them, and trudged onward in the cold.

"Is something wrong?" one of them inquired, then dismounted his horse. He limped toward Ellia.

"Lord Ronn, we should get going," said another horseman.

Ellia looked up to see Ronn. He had trouble standing straight and had to support himself with a cane. His leg was crooked. "It's you," Ellia said with a bitter frown.

"My lucky day." He backhanded her, sending her to the ground. "You'll help me find Kyle and get revenge for my father."

Did Kyle really kill Breneon? Ellia thought. "Did Kyle get the last Blessing?" Ellia asked.

Ronn hit her again. "Gentlemen, grab her."

Ellia stood up and tried to run. Ronn stretched out his hand in time to grab her hair. He pulled her back, and Ellia screamed, falling to his feet in the muddy snow. She didn't want to fight. The mana within her was calm and motionless. She didn't want to kill.

A horseman chuckled.

Ronn lifted his boot, ready to bring it down on her face. She saw his nasty grin.

A spike emerged from the ground beneath Ronn. He let out a faint groan as it pierced his head. His limbs fell down. Blood spilled from his nose and open mouth.

The horsemen all froze.

Ellia didn't want to fight. Deep down, she wished for them to just walk away.

One of them gave the order to attack. They dismounted and readied their weapons. Before they could make a move, Ellia imagined their deaths. When she opened her eyes, she saw their corpses impaled before her, the startled horses dashed away.

The sight didn't disgust her anymore. At first she really didn't want to fight, but now that she did, it didn't feel wrong. She felt powerful and confident. There was peace within all the chaos of a fight. As long as she was the strongest, she didn't have to fear anything that came her way.

She looted their bags for anything useful. She grabbed the food, the gold, and a map of Narilan, then strode away. She felt like a thief, but the feeling lingered only a moment.

The world is already rotten, Ellia thought. *I don't need to be any different.*

She looked in the direction of Locklair's Keep.

CHAPTER 40

INSIDE HIS MIND, Kyle could feel his entire body intact. He clenched his fists until all the blood escaped from his knuckles, and they turned white. He found himself floating in the darkness. Steadily drifting, eyelids sealed, his muscles were not reacting. He panicked.

"Why did you bring him here?" a female voice from the outside rang in Kyle's ear.

"You are to take care of him, Delora," Reave said. "Preceptor's orders."

"What is this?"

"Medicine. He'll probably die without it."

"Herbs?" Delora asked. "That's forbidden in Narilan. Where did you get these?"

"That's none of your concern."

"It is my concern when your brother is scheming and breaking the rules."

"Look, you do as we say, or you'll regret it."

"Will the Celestial King bestow upon me the Gift of Misfortune?"

"If that's what you want," he said.

"It should be you, Reave Sahne, who should be cursed with misfortune. I'm sure once a new Celestial King is crowned, he will agree with me."

"Just nurse him back to health. He is to be ready soon."

There was a sound of footsteps. A door squealed, then fell silent as it closed.

Kyle's senses came back slowly. The darkness blinded him, his vision distorted and blurred. The air was heavy. He could hear banter in the distance, but he couldn't understand it. He wanted to sit up. He tried. Yet, his body declined servitude, throbbing with tremendous pain. He fell on his back again, gasping for air. With every breath, his chest ached. A fleeting scream filled the room.

"Where am I?" Kyle murmured, his body burning up.

"Don't move," Delora said. "My name is Delora. You have a few broken ribs." There was no worry or concern in her voice. She seemed to have no trouble ignoring the loud screams, too.

Kyle closed his eyes. He could no longer feel his arm. The thought made him uneasy at first, but he was too weak to think about it. A wet cloth was put over his forehead. It was cold, just like the darkness. For a brief moment, he thought that he could see the sea of stars above, shining without a tinge of worry.

◆

Kyle felt a few cold drops on his face. He opened his eyes to find Delora standing over him. She was a big lady with a square-shaped body. She had a big, round head and a huge nose, as well as a few moles on her forehead. Her eyebrows were bushy, and her face was stuck in a constant frown. She wore white robes just like Audene.

"I thought that you might have died," she said in a hoarse voice.

Kyle wanted to turn on his side, but even the most subtle movement made his whole stomach throb with pain. "How long was I out?" he whispered, his forehead hot.

"Only a couple of days," Delora said. "You had a bout with Reave?" Kyle was silent. "He must have had a bad day. I've had people here before, but none with such injuries. None that were alive, anyway. Broken ribs, lost arm..." She fetched some herbs from a bag that hung on the wall and came back. She inspected Kyle's chest. He didn't know what she was doing. He couldn't feel anything.

Then it hit him again. He could not feel his forearm. He looked at his limb, leaves wrapped around his elbow—the rest of his arm lost. His heart started beating faster. He felt angry and helpless. He wanted to get up, but the pain was far too great.

He tried to restrain the stream of emotions—the panic and the fear. He recalled his fight with Reave. The thought that he took his eye soothed him a bit. He let out a helpless smirk. The idea that his dream was lost overcame him.

A scream resounded. He remembered Dorrell talking with Reave about donors. "Where am I?" he asked.

"Don't worry about it for now."

Another scream echoed through the room. Kyle could hear a whistle. Applause. He recognized the sounds of a fight, sword hitting shield, and the shriek a novice makes when faced with a merciless opponent.

"I heard about you, but your name escapes me." Delora tossed some bloody bandages to the floor.

"My name is Kyle," he said, trying to keep himself awake. But his eyelids were heavy, and his mind clouded. There was nothing he could do; his consciousness slipped away.

◆

Reave leaned back in the chair in Dorrell's quarters. The overwhelming scent of gardenia bouquets irked him in many ways. He looked around to see the decorations. He thought they were too beautiful, too perfect, just like all things in Zardan. Even the chair that he sat in had complex carvings and was made from expensive wood. Everything was well-ordered and had its place in the city. It irritated Reave, as if telling him that he didn't belong. And it was true. He always preferred simplicity and some chaos in the world.

His brother retreated to the top of the Great Tower some time ago, claiming he had some things to attend to.

Why did I come back? Reave wondered. The sole reason for his return to Zardan was his brother—the only human being he managed to establish a real connection with. They were always together, working, helping each other. They had no secrets.

Reave noticed a mirror on the wall. He came closer and untied the bandage around his right eye. It stopped bleeding, but there was an empty hole where his right eye once was. He didn't want to believe it. The loss of his eye was something that he could live with, but he couldn't get used to his new blind spot. It made him feel weaker and vulnerable.

The lift grated. "Ready to go?" Dorrell asked, striding out.

"Yes." Reave joined his brother.

"Sorry for the wait. I just have to grab something."

Dorrell stepped on a few specific tiles, and the floor groaned. Puffs of dust covered the room, and after they settled, stairs appeared, leading down to the basement.

Dorrell made his way down, lighting the torches with his mana.

Reave didn't follow. He knew all of Dorrell's secrets.

When Dorrell returned, they boarded the lift and ascended the Great Tower in silence. They stopped somewhere close to the top floor. With a determined pace, Dorrell led the way through a corridor to a lone chamber at the end. The door opened, inviting them in.

The chamber was very spacious and dark. There were a few lone rays that sneaked in through the arrow slits. The sound of water's soft murmur resonated through the empty chamber. Thin carvings were engraved in the floor, and there were countless pools of water around.

"This is just like the Celestial King's chamber," Reave said.

"It's connected to his chamber. The Celestial King will be able to freely use the mana that will be gathered here." Dorrell said proudly. "I have all the necessary donors to support even the weakest successor to the throne."

"You haven't been wasting time." Reave strolled around.

"You always knew that I would go this route, that I would start gathering donors," Dorrell said. "Back when I first told you about this idea, you told me that when the right time comes, I'll forget about all of Narilan's laws and tradition, and do what I think is right."

Reave nodded with a smile. Despite having some differences, they were twins—same blood. Reave knew that Dorrell would start collecting donors to help Narilan because that's what he would've done. That's why he brought Kyle. He knew that when times became grim, Dorrell would make the choice.

"You don't look impressed?" Dorrell asked, his enthusiasm withering.

Reave sighed. "Why should I be? You made all this progress, yet people are suffering out there. Zardan is in a pathetic state."

"It's not so simple." Dorrell stepped forward "There are those that suspect me. I already had to deal with one vermin. What do you think the Grand Court would do if they found out about this?" He pointed to the pools of water.

Reave shrugged, strolling around the chamber. He was surrounded by pools of water. Several were still empty, but the vast majority were occupied. He saw a blond man submerged in the water, sleeping. Then another man and another. "I understand, but look what happened to the lake. There is a chance this water might be infected too."

"It's not. I made sure of it."

Reave glanced at Dorrell.

Dorrell frowned. "Listen Reave, the Celestial King has no mana. He's practically a corpse. The reason the Dominant Veil hasn't gone down and the kingdom is still functioning is because of these men here. Without them, Narilan would be no more." He came closer and put his hand on Reave's shoulder.

"Then get rid of the Celestial King. We have enough donors, Narilan doesn't need a false god anymore."

Dorrell looked down. "We can't. He is a divine figure. We can't toss him out like a piece of trash. Never has Narilan abandoned the Celestial King."

"Let's do it together," Reave said with determination. "No one has to know. Let's fix this."

Dorrell shook his head. "I can't."

Reave shoved him back. "Why do you care for him so much?"

Dorrell didn't answer.

The chamber fell silent.

Reave wanted to smack Dorrell across the face, but he held back. "Fine, but whatever happens, it's all on you." He understood Dorrell's devotion toward the Celestial King, but he couldn't fathom why his brother would hold on to it at such a dire time.

If only I was the preceptor, I could fix this. Then Reave realized that he really could make a difference. He could become the Celestial King; he just didn't want to, knowing what it meant. "I'm sorry, brother," Reave finally said.

"Don't be sorry." Dorrell sighed. "You're right. I should have done something."

"You said you have more donors. Let's continue." Reave pointed to the pools of water.

Dorrell nodded with a comfortable, soft expression. "Do you think it was a good idea leaving Kyle there?"

"I do." Reave nodded. "The Grand Court will have something to talk about. If Kyle tries to escape, he'll be executed. If he survives, we can always use him as a donor later. Corbit reassured me that he'll take care of things."

"And you trust him?"

"Corbit reveres power. I defeated him. He would do anything for me."

Dorrell paused. "You're probably wondering why I chose to save Kyle. You see, I don't want you to turn into a cold-blooded killer, Reave. I thought that if I allowed you to kill him, you would lose a piece of yourself. I saved him for your sake."

Reave frowned.

They walked back to the lift. Reave poked Dorrell in the side. Dorrell retaliated with a powerful blow to the back with an open palm, then grabbed Reave under the arm and tousled his hair. Reave quickly shoved him back.

Dorrell put on a childish smile. "It's good to have you back, brother."

◆

The following day, Dorrell left the courthouse with a stack of papers under his arm. The members of the Grand Court were particularly inquisitive today, which irked him in a disgusting sort of way. They had doubts he was fit to be the preceptor. They also complained about his inability to find a worthy successor. And so the meeting ended with a loud argument.

Dorrell feared there would be consequences, but he managed to persuade the Grand Court that he had everything under control. It was all thanks to his scheme. It was the only reason the disease was gone from the water, and Zardan was still protected.

He looked around the central plaza to remind himself why he was doing something forbidden in the kingdom. He noticed the empty streets, the beggars clustered in a side alley, and the rotten fruits and vegetables. Deep inside, he truly believed he cherished every human life and would never sacrifice anyone. Yet here he stood with a room full of victims. As much as Dorrell wanted to be coldhearted, he wasn't. Reave always told him he was too soft.

Dorrell gazed at the Great Tower, where a thick dark cloud of dust gathered—slowly growing.

Within a few of minutes, he was back in his chamber. The Great Tower was empty; Albert was off on an errand, and Reave wandered off somewhere on his own. Dorrell left the stack of papers on the desk and turned the walls invisible to reveal a view of Zardan. He pulled his chair closer and took a seat. He began meditating, the sun burning red on the horizon.

CHAPTER 41

EVEN THE TINIEST whisper resonated through the mute cave like a powerful chant. The people sat on the cold floor, legs crossed and palms up. Their eyes were closed; the people were lost in meditation. But not everyone was at peace. There were those who murmured to themselves, and others who struggled to keep from weeping.

Kyle took note of his sweaty hand. He looked up to see the withered, gnarled figures around. Perhaps it was his young age that kept his mind clear, or maybe his destiny was to end up like these figures—withered and mindless.

"They're here," an old man called out. "I can hear them!" His thick beard and long hair covered his dirty face. He stood up and ran to the closest guard. "I can hear them."

"They're in your head, old man," the guard said. "Get

back to your station." The guard was used to this kind of behavior. Feeling no sympathy was a prerequisite for taking the job. When the old man didn't obey, the guard took hold of his sword and drove the pommel into the old man's neck. The man fell to the floor lifelessly like a corpse—eyes wide open.

Someone applauded the guard. Most of the people refrained from looking and kept their eyes closed. Yet, Kyle couldn't stop himself. He looked over his shoulder and saw a man dressed in royal robes, a ring with a huge gem on each finger and countless earrings dangling from his ears.

The man noticed Kyle's hateful stare. He whispered to a guard, then left. The guards dragged Kyle away deeper into the cave. He struggled against them, but he didn't scream.

◆

Kyle thrashed around with all the strength he could muster. Then he plunged downward in pain. He opened his eyes to see his bloody palm. He was coughing out water. He tried to breathe, but both the pain and the water in his lungs made it difficult.

He heard laughter.

After everything came back to him—his location, problems, and goals—he saw the people looming over him. Two guards were full of mirth. The elderly guard held a piece of cloth drenched in water. The other one held a bucket.

"What is going on here?" Delora roared.

Kyle found himself on the floor. He tried to stand up, but he had no strength. Forced to crawl, he gritted his teeth.

The anger that was boiling within his chest was suffocating. He could think of nothing but the overwhelming rage that he had to endure. He closed his eyes to use mana, but nothing happened. His thoughts were too chaotic. He knew he couldn't use mana because he lacked harmony.

If only I could use mana, he thought. *I would kill them all.*

Delora said something, and the guards bowed over Kyle. They pulled him up and carelessly shoved him on the bunk. His chest was full of pain and bleeding.

They left chortling. Delora didn't say anything more. She returned to her duties.

The situation reminded Kyle of his life in the cave. He felt trapped and powerless. This disgusting feeling infuriated him. He once promised himself that he would never be enslaved again. Yet, striving to reach his ultimate freedom led him to be trapped again. He hated the feeling that his life ran in a circle. Before drifting off, he promised something to himself. He promised that he wouldn't perish here, that he would make it out no matter what.

His thoughts vanished as he fell asleep. Nothing mattered anymore. Sleep was his only sanctuary, a safe haven where he didn't have to fight.

The next day, Delora came back with something to drink. The mixture of herbs was strong and bitter, but Kyle didn't complain.

◆

Kyle lost track of how many days had passed. Eventually, the fever went down and he felt better, but the pain didn't diminish. Many times he found himself lying there, staring at the ceiling. He tried to keep his mind from wondering. The moment he started thinking of his helpless situation, he couldn't subdue the flood of emotions that spread chaos through his mind.

Whenever he faced the notion that the only reason he was saved was to languish and give up his mana, he felt sick. That's when he would rehearse the same line over and over again.

The world is waiting for me, he thought.

He would think about his mana. The reason for his inability to use it was obvious. Yet, he didn't know how to handle it. And so he started listening to the sounds in the distance.

There was a bizarre tranquility in the hectic noises that echoed around him. A subtle sense of order. He came to listen to the battles and recognize all the sounds. The swift sword attacks, the grouts, the laughs, he knew them all. They reminded him of the outside world.

The vicious world that he lived in was out there. He didn't fear it.

He yearned to return, to fight.

CHAPTER 42

THE SWORDS WERE ready at sunrise, at the same time the knights started their training. Their scuffles could be heard all over town. Satia was worn out from her use of mana. In truth, she rarely used mana, despite her love of knowledge and experimentation. She much preferred fiddling around with all the different herb combinations or alchemy.

The weather was strange. Gone were the cold winds and the gloomy clouds, and in their place was a plain blue sky and a powerful sun.

Udall loaded a cart with all the swords, and they dragged it to the armory. Used as a training ground, the grassy field behind Locklair's manor was full of knights. That's where the armory, a dilapidated shed full of weapons, resided. When they delivered the swords, Udall searched for Locklair. He wasn't around, so they entered the manor.

Locklair's servant, who was obliviously standing behind the counter, said that Locklair was busy teaching his knights to fight—too busy to bother with meeting a depressed blacksmith. Udall insisted, but no matter how hard he argued, the servant had no intention of being helpful. The only relief was that the servant gave them a written declaration, which stated that Udall's debt was paid in full.

As they left, Udall perked up.

"You're a free man, Udall." Satia tossed her hair back.

"Not even close," he said, "I owe you now."

Satia shrugged. She knew Udall very well. The flashes of gloom were his signature behavior. Often he was just like any other man, but from time to time, he would enter this state of unhappiness and utter pessimism. Satia had no intention of cheering him up. It would be a waste of time and energy.

They returned to Udall's hut. After a hefty meal, Satia prepared her horse. She waited outside while Udall stayed for a talk with his family. He came back with a big sack over his shoulder, ready to go. Satia saw Udall's wife looking her way and nodded.

In the center of town, a crowd of people gathered. A shipment of goods arrived, and every one of the residents wanted to take advantage of the opportunity to get food and other supplies. Satia and Udall pushed their way through the crowd.

"Where is your horse?" Satia asked at the gates, pulling her horse behind by the reins.

"I don't have one," Udall retorted with a disinterested look.

"And you didn't think that was important to tell me about earlier?" She frowned.

"I sold my horse." Udall shrugged. "We can buy one somewhere else."

She shook her head, then sighed. "I left all my gold with your family. We barely have any for travel."

Satia gave Udall a hard, long look. He wasn't bothered by it. "I'll walk then." He smiled, looking away. "And you're light, so we can always…"

"I know. One horse should be enough for both of us." Satia climbed her mount. "But for now, you can keep walking," she said in a childish tone. She liked teasing Udall. Despite his frequent lack of reaction, she knew him well enough to determine when he was listening and when her teasing reached him.

Udall looked away. "Looks like there is someone coming." He pointed to a lone figure striding toward Locklair's Keep.

Satia couldn't make out the figure in the distance. It was distorted by the heat of the sun. Yet, a lone traveler wasn't something uncommon in these regions, so she ignored them.

"So where are we heading?" Udall asked.

Satia looked down at him. "I'd like to have one more trusted person by my side… and a couple of thugs."

"Do you have another person in mind who is foolish enough to come along?" he asked cynically.

She tried kicking him in the shoulder, but she wasn't fast enough and he sprung away.

"Keep your eyes on the road instead of trying to attack me." Udall rubbed his nose with a smile.

Satia ran her hand through the soft mane of her horse. "There is one person, but he's in Razan."

"That's too far. I don't feel like trekking across the entire kingdom." Udall paused. "I have a suggestion, but the man lives in Hunt's Hamlet. It's still quite a journey from here, but it's closer than Razan."

"Is he dependable?"

"If there is still a man in Narilan with a bit of honor, it's that man."

"Fine." Satia looked at the elaborate silver ring on her finger.

The figure was closer now. It had a timid stature with a hood over its head. It froze in front of Satia's horse, then took down the hood.

"Hello, Satia," Ellia said in a serious voice.

Satia fell silent. She knew she left Ellia in the woods with Raun. Since then, she never once wondered what happened to Ellia, and it made her feel guilty. "Hi, Ellia."

"Good to see you're well... after leaving me," Ellia said, but without any bitterness.

"I'm sorry for abandoning you in the woods," Satia said. "It's good to see that you made it out."

Ellia gazed at Udall, then at Satia. "The same thing can't be said about my aunt, Hilda, but I bear no ill will. You had no obligation to help me." Ellia nodded with a faint smile. "I would run away too if I was in your shoes."

I didn't run away, Satia protested within. *Does she really think so? Maybe it's for the best.* Satia decided that it would be foolish to admit she left Ellia due to a selfish impulse. "So why are you here? Are you not traveling with your companions anymore?"

Ellia looked straight at Locklair's Keep. "I can't travel with them anymore," she confessed. "Something terrible happened, and I don't think they would want me back."

Satia brooded over Ellia's confession. She yearned to know more, but something about Ellia seemed different. It left her unsettled. "Why don't you travel with us?" Satia said, eyeing Ellia's dirty hands.

Ellia shook her head. "I have things that I need to do."

Udall pulled on Satia's sleeve. "Is that blood under her fingernails?" he whispered.

Satia dismounted her horse and came closer. She grabbed Ellia's hands and saw the blood and the dirt. She gazed into Ellia's cold eyes; they were devoid of the warmth they had in Relien. Ellia was very different, and Satia recognized it. "What happened to you?"

Ellia wrestled her hands out of Satia's grip, then retreated. "Nothing."

"You can tell me," Satia reassured her. "I'm not your enemy. Whatever it is you got yourself into, I'll help you."

"Tell your thug to take his hand off the sword," Ellia said, staring at Udall.

Satia motioned to Udall to back away. She saw the surprise in his eyes. He probably wondered why she was so concerned with Ellia. All Satia knew was that she wanted to help Ellia and soothe the guilt of leaving her in the woods. "This is Udall. We are traveling together. We're not your enemies. If you'd like, you can join us. We can travel together."

"I already told you I must do something."

"Locklair's Keep isn't a place for a young girl, such as yourself," Udall said.

Ellia ignored his comment. She passed Satia and continued walking.

"At least tell me what you're doing here!" Satia called out.

Ellia stopped, then turned around. "I'm here to kill Locklair."

Udall faced away, glanced at Satia, and then covered his smile with his hand. "Let's leave her, Satia. It's not like she can succeed anyway."

Ellia watched Udall. The dirt gathered around his feet, clinging to his boots and merging with the fabric. He thrashed around, but couldn't free himself. Looking at Ellia, he drew his sword.

"Ellia, stop!" Satia said, walking closer.

Ellia pointed to Satia, and a powerful gust of wind blew across the land, shaking the treetops. It was cold and fierce. The horse bolted away, frightened by the very first whistle. Satia was barely able to hold against the harsh gale, which ripped her cape off.

The archers gathered at their posts, staring at the commotion.

Udall tried to free himself, but with just a single clumsy swing, his sword was stuck in the soil. The soil, under Ellia's control, grabbed it and ripped it out of his grip. It then vanished underneath the surface. Stunned, Udall looked at Ellia.

Satia stood astonished as well. An arrow fell right at her feet, but she continued to gaze at Ellia. She could hear the archers yelling, but she couldn't understand their words. She ignored them.

Ellia spread her arms out. The ground quivered and murmured. The soil was set in motion. Satia sunk, knee-deep. Udall continued to thrash around, but the more he struggled, the faster he was swallowed up.

A horn suddenly blared, and a sea of arrows covered the sky. Udall closed his eyes, praying. Satia was mesmerized by Ellia's power. She rarely saw Dreamers, of course, and when she did, she never had an opportunity to observe their full might. That's what she saw in Ellia—a fierce power that just awakened. Her eyes were glued to Ellia's outline, which was drenched in a pale, white light, her cape twirling.

Then a great gust of wind swept the arrows away.

Udall looked up, gritting his teeth. The soil was up to his neck. "And here we were planning to travel to Hunt's Hamlet," he muttered, then his head sunk beneath the surface.

Satia thought it was her imagination, but then she saw it again—the pale light coming from Ellia. It was subtle, like the hesitant first ray of the morning sun, but it was vibrant and strong too.

Satia didn't try to fight it. She closed her eyes as the soil swallowed her. Then there was only darkness.

CHAPTER 43

JUST LIKE EVERY single day, Cwen was seated in the lecture hall, listening to Dorrell. Although composed and focused, her mind was somewhere else. She looked around at the other scholars. Some were furtively chatting while others were absorbed by their studies and a sole desire to become the next preceptor. Anson was absent.

"I believe in intuition," Dorrell declared, standing on the podium. "When you feel something deep down, you should follow that voice. It's the only right thing to do. As a preceptor, you will be required to make difficult decisions, and without that voice, you'll be blind. You need to learn to listen to what's inside of your heart."

You should practice what you preach, professor, Cwen thought. She raised her hand, and Dorrell nodded.

"While an individual's unique identity and desires are important in Narilan, there is emphasis on collective decision-making too," Cwen declared, playing with a bracelet around her wrist.

"Please listen to Cwen," Dorrell said to the other scholars, strolling away from the podium. "She has the making of a true preceptor. She's absolutely right. That's why the Grand Court is there. It's implemented to make sure a preceptor doesn't abuse his power."

One of the scholars raised his hand. "Did that ever happen? That a preceptor overused his authority?"

"There are no records of that, but do remember that our history is only being written."

Cwen observed Dorrell's fatigued movements, strained voice, and tired eyes. She saw a man unlike the one she remembered. Before, she saw Dorrell as a preceptor who cherished his love and dedication above all else. Now she saw a man overcome by bad decisions and a false sense of righteousness. That's how she felt, but she had no proof. Her intuition was the only thing she had, and she hoped it was wrong.

She couldn't imagine a world without Dorrell.

A time of sorrow and pain was a fair price to pay for a century of peace, she recalled Dorrell's words. He had a lot of mantras and after listening to his lectures for the past few years, it was hard for her to forget most of them. *Harsh times demand initiative,* she thought about one of his favorites.

The words stimulated her to take action—gone were the doubts, the fears, and the lack of determination. All thanks to the words of the person she had to confront.

◆

In the evening, Cwen took a carriage to the Great Tower. Each day she noticed people gathering to donate their mana to the Celestial King. It was an honorable gesture, but she was too cynical to think so. Ever since the water became contaminated, people have started to give more mana. Fear and anxiety were driving them. As much as Cwen didn't want to admit it—she never viewed people in a good light. There was always that strong pessimistic voice in her head questioning everything.

The carriage pulled to the side. She paid with gold, then entered the Great Tower. Albert greeted her as she called for the lift. It groaned on arrival, welcoming her inside.

"The preceptor is waiting for you," Albert said, stepping on a few specific tiles.

The lift murmured as it climbed up.

Is he expecting me? Does he know why I'm here? Of course he does if he had anything to do with Anson's disappearance.

The lift stopped and opened to reveal a dark room. Cwen saw a man standing deep inside. "Is that you, Dorrell?" she asked.

Cwen tiptoed ahead as the murmur of water redoubled. She saw pools of water and many bodies submerged up to the neck. All of them had their eyes closed as if they were sleeping, docile and tranquil.

"What do you think?" Dorrell asked.

Cwen sighed. She looked up at Dorrell, the man she admired. All that admiration was gone, and it was replaced by a profound sense of pity.

"Are you not going to say anything?" Dorrell asked, turning around. "I was prepared to face all the accusations."

Cwen hesitated. She wondered why she waited this long to confront Dorrell, but she knew the answer. She didn't want to hear the truth because she didn't know how to handle it. She respected Dorrell as the preceptor and a teacher. She knew he wasn't a bad person. All this time she had hoped that her suspicions would be just fake misgivings, but now—

"All of them," Dorrell said, pointing to the bodies, "are individuals that wanted to become the Celestial King. They would have given up their life for Narilan anyway. If you think about it, their fate isn't so different from…"

"Stop," Cwen whispered, then fell silent. "Can they hear us?"

"No," Dorrell said, "but he can." He motioned to Reave, who was standing by the wall. Reave snorted and strode out. Now Cwen and Dorrell were alone. "My brother was helping me with another donor."

"Is that what you call them, Dorrell?" Cwen looked into his sad eyes. He looked ashamed as if all his pride left him. He nodded. She wanted to ask him why he would do such a thing, but the question seemed pointless.

"I have no intention to justify what I have done. I made my decision."

Cwen looked around the chamber. She couldn't recognize any of the donors because of the darkness. They didn't look like they were in pain. They looked fragile and submissive. "Who else knows about his?"

"Albert and Reave."

"Does it work?" Cwen walked around, playing with her bracelet.

"Thanks to them, the disease that nearly destroyed Narilan's main water supply is gone. They gave Narilan stability. When this is finished, everything will be back to normal."

Cwen crossed her hands in front of her chest. The place was cold. Dorrell walked closer, taking off his cloak, then handed it to her.

"Was it really so hard finding a successor?" Cwen asked.

Dorrell sighed. "I know only two men powerful enough to bear the weight of the world. There is no way my brother would do it. As for that common brute... Kyle... I can't allow him to desecrate this sacred place."

He did all this for the sake of Narilan, Cwen thought. *This wasn't a selfish act. It was his devotion speaking through him. Without him, Narilan would be no more.*

"So are you going tell the Grand Court about this?" Dorrell asked as he went to an arrow slit in the back of the chamber. The light illuminated his tired face. He leaned against the wall, staring outside. It was some time since he last saw the land so peaceful.

Cwen hesitated. "What happened to Anson?"

"He's in the basement. Alive and well. I just had to imprison him since he would never stop poking around." Dorrell turned to Cwen. "I don't know what to do with him, but I can't let him out... not yet."

"Are you going to execute him?" Her voice trembled.

Dorrell paused. "I don't want to."

The chamber fell silent.

"Promise me you won't," she pleaded.

"I can't do that. He will never join my cause. He'll do everything to take me down the moment he is a free man."

Cwen played with her bracelet, undecided and tormented by what to do.

CHAPTER 44

KYLE COULDN'T SLEEP, lying flat on his back. A cry kept him up all night. Lost in thought, he sometimes became deaf to it, tricking his mind into thinking that it had stopped. Yet it continued, only in a much feebler way. It started as a powerful cry, and now, it was only a pathetic, incoherent whimper.

Kyle turned on his side. The bunk was hard and uncomfortable. It bothered his ribs, but he wanted to look at the door. It was shut, but light sneaked in at the base.

No matter how much he meditated, he couldn't use mana. After the first few hours he spent igniting it, he gave up. The more he tried, the more the anger seethed within his chest.

His bleeding stopped just yesterday, and his fever was gone too. He wondered if the herbs he was given were the same ones Ellia used, but he quickly dismissed the thought.

Kyle dropped his feet to the ground, and pushed up with his only hand. When he managed to sit up, he took a deep breath before using all of his strength to stand up. It felt unnatural at first, but only for a second. It was his first time up after battling Reave.

He looked around the claustrophobic room and noticed a window. A tiny, barred opening at the ceiling. The bars were rusty, almost red.

He hobbled to it, then stood on his toes to see out. The window overlooked a narrow corridor. He could see two guards playing a board game at a wooden table. He recognized them as the ones who nearly drowned him. They were gossiping about a monster.

"Did you see that monster rip that thug apart?" the elderly guard barked. He had a thick mustache.

"You should've seen him last week." The other rubbed his chin. "Now, that was something. Bones sticking out everywhere, the skin like a cape, the thug begging for his life."

"Too bad I missed it." The elderly guard shook his head.

"You should come to work more often." The other rubbed his eyes, then cocked his head as if his neck was stiff.

"Watch who you're talking too."

What is this place? Kyle thought. *What is the preceptor planning? Does he want to become the Celestial King? No, that wouldn't make any sense. I heard of his devotion. He wouldn't do such a thing. Maybe he's trying to handpick a successor? If the successor is weak, it would explain the need for donors.*

Kyle walked to the door. As he stretched out his hand to reach for the knob, he froze. He was always right-handed. That's just the way his mind worked, but that was all in the past. With his right hand gone, he had to start using his left for such an elementary task. The thought was dispiriting, and it lingered in his mind. He reached out with his left hand. Just as expected the door was shut, locked.

He sighed, thinking of Reave. At that moment, he wanted nothing more than to sink his blade into Reave's heart. He subdued the feeling. It was too powerful to nurture while waiting here. He knew it would ruin him. Like a disease, it would slowly destroy him from the inside if he allowed it to run freely.

He returned to the window. "Hey," he called out to the guards. "What is this place?"

"The place where you die, scum."

The guards chuckled together.

Kyle frowned, stepped down, and then leaned against the wall. He took a seat on the cold, stone floor, legs crossed. The pose felt natural.

The world is waiting for me, he thought. *I'm not ready to die.*

CHAPTER 45

ELLIA WALKED IN a determined pace, the fortifications before her. The road was covered in arrows like a field covered in grass. The arrows came in waves, but no matter how talented the archer, Ellia would just blow them all away. She didn't have to put much thought into it.

Knights gathered at the gates. They formed a tightly packed line with their shields up. They kneeled to reveal a second line behind them composed of archers.

The arrows whispered in the air as the archers fired. The gale swooped them up with ease. It tossed them in the air back at the fortifications and the knights. The knights screamed, putting up their shields as the archers hid behind them. The rain of arrows chinked against the shields, bouncing off and dancing at the gates. When it was over, the knights grabbed their swords, then bashed them against their shields in anger.

Ellia stopped before the gate. "People of Locklair's Keep, listen! I don't want to fight you. I only want Lord Locklair." She paused, waiting for an answer. "I only want to challenge Locklair. Nothing more."

There was only silence.

"I knew I could call Locklair many things," Ellia continued. "But I didn't know coward was one of them."

"Such strong words coming from such a puny girl," Locklair said, hiding behind the knights. With a wave of his hand, the line broke, and he walked through. "I heard there was a commotion, but I thought my knights could handle it."

"Looks like their instructor is incompetent," Ellia said.

"Look at you," Locklair said. "So insolent, but I like you this way. Say, where is your companion?"

"Dead," Ellia said quickly.

"That's why you're making all this fuss." Locklair turned to his knights. "You're scared of a girl who had a bad day. All of you are a disgrace! You'll be fighting on the front lines in our next battle, no matter your rank."

Ellia sprung forward. As if she was gliding on the wind, the gust shoved her forward with immense speed. She clenched her fist, staring at Locklair, who faced away.

"Watch out!" a knight yelled.

At peak impetus, Ellia channeled all the energy into her fist, then jammed it into Locklair's gut. She heard a faint crack as her knuckles dug deep, scuffed. Locklair groaned and bowed. His look was full of surprise, but also fear. His sword shrieked as he drew it, swinging chaotically. Ellia evaded, the wind pulling her back. Then Locklair fell to his knees and gasped for air.

"I must say I like you better this way," Ellia said with a self-satisfied smile.

Locklair gritted his teeth, spat, and stood up. "After we're done with you, you're going to beg for mercy," he said, his voice hoarse and tense.

The archers were ready, their aim steady and determined.

The wind veered and gusted the fortifications. The knights dug their shields into the ground, struggling to withstand it. It lashed the archers, pushing them off balance. One of them slipped, and his arrow was released. It darted ahead as the wind whistled. Someone screamed, and the knights froze in shock. As the arrow grazed Locklair's temple, he bowed with an angry look.

Ellia smirked. "It would be quite miserable to die at the hands of one of your own archers." She walked closer. Seeing his astonishment was like a breath of fresh air. She relished the power, the fear, and the freedom. She felt as if she was in the right place, the exact spot where she should be. There was nothing else that mattered to her. She had everything she wanted.

Locklair relaxed. Ellia recognized his intentions, grabbed his armor with her mana, and then pulled down on him. He plummeted headlong, screaming. His body was shoved against the ground with a loud thud. There was a crack of bones and a feeble murmur as the impact sent him into a dazed state. His limbs tangled together, he twitched in pain without any strength to stand up.

The second-in-command screamed. The knights didn't hesitate, despite the obvious fear that was on every one of their faces. They advanced, then surrounded Locklair, their shields up.

Ellia thought about ending it all at that moment, but hesitated. *They don't need to die,* she thought.

The knights retreated inside the fortifications, and Ellia followed. A few of them struggled to close the gates, but she just shoved them back. She could see some of the knights cower in fear. Others tried to mask their distress under a frail veneer of strength.

Ellia followed the knights into the town square. All the knights gathered to surround her in a thick ring. In the windows, she saw villagers with blank stares and their faces spiritless. The roofs were covered with archers, aghast.

Locklair looked up and grunted. He stood up, pushing the second-in-command back. Then he let out a pitiful scream as he collapsed, unable to stand. His leg was broken, with a piece of bone sticking out and a stream of blood trickling from it. The knights struggled to help him up. Locklair was bleeding from his forehead as well, the blood flowing into his eyes. He wiped it with his hand, barely standing.

"What do you want?" he called out to Ellia.

"You have caused me pain," Ellia confessed. "I had to prove to myself that I am not afraid of you."

"You have proven yourself," he rasped. "What else do you want?"

Ellia looked at the manor. The ground trembled and murmured. The manor shook like a wooden hut in the wind. The glass shrieked, then cracked, chipped, and rained on the ground. The image of the king and queen was gone.

Locklair looked at his manor, agape. "Father, mother," he mumbled.

Ellia picked up a sword that one of the knights must have dropped. She attempted to flourish it, but it felt unwieldy in her hands. Perhaps because she never handled a sword before.

Locklair frowned, then whispered something to his second-in-command. A few knights helped him stand up. He placed his hand on one of their shoulders, balancing on one leg. "If you want me so bad, I'm here. Spare my people and be done with it, witch."

Ellia swung the sword and Locklair shrieked, falling to the ground. She grinned. "Time to die."

"Father," a young boy called out from the crowd, then hurried to Locklair, but before he could reach him, the second-in-command took hold of the boy.

Ellia hesitated. She looked at the pathetic man lying at her feet. She held her sword point-down over his head. Then she looked at his hand.

The knights were ready to charge at her, their hands firmly holding their weapons. The archers were awaiting command. The second-in-command drew his blade, and screamed as she attacked.

Arrows rained on her. Dust covered the town square.

There was blood, screams, and chaos.

The battle escalated, but Ellia just continued to smile in the face of danger. She feared nothing.

Yet at the same time, everyone feared her.

CHAPTER 46

SATIA AWAKENED TO the deafening blare of a trumpet. A few horsemen arrived at a village in the distance, but to Satia's weary gaze they appeared only as indistinct shapes. The wind soughed, picking up some of the sand and blowing it in her face. She grimaced, then slowly dug herself out. The soil was dry, and she was just at the surface of it, so it didn't take much time. She spat out the sand that was in her mouth and on her lips. Then she tossed her hair to get rid of the sand, and searched for Udall.

He was buried nearby. His body was covered by a thick layer of sand, making it almost invisible. He was moving slightly, as if he was shaking in his sleep. Satia uncovered his face and pulled him up.

"What happened?" Udall asked, sitting up. "I thought she intended to kill us."

"No, she isn't like that." Satia patted him on the back.

Udall stood up, and noticed his flask was uncorked. He tried to drink from it, but he was forced to spit the mead out. There was sand everywhere.

"We should get back to Locklair's Keep," Udall said. "I have to get back."

"Listen, even if you leave now, you won't make it any time soon. Besides, you saw what Ellia could do." A childish grin crept up Satia's face. "Locklair doesn't stand a chance."

"But my family could be hurt in the battle." Udall turned away to look in the direction of Locklair's Keep. He could barely make out the shape of it. It looked bleak and unimpressive from here.

"See that village over there?" Satia pulled him by the arm. "We're in the Tranquil Meadows. Let's go."

Udall hesitated.

The humble village was surrounded by a vast meadow. There was no wind, so the grass was still. It was knee-high, and had a pale green color. Yet, the closer to the village they came, the more vibrant the green color became. Soon, it was rich and bright like the color of an emerald. The meadow was scattered with enormous rolls of hay.

"Looks like we'll never get to Hunt's Hamlet." Udall sighed. "Do you know anyone in the village?"

"Sumin lives here, but I don't know if he'll help." Satia led the way.

"Why? I thought thugs would do anything for a gold coin?"

"Well, he's kind of like you—moody and..."

"And what?" Udall demanded.

"You'll see."

At the entrance, the gatekeeper greeted them with a spear by his side. He was wearing a tattered tunic and an old pair of trousers. His hair, tied into a neat ponytail, was the color of hay.

"What brings you to the Tranquil Meadows?" he asked in a husky voice.

"I'm looking for Sumin," Satia said.

"Why visit such a scumbag?" the gatekeeper asked with a stoic face.

Satia smiled. "The scumbag is needed somewhere."

The gatekeeper couldn't fight his amusement and burst out a wholehearted laugh.

Udall rolled his eyes.

Satia frowned. The behavior irked her the wrong way. Her reply wasn't a joke. As the man's mirth spiraled out of control, she looked around for someone else to talk to, someone normal.

"I apologize," the gatekeeper finally said, holding his stomach. "You should talk to the chief."

Satia gave a single nod. "Please lead the way."

The gatekeeper beckoned to them as if welcoming them, but the gesture came out stiff and uninviting.

"What was that all about?" Udall whispered to Satia.

She shook her head.

The gatekeeper stumbled upon one of his relatives, a young woman, and after a brief exchange, he told her to take his place at the gates. The woman agreed without a second thought. The gatekeeper took Satia and Udall around the back of a middling hut with a round roof. The narrow alleys led them to the remnants of a destroyed dome, with villagers chanting inside.

Satia couldn't stop herself from peeking in. She saw a ritual ground with two concentric rings of people. In the center was the very spot that would be illuminated by the oculus had the dome been functional. The inner ring was meditating, their hands bleeding. The blood slowly evaporated up into the air. The outer ring was only chanting.

Satia looked above into the clouds. They were veering in the direction of Relien. *Maybe that's the reason for the rain of blood in the woods.*

"May I ask what they are doing?" she turned to the gatekeeper.

"You may not."

Satia pulled Udall closer. "See the clouds? Just like the rain of blood in Relien."

He nodded, then paused, making sure that no one else was listening. "That was a cleansing ritual. Some people think that draining some of their blood helps them enter a deeper state of meditation and connect with their mana. The inner ring meditates as normal while their blood is drained. The outer ring serves only one purpose; they make the blood evaporate."

Satia looked at him. "I didn't think you would know all that. Thank you for sharing."

"I had a good teacher," Udall said, smiling.

The gatekeeper led them through a string of alleyways and corridors. Most were filled with people bantering and children fooling around. There were also alleyways stuffed with goods, narrow and packed.

"Are you not scared of thieves?" Satia asked.

"Only one such person here." The gatekeeper frowned.

They entered an open area with a taller, bulkier hut which had a chimney spitting dense clouds of smoke. The gatekeeper insisted that they wait. He entered, and after a brief moment, he appeared from the darkness. "Only one person can enter. The other waits."

Satia looked at Udall. He nodded with an indifferent look.

When Satia entered the hut, the ambience inside gave her a familiar feeling. It reminded her of the suffocating workshop she had in Relien. It, too, had heavy air, very little space, and a musky smell.

The warlord was sitting inside. He had a tiny stature, resembling a child. The pipe in his mouth was short and ornamented. His robes were handmade from the skins of various animals. They looked elegant and expensive, but they didn't bear the same royal significance as the robes in Relien. Here, the robes were a mark, a symbol of being a true warrior.

Satia wondered why the gatekeeper would allow her a private meeting with the warlord, but she already knew. The warlord had enough mana to obliterate more than a dozen men. He wasn't as strong as Kyle, but he was intimidating still. She could sense his might.

"You've come to take Sumin," he said.

"Yes, I need his help, my lord," Satia confessed.

"The pest had me itching to get rid of him for quite some time. Your arrival must be a sign that my prayers to the Celestial King have been answered."

"Honestly, I hope that's not the case," Satia said. She heard stories of the Celestial King being all-knowing, but lately, she didn't hear of anyone being punished, and she preferred it stayed that way. She didn't want to tempt fate.

The warlord chuckled. "So why do you need a miserable vermin without honor? You do know Sumin is like that?"

"I must confess that my mission is very difficult. I don't think a lot of people would want to join me."

"Well, don't count on Sumin. He will abandon you at the first sight of danger."

"I understand," Satia agreed. She didn't need the warning as she knew who she was dealing with.

"Well, you are free to take him. Just circle around to the right. You'll stumble upon a devastated shed. That's his dwelling."

"You have my gratitude, my lord." Satia bowed.

The warlord nodded and continued smoking his pipe.

Satia left and returned to Udall. They followed the warlord's directions and found a shed with a sunken roof. Flies were drawn to it by the heavy stench coming from the inside. Their buzzing infuriated Udall.

"Don't look at me," he said. "I'm not going inside. I hate bugs."

Satia frowned. She went around to the back of the hut.

On the grass was a man on his knees, his head on the ground. His tattered tunic was squalid and tattered. The man turned around at the sound of Satia's footsteps. She saw his lifeless face, ghastly eyes, and dry skin. His forehead was burning up with a fever. The moment she looked him in the eyes, she knew that this was not the man she once journeyed with. This was a man whose deeds angered the Celestial King and earned him a very special Blessing—a Gift of Misfortune.

CHAPTER 47

THE GUARDS LUGGED Kyle back to his cell, his legs dragging on the floor. He lifted his head. It was throbbing with intense pain. He knew he should have come quietly, but he couldn't fight the urge to disobey the guards. He even tried to steal one of their swords, but he was in no position to fight one swordsman, let alone three.

The last rays of the sun were joyfully illuminating the corridor, peeking in through the cracks and gaps in the wooden ceiling. But before they made it to the wooden door at the end, the sun was gone, consumed by the clouds.

The wooden door squealed, and the guards hurled Kyle onto the floor. The sudden descent was painful, his ribs still aching. Yet, it sharpened his mind. He was fully awake now. He stood up without much trouble. It made him feel confident that he was slowly regaining his strength, but he still felt weak.

"Show respect to the warden," one of the guards said as he shoved Kyle in the back.

He groaned, looking around the room.

There was a bulky desk full of scrolls with a woman seated behind it. She dipped the tip of her feather in the ink, then continued to write. She looked at Kyle from underneath her tiny glasses and turned to the scroll again. The sleeves of her plain white shirt were rolled up, revealing numerous tattoos. Her hair was wrapped in a plain orange bandana. She had a dark complexion, and her large, beautiful eyes were blue.

"Today is your day," she declared.

"Who are you?" Kyle asked.

"You don't need to know my name." She cleared her throat. "Know me as the warden."

Kyle frowned. "Where am I?"

"Doesn't really matter, does it? What is important is why you are here." She fixed her glasses.

"Spare me the trickery, and end my life if that's what you want. If not, get to the point." Kyle spat on the floor. He noticed an old wooden chest in the back. His armor and belongings were on top of it.

"I doubt you've got a sense of duty, but I'll explain it to you. Narilan needs mana. Even if a successor is chosen, we were told that the more mana we gather, the better. Your only purpose here is to be a donor." The warden relaxed in her chair.

"So you work for Dorrell? He's gathered quite a group of people. A few guards, a priestess, and you. I wonder if he forced you to work for him, or if you all politely agreed."

The warden remained silent. "That's Preceptor Sahne to you, scum." Her words were cold and serious. She didn't let her emotions get the best of her. It was probably the reason she was in charge.

The warden didn't deny Kyle's statement, which made him realize that he was right. He was here because Dorrell wanted him to be.

Kyle forced a bitter frown. "Anyway, tough luck. I can't use my mana."

"Would you like me to tell you why?"

The warden smirked, and it irritated Kyle. He gnashed his teeth. Just looking at her, he knew the implications of her question. *It's this place. It must be.*

"You've heard of the domes and the caves, right?" The warden took off her glasses and rubbed her eyes. "Just like all those places, this is a ritual ground. It saps the mana of all of us. The good news is that it works mostly on the strong… the very, very strong."

Kyle's hand quivered. The thought that his life went full circle, that he ended up in the very place he wanted to escape, infuriated him. He had trouble holding on to his anger. "So useless thugs, such as yourself, are not influenced?" He put on a bitter grin.

The warden snorted. "I'm glad you're in a good mood. Today is your first fight. I ask you to do everything in your power to entertain the Grand Court. Oh, and don't mention the ritual. They don't know about it."

A guard grabbed Kyle by the arm. Kyle wrestled out of his grip, and shoved his elbow into the guard's face. The guard groaned and retreated, his nose bleeding. As he attempted to draw his sword, the warden waved her hand.

When the guards finally managed to restrain Kyle, they pulled him back and out of the door.

"Don't worry," the warden called out. "You won't die, but you might lose another limb or two."

The warden reminded Kyle of his tormentor from the cave. Yet she didn't scare him.

His tormentor had this blank stare. He didn't care about anything. He wasn't angry or happy. There was a profound emptiness within him as if he was merely a living corpse. He didn't care if Kyle lived or died. Facing someone like that was frightening as Kyle could never predict what would happen. That uncertainty, combined with despair, nearly destroyed Kyle, but it also made him stronger.

The warden didn't evoke any of those dreadful feelings.

◆

Kyle was sitting on a bench, cape covering his lost forearm. Sounds of a struggle came from the door beside him. He looked at the dull knife he was given, rust gathering on the handle.

From the other end of the hallway, Kyle heard heavy footsteps. A man trudged in his direction like a massive chunk of meat. The huge man had an axe for a weapon. He had a muscular stature and wore no armor. His bald head and thick beard gave him a savage look.

"How's life, young man?" the man asked. "They call me Ned."

Kyle looked at the axe Ned was holding.

"I only came here to see my opponent. I'm disappointed." Ned gave Kyle a pitiful look. "I was expecting a true warrior, and I get a half-broken man."

Kyle looked at the knife in his hand. The thought that he was being used by the kingdom made him sick. He felt powerless and defeated, chained by Narilan.

Ned took a seat next to Kyle. "I have only one rule that I follow to the letter. You've got to enjoy life every chance you get, as any moment you might die." He rested the bloody axe-head on the floor, holding the haft to keep the axe upright. "At least that's what I think every time I look at my axe," he chuckled.

Kyle grimaced. He pushed aside his cape, his only hand gripping the knife.

Ned's eyes wandered around the hallway. "Don't worry! It will be a quick death."

"Do you enjoy mindless killing that much?" Kyle asked, staring at the brute.

"Mindless killing? It's not like that. This place is important."

"Enlighten me."

"There are those of us who enjoy fighting, bloodshed. Narilan doesn't have much to offer to such people, but warriors come here." Ned scratched his beard.

Reave must know about this place, Kyle thought. *Instead of traveling, he could sate his hunger for fighting here. Maybe he couldn't find a worthy opponent.*

"We don't have a lot of spectators," Ned continued. "But members of the Grand Court do come to watch."

"Didn't think they would enjoy it." Kyle played with the knife in his hand. He heard of the Grand Court, the group of scholars that made decisions about everything that happened around Zardan. He wondered if they knew about Dorrell's plans. "Do the citizens of Zardan know about this place?" He turned to Ned.

"I don't think so, or maybe no one cares." Ned leaned back against the wall, heavily placing his hand on his knee.

"What about the ritual?"

"What ritual?" Ned glared at Kyle.

"Never mind." Kyle felt his breathing become strained as if the anger was overpowering him.

"You know there is something about fighting," Ned said with a serious expression. "Nothing beats seeing your opponent run in fear. I still remember my first fight."

Kyle was sick of Ned's yapping. His hand trembled.

"Anyway, there is this man," Ned continued. "A true freak, a disgusting creature, who sacrificed his body for power. No one has ever defeated him. When no one wanted to fight him, he swore that he'd use his mana to grant the victor's wish." He chortled.

Wish? Kyle thought.

"What is your name? I'd like to know the name of my victim."

"My name is Kyle."

"Kyle from?"

Kyle took a big breath of air.

As Ned looked away, Kyle sprung up with the knife in his hand and jammed it into Ned's throat. Blood poured out slowly. Ned reached for his axe, eyes wide open. Kyle pushed the knife in deeper. The axe slipped out of Ned's grip and dropped to the floor. He groaned, trying to shove Kyle back. All strength was now gone from Ned. Kyle twisted the knife, then ripped it out, blood spattered the wall. Again and again, he shoved the knife into Ned, the anger seething within. Blood sprayed Kyle's face. Ned collapsed on the bench, leaning against the wall. Kyle left the knife still intact, his breathing heavy and fast.

Kyle spat on the floor, leaving a trail of blood as he walked away.

"You were right," Kyle said. "Any second you could have died."

The sounds of battle on the other side of the door ceased. Guards surrounded Kyle, but he surrendered without a fight. He was tired and dizzy, but his anger was gone.

CHAPTER 48

SATIA KNEELED NEXT to Sumin, pitying him. He didn't pay much attention to her. He just kept staring blindly ahead. His will to live was gone, and in its place was despair. He looked like a living cadaver.

"We need your help," Satia said.

Sumin remained silent.

"Come on," Udall interrupted. "He's not going to come with us. It's obvious. Besides, I don't think he would be helpful in his current state."

Satia gave Udall an angry look. She was hoping to hear Sumin say one of his pesky remarks that she so vividly remembered. She could rehearse most of them in her head, and while they were nothing short of irritating, they seemed to have a peculiar effect on her. They would lighten up her mood, no matter the situation. She wished to hear them once more.

"I mean, look at him," Udall said. "He is a shell of a man."

Satia ignored Udall's complaints. She turned to Sumin. "We're on a mission. The future Celestial King assigned it to us."

"Going on a journey with you is pointless," Sumin uttered. "I will only be a burden. Your friend is right."

Satia frowned, but she wasn't going to give up. His response was disappointing, but she was happy he finally spoke. It felt like she made a connection. It was a glimmer of hope that stood against the despair that surrounded Sumin.

Satia drove away a large, nasty fly. "Pointless, you say? So is staying here, Sumin. Leaving could give you an opportunity."

A villager stopped by Sumin's hut and gave Satia a disgusted look. He spat on the doorsteps, then continued.

Satia looked at the tattoos on Sumin's arms and legs. They resembled shackles that wrapped around his limbs. They were a symbol of the Gift of Misfortune, which had many ways to take shape. Sometimes, it made disease destroy a person from the inside, but other times, it delivered more creative punishments. Satia once heard of a man whose whole family died, and he was left to languish in his solitude after every one of his friends left him.

"What did you do?" Satia asked.

"You saw the dome? That's my doing."

"What happened?"

"I tried to steal from the dome," Sumin confessed. "There was a fire. I fought some villagers." He took a deep breath. "I used mana, and I destroyed the dome. I was cursed on that day."

Satia paused. "I can try to help you. Maybe I can find something to make you better."

"I don't want your help," he said. "You should leave before you get cursed too."

"It's a waste of time trying to persuade him," Udall whispered behind Satia.

Sumin looked over his shoulder. "Listen to your friend. I'm serious."

"I don't understand you, Sumin." Satia frowned. "This could be your opportunity to get your life back."

"You don't think I tried, witch?" Sumin lashed out, but his powerful voice was stifled by his weak body. "I tried many times to make up for what I did. I'm tired of even trying anymore." He coughed, then sighed.

"So that's it?" Satia waited for an answer, but it never came. "You're done? You're just going to wait here until you die?"

"You don't know how it feels being cursed," Sumin whispered. "The suffering, the misfortune. There is not a day in my life that I don't regret my decisions."

Satia stood up, frowning. "It's all in the past now. There is no point in crying endlessly about what happened. Get up, let's go. You can make a difference." Seeing Sumin's depressed look evoked a sense of pity in Satia at first, but the only thing she felt now was frustration from hearing his pointless lament.

"I'm not going." Sumin shook his head.

There came a murmur from the street. People gathered to eavesdrop on their conversation. Some of them were curious, but most of them just wanted to see if Sumin would leave. Satia recognized their disdain. She remembered how the people of Kelien looked at her every time she used herbs. It was the very same bitter look.

"I'm disappointed. I took you for someone else." Satia brushed the dirt off, then walked away. "Let's go, Udall."

She remembered the old Sumin, a trickster without a care in the world. Back in the old days, Sumin was a man untainted by worry and with an undefeated spirit. Yet that man died some time ago. Satia felt upset that such a man was defeated. If a stubborn fool such as Sumin could be broken, Satia began wondering how she would handle the Gift of Misfortune.

Udall looked at Sumin for a moment. Satia saw the pity in Udall's eyes.

As they left, the crowd scattered. They decided to stay the night at the village. The next morning, they bought some fruits and a horse. Satia had no gold left after that.

Outside of the village, Satia asked, "Why are you so sad? I thought you didn't want to work with Sumin?"

"I didn't, but seeing him there made me feel miserable. The man gave up on life." Udall looked in the direction of the village.

A few villagers gathered at the gates to see Satia and Udall off. Their faces were disappointed that Sumin chose to stay.

"When we came here you said that he was like me. I still don't know what you meant."

Satia looked away. "At the time, I thought that he was brave just like you, but I was wrong." She turned to him with a smile. There was sadness in her eyes.

CHAPTER 49

THE WARDEN SAT behind the bulky desk. She had a vexed frown that she tried to hide, but couldn't. She finished writing on a few more scrolls, then took off her glasses. She rubbed her eyes, leaning back in her chair.

Kyle stood in the center of the room, the guards behind him. It was only his second time in the warden's office, but each time he had the chance to walk around, even with guards by his side. He now had a better idea of the layout of the entire location. Unlike his early impressions, he believed that this was a very small place. There was only a single corridor that led to the warden's office. The corridor had many doors, all of them shut. They must've been cells just like the one Kyle was kept in. There were also the guards' quarters, and a single, larger chamber, where all the screams and noise came from.

"What do you think you've done?" The warden stood up.

Kyle snickered. "Survived."

She slammed her fist into the desk. "You should be thankful. If it wasn't for the preceptor, I would have you killed on the spot."

"Everybody seems to listen to him. Why?" Kyle looked at the warden without any fear. "Why bow before the preceptor?" One of the guards shoved him in the back, sending him off balance. The hit was painful because of the injuries Kyle sustained. He let out a short groan, then straightened up.

The warden snorted. "I'm not bowing to anyone. I'm helping a cause. If it wasn't for the preceptor, we wouldn't be here. You wouldn't be here. You'd be dead."

Kyle stepped closer. "What is on the other side of the Dominant Veil that you are all so afraid of?"

The warden turned around. "I'll tell you the story of our savior. Take a seat."

Kyle grabbed a wooden chair.

"Unlike the caves, this place wasn't meant for gathering mana for the Celestial King. It started as a place for all sorts of warriors to gather and fight for gold. The Grand Court likes watching fights. They like it a lot." The warden bared her teeth in a fleeting smirk. "Then came Dorrell Sahne. He didn't want to use the people of Narilan any more than he was forced to, so he decided that he could use this place."

Kyle listened.

The warden called for a servant. "The preceptor came with a priestess. She turned this place into a ritual ground, which saps mana from the people inside. The preceptor then chose a champion that no one has ever defeated, and to attract participants, he spread a rumor of a prize. A wish will be granted to the victor. Of course, it's a lie." She smiled softly, but it wasn't a pretty smile. It was filled with malice and a tinge of pleasure at the pain others suffered fighting for a wish that would never come true.

"Anything else?" Kyle asked, unimpressed.

"If you lose, you stop fighting. You become a mana donor for life." She smiled, her teeth pure white.

Kyle sat, wondering about all the things going on in Narilan. He didn't know if it was like this all the time. As a child, he heard people talking about Narilan as the perfect kingdom without any problems. Yet, now all he saw was chaos. *Is it the fault of the dying Celestial King? Or is there something else going on?*

A servant appeared with a salver. It was filled with vegetables, fruits, and a large chicken. He left a bottle of white wine and a glass before leaving.

The warden opened the bottle and poured some wine. "The Grand Court wants a true spectacle. I know who you'll fight next." She looked at the guards, and they laughed.

Kyle gave the warden a long glare. His indifferent approach irritated her. He could see it in her, and it made him feel triumphant. So much so that he had to fight to conceal his mirth.

◆

Kyle was sitting in his room. He could hear the faint whispers of the wind outside. The pain was gone, and his strength was coming back. The anger that clouded his mind was under his control. He took a few deep breaths, then entered a state of meditation.

For a moment, he was thankful that Avril had left him. He was content, thinking that she found her way in life, and she didn't have to suffer in Zardan just as he did.

Then he emptied his mind of all unnecessary thoughts, and his heart slowed down. He felt his whole body become heavy, and then it felt as if something pulled him downward. His mind was clear, and he felt in tune with the world around him. A stream of energy flooded his whole body.

He opened his eyes. He didn't know if he should try to use his mana.

He wondered if there was a Spectator around and who it might be.

They must have one, he thought. *It would be wise to refrain from using mana until I know who it is... unless I'm forced to.*

Kyle stood up, then stretched. He took a seat on his bunk and sighed.

What does becoming the Celestial King really mean? he wondered. All this time, he wanted to become the ruler of Narilan in order to keep his promise, as well as to escape. Witnessing the world outside the Dominant Veil was exactly that—a means to forget about the cave, and at last, have the past put to rest. He didn't want to believe Ellia when she told him that there was something hostile on the other side of the Veil. *It might very well be that Narilan is the only world for us,* her words echoed in his mind, making him frown bitterly. His desires were questioned many times before. Many tried to dissuade him. Yet in this moment, he didn't know what to think anymore.

He wondered what it would be like to be the Celestial King. *It might be something very different than what I'm expecting. It might be a struggle. It might be a lie.* Yet all his thoughts, no matter how depressing, didn't discourage him. Even if he decided to turn back, he couldn't. He came all this way, and there was nothing left for him to do. Then, he made a promise to himself. Whatever awaited him at the top of the Great Tower, he would face it head on.

I will take pleasure in killing Reave.

I will slaughter anything that stands in my way.

I will become the Celestial King.

CHAPTER 50

DORRELL STOOD BEFORE the Grand Court. The scholars hid their faces behind various masks, as always. He was summoned suddenly and forced to wait as the scholars spoke among themselves in whispers. They gave Dorrell long, patronizing stares, which made him uncomfortable.

I'm prepared for whatever comes next, he thought.

Dorrell knew that they made him wait on purpose. It was all to make him uneasy. They watched his every move, waiting for him to make a mistake.

"Gentlemen, I would like to know why I was summoned," Dorrell said, mustering enough courage.

"How is your mission coming along?" a headstrong voice asked.

"I am attending to all my duties, if that's what you want to know," Dorrell said, but his answer sounded more like a provocation. He regretted not choosing his words with more care.

"We demand to know if you have picked a successor," a panic-filled voice echoed through the chamber.

Dorrell paused. He could see just how anxious the members of the Grand Court really were. Most of them were silent, but some couldn't hold back their panic.

"The people live in fear. The disease in the water, the unnatural weather patterns, what do you think you're doing?" a tedious voice called out.

Dorrell fell silent, but not because he didn't know what to say. He just realized that the scholars were slowly losing their bearing, and it would be very hard to satisfy them. There was only one thing he could say.

"Speak," a different, deeper voice demanded.

"I have chosen a successor," Dorrell announced. It was a lie, but it came easy, which made him think that his brother was probably right. Maybe he just needed more practice.

"Who have you chosen?" the headstrong voice asked.

"His name is... Graeme," Dorrell said, recalling the name of the only donor he could remember.

"Do you think he will be strong enough to bear the weight of the kingdom?" the panic-filled voice asked.

Dorrell hesitated. He reminded himself that with the other donors, anyone could become the Celestial King. "Yes, he is strong enough. He's the best candidate. Unlike many, he's noble and kind." Dorrell realized that, in fact, Graeme wasn't a bad choice. With some work, he could mold him into a benevolent, obedient ruler.

The scholars whispered among themselves again.

Dorrell hated the Grand Court. More and more, he

could see them as a group that only talked and gave out commands. To him, the Grand Court was useless. The scholars criticized him and pushed him around, but they didn't do anything for Narilan. They depended on Dorrell to do all the dirty work. However, he refrained from voicing his thoughts. The last thing he needed was a quarrel with the Grand Court.

"We approve," the voices said in unison, then the chamber fell silent.

"So," the headstrong voice said slowly, "when do you intent to crown Graeme?"

"The Celestial King's birthday is coming up in five days," Dorrell said.

"He'll be a century old," a soft voice added.

"Yes," Dorrell agreed. "If you approve, I'd like to wait five more days. After that, Graeme will ascend the throne."

"I believe that we were very lenient with you, preceptor," the headstrong voice said. "I don't have anything against waiting as long as there is no imminent danger to Narilan. If you can promise me that, I think I can speak for the rest of my colleagues when I say that we can wait."

Dorrell looked down. He felt belittled asking them for permission. He believed that they owed the current Celestial King respect for all the years of peace and stability. Yet, these men felt no such thing. If Dorrell wasn't around, they would throw the current Celestial King into a ditch and crown someone else in order to save themselves. After a long pause, Dorrell looked up. "I promise you that," he declared.

"You have five more days, and after that, a new Celestial King will be crowned. But make no mistake, we make this exception not for you, but in reverence of the King."

The other voices nodded at the announcement.

"May I leave?" Dorrell asked.

"There is another matter," a deep voice said. "I think I'll speak for everyone else. Is there something amiss?"

Dorrell kept eye contact with the man behind the voice. "Explain."

"There are problems whenever a new Celestial King is chosen, but this time, things have been particularly turbulent. Is something wrong?"

"No, there are no problems." It was the second time Dorrell had to lie. He felt uncomfortable and didn't know how much longer he could keep going. "The only issue is that finding someone strong enough is problematic. I don't suppose you would want someone like Kyle at the helm of Narilan?"

The deep voice didn't reply.

As Dorrell walked away, he could feel their suspicious glares and hear their whispers. They never trusted him.

And he never trusted them. A growing part of him wanted the Grand Court gone.

Dorrell returned to the Great Tower. He took the stairs this time. It was something he only did when he needed to clear his mind. There was something about movement that helped him cope with all his problems. The only issue was Dorrell's lack of stamina. After only two floors up the enormous staircase, he was gasping for air and had to take the elevator.

He remembered the meeting with the Grand Court. The only thing that kept him in control was the idea that his scheme was working. It was in place, and it already

saved Narilan. Without it, he knew there would be consequences. He found it ironic that the very thing that he tried
to avoid saved him.

When Dorrell reached his chamber, he fell onto his
bed. He looked at the ceiling and sighed.

Albert came over, pushing a cart with fruits and vegetables. "How was the meeting, young lad?"

Dorrell grabbed a vine of grapes. "I had to lie... twice."

"Don't make that face, as if this was the end. This is
merely the beginning."

Dorrell put his hand under his head. "I never thanked
you for being by my side all these years."

"Hearing you say that makes me consider your well-
being." Albert took a seat in the corner.

"I'm just not like my brother. I get too attached, and I
think too much about the things that are going on."

Albert rubbed his eyes. "The world needs people like
you. The mistakes of weak men sometimes craft great men.
The mistakes of great men sometimes craft broken souls.
That's what the Celestial King said to me on the fifth day
after he was crowned."

Dorrell nodded, eating a grape. "I looked through all
the books. Yet, I can't seem to find any details about how
the throne was created. All I find are stories. I wanted to
know if it's still working as it should."

"You're worried that it's weakening?" Albert asked.

"I keep hearing people complain about how tough
these times are. I know it's always been like that, but still."
Dorrell paused. "Do you think it was a good idea, imple-
menting our plan?"

"Now that's just self-doubt speaking through you,"
Albert said, crossing his arms. "I think we've made the

best decisions we could. If you could speak with the Celestial King, he would tell you the same thing."

There came a knock on the door. The door groaned and Reave appeared. He strolled inside, took an orange, and then jumped into a chair. "Looks like things are slowly returning to normal."

"See?" Albert looked at Dorrell.

"What's going on?" Reave asked.

Albert unbuttoned his vest at the neck. "Your brother is doubting himself. He just had a meeting with the Grand Court."

Reave frowned. "The Grand Court does nothing. They celebrate, watch fights, and eat. If it were my decision, they wouldn't exist."

Dorrell considered Reave's words. He wanted the Grand Court gone. Yet, he realized what that turned him into. He would be no different than Kyle or Locklair, a savage that would do anything to secure power.

Dorrell felt something pull on his leg. He tried to sit up, but he slipped and landed on the floor. He saw Reave standing over him. "What are you doing?" Dorrell roared.

"Stop feeling sorry for yourself." Reave took a seat on the bed. "You already made your decision, now you just have to continue. It's easy. You don't see me crying about my eye."

"Maybe you should," Dorrell said, standing up.

Reave shrugged. "What is that supposed to mean?"

"Calm down, both of you," Albert interrupted. "I agree with Reave. There is nothing to think about. All we have to do is continue."

Dorrell shook his head. "I'm not doubting myself. I just feel the pressure. It's almost like I'm hiding something. I feel like a thief or a thug. I'm just tired of that." His confession was honest. He knew he didn't have to hide anything from Reave and Albert. "Today I had to lie to the Grand Court. I took an oath that I would tell nothing but the truth. I broke it, that's why I'm…"

"Just get used to it." Reave shrugged.

Albert kept quiet, listening.

Dorrell looked at both of them. Their presence seemed to help him slightly. Up until now, he knew that he helped a lot of people. Yet, the doubt was there. It would always be there like an abandoned part of his character that he'd like to forget. He was fine with that, but he didn't know how to handle a broken oath.

He took a seat, tense. The broken oath was his own problem, a burden that he had to bear for the rest of his life. It was something he had to deal with alone.

If they want to question me, let them. I will do what I think is right, even if the Grand Court is against me. I will care for Narilan every day of my life. That's what a preceptor should do. That's what I'll do. He tried to justify his actions to himself. It helped, but not very much.

"Thanks, brother." Dorrell faked a smile. "I needed that. I don't need pity. What I need is someone to listen. Despite your unconcerned nature, you listen." He bowed his head, and Reave frowned. "Now get off my bed." He shoved Reave off. The white sheets were all dirty.

"I had a bit of a scuffle outside," Reave said.

Dorrell frowned. His brother was a nuisance sometimes, but he felt good having him by his side.

Chapter 51

SATIA DISMOUNTED HER horse and crossed the bridge, the bulky water mill murmuring by the riverbank. The water was clear, the fish joyfully swam around. The villagers nodded as she entered Aylmar, a southern town on the outer reaches of Narilan. With wooded fortifications only slightly taller than an adult man, the town wasn't impressive. Even the castle looked quite humble when compared to the likes of Castle Relien. It was as if the place was built with temperance in mind, and in some ways, it appealed to Satia.

She turned to look back. Udall stopped to talk with a guard. Their chatter continued for some time before Udall joined her.

"The tavern is to the left," Udall said, and Satia nodded. "So how do you intended to convince anyone to work for us without any gold?"

"I'll leave that to you." Satia patted Udall on the back.

He didn't reply.

They left their horses in the stable and continued. The tavern had no name and no sign. It reeked of fish and the only thing that alleviated the stench was the soft aroma of mead. The dirty, wooden floor creaked with every step. The only young lass dashed around, taking orders and delivering food. There was discordant music coming from the corner as a group of amateur bards tried to string together notes.

Satia noticed a group of five warriors, their weapons placed on the floor at their feet. Their loud banter echoed through the tavern. All of the warriors wore animal skin, although one of them had some metal around his arm too. The loudest one of the warriors had a round helmet with a single horn in the front.

Satia motioned to Udall, and they came to the table.

The loudest warrior stilled and stared at Udall, then at Satia. "What do you want?" He scratched the scar that ran across his left cheek.

"We were looking to hire some warriors," Udall said, placing a sack on the table that clinked like coins.

The man lifted it, shook it, and then laughed. "If you need our help, you have to bring more." He tossed the offering back on the table.

Satia looked at Udall with suspicion. They had no gold, so she wondered what was in the sack.

Udall watched the warriors. "I'll triple that," he said, sliding his offer back across the table. "You keep it."

"Chief, take the job," a warrior with a very dirty face said to the loudest one of the group, who appeared to be the leader.

Then the warriors fell silent.

"What would you need us to do?" the chief finally asked.

"All you need to know right now is that there will be fighting involved." Udall pulled a young lass aside and ordered some ale.

"That's not how it works," the chief grumbled.

Udall paused, and Satia sprung forward. Before she could say anything, he looked at her and shook his head. She decided not to intervene and retreated.

"Really?" Udall asked the chief. "What I see here are men looking for a challenge. When was the last time someone promised you a real battle?"

All the warriors fell silent.

"Sure, you can wander the woods in search of a wild wolf or a bear," Udall continued. "But where is the fun in that? We are confronting a real danger. Are you coming or not?"

Satia smiled. She knew Udall could handle it. He knew such men—warriors, savages. He knew their priorities and their desires. He was one of them in the past, but now, he was just an exhausted human who wanted to put his past behind him. Yet, that past was the sole reason he knew what to say to the warriors to spark their enthusiasm. Satia was glad to have Udall by her side.

The warriors leaned forward until their faces almost met in the center of the table. They whispered and nodded.

"Fine," the warriors said together.

"You can call me Chief," said the loudest warrior. "So where are we going?"

"Do what you were hired to do," Udall said. "We leave at sunrise."

The young lass brought Udall a mug of ale. He gulped it down before leaving with Satia.

"I'm impressed. You might not be a true warrior anymore, but you still know how to talk with brutes." Satia pretended to applaud him with a smile.

Udall frowned. "I just did what I had to. I want to return to my family as soon as possible. These men are as good as any other."

Satia put her finger to her lips. "I'm wondering how you intend to pay them when their mission is complete."

Udall hesitated with a worried look, his cheeks red. He wrapped a piece of cloth around his face. "Maybe I won't have to if our opponent is as vicious as you say. I'm just hoping they don't find out the sack had fake gold that I created with my mana."

Satia looked at Udall with a nostalgic smile. When she first spoke with him, he was a completely different person. He abandoned and forgot his nature as a fighter, but now, she saw that glimmer in his eyes. It was the will to struggle, fight, and survive anything that the world threw at him. Udall, her Udall, had returned.

◆

They traveled southwest from Aylmar to a hilly region that neighbored the Tranquil Meadows. The hills were bare, with only small patches of dry grass. They were, however, peppered with rocks and weeds.

On the first night, Satia nervously adjusted the ring Kyle gave her. She wanted to know if he succeeded. Yet, there were no signs that a Celestial King was crowned, so she knew that much. The thought that Kyle could fail made her feel a strong sense of disappointment.

Surely he must've succeeded, she thought.

The warriors gathered wood and made a fire. Then they bantered and cheered. One of them turned out to be a cook. He made a spiced stew. It was edible, but the taste was too strong.

Satia was tired. She rested on the ground with her pouch under her head. Udall was by her side, sitting by the fire.

"One of us should be up at all times," Satia whispered to him. "Wake me up when you feel tired."

◆

Satia pulled up the blanket over herself. The mornings were cold. Three days have passed since they arrived, and nothing was happening. She sat up, tossed her hair back, and eyed the warriors. They were talking among themselves, whispering. The fire was smoldering, leaving a thin cloud of smoke that nearly tore the sky in two. She searched for Udall and noticed him come up one of the hills. He was looking at the Veil.

Satia took a scroll out of her bag. She unrolled it and started writing her thoughts down. The scroll was one of many. She must have left hundreds of them back in Relien. Each day, she would write down what happened— as well as her unplanned adventures and her wild ideas. She hadn't done so in a while, which made her feel awkward.

Udall returned, and took a seat close to her.

The chief came up to Udall, "My men are getting impatient. They're bored."

"Well, go hunting for some wild boars," Satia said. She was never tolerant of those who were impatient.

The chief frowned. "Tell your mistress that she should keep her mouth shut."

Satia and Udall looked at each other. Satia had a faint smile, restraining her urge to retaliate by saying something nasty. Udall had a silly grimace as if he ate something sour.

"Look," Udall said. "It's only a matter of time. Please tell your men to be patient."

"Maybe we should just kill you and take the rest of the gold." The chief put his hand on the pommel of his sword.

"You can try." Udall crossed his arms. "But you will find nothing. You can search my bag if it makes you happy." He tossed his bag at the chief's feet.

The chief stamped on the bag, then unsheathed his blade. "You promised us gold. What did you do with it? Speak."

The other warriors were drawn to the commotion and watched the scene.

"You didn't think I'll be carrying around so much gold with me, did you?" Udall smiled.

The chief gnashed his teeth.

"Calm down," Udall said. "It's gone... for now. I told you, you'll get much more, and you will... when the time comes. So how about it? Tell your men to relax and wait a little longer."

The chief swallowed. His grip relaxed. He nodded with a serious expression, then walked back to his men.

CHAPTER 52

KYLE WAS PLAYING with the knife in his hand. Ned's blood stained the blade. His hand was cold and unsteady. He wondered how he would fight if a knife was all he had to defend himself. He was curious who his opponent would be. Seated in the same spot where he killed Ned, he listened to the sounds of battle slowly fading.

Kyle was unprepared. Yet he did everything he could to get ready. He practiced fighting with his left hand every single night. Even though fighting with it became more natural and the movements easier, the thought that he would never be on par with his former self rattled him. He felt weaker every time he thought about his lost arm, and rightly so. He was weaker, and he had no doubt about it.

He thought about the *monster* that the guards were talking about. The thought of fighting a mindless and powerful creature frightened many, but Kyle wasn't one of them. More so, he hoped he would fight a monster. He knew he would stand no chance against someone skilled in swordsmanship, but fighting a monster was a different story. Monsters were mindless, and that was a weakness that he could exploit.

Kyle took a deep breath, the metal gate grating behind him. He stood up, fixed his mantle, and entered. The intense light blinded him. He put his hand up, but it didn't help. When his eyes adjusted, the first thing he saw was a tired, unassuming man.

The man stood in the center with a bare chest. His body was covered in bruises, many about the size of a fist. His unbound hair—disheveled and dirty—fell over his long, narrow face. He looked as if he was in a trance. His eyes were open, but he seemed blind to the outside as if daydreaming, as he vacantly chewed on some willow bark. He was loosely griping a bizarre weapon that resembled an oversized axe; it was a thick and large elephant tusk fastened to a big piece of wood.

This isn't a monster, Kyle thought, then took a step forward. He was careful and patient as his heart started to beat chaotically.

The floor was covered with white alabaster tiles, the ridges between them stained in red. There were guards around, but they hid behind the metal gates. The oculus above reminded Kyle of the many heavenly grounds he visited. Yet, this oculus was much smaller, and the light felt artificial. It wasn't sunlight. Kyle was certain of that.

Up above, there was a balcony. The masked people above laughed and gossiped, surrounded by food. Seeing their masks, Kyle knew they were members of the Grand

Court. The priestess that nursed him back to health was there as well, and so was the warden. They were seated away from the Grand Court in a little alcove.

The Grand Court is here, Kyle thought. *I wonder if Reave and Dorrell are around too.*

Trumpets blared. Kyle's name was called out, and his opponent was introduced as Corbit.

Corbit spat out the willow bark then lifted his hand as if pointing at Kyle. The skin withdrew from his arm before drooping down. His bare bones were drenched in bodily fluids. He snapped his fingers and one of his bones whizzed through the air.

Kyle swung his sword and the bone bounced off, vanishing somewhere on the white tile floor.

How? Kyle thought. *Is he using mana on his own body? He must be.* Kyle heard of many bizarre feats with mana, but to him, this was unimaginable. When he faced the recluse who controlled the creatures in Mount Nakroh, he thought that he had seen everything. He was mistaken.

Corbit rested his skeletal hand on the floor, putting his other hand behind his back. The floor trembled, and the tiles cracked. The ground burst open to reveal a small fissure. Kyle evaded as a skeletal arm rapidly sprung out of the ground before vanishing underneath.

"Is that it?" Kyle asked, then smirked.

The ground quivered. Kyle waited, firmly gripping his sword. When the tremors redoubled, he sidestepped. The skeletal arm reappeared, and with a swift kick, he shattered it into pieces. The bones, like pebbles, danced on the ground.

Corbit grimaced, then stood up. His skeletal hand was whole once again. "Why are you not using mana?" he asked in a fragile, sleepy voice.

Kyle frowned. "I figured there is a Spectator nearby."

"Everyone is here for a show. As long as you don't escape, there are no rules. If you have mana, knock yourself out." Corbit revealed the hand he hid behind his back, the skin sagging and the bones gone.

Kyle lengthened the knife until it was sword-length, and reshaped the handle into a hilt that felt comfortable in his hand. He wanted to ask Corbit who the Spectator was, but he couldn't with all the people watching. "I've never seen anything like it. Your power is astonishing."

Corbit nodded, but there was no pride on his face. "I've heard of you," he said, removing a fresh piece of willow bark from his pocket and putting it in his mouth. "Stories say that you're the strongest. You were aiming to become the Celestial King."

"Where did you learn to do this?" Kyle insisted. "Is it painful?"

Corbit came closer and hesitated, looking at the balcony. "I didn't learn it. I'm forced to use it every single day. I earned myself the Gift of Misfortune. And you have no idea how painful it is."

Kyle shrugged. "So? How is it you're still alive?"

"My transformation can't kill me. I'm here to suffer. That's what the Celestial King wanted."

Someone from the balcony hurled an apple. "Fight!"

"You must have done something terrible, killed a few people dear to the Celestial King maybe?" Kyle asked, but Corbit didn't answer.

A few more people expressed their discontent with the lack of fighting.

Corbit turned around. "Don't disappoint me," he whispered.

Kyle readied his sword. Corbit spun, swinging his bizarre axe with immense speed. Kyle evaded as the axe clashed against the floor, sending a subtle quake as the tiles cracked around.

Kyle attacked swiftly, but Corbit lifted the handle of his axe and hid behind it. His sword sunk into the wood. His attack was weak and lacked finesse. It was clumsy and naive. Corbit tightened his grip, the axe-head resting on the floor, then used all his strength to move it. The axe-head grated as it slid along. Corbit lifted the axe and made a wide swing. Kyle retreated, nearly tripping, and waited for the attack to conclude. The momentum of the attack pulled Corbit's body with the axe. As the axe landed on the floor with a heavy thud, Corbit's back was wide open, and Kyle didn't waste this opportunity. He leaped in with an attack.

Kyle's movements were delayed and clumsy. As he swung, he felt something pierce his thigh. He screamed as his attack was interrupted. His knees hit the floor, sword sunk in the ground between a few cracked tiles. A bone whizzed, and Kyle was forced to fall on his back to evade. He saw what looked like a bone fragment drenched in blood on the floor close by. The bone had been reshaped into something resembling an arrowhead.

Kyle gnashed his teeth. He disliked being forced to his knees. Long ago, he promised himself that he wouldn't bow to anyone, that he wouldn't be defeated. Yet, he was forced to bow—to crawl like a worm. The thought disgusted him.

Corbit stood over him, lifted his axe, and obscured the light with the axe-head—the large tusk. His hands quivered, blood dripping from his eyes.

There was no way Kyle could block the attack. He could try to crawl away, but he was too slow. *The thin layer of stone will not hold,* he thought after using mana to form a barrier.

I won't die here, Kyle thought, watching the axe.

The wooden handle creaked as the axe plummeted down.

CHAPTER 53

THE ATTACK WAS quick, despite the weight of the axe. It crashed into the stone barrier around Kyle, cracking and piercing it. His scream echoed through the chamber. The people cheered, and soon, their mirth turned into a joyful applause.

Kyle sat in the darkness, his heart pounding. Blood trickled from his shoulder. The pain was as vibrant as ever. Fragments of stone gathered in front of him. He molded them into a sphere, a fist, and then a hand. He imagined a forearm, and then it connected with his right elbow. He made a fist and grabbed his sword. The hand of stone felt natural, just like the right hand he lost always did.

Kyle was sick of playing. He wanted to finish this quickly. He observed that Corbit was strong, but his reactions were late. That could be his downfall.

Corbit pulled out the axe, the tusk dripping in blood.

Then he peeked through the gap that he made with his attack.

Kyle pressed his hand against the stone barrier that enveloped him. It burst into a cloud of dust, covering the entire chamber. The dust was soft—white.

Corbit didn't react.

Kyle sprung forward. His attack was quick. Corbit put out his skeletal hand and blocked. The sword hit the bone, and then slid across his arm, cutting through the flesh wrapped around his waist. A big piece of skin fell to the floor, blood dripping from bone.

Corbit groaned. He made spikes emerge from the floor, but Kyle easily evaded. A few bones whizzed through the air.

Kyle was hit again, the pain fierce. He ignored it, putting all his anger into his next attack. He crashed his sword into Corbit's forearm with all his might. The attack was fast and decisive. The impact sent a crack through the bone. Corbit reached for Kyle's chest with his other skeletal hand, but Kyle imagined a knife and blocked with his left hand.

The two were at a standstill.

Kyle panted. He knew he couldn't hold for much longer. He was still weak from his previous injuries, and Corbit was particularly resilient. The dizziness started to kick in.

Corbit carefully noticed his opponent growing weary. As he was about to make a move, Kyle took the opportunity to headbutt him, breaking Corbit's nose and sending him into a dazed state. In a wild coughing fit, Corbit spat out the willow bark, blood gushing down his mouth and chin. Kyle shoved him back with a kick, then imagined a second sword in his left hand. He sprung forward, lifted both swords high into the air, and brought them down hard.

In that moment, Corbit shed his skin. It slithered off his bones to reveal his scratched skull, his lidless eyes, his bare skeleton, as big flaps of loose skin gathered around his waist, organs crammed within them. It all happened in an instant just before Kyle's swords struck his shoulder.

Astonished, Kyle didn't stop. It was all he had left. He was almost at his limit. The dizziness began overpowering him as the headache started. He spun, blades parallel, his attack aimed at Corbit's spine.

Corbit tried to block, but his reaction time was impaired by the pain. Aghast, he groaned as the blades tore through his spine, sending vertebrae across the tile floor. His posture crumbled, and his torso scattered across the floor. His lower half held together, but dropped down as well.

The audience fell silent.

Kyle pulled out the bones that were jammed into his flesh. He was about to throw the last one to the floor when he felt a faint vibration coming from it.

Kyle realized what it meant, but he didn't want to believe it. His headache redoubled, sending a powerful echo through his mind.

The bones scattered everywhere and were magnetized to Corbit's bloody half-corpse. They gathered into a pile, and slowly reassembled into a skeleton. The skin crept up the bones until it covered his entire body, except for a single arm.

Corbit lay on his back. There was blood in his eyes, and it was dripping from the corners of his mouth too. "Would you..." His eyes wandered downwards.

Kyle cautiously walked over. He knelt and removed a piece of willow bark from Corbit's pocket. He then placed it in his mouth.

"Your wish?" Corbit wheezed. "A lie. Nothing more. But... thank you for not disappointing me."

Kyle frowned. He knew there was no reward for winning. He was cautious about approaching his opponent for fear of falling into a trap, but upon looking at Corbit, it was obvious the man was defeated. Kyle kneeled by his side. "You said there is a Spectator here. Who is it?"

"The guard..." Corbit's breathing was slow and weak.

"Which guard? Tell me."

"Mustache," Corbit whispered, closing his eyes. His body relaxed. His heart stopped beating. His pain was no more, and his torment was over.

Kyle stood up, gazing at the balcony. The people gaped at the death of the champion. The gate behind him opened with a groan. He turned and walked back at a steady pace, leaving his swords behind. His arm fragmented into dust. The guards were waiting for him, ready to fight, surprised and frightened.

The whole way back to his cell, Kyle was struggling to restrain his laughter and the disgusting smirk creeping up his face. He even forgot about the dizziness.

◆

Kyle rested in his cell. He watched the guards each day, waiting for the perfect moment to attack. He wanted the guard with the mustache to be alone, but he was almost always accompanied by another guard at the table.

Then one day, he awoke to the sounds of trumpets and cheers. There was a huge celebration outside. The priestess was gone, and so were most of the guards. When the guard with the mustache was alone, Kyle called out.

The guard made his way from the end of the hall. Before he could make it past the halfway point, a sword emerged from the wall, beheading him.

Kyle unlocked the door with his mana and walked outside. He dragged the body into his cell, cleaning up the trail of blood and any signs that something happened. He sneaked into the warden's office to reclaim his belongings. Putting on the ring from Avril made him smile. He returned to his room and looked at the tiny window above. The wall murmured and opened like a secret passage. Steps formed leading up into the sunlight.

Kyle smiled. He was finally free.

He strode into the light.

CHAPTER 54

REAVE RETURNED TO the Great Tower. The cheers and screams of joy died as the doors closed behind him. The mirth that was in the air was foreign to him. He could understand it, of course, but he couldn't identify with it. It felt as if it was out of reach, as if he was unable to feel it. He sighed.

He stopped in front of the door to Dorrell's chamber. The door was ajar, and he could see inside. It was dark. He heard Cwen preaching and helping Dorrell with a speech. Reave thought it was needless as his brother was skilled enough at public speaking. He didn't want to be considered a spy, so he knocked.

"What is it, brother?" Dorrell asked.

Reave entered. "Is your speech finished?" There were only two chairs in the room—both occupied—so he leaned against the wall.

Dorrell stretched. He looked tired. "Just a few more final touches."

Cwen sat in a chair in the corner with her legs up. She was perusing the text written by Dorrell. She looked tense, eyes nervously running across the page.

"Is there something you need?" Dorrell turned to Reave.

Reave hesitated. Even though Dorrell told him the night before that Cwen knew of their plan and wouldn't interfere, when it came time to speak openly about it, he hesitated. "It's finished," he declared. "Our kingdom is again in a state of stability."

"It's good," Cwen interrupted, handing Dorrell the speech. "It's better now. Before it was too pompous, and now you just convey your dedication and sacrifice."

Dorrell nodded. "I'd like to see the Celestial King once more before I go." He went to the door.

Reave grabbed Dorrell by the arm before he could leave. "Do you really trust her?"

Dorrell shook his head. "I have no reason not to. Now would you let go of me?"

Reave released his grip, then looked at Cwen in disgust. He shunned her. She shared the dedication to Narilan that Dorrell always had, but there was another layer to her character. She always followed rules. That's why Reave disliked her. He preferred people who depended on personal judgement when making a decision. As important as laws might've been to Narilan, they meant nothing to Reave.

Dorrell left in a hurry. Reave took a seat and eyed Cwen playing with her bracelet.

"What?" Cwen asked in a grumpy tone.

"I can't figure out why my brother would trust you."

"Perhaps he has spent more time with me than with you. Maybe I'm like family." She pressed her legs to her chest and put her chin on her knees.

Reave frowned. "He seems upset and down ever since you arrived." He grabbed an apple from the tray on the table and leaned back. "I'd like to know what you said to him."

"Or what? You'll kill me?" Cwen asked without much worry.

"My brother wouldn't want that." Reave took a bite.

"Everything you do is for the sake of your brother? Such a pity."

Reave wasn't bothered by the gibe. "What do you think of the donors languishing above?"

Cwen frowned. It was obvious to him that she didn't support them.

"You love my brother," Reave said, watching her closely. There was no other reason someone like Cwen would stand by Dorrell, allowing him to break the laws of Narilan. "Did my brother make any promises to you?" Reave asked, and Cwen looked away. He laughed. His mirth seemed to irritate her.

Cwen snorted. "You wouldn't be laughing if you knew what he promised."

"Let me guess." Reave stretched. "He promised that he would confess his transgressions to the Grand Court." Reave waited until Cwen nodded. "You do realize what that means? He will be cast out of Zardan. He will be branded with the Gift of Misfortune. Ultimately, he will be betrayed by the kingdom if he does that."

Cwen swallowed, then turned away.

The trumpets blasted outside with tremendous force. They reminded the people of Narilan that the celebration was underway. The Celestial King, a century-old man, would make his appearance soon. At least, that's what everyone outside hoped for. Reave knew it wouldn't happen. That was the whole reason why Dorrell wrote his speech. He intended to speak on behalf of the Celestial King.

"That punishment would be nothing to a person such as myself," Reave said as the noise outside faded. "But it'll destroy Dorrell. He'll be like a child abandoned and without purpose."

"If you're trying to convince me to back off, I want you to know that I made up my mind," Cwen rasped.

Reave smiled. "You see, there is no point in trying to change your mind because that would change nothing. My brother is a very peculiar character. To him, a promise is something sacred. If he really made that promise to you, he will most likely keep it. There really isn't anything I can do about it."

Cwen had a triumphant smile.

"But I think that not everything is lost." Reave placed the core of the apple on the table. "I think that my brother loves being a preceptor, and he will never give that up. He loves working for Narilan, and deep down, he knows he has done the right thing." Reave tightened the bandage covering his eye. "Before long, you will end up with Anson."

"You don't know Dorrell," Cwen said. "He is a man of honor. If you think he will break his promise, you're mad."

"It wouldn't be the first time." Reave left with a joyful step. He believed everything he said. He knew Dorrell was just like him. He could see it in his eyes sometimes. He was confident that Dorrell wouldn't surrender, no matter what. His brother already broke one of his oaths. He went against Narilan's laws and traditions when he implemented the idea of the donors in the Great Tower. Doing so, he interfered with Narilan's natural ways.

Reave knew better than anyone that everything was easier the second time around. He believed in his brother.

◆

Dorrell was looking outside from an arrow slit. He could sense the Celestial King's presence, even though the Celestial King wouldn't speak and the only sound that he ever uttered was a feeble mumble. Dorrell was deaf to the sound of water and wind. His mind was somewhere else.

Sometimes he found himself worried what would happen to Narilan if he was gone. The only time he felt at peace was when he was taking care of the kingdom. He wondered what would happen if someone else took over. *Would the kingdom survive?*

He loved Narilan. The kingdom meant everything to him. It was his job, his passion, and his life. He couldn't imagine what life would be like for him outside of Zardan. Life as a preceptor was all he ever knew.

Perhaps living as an outcast with the Gift of Misfortune would be the ultimate punishment for him. *And for what? All I ever strived to do was save the kingdom.* The thought of punishment felt overwhelming and unfair. He couldn't accept it. He wanted to fight it, struggle against it, and escape.

Yet, Dorrell made a promise. He swore to Cwen that he would turn himself in because it was the only way to continue his scheme and keep her alive at the same time. He didn't want to kill. He couldn't kill for selfish reasons.

The thought of Cwen angered him.

He was boxed in. He only had one choice, a single question waiting to be answered.

Keeping a promise or being a preceptor? he wondered. *What is more important to me?*

◆

Cwen sneaked downstairs. The tower was empty and still. She lit the torches with her mana, then carefully descended. It was her first time in the basement.

"Cwen," Anson called out. He was pale and tired, his clothes tattered.

"Listen, I spoke with Dorrell. He will release you soon."

"The man is a lunatic. Get me out." Anson shook the cage, screaming.

"He will confess to the Grand Court. He did it all to protect Narilan."

"You believe him? How can you believe him after he trapped me here like an animal?"

"Trust me," Cwen said, confident in her words. Looking at Anson made her worried. She heard Reave's words in the back of her head. And then there was nothing but doubt.

CHAPTER 55

KYLE WANDERED THE crowded streets, disguised by his cloak and listening to the mirth. The people swarmed the town square, dancing to the music of the minstrels. There were tables everywhere, most occupied. Young girls in colorful dresses walked around with salvers in their hands. Kyle stole a drink, but he wasn't quick enough, and the girl noticed it. Her reaction was unexpected as she greeted him with a smile.

Kyle made his way through the crowd, jostling a few bystanders, and then, he heard a commotion. The merchants gestured and screamed, trying to outshout the customers. The fruit-filled carts were pushed into a side street, which made the merchants angry.

Kyle came closer and snatched an orange.

What is all the commotion? Was a new Celestial King crowned?

Kyle felt disappointed by the thought. Yet, his life taught him that there was no point in questioning the way things were, no point in brooding over the past. Things just happened, and the only thing that really mattered was making the best of the situation.

He passed the tavern on his way to the Great Tower. A man was hurled out the door. He landed on the cobblestones, groaning. His face red, it was obvious that he was drunk. "Hail to the Celestial King," the drunkard said, wiping his nose.

Kyle circled around him, then looked around. He came to a table.

"Gentlemen, what are you celebrating?" Kyle asked.

The men all looked up.

"Where have you been?" one of them asked. "The Celestial King is a hundred years old. How could you miss that?"

Kyle shrugged, then left without a word.

◆

The courtyard was bustling with life. The music was lively, the dancers seemed more energetic, and even the guards had a smile instead of the usual angry frown.

Kyle climbed the steps, dodging the people sitting there. He felt an overwhelming sense of anticipation, which he stifled. He couldn't afford to lose sight of his goal. His most important battle was yet to come. The Great Tower stood before him.

"Who goes there?" one of the guards asked, striking his lance against the ground.

"A challenger," Kyle said and rolled up his sleeve to reveal his final Blessing. He didn't know if he would be able to enter the Great Tower again, but he didn't hesitate.

The guards glared at him before standing aside.

Kyle placed his hand on the door. It slowly lit up, groaned, and began to open. He felt a profound sense of defeat. He was reminded of the last time he entered the Great Tower. His heart started beating, and all the strength left him.

Kyle took a breath of fresh air. Downcast, he looked back. There was nothing left for him in the world. Either he would become the Celestial King, or he would die; those were his only options.

Kyle reminded himself of the humiliating defeat at the hands of Reave. The anger fortified him. His will to fight was back, ignited by the hatred. His heart began beating wildly as he entered the darkness.

The Great Tower was still and empty. Yet, Kyle could hear whispers and pleas. They were weak and pitiful as if a tortured soul was languishing nearby. He drew a circle around himself with his mana. The ring rose up while he was standing on it. It only stopped when he almost hit the ceiling. Kyle stepped on the railing, and leaped down on the stairs, turning the ring into a cloud of dust.

The next floor above was the battleground. Kyle leaned against the wall and imagined an arm. The stone wall flaked, and its pieces reformed around his elbow. He placed his stone hand on the pommel of his sword and continued. He remembered the exact spot, where he lost his arm. The blood had already dried up. He strode around the cloven armors, broken swords, and blocks of stone before ascending the stairs on the other side.

Kyle was suspicious of the silence. The emptiness didn't grant him peace of mind. It made him wary as if some great danger was lurking nearby. The thought that he didn't sense anything made him even more uncomfortable.

The stairs spiraled around the Great Tower. There were numerous doors, most of which Kyle ignored. Yet, there was a single door that he was drawn to. He was almost at the top, but he couldn't ignore it. He could hear a myriad of voices, a convoluted barrage of pleas and begging that echoed in his mind. Yet the most bizarre feeling was the sensation that it all came from within his mind, not from the outside.

He bowed forward, head pounding. He put his hand to his forehead. The voices redoubled.

Silence, he thought, and the sounds were muffled. He could still hear them, but they weren't so overwhelming. *What was that?*

Kyle waved his hand, and the door opened. Inside, he saw many pools of water and countless unconscious faces. He stepped forward, then leaned over to take a closer look. *The donors,* he thought, feeling disheartened. All of these men had their lives stolen. It wasn't just that they were Narilan's slaves; they couldn't think, couldn't feel, and there was not a moment of peace for them. The thought that these men were enduring a fate much worse than the one Kyle faced in the cave unnerved him.

The voices he heard were their calls for help, just like the begging of the Celestial King he heard during the ritual. Kyle was somehow connected with this place, with the Great Tower. *Was it because of the Blessings?* he wondered.

He left the chamber and continued his climb. When he was at the summit, he faced a huge, lone door. The wood was engraved with carvings. They were different than the ones he saw below. Their purpose was unknown to him.

He waved his hand, but the door didn't open. Surprised, he pressed his hands firmly against it and pushed with all his might. The door gave in, then opened. A faint but cold breeze hit his face. He felt the Celestial King's presence inside. It was soft and withering.

Kyle entered. It was too dark to see anything, except for a thick red veil in the center. He came closer, then drew the curtains. He retreated, seeing a ghastly sight.

The Celestial King sat in his throne, looking skyward. He had a short beard and thinning hair. His eyes were wide open, and tears were dripping down his pale cheeks. He was whimpering, saliva dripping from the corners of his mouth. His gnarled hands were tightly grasping the throne's arms.

Kyle frowned, puzzled.

All the stories he heard as well as his own personal interpretations of the benevolent Celestial King spoke of an almighty ruler, an omnipotent man with unlimited mana who graciously ruled Narilan from the Great Tower. This perfect image was ruined as he saw the real Celestial King. There was no glory or power here. All that Kyle saw was unfathomable despair.

"It's not what you expected?" a voice came from behind Kyle. The Celestial King replied with a brief mumble.

Kyle recognized the voice. Reave was leaning against the door, a bottle of mead in his hand.

"I was hoping you would defeat Corbit and escape," Reave continued. "I was getting bored here. So tell me, how does it feel losing an arm?"

Kyle's hand quivered with an uncontrollable urge to kill. Looking at Reave's bandages, he reminded himself that they both lost something in that fight. "What is this?" he asked, pointing at the throne.

"The truth."

"Explain," Kyle demanded.

Reave chuckled. "It's ironic, isn't it? You were striving to become the Celestial King in order to gain true freedom, but when you become the Celestial King, you will live your life in shackles, languishing here in this chamber."

"What happened to him?" Kyle asked.

Reave sighed. "I guess there is no harm in telling you. See these markings?" He pointed to the intricate ridges around the chamber, a sign of a ritual ground. "The throne was created a long time ago. It intensifies the mana of the Celestial King, so that he can care for Narilan. But it's also very straining. It pollutes the mind and strips you of your consciousness. But don't worry, he can still obey basic commands... that's why Narilan still exists."

Kyle gnashed his teeth. His goal was a lie. The Celestial King was a mere puppet in the hands of the kingdom. At that moment, Kyle realized that he should have known better. He always saw Zardan as an entity that used others. He sighed, defeated. "Was he always like this?"

"Earlier he was conscious more frequently, or so I heard. Now he's..." Reave trailed off, shaking his head, smiling.

"How long does it take for a Celestial King to lose his mind?"

"The process is slow. I heard it takes a year... maybe less."

One year, huh? Kyle wondered. He didn't trust Reave at all. "So the Celestial King is just like those people in the caves. He is a sacrifice so that Narilan can continue to exist."

Reave nodded, then sipped his mead. "He is much more than a sacrifice. The man behind you, the Celestial

King, has endured years of agony. He suffers for the sake of the kingdom. He is a true martyr." His voice was brash and proud.

"What of the people below?"

"They also decided to sacrifice their lives for Narilan. They lost their chance to become the Celestial King, but they can still be useful. They came to us so that they can help the kingdom. We have honored their request."

"That's what you tell yourself to justify your actions?"

Reave nodded, without shame. "Don't feel bad for them. You'll join them soon." He smiled again.

Kyle stood still, his world turned upside-down. Every single time something happened, he had his dream to fall back on. Now he was stripped of that. He was truly defeated. Like a pawn, he chased after a dream that didn't exist.

"Let's talk about your life," Reave said abruptly. "No matter what happens, you will suffer. Either I'll kill you, or I'll watch you languish from the heavens." Reave smiled. "Tell me, do you still want to become the Celestial King?" He licked his lips.

Kyle slowly grasped his sword. He felt the anger inside his chest. He was seething with rage, and could barely control it. Reave's behavior infuriated him until he couldn't focus on anything else. He looked down, sighed, and then lifted his sword. He retreated to the Celestial King, and with a single swift thrust, stabbed him in the chest.

"What are you doing?" Reave sprung forward.

It was too late.

Kyle ripped the sword out, blood dripping from the tip of the blade. The Celestial King let out a final breath, the heavens thundering. The Great Tower trembled and swayed. Dust fell from the ceiling as stone blocks quivered. A bolt of lightning fell from the sky, and a vicious gale passed through the chamber. The streams of water ceased to move.

Reave covered his face in the wind.

"You could have become the Celestial King long ago," Kyle said. "But I assume you didn't want to, and I don't blame you. Now let's see if you cherish Narilan as much as your brother. If you kill me, you will be forced to ascend the throne and suffer."

Reave drew his sword, his robe twirling in the wind. "Ready to die?"

"I have made my choice long ago," Kyle confessed. "If I must die here, so be it. But as things stand, I'm happy we're both doomed." He had a triumphant smirk on his face.

◆

Dorrell was seated at a table in the tavern. He was sipping some cheap wine and eating a juicy piece of chicken. He liked to watch the celebration. He enjoyed the music and the various dances, although he never tried to dance. Watching helped take his mind off of the problems he faced.

He thought about Cwen, but he couldn't despise her. More so, he understood her. They were friends, and she still urged him to confess to the Grand Court. She pushed him to do the right thing. If anything, he was impressed.

She wanted to come along with him today, but he told her that he wanted to be alone. The last time he was with her, she was walking around Zardan.

A cacophonous string of noises came from the outside. Dorrell didn't pay much thought to it until he heard screams. The crowd from the tavern spilled onto the street. He pushed his way outside.

Horrified, he saw the Great Tower crowned in dust, trembling as if ready to collapse.

CHAPTER 56

SATIA AWOKE TO the sound of a scuffle and laughter. She watched as one of the warriors toppled Udall to the ground, pounding him with his bare fists. She did not pay much thought to it, thinking that it was just the type of thing men like to do to kill time. Yet when she noticed Udall's angry gaze, she knew something was wrong.

"What is going on?" she called out. The warriors didn't react, so she came closer.

"Finally awake," the chief said. "We needed some entertainment."

Satia frowned.

"Fetch us some mead, would you?" a warrior said, giving Satia a belittling glare.

Satia snorted, but then she gave a benign nod and walked off. She grabbed her pouch and pulled out a vial of green powder. She snatched a few bottles from the chief's private stash of mead and sprinkled a bit of the powder into each bottle. As she shook each one, the green power vanished, dissolving completely. She knew the taste wouldn't be any different, but there was a subtle scent in the air that she hoped the warriors wouldn't notice.

She questioned her actions, but she was tired of the warriors, and this was the only way she knew to stop them. When she was ready to hand out the mead, the sky dimmed.

The warriors froze.

She looked over her shoulder to see the Dominant Veil flicker for a second. It turned invisible, glowed, and then burst like an air bubble. Her eyes sparkled as she saw the horizon.

One the other side was a vast landscape of deserts and forests. Far in the distance, there were monstrous mountains with snow-crowned peaks that shamed the Great Tower. The two tallest mountains were divided by a ravine, and the only way across was a stone arc—an enormous bridge. In the rocky hills further in the distance, there was a majestic castle, its massive walls were decorated with various flags that swayed in the wind. The water from the moat seemed to be slowly evaporating as if burning hot.

The sight made Satia ecstatic. The thought that the world was so vast reinvigorated her. She wanted to explore it all, to experience it for herself. Her body burned with excitement.

"What is going on?" one of the warriors asked.

"Satia," Udall called out, watching her wander off.

Satia stopped right at the edge of Narilan, where the Veil met the ground earlier. She looked at the soil on the other side. It was the same, yet very different. It was colder… neglected.

Hooves pounded on the ground. There were six hooded figures coming her way. Consumed by her thoughts, Satia ignored them at first.

The figures rode into Narilan and stopped, their horses neighing. Each figure was dressed in leather armor, with a cape over the shoulders and a hood over the head. They were outlined by a faint flash of light. All but one had a sword. They looked around as if astonished.

Satia stared at them with amazement. Part of her was fascinated with them, but another part of her feared them. There was something mystical about the mysterious figures standing before her. Their knowledge, their power, everything was on Satia's mind. Yet, she did not dare to speak.

"So this is Narilan?" the first figure asked in a masculine yet pleasant voice. "I expected something different."

"It's not impressive," the second figure said.

The other three nodded. The third figure spat in the grass. The fourth and fifth looked at each other.

Satia kept looking at the soft light emanating from them. It reminded her of Ellia.

The first figure looked at Satia. "I'm speaking to you."

"Welcome," Satia finally said. "Welcome to Narilan. My name is Alsatia Appledawn." Her voice was hesitant and lacked strength.

The figure took off its hood to disclose a face of a young man. He had a neatly trimmed beard and a short cut. There was a pendant around his neck, hanging over his armor.

He's no different than a regular human, Satia thought. Despite the fear, she hoped to face a being of unimaginable knowledge and power. She wanted to learn, but all she found looking at the man was dissatisfaction. "What is your land called?" she asked.

The young man ignored her, staring at Zardan. The other figures remained hooded. The man signaled to the others. One of them quickly galloped back from whence they came. The others dismounted.

"Where do you come from?" Satia asked.

The young man gave Satia a sympathetic look, his eyes blue. "I come from a land of conquest and war. I was hunting. When the Veil opened, I reckoned it might be my only chance to see Narilan. I'd like to see the ruler of this kingdom."

Satia hesitated. "Do you come in peace?"

There was a whisper in the air. An arrow whizzed and hit the young man in the chest. Surprised, he slipped off his horse and dropped to the ground. Blades shrieked as the young man's escorts prepared for battle. Satia looked back to see one of the warriors holding a bow, tottering by a tree. His movements were unsteady, most likely from too much mead. Then she saw Udall running her way.

The first swordsman sprung forward, and Udall crossed swords with him.

Satia gathered powder into her hands and blew it at the second swordsman as he tried to attack. He tripped, falling headlong. Satia opened a hole in the ground with mana and closed it when the swordsman fell in.

The first swordsman kicked Udall back and spread his arms out, glittering white. The ground quivered. Udall lost footing. He stuck his sword in the ground as he sunk in, vanishing in the sand.

Satia grabbed Udall's sword, and before the first swordsman could react, she stabbed him in the back. She pulled the sword out as he groaned. She flourished it, blood spraying the ground. It was some time since she had a blade in hand.

Then the warriors charged, screaming. They pummeled the third swordsman, overwhelming him, while the fourth swordsman—the last one—stood meditating. Spikes suddenly impaled one of the warriors. The swordsman dodged an axe swing and beheaded another warrior. He spun, dodging sword swings and twisting around attacks. His movements were delicate. When his dance was over, the chief was bleeding on the ground with his warriors dead by his side.

Satia readied her sword.

The swordsman leaped forward. He easily dodged Satia's attack. He forced his pommel into Satia's stomach, sending a powerful tremor through her body. Satia spun, then fell. Hitting the ground, she accidentally released some of her powder into the air. She sat up, but before she could react, the swordsman stamped her leg with his foot. She screamed as an incredible flood of pain arose in her leg. The swordsman coughed, inhaling the powder. He hobbled as an arrow hit his back.

It was from the drunken warrior by the pine tree.

The swordsman opened his palm, then made a fist. The tree swelled, its needles bristled like an angry dog's fur. The warrior hesitated instead of running. He stood petrified, motionless. The tree then exploded in a rain of needles, which whizzed everywhere. The warrior collapsed. Satia looked at her shoulder, which was pierced by three thin needles. She felt no pain, yet she fell on her back.

The last thing she saw was the swordsman collapsing as well.

CHAPTER 57

THE FLOOR OPENED beneath Kyle, and he fell into the darkness. Pulled downward, he plummeted one floor and another, until he landed on a block of stone in a puff of dust. His landing was nimble and calculated.

Reave descended from above, balancing on a tiny stone disk. As he stepped down, he flourished his sword. His movements were sharp and fast. He didn't say anything, and it was the first time Kyle noticed that Reave was serious about fighting. There was no air of mockery around him, and his smirk was gone.

Kyle closed his eyes, mind clear. He set aside his anger. It was hard to meditate inside the unstable Great Tower, its murmurs intensifying. He felt his heartbeat dying down, and his whole body became heavy.

Then he leaped forward, sword in hand. Reave side-stepped to avoid the attack, then countered. His movements were swift. Kyle blocked with his stone arm. His blade caught Reave's glass of mead, shattering it. The liquid flickered in the light, hardening around Reave's legs into ice. It emitted a cold mist.

Then Kyle imagined another blade and unloaded a barrage of attacks, each heavy and fast. Reave was immobile and forced to struggle against the flood of swords that nearly sent him to his knees. With each sword clash, there was an echoing chink. Kyle hammered with his swords until one of them chipped, the tiny piece dancing on the tiles. Reave thrust his weapon forward, but Kyle dodged, imagining a spike.

Reave pressed his hands on the floor, forcing his mana into the ground and hindering Kyle's attack. Timid fires circled around him, melting the ice.

Kyle looked up at the ceiling. The Great Tower shook, murmuring. Dust fell and stone blocks loosened, Kyle pulled one down. The block plummeted with immense speed, pulled by its weight. Reave rolled out of the way. The block crashed into the floor and sank in, cracking down the middle. It sent a tremor through the floor and a cloud of dust across the chamber.

Kyle charged as he saw Reave cough. It was his opportunity to get the upper hand. Reave parried clumsily, and Kyle blocked his counter with his stone arm, passing his sword to his left hand. Reave's blade, imbued with mana, ripped through Kyle's artificial arm, shattering it into pieces. It seemed as if nothing could stop it. The pieces bounced on the floor as Kyle ducked, dodging Reave's next attack, blade passing just above his head.

Then Reave continued his assault. It was fast and decisive, with each attack increasing in momentum. Kyle knew

Reave's intention—all of his vicious attacks were aimed at his left hand.

Kyle relinquished his sword, retreated, then pressed his hand against the floor. His sword rang against the tiles. It shined red, then exploded in a bulging mass of crimson flames. Reave covered his face, the fire burning bright. Yet, the fires were short-lived, dying within a moment.

The ground quivered, and a thin stone pillar sprung from the ground. Reave attempted to dodge, but the pillar hit him in the side of the face, grazing his temple.

"I never took you for a trickster," Reave said, spitting blood.

Kyle forced a smile. *I can't beat him in a sword fight,* he thought. *Mana is all I have left.* He wondered about the headaches that he had many times before. They always unnerved him, but he knew this wasn't the time to be frightened. He had to use all the mana he had left.

The tiles cracked. Kyle instinctively sprung away as the floor opened up to reveal a dark pit filled with fire. The scorching flames burned with a subtle intensity. He circled around a stone block until he lost sight of Reave.

Another one of his tricks, Reave thought. "Hiding won't do you any good," he proclaimed aloud.

Kyle gathered all the mana that he could muster and forced it into the stone block. He felt pounding in his head and a profound aching in the skull, as if it was slowly being cracked open.

"Hiding worked for you, so I figured I'd try it too," Kyle said, thinking of their journey.

Reave frowned, came close to the stone block where Kyle was hiding, and then thrust his sword. His blade sunk up to the hilt, yet his mana had no effect. The stone block didn't explode. Nothing happened. Reave pulled on the sword, but it was stuck, trapped in stone.

Then the stone block burst like an air bubble, splitting into specks of dust. The wind gathered right at the tip of Reave's sword into a tiny orb. Like a meaningless spec, it was almost invisible. Reave pressed his feet firmly on the ground, trying to free his blade, which was still held by something.

Kyle formed a shield of stone and hid behind it.

The wind whispered and howled as it strengthened around the orb. It yanked the cloth from Reave's hair, turning it into nothingness. His hair unbound, he fought against the powerful wind, but he could barely hold his ground. The orb swallowed the swords, the armor, the tiles, and anything else it could find lying around. Then the wind ripped the bandages from Reave's eye, revealing a deep wound that was slowly healing.

Kyle stood behind cover, watching.

Reave was losing strength. As he was pulled closer to the orb, he groaned. His fingers, nearly touching the orb, oozed with blood. He grimaced, gathering his mana. He summoned a powerful gale that passed through the chamber, pushing the orb away. He let go of his sword as a stone wall emerged between himself and the orb.

The orb drifted away devouring everything in its way. It collided with a lone column and swallowed it. The Great Tower trembled as the orb ate a chunk of the wall and the ceiling, water pouring from above. A body fell down. *One of the donors,* Kyle thought. Pulled by the wind, the corpse vanished in a stream of blood — devoured by the orb.

"What did you do?" Reave panted as the orb's soft

touch swallowed a portion of the stairs. He lifted a worn-out sword from the ground.

Kyle watched as the orb drifted away. He tried to pull it back and soothe it, but he didn't have enough mana. He heard Reave coming up behind him, the sword grating against the floor. Reave slashed at his back, but Kyle was ready. He knew what to expect. He evaded, spun around, and stabbed Reave in the stomach with a knife—Avril's knife. Then he shoved Reave back, holding his hand to his pounding head.

Reave dropped his sword, spitting blood. He looked at Kyle for a moment before turning his attention to the orb. "At least now, I won't have to worry about Narilan. Everything falls on you."

They stood still, looking at each other for a brief moment. Without saying a word, the two Dreamers acknowledged each other's might.

Then Kyle concentrated on the orb, and Reave joined him soon after. The wind dropped. It howled as it died. Then the orb lost shape, fading away.

"I didn't take you for someone concerned about the well-being of the people," Kyle said, watching the crowd below. Their screams were vibrant and loud.

"My brother would be really disappointed if something happened to the innocent people down below," Reave said, wiping the blood from his face.

The floor vibrated. The stone blocks that made up the Great Tower started coming loose as if the whole structure was about to collapse. Reave pushed his hands against the floor. He tried to steady the Great Tower. Chunks of rocks fell from the ceiling as a powerful tremor passed through the floor.

"I can't do it alone," Reave called out.

Dizzy, Kyle panted. He came closer and took a seat on the floor, legs crossed. He imagined the Great Tower as it was before the fight. A single block slipped down from the ceiling and slammed into the ground next to Kyle, shaking him out of his meditation. He opened his eyes, but the dust obscured his vision. He could feel the whole place crumbling.

He closed his eyes again. A column erupted, slowly. Another tremor. Pebbles covered the ground. Another block fell down, shattering into small fragments that bounced around. The gap in the wall closed up. The Great Tower slowly calmed down. The violent tremors faded.

Kyle felt his heart pounding in his chest, his mind dazed. He opened his eyes to see Reave slumped, his head down, his chin against his chest.

Just a little more, Kyle thought.

A huge piece of rock plummeted, and Kyle did everything he could to concentrate. He watched Reave as the rock crashed into the ground, sending a wave of dust his way.

Kyle's mind became cloudy. All his bad memories relished the chance of tormenting him. The Great Tower fell quiet again. The structure stopped moving, but the ceiling was still unstable. And then there was another powerful tremor. As Kyle staggered up, pebbles dropped around him. He couldn't hold it anymore. A stone block came loose from the ceiling, crashing into the floor with a thud. The whole chamber was consumed in a cloud of dust.

Kyle coughed, wobbling to the stairs. He couldn't save the Great Tower in his current state. Pressing his hand on the railing, he ascended, swaying with every step. At the top, he entered the Celestial King's chamber, but hesitated before the throne.

Then he grabbed the crown and pulled the corpse off the throne.

He took a seat and placed the crown over his head.

Everything went dark.

CHAPTER 58

KYLE DRIFTED IN his mind. He felt the mana pulsing through him. He was fully conscious. He saw nothing, but a pale, waning light that surrounded him. He plunged into the light when he took the throne and sank deeper into it ever since. He could not feel his body anymore, although he could feel a comfortable warmth.

As if drifting in the clouds, he was lost without a sense of direction or purpose. He couldn't determine if this place was a world within his mind or the world of the Celestial King.

He panicked at the thought of not being able to come back to Narilan, of losing his mind. The impulse shook him awake. Then the light died, and the clouds were blown away. Kyle saw Narilan from a bird's eye view.

He heard voices, but very different from the ones he heard in the Great Tower. They were subtle and soft like a shy whisper. There was no deeper meaning to them. They were just conversations all across the kingdom. He could hear them all—merchants trading, travelers whistling, lovers confessing, and so much more.

Like never before, he felt connected with the kingdom. He could feel the mana pulsing through all things. He felt in touch with nature and all life. Weather was at his disposal. With a single thought, he could summon rain, snow, wind, or something much worse.

He restored the Great Tower to its former state with ease. Then he looked outside the Dominant Veil. He didn't know he could do that. His vision was out of focus, but he saw kingdoms at war. He heard screams and felt panic. He saw vicious rulers, who craved power. He could see castles that acted as prisons for beings far too powerful to roam the world freely and lands filled with chaos. The mana that pulsed through the land wasn't delicate like the one in Narilan. It was throbbing, beating chaotically, and out of control.

Kyle restored the Dominant Veil and strengthened it. It was obvious why it was there in the first place. Narilan could never measure up to the power of the kingdoms outside. The Veil was a means of ensuring that Narilan survived.

Kyle felt the weight of the entire kingdom. It was a huge burden, but he could bear it.

He saw all and knew all.

◆

The water murmured softly. Kyle opened his eyes. He was slouched on the throne. He lifted his head and moved his arm. His body felt heavy, heavier than before. He looked to the side to see the preceptor.

Dorrell, tears dripping down his face, was kneeling by the dead Celestial King. His hands quivered. There was anger and despair in his eyes. "How does it feel?"

"Overwhelming," Kyle admitted.

"In one day, you took two of the most important people away from me."

Kyle leaned back, thinking about Reave's sacrifice, yet he said nothing.

Dorrell frowned. "Look what you did to the Celestial King. Don't you have any respect?"

Kyle challenged his gaze. "That's not how you should speak to the Celestial King." He smiled.

Dorrell hesitated, gnashing his teeth. Then he put his thoughts aside and bowed. "I apologize. How may I serve you, Your Majesty?"

Kyle wasn't convinced by the farce. "I have some questions. Why do I feel like I'm carrying some great burden?"

Dorrell looked at Kyle with disgust. "The throne is a ritual ground. It offers great power, but it also takes a toll on the body. You are connected with all of the mana that's in the kingdom. You can influence the land, listen to people's thoughts, and more. You will feel burdened… that's unavoidable." Dorrell narrowed his eyes, as he watched Kyle nod. It wasn't what he wanted to see.

"I've seen the donors."

"I can't explain it," Dorrell said with a frown. "But it's been ages since our first Celestial King created this ritual ground, the throne. It might not be as strong as before. Its power to enhance mana is fading. That's why we need more donors. That's why I turned the caves into ritual grounds as well."

Kyle bit his lower lip. Dorrell's confession reminded

him of his suffering. "You do realize that I would kill you for what you said if I didn't need your knowledge. I languished in one of those caves."

The chamber fell silent.

Kyle snapped his fingers and the place lit up in sunlight as the walls became transparent. "So I'm connected with the kingdom. What happens if I want to travel?"

"As long as you have the crown with you," Dorrell said with a pause, "you can still control Narilan."

Kyle took off the crown and looked at the blue gem. It glittered in the light. "Fine. Take me downstairs. I'd like to see the donors."

"Do you know what this place is called?" Dorrell interrupted, but Kyle didn't stop him. "It's called the King's Fall. That's what everybody secretly calls it. Would you like to know why? Because the Celestial King awaits his death here. It's the place where he spends most of his time until he dies... it's the place where he falls."

Kyle didn't respond. He saw Dorrell's words as a mere provocation. There was no point falling into his trap, yet the words were true. They were so true that Kyle had difficulty fighting them off. Filled with despair and dread, they reminded him of the weight of his decision.

Kyle stood at the door. He thought about what he should do with the donors. After what he heard from Dorrell, he thought that he might need their help, yet he also wanted to free them no matter what. They didn't deserve to spend the rest of their lives like this, waiting for death. Kyle pitied them, thinking about Avril. It was an opportunity for him to do the right thing.

"Free them," Kyle said as he entered the chamber.

"What?" Dorrell asked in a loud voice.

"You heard me the first time. Do it."

Dorrell walked to the center of the room. His step was slow as if he was in no hurry. He kneeled, then chanted. The water halted. Slowly, the men awoke.

"Where am I?" Graeme said in a dazed tone.

"What is this place?" another man said.

"You!" A slim man sprung out of a pool of water. Dorrell retreated, his step nimble. The man slipped on the wet floor, falling and grazing his knee.

"You imprisoned me," a disfigured man yelled in the back of the room at the first sight of Dorrell.

"Stop," Kyle commanded as a fight was about to break out. "This is not the time. If you want to exact your revenge on the preceptor, you can do so later."

"And who might you be?" the disfigured man rasped.

Kyle felt irritated by his lack of respect. The ground vibrated subtly, and the disfigured man slipped, plunging into the water, where he spent the last few weeks if not months of his life.

"I am Kyle of Darga. I am the Celestial King."

The men froze, then all of them bowed. The disfigured man showed signs of shame. After climbing out, he wouldn't look up, staring at his feet, kneeling.

"You were here because the kingdom needs mana. If the Dominant Veil falls, Narilan is lost. There are powerful kingdoms outside who await that moment." Kyle paused. "I have a proposal. You are all free to leave, but I ask one thing of you. When the time comes that I'm unable to provide for the kingdom, I'd like all of you to freely give your mana."

The men murmured, looking at each other. Shaken by doubt and fear, their eyes wandered around the chamber.

The thin man strolled passed Kyle. "I'm sorry," he said, his drenched tunic and trousers leaving a trail of water behind him.

The chamber fell silent.

"I agree," Graeme declared. "My name is Graeme of Elra, and I swear to protect the kingdom."

Kyle continued to watch as the other men whispered among themselves.

"Remember why we are all here," Graeme said. "We wanted to help Narilan. Now is our chance. But not as slaves, as free men, as warriors."

"Fine," the disfigured man declared. "My name is Waylan of Aylmar. Anytime you need my help, I'll be there."

"My name is Deryck, and I offer my mana as well."

A few more men left, then the rest swore to help Narilan in unison. Kyle smiled triumphantly. Before him, he saw men of devotion, strength, and pride. Within them, he saw the unyielding strength that humans possessed. They weren't so different from him; they traveled the same road. Having them by his side was an honor to him.

Kyle nodded, then left. He already had another idea about what to do with the empty pools of water. He smiled at the thought.

CHAPTER 59

DORRELL STOOD IN front of the Grand Court. The members whispered, waiting for his confession, hiding behind their masks. He could feel their patronizing eyes glaring at him. He had yet to say a word. All his thoughts were clustered and muddled. He was defeated and bitter, but he knew he was making the right choice.

The thought that Kyle was the Celestial King made him angry, but it was until he thought of giving up his title that he felt sickened. *I won't be able to help Narilan anymore,* he thought. *I lost everything... everything.*

Dorrell remembered Reave and the former Celestial King. He felt at home back then. Now, Zardan felt foreign, but not like a long-lost friend; it felt like an apple left to the world—rotten. Yet, he still wanted to care for it.

"We're waiting," a strong voice said.

Dorrell looked up. "My name is Dorrell Sahne, and I'm

the preceptor. I have betrayed the Kingdom of Narilan." His heart started beating, his thoughts chaotic. He tried to catch a breath as he prepared to speak. "I have dishonored the Great Tower, and I have abused my power. I have ignored traditions… and the laws that hold our kingdom together."

The whispers intensified.

Dorrell noticed Cwen in the corner. She had a sad look about her.

"I wanted to handpick a successor to the throne," Dorrell continued. "Even though there were people like Kyle that were powerful enough, I believed that we could do better, that a brute without a drop of remorse shouldn't ascend the throne. I gathered donors of mana against their will, and they languished for weeks in the Great Tower. I imprisoned Anson, one of my students, and lied to you all. I tried to cover up what I did. I broke an oath. People died because of me."

Dorrell thought about the food shortages, the storms, and the disease. People died because of him, yet he kept pushing on, thinking that the Celestial King deserved to spend his last days on the throne, that the Great Tower deserved a better successor. He wondered if things would've been different if he had selected a powerful successor earlier, ignoring his own judgements.

The chamber fell silent.

The members of the Grand Court exchanged glances. They nodded, then frowned.

Dorrell's hands were cold. His heart kept beating, his chest tense and his breathing hard.

"We have come to a decision. You are stripped of your title; you are preceptor no more. You will be exiled from Zardan, but before that, you will be branded with the Gift of Misfortune."

Dorrell swallowed. He sighed, then heard applause.

"I would say the preceptor is already suffering from misfortune." Kyle's voice spread through the chamber. He was wearing a simple white shirt and black leather trousers. "He lost everything... well, almost everything."

"Your Majesty," the scholars said together, then stood up and bowed.

"Don't pretend to respect me," Kyle said, his voice cold.

The chamber fell silent.

"What makes you say that, Your Majesty?" a headstrong voice finally asked.

"You might wear masks, but I recognized all your voices. The Grand Court was there when I fought Corbit. You laughed and cheered as I bled." Kyle took a seat and crossed his legs, leaning back.

No one dared to speak.

Dorrell kept staring at Cwen. She eyed Kyle, playing with her bracelet. She had a frightened look as if she had never seen someone with such a presence. Her hands then tightened around her white dress.

"But that's in the past," Kyle said. "I'm here now, and I have to know if you are willing to sacrifice your life for Narilan. If not, then you're worthless."

"Of course, Your Majesty," the headstrong voice declared. The others agreed.

Kyle stood up. "That's what I wanted to hear."

Chains chinked and shrieked as they snaked through the door and into the chamber. As a single chain shackled a member of the Grand Court, the others panicked. They tried to run, but it was futile. Some used mana, but they were too weak. Others tried praying and meditating. When every single scholar was shackled, the chamber fell silent.

"What is this?" the headstrong voice was the only one brave to ask. The others cried and whispered.

Dorrell clenched his fist, knowing what would come next. He hated the chaos that was Kyle's way of doing things. Yet, he knew there was no point in arguing. *Only a few months,* he thought. *That's how long it'll take.*

"We are in desperate need of mana. You will become donors." Kyle started walking away. He grabbed Dorrell by the collar and dragged him along. Then he looked over his shoulder at the Grand Court. "It's ironic how things ended up. If Dorrell succeeded, you wouldn't end up like this." He chuckled.

Outside of the chamber, Dorrell wrestled out of his grip, grimacing. "What do you think you're doing?"

"I have no need for the Grand Court. Make sure they become donors."

"What about their decision?"

"After I learn everything I want to know, you can leave," Kyle said. "For now, you're still the preceptor."

Dorrell snorted.

"There is something else. The caves... I want all the people freed. If I hear of one person kept there against his or her will, I'll kill your girl." Kyle pointed to the chamber.

Dorrell leaned against the wall, breathing deeply. He knew he could ignore the order if his life was on the line. Yet, Kyle noticed Cwen. Dorrell had no choice. He was boxed in between the circumstances that surrounded him. He was on his knees, with a single choice of submitting to the rule of the new Celestial King.

Only a few months and you'll be just like any other Celestial King... docile and obedient, he thought.

CHAPTER 60

SATIA AWOKE TO the shaking of the carriage. She was lying flat on her back between two big bags of grains. She sat up to see the mountains stretching across the land, the Dominant Veil restored. A peasant with a red shag was snoring nearby.

Satia tried to move, but the pain in her leg stopped her. Then she remembered what happened. Her broken leg was wedged between two wooden planks. She poked the peasant in the arm.

"Where are we?" she asked.

"You're awake, miss. We are heading to Zardan. We should be there soon." He smiled, revealing a broken tooth. "Udall wanted me to tell you something." The peasant paused as if waiting for Satia's full attention.

"I'm listening," she said, grimacing from the pain that pulsed through her leg.

"After Udall found you, he left to return to his family. He said he will join you in Zardan."

"Thank you." Satia forced a smile.

"Don't worry about the injuries, miss." The peasant tittered, then loudly cleared his throat. "They'll heal, and you'll be able to frolic at your wedding to your heart's content."

Satia smiled honestly at the peasant's ignorance. She knew enough about injuries to realize that her wounds were not severe. *Thankfully,* she thought. She fell on her back and closed her eyes, her cape pulled tightly around her.

◆

When Satia arrived in Zardan, there were people waiting for her. She only saw strangers, but they acted as if she was someone important, as if she was family. They greeted her with smiles and told her that the Celestial King was waiting for her.

An elderly couple led her to a chamber in the Great Tower, where she could ditch her dirty clothes and get a pair of elegant blue robes. But before that, she wanted to bathe. A pair of women had to help her as she was helpless with her broken leg. Afterward, they dressed her, and she was forced to sit in bed.

A knock came at the door, and Kyle entered.

"Look at you, a true Celestial King." Satia smiled, looking at the crown, although she disliked the shirt and everything else. It was too messy… too ordinary.

"Not everything is as it seems." Kyle returned a grin. "Although I do like the power."

"Tell me about it," she demanded, her eyes glistering.

"You first."

Satia shook her head in disapproval, but then surrendered. She told him of her encounter with the hooded figures, the light, and the view of the world outside. "I'm not sure but I think they were all Dreamers, or something stronger. Yet they were human just like us."

"What do you think of the light?" Kyle asked. "I saw a pale light as well when I became the Celestial King."

Satia wondered for a moment. "I think the light is a sign of mana. I've seen it before. When a person overuses mana, they start to exhibit certain symptoms. I think it starts with a headache. I've heard of people hearing voices too. Then there is the light. Whatever follows is the stage that those figures were in. They were pushing their mana to its limits."

Kyle nodded. "As the Celestial King, I could get a glimpse of what's outside the Veil. I could feel powerful beings. Men hungry for power. It's a chaotic world out there, and Narilan isn't strong enough to be a part of it."

"So what was the point of my broken leg, huh?" Satia crossed her arms.

"I didn't know I'd be able to see outside the Veil." Kyle called for Dorrell with his mana. Then he came closer and took a seat on the edge of the bed.

"How is it?" Satia whispered. "How does it feel being the Celestial King?"

Kyle had a childish smirk as he explained everything he found out.

"That's not what I was expecting. The Celestial King was a puppet?" Satia frowned. "That's... sad. But does that mean..."

Kyle shrugged. "There was nothing else left for me. I

thought that even though the fate of the Celestial King is grim, I can make the best of it. That's what I intend to do."

"You're going to make a great Celestial King," Satia whispered. "I know it."

Kyle smiled softly. Satia put her hand on his shoulder, and then noticed the half-empty sleeve under his cloak.

"What happened?" she asked.

"I was injured during a fight."

Satia wavered a moment. "We could... you know."

"I think I'll pass." Kyle grinned. "Do you need anything? I'll tell the servants to bring books from the preceptor's library, how about it?"

Satia smiled. "I'd like that. I also have two wishes."

"Go on."

"There is a man, Udall. He helped me on my journey. He would like to live in Zardan."

"Done. What else?"

"There is also Sumin. He was cursed with the Gift of Misfortune."

"When you figure out the correct ritual, just let me know."

Satia smiled. She was content that Kyle kept his word. More so, she was at peace that she wasn't wrong. She could really trust Kyle. There was honesty in his heart as well as strength and courage.

A knock came at the door, and Dorrell entered. He bowed, but his behavior lacked respect and seemed forced.

"What do you know of life outside the Dominant Veil?" Kyle asked.

Dorrell rubbed his eyes. "The Veil was implemented because the power of Mind Mana can bring chaos. If you abuse mana, there are consequences. With each use of mana, you are able to gather even more of it and use it more effectively. Therefore you become more powerful. But mana also clouds the mind. There would be no way to stop someone like that. That's why most people are told to use very little of their mana. It's why the Dominant Veil is there. Without it, nothing could protect us from the Dreamers outside. We're nothing compared to them. Yet at least we can think clearly, and we're not hungry for power."

"What do you know about mana overuse?" Kyle asked. Satia noticed their extreme dislike of each other.

"Dizziness, headaches. Some people hear voices… most likely a sign of going mad. Light is the physical representation of mana. The more mana you use, the more it manifests itself. At that point, you either die, or you become something else. It all depends on the person." Dorrell's words worried Satia. "But overusing mana ultimately clouds the mind, makes you lose control, maybe even go mad."

The chamber fell silent.

"Why haven't I lost my mind then?" Kyle asked before Dorrell could sneak out.

"You probably will, eventually. But a Dreamer such as yourself is more resilient. It's usually weak-minded people who are prone to it."

Kyle paused. "What about the Celestial King? He should be the first one to go mad with the amount of mana he uses."

Dorrell smiled bitterly. "That's true. But usually before the change occurs, the Celestial King has lost his mind… and becomes a living corpse."

Satia saw worry within Kyle's eyes. She wanted to ask him about it, but hesitated. She could easily guess what was on his mind, but she wanted him to find answers for himself.

When Dorrell left, the chamber fell silent. Kyle stood up, ready to leave.

"There is something else," Satia said.

CHAPTER 61

THE GRASS SWAYED in the gentle breeze. The apple trees cast vast shadows. The dense treetops jostled against each other, leaves falling. Occasionally apples fell down as well. Rabbits jumped around the orchard, playing around, their eyes huge and innocent.

Ellia was cuddled up by a tree, her dress sprinkled in blood. Her hands were trembling, and she was glowing in a faint white light, bloody sword by her side. Tense, every time she tried to breathe, her chest hurt. The voices in her head echoed.

She heard something coming and almost jumped. Hooves were hitting the dirt road in a rhythmical way. Two riders. She recognized both—Kyle and Dorrell.

As they arrived, Kyle dismounted, then turned to Dorrell. "Why did you follow me?"

"Matters of the kingdom are important to me." Dorrell

dismounted and fixed his robes. "She is dangerous."

Ellia sprang up, grabbed the sword by her side. Her whole body was hurting. The first thing she thought about was Avril. She felt scared.

"I heard what happened in Locklair's Keep," Kyle said to Ellia as he approached her.

"You're going to imprison me?" she barked.

Kyle frowned. "Your mana is unstable. That's why I'm here."

Ellia tossed her hair back. "And you brought the person responsible for my misery." She sprang forward with her sword aimed at Dorrell. At once, Kyle drew his sword as well and parried, knocking hers away from her hand.

He sighed. "I still need him, but you can have him later."

"What are you talking about?" Dorrell interrupted, staring at Ellia.

"A village in Nalza. That's where I come from." Ellia recognized defeat in Dorrell's eyes. "Are you not going to justify your actions?"

"Are you going to feel any better if I tell you that Narilan has been shrinking all along?" Dorrell asked with a dejected look. "Slowly. Inevitably. It happens whenever the Celestial King grows weak."

Ellia fell silent. She was tired and hurt. Far too exhausted to strike down the preceptor, to carry out the only act that in that moment seemed to be able to grant her an ever so fleeting solace.

Kyle watched the exchange patiently, his eyes devoid of sympathy.

"You should take this chance and finish her off," Dorrell whispered to Kyle. "She's nothing but an unfettered monster. You would do well to heed my warning."

Kyle gave Dorrell a scrutinizing glance before turning to Ellia. "If you make a promise to stop using mana, I can let you go. I actually enjoyed hearing of Locklair's defeat." He chuckled.

"You can't be serious," Dorrell calmly protested. "She's a threat to the kingdom."

Ellia panted. "I love mana. I will never cease to use it." She made the earth tremble, but as she had her eyes closed, an image of Avril flashed in her mind. It was vivid and alive as always. "I love to fight," Ellia confessed.

Kyle waved his hand, and roots came out of the ground. They circled around Ellia, wrapping around her arms, pulling her down. When her knees hit the ground, she screamed.

She had Avril before her eyes again. She couldn't make the image go away. It lingered in her mind ever since Avril died. She could never forget it. It was there, reminding her of her transgressions. Then all of the sudden, unable to bear the weight of her past, Ellia called out, "I killed... Avril."

Kyle stilled. Ellia could see the same bloodthirsty gaze he had in Mount Nakroh. Yet, she was not scared. Liberated by her confession, she bowed her head down, breathing heavily.

Kyle came closer, clutching his sword.

Ellia closed her eyes. She knew she could fight, but she didn't want to. Killing Avril was an accident, but she still felt guilty. There was no point justifying her actions, no point struggling.

"What did you say?" Kyle snapped, his voice cold and cruel.

"I... killed Avril."

"Where is she?"

"The waterfall. She's buried in the dirt."

Kyle grabbed Ellia by the shirt and pulled her closer. "You buried her like a piece of trash in the road?" There was madness and hate in his eyes.

"It was an accident. It was the first time… I just started to use mana." Ellia's emotion ran wild. She didn't know if what she felt was fear, surprise, or anger.

Standing behind Kyle, Dorrell lowered his voice. "See? Her existence only leads to tragedy. She deserves death."

Kyle shackled her down. He instinctively steadied his blade. He took a deep breath and waited a moment. His gaze was controlled yet ruthless.

Ellia looked him straight in the eyes. She didn't turn away. She wanted to let the events unfold, but she had no intention of falling apart.

This time, they were equals.

The sword in Kyle's hand trembled, before dropping to the ground. Kyle sighed, then frowned. "I don't want to see you ever again," he said, but his voice was a mere whisper. "But I can't just let you go."

"I know." Ellia nodded.

The two stared at each other without another word, yet both of them could only think of one person: Avril. Kyle remembered her smiling or musing mysteriously, yet Ellia could only see the face Avril had when she died.

"We should execute her," Dorrell insisted.

With perfect silence, Kyle slowly picked up his sword.

"She took someone dear away from you, didn't she?" Dorrell growled. "She will only cause more pain. She must die."

With one clean cut, Kyle effortlessly slashed Dorrell.

Eyes wide open, Dorrell fell to his knees, grasping his throat as blood trickled between his fingers. His eyes stared at Kyle, filled with resentment, shock, and malice. He attempted to speak, but could only let out a faint gurgle.

"You have no right to speak, after everything you've done," Kyle said calmly.

Dorrell attempted to mutter something once more, but his rage was smothered out as he collapsed in the grass.

Kyle loosened the roots around Ellia. She stood up in silence and looked intently at Dorrell's body. She felt absolutely nothing.

Kyle gave her a long look. "You can either come with me to Zardan and spend your life imprisoned, or you can leave Narilan forever."

"I think you already know my answer." Ellia's smile was faint and very, very sad.

Without a word, Kyle mounted his horse. Ellia stole Dorrell's mount, and they traveled in the direction of the Dominant Veil, leaving Dorrell's body behind.

Riding along Kyle, Ellia felt just like she did during her early travels with Hilda. She felt content and at peace, as if she had a purpose. Instinctively, she looked back to see Hilda, Avril, and Reave. They weren't there anymore, but Ellia wasn't sad. She had all those memories that she could cherish.

When they arrived, she dismounted.

"I always believed that there was goodness in everyone. Thank you for proving me right."

Kyle hid a bitter sneer.

Ellia glanced at his right arm as the wind lightly pulled aside his dark cloak. "I wish you the best of luck as the new Celestial King." Ellia hesitated. "Remember what you told me in Elra. I think I have a wish. Please make sure that Nalza will be safe."

Kyle nodded. "As long as I'm alive, you have my word."

The Veil rippled and opened. A faint ray of light hit them. Ellia didn't hesitate. She walked through the opening, knowing that she would be fine. The thought of having the world as her playground kept her uplifted. No matter what she would be forced to face outside the Veil, she knew she would be able to grow stronger. That thought alone kept her moving.

Kyle suddenly felt his numb hand, tightened into a fist. He flexed it, then he let it relax. It felt unnatural.

He looked up once more to see Ellia's figure, her mantle twirling in the wind.

Then she vanished in the light.

A flock of birds covered the sky, singing. The sun retreated, almost vanishing behind the horizon. The stars above peppered the blue sky. The moon was already visible.

Kyle kneeled next to Avril's grave. He still couldn't shake off the feeling he had when he dug her out. The overwhelming fury that rooted itself in his psyche—a profound echo of despair was lingering, growing. He didn't want it to go away. He treasured Avril too much to just brush it aside.

He bowed and chanted the only song he ever knew.

Audene, Rosa, and Fay were right behind him.

He buried Avril behind the dome near Relien. It was the only spot he could think of. They had no family, and their hometowns were just remnants of their forgotten pasts. Yet Relien, despite being a hostile place, was also the very first place they visited together. It was where their journey started.

A tear dropped down Kyle's cheek. And he fell silent.

Without Avril, he wouldn't be the man he was. She was the one who urged him to become the Celestial King, and the one who held him back from becoming a monster.

When he faced Ellia, he could think of no one but Avril. He really wanted to kill Ellia for all she did—for her foolishness. He could barely stop himself. But Dorrell's urging reminded him of his own suffering. The struggles he was forced to endure. The challenges and enemies he had to face. They have all suffered enough. He wanted it all to end—to come to a tranquil, ceaseless stop. He had simply had enough. He hoped Avril would understand.

When he rushed up to become the Celestial King as the Great Tower was ready to crumble, deep down, he considered leaving, forgetting about becoming the Celestial King. He wondered what the people would do without their beloved ruler. Sending Zardan into chaos was a very enticing thought until he remembered the possible danger outside of the Dominant Veil. If it was real, it would mean that countless people would suffer and die. Bringing chaos to Narilan would be the only deed Kyle would be remembered for, and that wasn't his intention. At the time, he knew Avril was out there somewhere, and she wouldn't want that to happen either. That's why he chose to become the Celestial King—to save Narilan in the very end.

He remembered the promise they made together. It gave him a sense of comfort, thinking that she would be proud to hear that the caves were destroyed. He wanted to think that fulfilling their promise was a way of honoring Avril.

"Thank you for being there for me," Kyle whispered. "Goodbye, my queen."

CHAPTER 62

STANDING AT THE top of the Great Tower, Kyle leaned over the battlement. There were crowds gathering in the streets of Zardan. It was the day celebrating his ascension to the throne. He didn't really have much interest in it. He even argued with Dorrell about it before they set out to confront Ellia.

"There you are," Satia came up behind him. She was using a simple wooden cane. It was only temporary though.

Kyle faked a smile.

"Quite the celebration. Have you seen the preceptor? He's not in his chamber, and I had a question about one of the books."

Kyle shook his head. "Last I saw him, he was lying in a pool of blood outside Locklair's Keep."

"I see..." Satia trailed off. "Are you by any chance seeking a new preceptor?"

"You read my mind. Consider yourself appointed."

Satia bowed gracefully and remained next to Kyle. She didn't say a word. She just stood by his side.

It's only been a few days since Kyle became the Celestial King, but he already found his favorite spot in the Great Tower. He liked standing at the very top, out in the open. He liked the breeze and the sight of birds within his reach.

He felt a brief semblance of peace. Despite the concern for what his future might hold, he already made up his mind. After seeing the chaos outside the Dominant Veil, he decided he would protect the people of Narilan.

Far off in the distance, Kyle saw one of the feral creatures he fought in Mount Nakroh. Its blue hide was paler. It dug itself into a ditch as if going back into eternal sleep.

Kyle lost himself in thought. Was this a pyrrhic victory? A hollow triumph of the will? Was his aim a meaningless fancy that refused to become a reality to the bitter end? Had his desire condemned him to a fate far worse than death? A fate where he was trapped, more than ever before? He had lost all of those that he had cherished. The ascent to the throne was just a return to the dark depths of the caves where he was to be sacrificed.

As he stood gazing at the horizon, at his kingdom, a sudden feeling lingered amidst the anguish and the emptiness. A conviction that he could be nowhere else. This was his destiny, and his alone. Many had perished before him, but they were not Kyle. He was, after all, a brute without remorse.

And he was the Celestial King.

MESSAGE FROM THE AUTHOR

Thanks for reading. I hope you enjoyed *The King's Fall*. If you did, please take a moment to leave a review on Amazon and/or Goodreads.

I would also like to tell you of a place, where stories are told and adventure awaits. The Unreal Castle is my website, where you can read short stories and poetry, as well as leave comments and offer suggestions. You can also become a knight of the Unreal Castle by signing up for my newsletter. With your adventurous nature, I think you'd fit right in. I hope to see you there.

www.unrealcastle.com

—Patrick Rain

ABOUT THE AUTHOR

PATRICK RAIN considers two domains to be truly limitless: the water and once's own imagination. It was in their freedom, during an evening swim, that the first idea for a story came to him, and he has been writing ever since. He devotes much of his free time to his passion for learning languages. He speaks English, Polish, and Japanese.